The Village Green and Other Pieces

Edith Miniter

The Village Green and Other Pieces

Edited by
Kenneth W. Faig, Jr.
and Sean Donnelly

Hippocampus Press
New York

Published by Hippocampus Press
P.O. Box 641
New York, NY 10156
http://www.hippocampuspress.com

Cover design by Sean Donnelly.
Hippocampus Press logo by Anastasia Damianakos.

First Edition
1 3 5 7 9 8 6 4 2

ISBN 978-1-61498-074-2

For our friends

Leland M. Hawes, Jr. (1929-2013)

Guy Miller (1926-2012)

CONTENTS

INTRODUCTION

It is indeed a tragedy that Edith May (Dowe) Miniter (1867-1934) was able to publish only one novel, *Our Natupksi Neighbors* (Henry Holt, 1916) during her long literary career. She virtually flooded the amateur world with her stories between her advent to the hobby in 1883 and her marriage to John T. Miniter (1864?-1900) in 1887. The struggle with *The Worcester County News* and her husband's alcoholism occupied the ensuing years 1887-91. Then, in 1893, after a brief New Hampshire exile, Edith Miniter, separated from her husband, returned to Boston to work for the society weekly *The Boston Home Journal*. She resumed her activity in the Hub Amateur Journalists' Club (founded 1890) and with her mother Jennie (Tupper) Dowe (1840-1919) entered into the whirlwind of its social and literary activities. It was only possible for Edith to concentrate greater attention on her writing when she left *The Boston Home Journal* in 1906 and with her mother rented a home in the Dorchester section of Boston. It was in the "observatory" atop their home "Stately Stairways" at 17 Akron Street that Edith composed most of her novel *Our Natupski Neighbors*. While her novel received a number of favorable reviews, the sales did not encourage Henry Holt to contract with Mrs. Miniter for a sequel.

The death of Edith's mother in March 1919 marked the end of an era in her life. In the fall of 1918, she and her mother had had to give up their home at 17 Akron Street and move in with fellow amateurs Charles and Laurie Sawyer in Allston, Massachusetts. Later, amateur journalists Charles and Augusta Parker in Malden, Massachusetts also provided shelter for Edith. But none of these living arrangements proved wholly satisfactory. The Hub Club more or less disintegrated following the effort of hosting the National Amateur Press Association convention in Boston in 1924, and by 1925 Edith had returned to her birthplace, Wilbraham, Massachusetts, to live in the home of her remote relation Evanore Olds Beebe (1858-1935). Only a few amateur journalists, including notably H. P. Lovecraft in 1928, were privileged to visit her in her refuge there. It was hoped that she might attend the Boston convention of the National Amateur Press Association in

1930, but her health did not permit. She felt well enough to attend the local Memorial Day celebrations on May 31, 1934, but died suddenly on the afternoon of June 4, 1934, and was buried in an unmarked grave with her ancestors in Wilbraham.

The tragedies of Edith's life were surely her broken love for John T. Miniter, whom she married in 1887, and her later relationship with fellow amateur journalist John Leary Peltret (1874-1938), who made his home with Edith and her mother during much of the Akron Street period (1906-1918), and often shared their vacation times in Wilbraham. While Edith was freed to marry again by the death of her estranged husband in 1900, the man she came to love, John Peltret, was himself not free to marry.

In addition to *Our Natupski Neighbors* and her wonderful short stories, many of the best of which we selected for *Dead Houses and Other Works* (Hippocampus Press, 2008), Edith left at least three novel fragments: *Love Without Wings* (serialized but not completed in Edith's amateur magazine *The Varied Year* in 1902-10), *Lydia 'n Gerald* (composed 1920-22?), and *The Village Green* (composed 1923-25?). Despite our concern for their fragmentary nature, we have chosen to publish all three of these novels in this collection, primarily because they reflect so directly the heart of the authoress. Surely in the toils of the young couple with a weekly newspaper in *Love Without Wings* we cannot help but recognize some of the circumstances of Edith's own troubled marriage. *Lydia 'n Gerald*, on the other hand, returns to the Wilbraham scene of her masterful story "Dead Houses" and her novel-length account of the immigrant Natupski family in *Our Natupski Neighbors*, with the same deep feeling for her ancestral roots that informed both of those masterful works. In *Lydia 'n Gerald*, Lydia Dutton, faced with an unfaithful and profligate husband, nevertheless seeks to make a future for her son Gerald despite her poverty. *Lydia 'n Gerald* shares the same episodic structure (essentially a gathering of virtually independent short stories) as *Our Natupski Neighbors*. In fact, Mrs. Miniter may have tried to market some of the chapters of of *Lydia 'n Gerald* as short stories—particularly those which exist in typescript form. But the editors have not succeeded so far in tracing any periodical publication for the surviving chapters of *Lydia 'n Gerald*. Because of its episodic structure, *Lydia 'n Gerald* suffers the least of Edith's three novel fragments from its incompleteness. It is in fact one of her surviving masterworks.

By the 1920s Edith had begun to redirect her literary efforts from short stories and novels to periodical articles focussed primarily on old-time New England life. Among her successes in this domain were appearances in *The New York Times* and *Antiques*. *The Village Green*, probably composed during the 1923-25 period during which she was transitioning to permanent residence with Evanore Olds Beebe in Wilbraham, is very likely Edith's last novel-length fiction. Her protagonist is Flora Hancock, a thirty-year-old Chicago career girl who inherits her aunt's somewhat decrepit home in the Boston suburbs. In a discarded fragment of *The Village Green*, she writes Flora's frustrated love for newspaperman Arthur Comyns:

> Well, she'd make this a turning point. Arthur Comyns should be effectively barred from any apartment which was hers to be in the vicinage of the Village Green. She considered the past and decided he had never brought her anything but sorrow. Even his brief time of fondness had brought sorrow; desire born of memory assuaged only by dreams; unassuageable until she hit upon the opiate of dreams. She did not consider his possible grief. She did not believe men felt grief, or any need of woman unless a bad one to satisfy a temporary passion. Strong in sex consciousness but weak in sexuality, she had set this man apart from humanity, making him a fetish and a devil. She did not know that he had done her a bit of good.
>
> Yet he had shown her the Bible people walking, not as gods, but as very mortal mortals, eating, drinking, squabbling, quitting one another cold, as Barnabas Paul when they fell out on itinerant missionarying. He had proved the iniquity of a split infinitive.

Perhaps Mrs. Miniter considered this passage too explicitly reflective of her protagonist's sexuality to pass the censors of her day.

Make no mistake—the editors make no exaggerated claims for *The Village Green*, whose portrait of a local literary club patterned on Edith's Hub Club never really jells into a coherent narrative. Perhaps if we were closer to some of the figures who played a prominent role in the Hub Club during the 1915-24 decade we could feel closer to Edith's narrative. Apart from the clear identification of H. Theobald, Jr.—"the man with the long chin"—with Howard Phillips Lovecraft, other identifications are harder to make at this remove. Club President Flo Sullivan is almost certainly modeled on Joseph Bernard Lynch (1879-1952), while Amelia Comyns and her lover Jim Jeffreys Hazelwonda are probably modeled on Elise Dorothy (Grant) McLaughlin (1889-1980) and George Julian Houtain (1884-1945), both of whom did in fact divorce their spouses to marry. Flora Hancock's legal advisor Herbert Trinkett is probably modeled on Hub Club member Walter H. Thorpe, who was in fact an attorney but died in court in Boston in 1918, before H. P. Lovecraft ever attended a Hub Club meeting. So, despite characters drawn from actuality, *The Village Green* is hardly a disguised attempt at Hub Club history.

Rather, *The Village Green* attains its few successes when it succeeds in engaging us in its characters. Of her protagonist Flora Hancock, Edith Miniter paints this sympathetic portrait:

> Flora was not exactly dumb, though she had done very little talking at Aunt Lury's funeral. Caution had been strongly developed in her school of regular work at small pay. Also, her looks had helped develop it. She was mighty good looking if one liked the type—of middle height, plump. A mass of reddish gold hair covered her head. It was disposed, from eyebrows to nape, in artfully arranged swirls. Her eyes were blue, the blue of the turquoise rather than of the forget-me-not.

Probably the next most sympathetically depicted character is Flora's man-hating tenant Etta:

> Etta's plainly disposed brown and brick-red hair, her high cheek bones, surmounted by small steel-colored eyes, her neat, upstanding figure and her brisk step, combined to express her principal characteristics. She was smart, that is, she was smart as the Village Green read the word. She could estimate the quantity of oysters needed for a church stew, and how much coke would carry a furnace through the winter as compared

to coal. She loved economy so much that she practiced it for other people. Not a trained nurse, she was able to carry out doctor's orders with absolute fidelity, and had done so in the case of Aunt Lury's rather unique jaundice. Making a virtue of the fact that she never read books—that not one was written which would keep her awake—she was lost without her 88-page *Saturday Transcript.*

While it is bony-kneed Belle Emerson who shares her bed with Flora the night after Aunt Lury's funeral, one almost imagines as one possible denouement for *The Village Green* Flora's and Etta's making permanent household together in Aunt Lury's decrepit mansion. The narrative is surely informed by a strong consciousness of contemporary sexual mores—from discussions of diaphonous women's lingerie to Mr. Posie's and Amelia's leaving a $5 bill in tribute for their illicit union in Flora's home. Like the young husband in *Love Without Wings*, Arthur Comyns must also draw considerably on Mrs. Miniter's own husband John T. Miniter. Lovecraft enthusiasts, of course, will delight over Mrs. Miniter's closely-lined portrayal of club member H. Theobald, Jr.

Stories about a sequel for *Our Natupski Neighbors* have been rummaging around in Miniter-land for decades. In the Brown University Lovecraft Collection—which holds the manuscripts of *Lydia 'n Gerald* and *The Village Green*—there are only several short outlines and a fragment of a chapter from the fabled *Natupski* sequel. W. Paul Cook and H. P. Lovecraft undertook the posthumous handling of the intestate Mrs. Miniter's literary affairs, and Lovecraft's holdings of Miniter material came to Brown University. Unless the *Natupski* sequel survives in more substantial form among the Cook holdings, it is likely that *Lydia 'n Gerald* and *The Village Green* as published herein will be the last-published novel-length (albeit incomplete) works from the pen of Edith Miniter. Fortunately, *Our Natupski Neighbors* itself is freely available on-line at Google Books and also available in several relatively inexpensive paper reprint editions.

We should add a few words concerning the incomplete state of the three novels that we present here. *Lydia 'n Gerald* is probably the most complex case. A "later contents page" preserved among the Miniter manuscripts at Brown University lists fourteen chapters as follows:

I.   Where Lydia Lived [check]
II.   Lydia Puts a Hen On [o]
III. Both Ways Across the Board [o]
IV. Helping God Out [o]
V.   Just Exactly Like Her [o]
VI. As Three Comforted Job [o]
VII. Poor Fish [check]
VIII. The Little Girl Who Died [check]
IX. A Petticoat That Rustled [check]
X.   Prodigious Beebes [check]
XI. A New Front Door [check]
XII. A Great American Poet [check]
XIII. Those Helion Students [check]
XIV. Craziness Better than T'other

Of these we believe we have all but Chapters III, V and VI. We derive Chapters II and IV from typescripts provided to us by R. Alain Everts. Chapter IV has the alternative title "A Successful Lumper for God" in the Everts typescript. Mrs. Miniter apparently originally contemplated extending *Lydia 'n Gerald* to twenty-two chapters but in the end decided upon fourteen. We hope that it is still possible that Chapters III, V and VI will eventually be recovered. Mrs. Miniter may have tried to market some of the chapters separately as stories, but we have not found record of any stories published under the chapter titles. Perhaps the chapters marked with "o" in Mrs. Miniter's "later contents page" were those which she tried to market separately as short stories and were separated from the main body of her manuscript. All of the chapters marked with a check mark in Mrs. Miniter's "later contents page" (plus Chapter XIV) are present in the manuscript at Brown University.

The Village Green, by way of contrast, seems to exist only in the manuscript at Brown University, which ends abruptly and is followed by an apparently unrelated essay on George William Curtis's *The Potiphar Papers* (1853). We have choosen to include the Potiphar essay for completeness. Perhaps some Miniter aficionado will eventually decide to undertake a completion of *The Village Green*. We can imagine Flora eventually reconciling with the man-hating Etta and continuing to share Aunt Lury's somewhat decrepit home on the Village Green although we cannot imagine the two as lovers. It seems harder to imagine that Flora might have eventually married Arthur Comyns, who once spurned her in favor of Amelia. It is harder to imagine destinies for the rest of the numerous cast of characters of this novel, although of course we know the life story of H. Theobald, Jr.

Love Without Wings was printed in installments in Mrs. Miniter's amateur magazine *The Varied Year* between 1902 and 1910 and was left incomplete when the magazine ceased publication. We do not know whether Mrs. Miniter wrote any further chapters. Since H. P. Lovecraft and W. Paul Cook shared the posthumous management of Mrs. Miniter's literary affairs, it is possible that further chapters of *Love Without Wings* survive in Cook's half of the literary estate. Lovecraft's half of the Miniter literary estate is held in the Lovecraft Collection at Brown University.

Out of concern that the incomplete nature of Mrs. Miniter's three novels *Lydia 'n Gerald*, *The Village Green* and *Love Without Wings* may leave some readers dissatisfied, we have chosen to add a series of ten short stories first published in the amateur press between 1885 and 1891. These stories, which include Mrs. Miniter's notorious "ultra-realist" stories "For a Big Roll of Money" (1890) and "Cindy's Child" (1891), reflect the growth of Mrs. Miniter's writing from the juvenilia first published in the amateur press in 1884-85 through an accomplished narrative like "A Tragedy of the Hills" (1891) (published by us in *Dead Houses and Other Works*). One can particularly note the development of Mrs. Miniter's vocabulary and descriptive power over the range of these early stories from 1885 to 1891. For lovers of the gothic genre, "Who Brought the Children Home?" (1885) and "The Other Elizabeth" (1888) both provide dark examples of an apprenticeship which finally culminated in the masterwork "Wonted Fires" (1905). The most notable development of Mrs. Miniter's short fiction between 1885 and 1891, however, is surely the increasing notice of sexuality. A married women envies a single women who was her spouse's first love, a married woman with an unfaithful spouse chooses suicide, another woman frustrated in her marriage flees with an old lover, friends entrap a young woman in an unwanted assignation in return for money, and finally in "Cindy's Child" the protagonist commit suicide on her wedding day when confronted with a lover's accusation that she killed her child. The ten short stories presented here can be seen as practice for the finer works presented in *Dead Houses and Other Works*, *Our Natupski Neighbors* (1916) and the incomplete novels presented here.

So as not to neglect other important aspects of Mrs. Miniter's writing, we present as "Book Ends" two examples of her work in other genres: "How to Dress on $40 a Year," her famous 1891 article in the *Boston Sunday Globe* (rediscovered by David Goudsward and shared with us for publication here) and "A Rearward Glance," Mrs. Miniter's affectionate look at her early years in the amateur journalism hobby, originally serialized in *The Varied Year* in 1909-10. Readers commented for weeks afterward in "Everybody's Column" after Mrs. Miniter's essay on dressing on a strict budget was first published; perhaps the entire discussion should eventually be reprinted. Many of Mrs. Miniter's best friends in the amateur journalism hobby are featured in "A Rearward Glance." It was probably the joy of those early associations which kept her faithful through all the tribulations of her later years in the hobby.

In closing, we hope that *Dead Houses and Other Works* (2008) and *The Village Green and Other Pieces* will succeed in staking a claim for Mrs. Miniter in the hierarchy of New England regional writing. We feel that a new critical edition of her novel *Our Natupski Neighbors* (1916), accompanied by the sequel outline and fragment held in the Brown University Special Collections, certainly ought to be published in time for the centenary celebration of its original publication in 2016. The following year, 2017, will mark the one hundred fiftieth anniversary of Mrs. Miniter's birth, and we hope by that time that a further selection of her short fiction will also have been published. While *Our Natupski Neighbors* may have been spurned by many of the residents of Mrs. Miniter's hometown in Wilbraham, Massachusetts when it was originally published, it is our hope that Mrs. Miniter's literary reputation will be so solidly enshrined in the New England literary pantheon by the two hundred fiftieth anniversary of her birth in 2117 that students in Wilbraham, Massachusetts will freely choose their "native daughter" and her works as the subjects of their school essays. In summary, we hope that Mrs. Miniter's trenchant observations of human character will continue to be appreciated by future generations of readers. We thank our publisher Derrick Hussey of Hippocampus Press for helping to realize our hopes for Mrs. Miniter's literary posterity.

Kenneth W. Faig, Jr.
Sean Donnelly

LYDIA 'N GERALD

I. Where Lydia Lived

Lydia Dutton lived in a house which was her own, and which had two chimneys. Both these facts made her very proud. And the view from her front window she considered the most beautiful in all the town of Holly. To you it would have been merely a green meadow with several walnut trees growing so near the line that at least two bushels of salable nuts were lost to Lydia every year. You would not have considered the view anything, either because of its unpleasant message about the walnuts, or by comparison with the really first class view of Mt. Tom from the room Lydia had once lived in down at "Father Dutton's." Ah— but this was her own, and sight of Mt. Tom had continually reminded Lydia that she had never visited Mt. Tom; that she would probably never get a bonnet handsome enough to go so far in. People who live near a famous object, as Bunker Hill Monument or Niagara Falls, probably feel free to drop in any day in a sun hat or without any head covering, but those from a distance feel different. Lydia knew. Once she had gone 2 1/2 miles to Holly Street with only an umbrella. She had hoped to be mistaken for a professor's wife who had just run over from Faculty Street to the grocer's with a parasol, but she felt the subterfuge was apparent. She never tried it again. She said she felt "too conspicuous." To really appreciate Lydia's house as she did you must have led the life she had as wife of Chris Dutton. Fifteen years, living with her folks, and his folks, and the underground part of Great Aunt Mari's with a place for a boy to sleep in the garret and two shelves in the pantry.

The way Lydia got her house was thus: she found the house was for sale, so she deliberately picked a quarrel with Mother Dutton, for the first and only time in their mutual and united protest against the tyrant man. The quarrel was over the pinning of Gerald's barrow coat, Gerald being the baby. Mother Dutton then told Father Dutton she was going to get Christopher's family out of the house. So Mother Dutton took $50 of Father Dutton's money and loaned it to their son

Christopher, actually handing it to Lydia so it would reach the right destination. Lydia made a first payment and the house was hers. The other $550 stood in the form of a mortgage held by Mother Dutton.

The house had started in life as a cobbler's shop. It had but a single chimney then, as the cobbler needed only one stove in which to burn his scraps of leather. Lydia had not only a kitchen stove, but one in the sitting room, and a chimney for each. The one in the kitchen had needed a lining for five or six years, and the top was cracked so that flames came into the room and it wasn't safe to go away and leave any fire burning. But then Lydia never did go away. Otherwise it was a real good stove, only the oven did not bake on the bottom at all and one was obliged to finish the pies on top of the covers.

The sitting room stove was a section of stovepipe set on end and would burn nothing larger than corncobs.

There were two outside doors to the house, also, both from the kitchen. The one opening on the piazza had a wire screen and was hooked in three places. Lydia never opened it except for important people, as the minister come to call, or her husband. The back door was screened only with pink netting, and flies were further discouraged by an army of fringed newspapers.

You must not consider this a house of poverty. There was a downstairs bedroom having a bed plump with feathers and ruffled pillow cases. There was also a bureau in which Lydia frequently kept the money for a cashmere dress pattern or a gravestone or a set of teeth. She never had the things themselves, owing to her husband's propensity to finding and spending money. In the sitting room was a nice rag carpet and a great many drawn in or hooked or braided rugs; also chairs made comfortable with interlacings of bright colored dress braid where the cane had broken. Every chair had a tidy and a cushion. On the table was a real good looking spread of red felt stamped with black, and in the centre a wool mat with bugle beads on which set one of those big lamps. It did leak considerably—that lamp—and Lydia was forever washing out the mat so it wouldn't be too smelly; but, oh, what a splendid light it gave. And Lydia thought a lot of that, because she loved to read evenings. Father Dutton had subscribed to the N.Y. *Ledger* and Mother Dutton gave her a great pile of them to put under the carpet, but Lydia used straw and kept the papers for a library. She never got tired of the long-continued stories by Mrs. Henry Wood and Mrs. E. D. E. N. Southworth. They would stand reading over and over again, because each was so long you had pretty well forgotten the one before—or else mixed it up with still another by Miss Braddon. Often Lydia tranced would be caught by her husband coming in at about dawn and how she would put out the light and hyper to bed and pretend to be fast asleep!

Lydia did not waste the daytime reading, because her housework kept her busy, especially the outdoors part, such as feeding chickens, hoeing the garden, picking berries, building fence, cleaning out the stable, and cutting brush. Then she liked to cook, which was a good thing, as the folks liked to eat, particularly between meals. It was quite a tramp from the kitchen to the pantry through the sitting room and bedroom, when she had cleaned up and put away the dishes and sugar bowl and so on it was only making your head save your heels to carry back flour and sugar and such and knock up a few pies. She never had a moulding board, but the table, well scrubbed, did just as well.

Luke, Lydia's oldest child, stopped but one night at his parents' house after they moved there when he was eight and Gerald a baby. Making his other shirt into a bundle he ran away across lots back to Grandfather Dutton's. It would have been much nearer on the road, but he went 'cross lots because he was running away. It not being a Dutton habit to compel any male to do anything he did not wish to do, Luke had lived ever since with his grandparents. He always referred to Lydia's house as "that homesick ole place up there."

Of course the house did have deficiencies—but then, said Lydia, what house doesn't have them? Even Father and Mother Dutton's mansion was dreadful short of closet room. For explanation of any peculiarities in Lydia's dwelling—as that the upstairs bedrooms weren't done off, or that the front door hadn't got itself out yet, or that the cellar entrance was out of doors and very inconvenient in times of summer rain or winter snow—one need only to understand that both Father Dutton and Christopher Dutton were carpenters.

Lots of neighbors remembered what shocking bad shoes had been worn by the cobbler's wife.

* * *

II. Lydia Puts a Hen On*

Lydia was just telling the cat it was a poor pie that couldn't grease its own plate, when she heard wheels rattle.

Two strides took her out of the back door, a few more, skirt wide, to the six apple trees sprigged up in dignity as the orchard. Well, the place looked as it ought to look in September after the fruit was gathered. There were a few dead leaves and twigs on the turf, and the trees had a dishevelled appearance, as of a woman whose children had lately gone to the city to work. Of apples only a smell remained, mixing with that of trampled grass.

Lydia returned to her piecrust. It is hard, however, to effect artistic triumphs with a divided mind. Thrusting into the oven—which baked only from the top of that side next the firebox—a matter badly crimped as to edges, she ran out, balancing a ball of dough from hand to hand, and banged on the woodshed. Gerald was changing to overalls. Lydia always made him change there since she once suspected him of a flea.

"Gerald," she called, "you can't—"

He came from behind a meager array of cut birch, and stood pulling a blue denim strap over his right shoulder.

"Can't what, ma?"

"You can't—" she stopped because she knew too well what she must say. And the honest trust of his eyes made it impossible to say it.

So in place of "you can't have school books," she made it, "You can't guess what your pa's done."

"No," said Gerald, pretty glum for eight years, "I can't."

"Picked the apples."

"No?"

"Every one. Cider middlings and all. And barreled 'em."

"Honest?"

"He has. And headed 'em up. And h'isted 'em into the wagon."

This was where she began to laugh. Choking, she went on, "And catched the hoss. And cl'ked. And drove off."

She kept on laughing, till her eyes blinded with tears. Gerald laughed. She helped him by a dig in the ribs. It was a wonderful joke.

The editors thank R. Alain Everts for a copy of the typescript of this chapter.

Because when the barrels rode away they took with them Gerald's school books and school pants and a barrel of flour and perhaps a set of teeth to replace the ones Lydia gave to get Gerald.

Suddenly Lydia was made aware, by the vexed countenance of the cat, that it wasn't proper nice for the mother of a family to be tossing a dough ball and threatening hysterics while the fire burned.

"Oh, this will never buy the child a dress," she sighed, and marched back to her baking. Five minutes later she shoved a superior pie into the oven and peeked from the window. Gerald had stopped laughing. She tapped on the glass until he looked up, shook her finger and made motions with her lips.

They said, "I've got a hen on."

But Gerald thought she had promised a turnover, and so came in to wear out his shoes kicking the woodbox. Therefore she made one, before scraping the table with the back of an old case knife—for the wood-working Duttons never provided their wives with molding boards.

"What's my thought like?" she asked, and answered herself, too impatient to wait—"Like your Gran'pa Dutton."

"If you put more wood in 'twould bake quicker," said Gerald.

"It would not. It would burn on top and soak below. Now why is my thought like your Gran'pa Dutton?"

Gerald considered a long moment and produced this, "Because Gran'pa did pretty good when he married father to us, so he needn't keep him to home."

Lydia looked wise like at the sky. "It's plain," she remarked, "you wasn't round then to hear the tow-row your Gran'pa made. But that's not the answer. It's 'cause you're going to have your face wiped off with the corner of a towel wet at the tea-kettle spout—so! And your hair brushed off'n your face—so! And your shoes give a lick an' a promise with your ma's apurn—so! And while the turniper finishes on top the stove you're going down to tell Gran'pa Dutton all about it."

Gerald produced a cap from some crevice of his anatomy and started. He had only got to the Parting Tree, halfway down the hill, when from a slat sunbonnet on top came sibilant orders.

"Remember—Gerald—not to ask for nothing. Don't let him—think—your ma's grew up to be a beggar."

He was a mere sliver, turning in at the gate under the cherry tree, when the last words floated down to him. Lydia nodded in contentment, and went back to her pies, now heaving as with ocean swells atop of the fire. He'd recollect. He'd been told often enough before. This running to the brow of the hill was only a ceremony.

Gerald was back in a short time.

"Well," said Lydia, who was stirring butter, the churn being broken since the year before Gerald was born.

"Oh, ma! You never put an oak leaf on it!"

Gerald referred to the turnover.

"It'll taste just as good when you set your teeth into it. Well?"

Gerald began to eat all around, like a cat trying something hot.

"I hate Gran'pa Dutton," he said. "I don't hate him like I hate Gran'pa Luther, but I hate him pretty good."

"Did you tell him you was lotting on school books?"

"Well, I did. And he was awful mean. He's just buyed Brother Lute a algibbera. And he was mad 'cause he'd buyed Brother Lute a algibbera. What is an algibbera, ma?"

"It's what he's buyed your big brother Lute. Your Gran'pa Dutton is a very forehanded man, only he's got to be handled right."

"He said algibberas was no use and a great note. When he was a boy he got to tare and tret and graduated. What is tare and tret, ma?"

"Your Gran'pa Dutton graduated at it, and he's a wonderful smart man. Don't forget that. The only man that could pile cord wood round the same stump year arter year and sell that stump over and over to the Boston & Albany Railroad. Did you have sufficient forethought, son, to tell him that like as not you'd never take algibbera?"

Gerald nodded, his mouth full. He dared not confess that in excess of zeal he had told his grandfather he didn't care much about school anyway, to which his exasperated elder had responded, "Very well, then, go home-alone and earn your—"

"Ma, how much salt do I eat?" was the query that gave Lydia a hint of the turn conversation had taken down in the big house.

"Oh, me; oh, my," sighed Lydia, setting her pies away in the pantry. "Anybody can toll a hen to a nest, the tug o' war's to make her keep on setting."

Yet in a few minutes she was back with a good natured inquiry as to Grandfather Dutton's apples. All carted away, were they? The men paying a great many dollar bills for them while Gerald was present.

Perhaps that accounted for the testiness of the old man. He was always pudjecky, Lydia knew, when anyone saw him acquiring anything. Like the boa constrictor, he wished to accumulate in secret. And then she flew to Grandfather Luther.

"No so forehanded with hisn, 'count of having no hoss."

Gerald wriggled in disgust at being called from contemplation of his own situation—schoolbookless, turnoverless, to pity a maternal grandparent, merely horseless.

"Now, Gerald, don't get twittery. Be a good boy and go pick up some your Gran'pa Luther's apples. Pick up a nice wagon load of 'em. Get 'em off the Gravenstein tree and the early Baldwin. Red cheeked apples catches the fancy of the mill folks. They don't know Greenings is a sight better pie filling."

"Oh, ma, don't ask me to pick up apples for Gran'pa Luther. There's enough work for us to do before frost and school. If I start helping the old folks our crops'll never be got in."

"Gerald, you stop talking so selfish. You ought to consider old bones. You should, so. Your Gran'pa Luther'll never be 70 again—or maybe 69. I ought to know, seeing's he's my pa. Anyway, it gives anyone over and above 25 a crick in the back to pick up apples. Such a slew of 'em as he's got, too. And such store as he sets by 'em. Specially the Gravensteins and early Baldwins. Always capital sellers, he used to say, with the mill hands."

Suddenly Gerald's anger broke bounds.

"Pa tooked the cherries," he whispered. "And then he tooked the raspb'rys. And then the peaches."

"Now, Gerald," said his mother, in the tone she usually kept for telling a well-spent neighbor woman that it was a fine boy and weighed nigh on to ten pounds, "we ain't got no time for discussing your pa. School takes up Monday week, and your books is over in Eastfield, and no idea in anybody's head that they were going to have Gerald Christopher Dutton District 7 written in 'em."

"Ma," said Gerald, bravely, "I don't want you to take on 'bout it 'cause I can't go to school. It ain't so much, going to school. I can go out and get me a job if you'll only say I'm big enough."

"You got a job right here on Holly Mountain. Picking your Gran'pa Luther's apples. A real honorable job."

Gerald had experience with his mother when she was set. He supposed he would have to go, and went. Lydia sped him on his way with a piece of cut pie and numerous admonitions.

"Don't let out anything about our apples being gone."

"Remember, I never told you. It's all your own doing."

"Ask pa how he finds his bronchitis. It's asthma, but he likes to call it bronchitis, 'cause sometimes they get better of that."

"Don't tell mother you had anything to eat since breakfast."

"Say I'm laying out to come over before a great while, and mention I ain't been to your Gran'pa Dutton's for more'n two weeks and they was in a stew about it."

Mr. and Mrs. Ithamir Luther lived very comfortably in a manner that shocked the town. They had made an opening between kitchen and stable and got the heat of the cow in the winter. Besides, Mrs. Luther saved up her dishes till she had enough to be worth washing.

Gerald was well received by his grandparents and fed up with doughnuts after carefully observing his mother's fourth precept. But when he began to pick apples trouble arose.

"I'll thank you, young sir," wheezed the old man, flourishing an impotent cane, "to let my fruit alone. I'm capable of harvesting it in my own time. And then I want it left on the trees till the leaves fall, so the sunshine can get to all sides and give better color. Besides, I've sold it, to be picked on shares."

The faded and fretful old fellow roused Gerald's contrariness. The boy never did like his Grandfather Luther, except perhaps for an hour on Thanksgiving Day. Lydia knew it.

"I'll pick half this tree and 'nother," said Gerald. "Your half, 'course."

Lydia was watching up the road with questions to meet him.

"How'd you make out? Get anything of a sufficiency? I hope you didn't ask for nothing?"

"No, ma."

"That's right. Never be a teaser nor a whiner."

"I ain't, ma. I never asked him if I could pick the apples. I went ahead and picked 'em."

"That's the boy. Now come in and draw to the table. The sun ain't quite round to the noon mark, but I guess you won't mind having twins.

8

Eat hearty, but don't dawdle. You got to go down and get your Gran'pa Dutton's hoss an' team that's hitched down by his barn while he's in swallering his dinner. He's laying out to go somewhere, I s'pose, which is real lucky, 'cause while you drive pretty good, you're too small to harness that great tall nag. You needn't say nothing to him till you're driving out the yard. Then you might mention you'll fetch the team back before sundown. Be sure and tell him, as otherwise he might be discommoded about going tomorrow where he's planning to go this afternoon."

Not until the vehicle, so borrowed, was filled with Ithamir Luther's Gravensteins and early Baldwins and the horse turned Mifflin Mills way, did Gerald see the beauty of the plan.

"Oh, ma," he cried, bouncing beside her on the leather thongs that made the seat, "we're using Gran'pa Dutton's team to sell Gran'pa Luther's apples so's to buy my school books. Oh, ma; you're pretty smart, ma!"

"N-no," said Lydia, judiciously applying the whip to flick the flies off old Ned. "I wouldn't go so far as to say that of myself. But I'm desirous, Gerald, that you shall grow up beholden to nobody. Just 'cause you got two gran'pas that's well-to-do, is no reason you should expect them to fork over at every turn. Your school books will be a real prize to you now, 'cause you can reflect you earned 'em honest. I don't want you to turn out, Gerald, one o' those tubs that can't stand on its own bottom.

IV. A Successful Lumper for God

It was a long winter and Christopher Dutton was due for a jolt. So his wife, Lydia, told herself, as she began to take violent measures to keep the boy Gerald from sensing the cold. Gerald had been sweeping the woodshed, but brought an empty dustpan for his pains.

"Nothing there, ma," he announced, with the unthinking sulkiness of eight years. "Jus 's I tole yer. We scrubbed it awful slick that cole spell long Thanksgiving."

"I wouldn't wonder," returned Lydia, airily, because she had merely sent the lad out with a view to utilizing a little sharp work toward a

The editors thank R. Alain Everts for a copy of the transcript of this chapter. We have determined this chapter to be identical to "Helping God Out" in Miniter's later contents page for Lydia 'n Gerald.

warming up. He was still pretty pale around the gills, but she said nothing about a great plan for making a real fire—a plan which had sprung full-grown during his absence. She just sat down on a chair that might very well have been painted with ice, and watched a few snowflakes that were drifting aimlessly, as if sluggish with cold. Gerald could not keep still. He dashed into the other room—all the doors had been reduced to firewood earlier in the season, which made it convenient getting about—and jumped with both feet into the middle of a calico covered couch. There was a sound of clattering springs and rending cloth almost human in intensity.

"Gerald, what are you a-doing?"

"I'm busting up the ole lounge, ma. It'll make a grand blaze, ma."

"Gerald Dutton, you stop such carryings on d'rectly," said Lydia, heaving herself up on her aching knees. "Just you think how that ole lounge pays for itself in haying season. So nice an cool to camp down on right under the open winder. Consider, my son, consider."

For answer, Gerald glared, but he did consider, and ceased operations on the furniture. Neither he nor his mother told one another the truth about the lounge, that it was used by no one but Christopher, either summer or winter. Indeed, Lydia hoped Gerald had never noticed this. But his next performance made her doubt much innocence. For he tramped upstairs and came down with a butternut heaped box. "Two barrels full, ma" he cried. "Guess you forgot about 'em, ma. Kind o' greasy. Bet they'd burn fine."

Lydia felt herself nigh stumped. For neither she nor her son ever enjoyed the butternuts, which Christopher Dutton was apt to carry away (cracked) by the sackful when he went to spend the evening out. Gerald was generally supposed to be asleep, what time his father left. But he was getting to a noticing age. Feeling quick action to be necessary, Lydia merely shook her head at the nuts, and began animatedly to carry out her plan for the jolt.

"Come, now, Gerald," she cried, "stick up your feet till I tie your pants tight down—now put this extry cloud right over your cap and lemme wind it round your neck and give it a good firm tie behind— now pull these mittens on over yourn—I don't need more'n a single pair, in the house here, all sheltered. Take this sharp little hatchet and git your sled. Hyper up the road and piece and cut some brush. Up front of Silver's is the best, I guess—between the road commissioners and us ain't much left down this way. While you're gone I'll start a fire. I aim to break up the woodbox. No sense having a great woodbox and nothing to put in it. Like Silly Sukey when she went to the fair and spent all the money she had to her name for a money-puss."

The child was gone. He looked very tiny and frail, as he breasted the rising storm. "Ain't much to him, spite o' three pair pants," Lydia told herself. She hoped she hadn't sent him out to catch his never get over, even if his father did deserve a jolt. But it probably wouldn't take long. Any father ought to get a good jolt when he saw his little boy trying to cut brush with two pairs of mittens on, after that father had not only neglected to supply his family with fuel, but had disposed of the three good cords of maple donated in October by the old folks.

Well, Gerald was back exceeding soon. He slammed up to the door with his empty sled, and began to undress instantly.

"Unwind me, ma," he yelled. "A feller doesn't need one scarve round his throat and nother on his head. And all these pants! I'm too tight, ma. Take me off some jackets, ma. And you hold all the cats, ma. Me—I'm burning afire."

The Duttons, like the child wife of Edgar Allan Poe, cultivated pussies as warming pans. Gerald's own particular mass of yellow fur was waiting to leap into his arms. Lydia nodded her head triumphantly. It had worked. The scheme had worked. At least, it had partly worked. Whether or not Christopher got a jolt, Gerald had seen something which saved him from shivering. "Good on my head," Lydia chuckled to herself, while calmly receiving the discarded articles of clothing. Some she put on herself, the others were folded away where they would be handy.

Quite suddenly a queer sound broke on the icy air. Gerald was cold. A chill crept over his young form, he trembled violently, his teeth chattered, he bit his lip until it bled. For the first time Lydia's generally stout courage showed signs of wear. Could she stand it? Would it not be as well to own herself beat? Then she looked once more in the face of her son and decided that the comfort of accepting defeat would be impossible. She must keep right on trying. Luckily, her eyes fell on the clock. It didn't go, because the works were gummed with cold, but it gave her another splendid idea.

"Gerald," she said, "what you about, having a conniption fit, and no wood? Didn't I tell you cut some brush? Stuffed twine into your pockets, so's you could tie it on the shed. And you ain't brang home so much as a twig. Lazy, lolloping, good-for-nothing—"

"Ma," interposed Gerald, quite passionately for an eight-year-old, "don't make me go back. I can't go back. I won't. Don't you go for to asking me why for, nuther."

"Gerald Dutton, don't you give me none your sass, or you'll get something you can't buy to store. You tell me your excuse and be quick about it."

"I won't," shrieked Gerald, his voice rising to a wail as he yelled, "won't, won't, won't."

"Say won't to me," muttered Lydia. As she spoke she reached back of the clock and took down a good birchen switch. With her left hand she grabbed the boy. "I don't care, ma," he shouted. "You can lick me, ma, if you're a mind to. But I'll keep right on saying won't." Then, after a ghastly pause, during which Lydia struck some pretty good blows, "I never thunk, ma, 'twould be you who was mean." Lydia, thus reminded of the time when she had rushed between the little thin boy and his father, on a day when the birch switch was first cut, when she had taken the blows meant for the child on her own skinny shoulders— the memory did its best to put the weapon of injustice back on the wall. Then conscience ceased to cower. Lydia saw her duty and did not flinch. After a terrible scene was over, and Gerald had refused any milk made lukewarm over a kerosene lamp, she sent him to bed. He clumped away, glum and sore, but with his thin lips set in a stern resolve. As he relaxed in the warmth of wool blankets, a strip of rag carpet and all the cats, he hugged his determination as for a lifetime. Never should his mother learn what he had seen!

His father and Mabel Silver, standing in Silver's front room, in the glow of Silver's great baseburner, laughing at the little boy's awkwardness in handling a hatchet in mittened hands. Well, there was nothing more for him to learn. He knew it all now—where the sacks of nuts went, all shucked; and the finest apples and peaches. And however much she might beat him, he would never tell his mother. Never!

After the boy had gone, Lydia concerned herself for half an hour with the old problem—did one sense the cold more sitting still and

EDITH MINITER

feeling it creep-mousing, or bustling about stirring up a breeze? Then she fell into a doze and on waking up saw moonlight repeating the pattern of the many paned window on the rag carpet. At this she knew it must be far after midnight. Christopher was not coming home. Christopher had not received a jolt.

As her stomach seemed about to slump in, she went to the but'ry and cut herself a slice of bread. Doubling it, she raised the morsel to her lips—then, perhaps because the dry bread reminded her of past communion tables, she felt it needful to pray. So she dropped her head and said quite humbly, "I beg your pardon, Lord, for taking on myself what I'd oughtn'd to. The jolts are yourn and yourn only to give, in your own time. I desarved not to succeed for my own pride and vaunting myself up, and you were perfectly right to show me my place and put me in't."

After which her head jerked itself high on its corded neck, and she reflected that having given God due thanks, she might rightfully pass a few words of praise to His good helper.

"Lyd Dutton," she reflected, "after all, you're a wonder. The child would probably have froze in his tracks if you hadn't had all them bright idees—fust, sending him out to see somewhat that got his dander up, so he was hotty quite a while, and then, when that wore off, devising a good switching to make him warm again."

These ideas, she knew, must be her own, as God could never be guilty of acting so wicked-like. But as she crept into her own bed, inadequately supplied with covers because Gerald was so well supplied, she gave her Heavenly Father one more chance.

"I'll admit," she muttered, "that if this keeps up nuther day I'll be done for. So you better have it moderate tomorrow. Just that, Lord, and I won't ask nuther thing. Whatever else is needful I can tend to myself."

* * *

13

VII. [Poor Fish]

The discovery was made that Brush Hill would support summer people. The summer people put up a bungalow with a field stone fireplace and the natives thought they would do very well when they realized they were merely squatters. No one really wished them ill, but it was a matter for secret gratulation that they attempted a driven well which in the end cost more than the house; also that when the first real August storm broke every pane of glass, it also blew the summer grandmother out of her elbow chair.

Mrs. Brookings wanted to be neighborly, and between weekends, when visitors from the city were back in the city, asked the country women, in parties of two, for a peculiar noon meal served at half past one and called luncheon. In course of time she got round to Lydia and Jim Fanning's wife, a bit of fluff whom he had rescued from a job in Mifflin Mills, cured of snuff dipping, and made a respectable woman of. Lydia put on a clean but far from new calico wrapper, a good white apron considerably patched, a slat sunbonnet, and went.

She was joined on the last bit of rising ground by Mrs. Jim, resplendent in pink muslin, fibre silk stockings and a hat mostly blue roses.

"Look who's here," cried Mrs. Jim. "Hullo, stranger. Where going? Huckleberrying?"

"I am not," said Lydia, succinctly.

"Ain't nothing but huckleberries this high," observed Mrs. Jim, lifting the muslin unnecessarily high, so Lydia could see her green petticoat was nearsilk if she wanted to look.

"There's the Brookingses."

"Oh, yes," admitted Mrs. Jim, taking sudden notice of the basket on Lydia's arm. "I s'pose they're good for a lot of eggs and garden truck."

"I presume likely they may be," said Lydia, vague as if speaking of the inhabitants of the Antipodes.

"Well, Over the River," cried Mrs. Jim, tripping nimbly up the immaculate (artificial) stone steps to the front door which bore a shining brass knocker and was protected on either side by a bay tree in a box. A sweeping gesture of the hand decorated with two garnets, a flawed turquoise and a rhinestone indicated to Lydia the path to the kitchen.

But while Mrs. Jim sought vainly for the bell-knob, Lydia reached right over her shoulder and thumped the knocker resoundingly. It couldn't awe her, that knocker, which had tarnished forty years on the thoroughly abandoned Webster place, known, for best of reasons, as the "small pox house."

While she was leading the simple life in the country, Mrs. Brookings opened her own door. Her hair was marceled, but she was dressed entirely in white linen and her shoes were merely canvas.

"How do you do?" gushed Mrs. Jim. "It was awfully sweet of you to ask me and I was tickled crazy to come. It's awful bad form to speak personal, I know, but you do look awful sweet in that get-up, and I must say your house is simply dandy."

"How d'ye do?" said Lydia, and nothing more.

Mrs. Brookings observed the patches and longed for some kindly way of offering two yards of dimity. She likewise noted the scant speech, and determined to give the awe-struck, middle aged woman at least one happy day.

The new bungalow was the completest thing possible, even to the Brookings set, with enameled bedroom furniture, a charming library, coaching prints in the living room, and kitchen ware entirely aluminum. Its possession put Mrs. Brookings into such a state of ecstasy that she could easily have supplied a ten-mile route with milk of human kindness. Today Lydia was to revel in the entire supply. Lydia interested Mrs. Brookings. Mrs. Jim was a type she had too often seen in city slumming.

The ladies took seats at a mahogany table adorned with doilies of white linen and real honiton.

"Well, Bessie," said Mrs. Brookings gaily to the neat maid, "what have you for my guests today?"

Bessie produced a shrimp wiggle, a basket of rolls and a pot of tea. At each cover was a small plate on which lay a tiny silver knife and about a teaspoonful of butter moulded into a wheat ear. A silver shell of salted nuts and a mould of crimson jelly completed the table equipment.

Those who knew Lydia's favorite attitude at table, her left elbow firmly planted beside her plate, while her right hand poured the steaming tea into a deep saucer over which her breath blew a constant, noisy

and cooling gale, would scarcely have recognized her in the Brookings'
dining room.

"Cream or lemon?" inquired Bessie.

"Oh, lemon for me," cried Mrs. Jim. "Lemon is simply dandy in
tea, ain't it, Mrs. Brookings? Before I was married and come out here
to live I just couldn't drink tea unless I had lemon for it. My landlady
used to say 'you are the greatest one for lemon in tea I ever did meet up
with.' I was a hauled mealer always, I never walked scarcely none till I
come out here to live."

Lydia's reply was brief.

"Yes, please," said she.

Mrs. Brookings could hardly eat for pitying the woman's nearly
speechless awe. All through the salad course (two lettuce leaves and a
slice of scream cheese smeared with *bar-le-duc*) she was devising plans
for showing herself in no way purseproud, and making poor Mrs. Dutton feel quite at home in what was so evidently the finest house she
had ever entered.

"Come right upstairs," she said, after Mrs. Jim had finished every
drop of her lemon sherbet and Lydia had left two-thirds of hers to
melt in the saucer. Mrs. Brookings supposed country women invariably sat in one another's bed-rooms when they sewed together after-
noons and swapped gossip. Really, of course, they did nothing of the
sort. In the spare chamber—possibly, if there had been cash and gumption to fix it like the *Ladies' Home Journal* said. But the room in which
one slept—why sit there if there was anywhere else to sit? It was not a
room for sitting in.

Before the shadows lengthened at four o'clock Mrs. Brookings
in every endeavor to break the icy reserve that presumably protected
Lydia's envy, made the two women free of her choicest treasures, as she
had made no other of her neighbor-guests.

She brought out her few bits of treasured old china and flatteringly
implied that Lydia ate off such daily. She asked advice as to the setting
up of a flax wheel, and whether or not gilding would improve it as a
hall ornament. She confided to them that her father, before he went to
legislature, was a farmer "too" and exhibited a picture of him milking a
cow. She opened to them her special pride, a wide drawer containing

pounds upon pounds of superfine chocolates, constantly renewed by a doting husband.

"Oh, how perfectly dandy," exclaimed Mrs. Jim. "I'm going to take a lot. I'm going to take two. Ain't you lucky to be hitched to such a perfectly grand man!"

"Like the stuff well enough," said Lydia, "but it doesn't like me."

It was her longest speech of the afternoon. After making it she went and looked out of the window. It was what she did in every room. Mrs. Brookings easily forgave her. Mrs. Brookings understood. The pitiable creature, once young and good looking, now worn with hard labor, wrinkled by worry, living in a hovel with a husband who beat her and a child she was barely able to find food for. She must have had her dreams, even as Cecilia Brookings (born Blodgett) had dreamed. But for Lydia no Prince Charming came riding on a white charger with a plume in his velvet cap. Indeed, a prince thus accoutred had been missing from before the Blodgett horse block. But there had come Hugh Brookings in a cute little horseless carriage (they called 'em that before they knew they were simply machines) and a knowing tweed helmet from London. So Cecilia forgave him his spectacles, which Prince Charming certainly would not have needed. Now she had a winter apartment in a hotel and the Brush Hill bungalow, hundreds of editions de luxe which she never read, and diamond ear-rings so large hardly anyone believed them true.

It wasn't fair—the way life's prizes were distributed. Mrs. Brookings, on the way to becoming a parlor anarchist, told herself it wasn't fair. In Lydia's place she would have rebelled at fate. She was quite ready, then and there, to help Lydia in such rebellion. Her active (and practically unoccupied) mind ranged over possibilities.

Mrs. Dutton, pried loose from the unsatisfactory Mr. Dutton, established in a tea room. The boy placed at some eleemosynary institution of education through Brookings' influence. Or if not in a tea room—because in a tea room a certain adaptability in meeting strangers is necessary—at least Lydia might be matron of a lunatic ward in some hospital. Or...anyway, slight amelioration might be tried here and now.

Mental starvation—Mrs. Brookings had heard of it as especially rampant in farming communities. Probably Lydia Dutton had it. She looked intelligent, though so inarticulate. Well, one might safely offer books. No slightest sting of an insult could lurk in a book.

"If I have anything you haven't read," she said, indicating carelessly the rows of O. Henry, R.L.S., British and American Poets, Robert W. Chambers and Gibbon's *Decline and Fall* in eighteen volumes rather more than fully illustrated, "I would be delighted to have you treat this little collection as your own."

Lydia, with the audacity of fright, picked a volume of Gibbon at random. A pamphlet, evidently once used as a bookmark, fell to the floor. After a glance Lydia slipped it into her apron pocket.

"Thank you," she said in a choking voice. "This'll do."

Mrs. Brookings couldn't recollect what pamphlet had ever been slipped into one of those learned books. Probably canning, during the conservation period, though what it was doing in Gibbon...

"Certainly, Mrs. Dutton," she responded, sweetly.

The two visitors went decorously down the hill between the rows of sticks that would some time be poplar trees.

"Weren't them doilies the dandiest?" asked Mrs. Jim. "Think of eating off'n real lace. I wonder was they part of her setting out?"

"One of them was put on crooked to another," observed Lydia. "There was a big burned spot on the table underneath. I s'picion it'd been ironed on more'n once."

Mrs. Jim stared her amazement.

"And I doubt me if she has that lemon sort of tea for herself. She has it to show off. One side the slice I got was waxened up. It'd been cut more'n yesterday. I took it to find out for sure."

"Good gracious grandmother!"

"As for chiny," Lydia went on, "she knows about as much concarning it as our ole cat. That mulp'ry sasser she showed us ain't nothing better'n flowing blue. Mother Dutton used up a whole dozen flowing blue plates last winter, baking pies on 'em. She said they was worth that to her when the Jew collector's best offer was ten cents apiece."

"I never see you so much as look at that saucer," commented Mrs. Jim.

"Oh, I was brung up not to be a gawpseed," returned Lydia. "At least not out in comp'ny. Re'ly I'm kind o' sorry for the woman. Didn't dast ask us to set in the parlor. I s'pose she was afraid we'd get rav'lings on the carpet, 'n the hired girl 'd make a fuss about extry sweeping. Her bedroom ain't much like mine—'n I guess not much like yourn, neither, M's Fanning. I keep mine real comfortable. There's his old shoes 'n rubber boots under the bed, 'n some ole quilts I'm getting the last wear out of before new covering 'em, on it; and I generally throw his overalls 'n dirty shirts behind the door. They got to go some place, and the kitchen has to be redd up with folks liable to drop in most any hour night or day. Then in the chair I got a whole lot o'pretty good things I shall make use of sometime or nother. As my husban' says, there's got to be some place in a house where a man can do as he darn please. But she took us completely over hern and I didn't notice a single identical room where she'n Mr. Brookings could shuck their ole clo's 'n pile their other shoes."

"No—there sure wasn't," said Mrs. Jim.

"N' her, poor thing, all laced 'n primped, though 'twas only forenoon."

"You bet yer she's dressed up all the time," agreed Mrs. Jim

"Sure-ly. An' how she must suffer. Did you notice when we was to the table how she couldn't pick up her own handk'chief? She poked round with her foot till she hit a little bell knob and when that Bessie come in she made her do it. I thought then, deliver me from being so stuck up in whalebone I can't reach to scratch a skeeter bite on my own laig."

"Anyhow, the eats was lovely," said Mrs. Jim.

"Oh, they was well enough, what there was of 'em. Though I would of preferred that sourmilk cheese hadn't fell into the preserves. But such a skimpy mess! Thinks I, 'f this is all she gives him for dinner, I don't wonder her man don't come home noons, but prefers to eat to a tavern. I got up hungrier 'n I set down. Won't I let into the plum cake 'n sass at supper!"

"N her father was a farmer, too," commented Mrs. Jim, remembering the picture of representative to general court and cow.

"Farmer!" barked Lydia, with a laugh. "I guess likely one them sort that raised Cain 'n not much else. Anyhow, he couldn't been much in the dairy line, or he'd knowed 'twas a queer cow'd let down her milk to a man on the off side."

"Gee!" exclaimed Mrs. Jim. "You're right. Wa'n't that funny? But I would like the recipe for that stuff we ate on the crackers. What she call it—wiggle?"

"Easy enough to guess at," returned Lydia, "only I think 'twas a gre't note setting canned peas before comp'ny this time o' year."

"Canned? Oh, but you can't be sure."

"Got a hunk o' sodder in my teeth," returned Lydia, valiantly.

They parted where the Brookings road joined the highway. Lydia strode homeward taking surreptitious glances at the pamphlet which had fallen from Gibbon. An innocent enough little booklet, advertising somebody's volume on birth control. The subject was one of general discussion whenever two or more women met in Lydia's or anybody else's kitchen, out of the men folks' hearing and when the children were at school, but that was quite different from seeing it as plain as day right out in print. Lydia was horribly shocked. She read the thing through carefully, twice, and then put it out of harm's way wrapped about a stone and flung into the disused well of the abandoned Webster place.

Deciding Mrs. Brookings to be more than an idle hussy, and that the coming of summer people in no ways boded good, "Gerald," she said to her son, on arriving home, "I forbid you to have anything to do with that Brookings boy. He's bound to be a bad one."

"You bet yer," replied Gerald, who was ably assisting his mother in her task of restoring nature after luncheoning out. "Sissy! What d'ye s'pose he done today down to the swimming hole? Jumped right in 'mongst all us boys—with a bathing suit on!"

VIII. The Little Girl Who Died

The little girl who died was not Lydia's little girl. Lydia never had a girl. A child of her own designing would doubtless have been female, but she had never felt financially able to afford the luxury of a planned—beforetime baby. Luke and Gerald were something in the nature of surprise parties, first abhorred, then endured, finally held fondly as causes of delight.

When the autumn winds did blow, and there seemed more sky than usual over the mountain—because at one time you saw the pale green of summer and the dense blue of cold winter, separated by vast cumuli of clouds in every hue from pearl gray to black—Lydia would talk about the little girl who died. To the cats, no other listener.

"My little sister, titnan o' the fambly. I come next before her, I was a gre't big girl of nine when she was born. Hannah Mari, mother's oldest, was married to Hank Hendricks and had one of her own besides all his young ones by his first wife and all his his first wife's by her first husband. So a baby to tend didn't present itself to me as anything of a novelty.

"I took a dislike to her because she ousted me from my place, next the wall on ma's side. I had to get what rest I could down 't the foot, dodging pa's kicking. The boys, that I'd had the kicking of before, got a trundle bed.

"I couldn't a-been meaner to that little baby if I'd set out to be. Ma'd say, 'Rock the cradle, Lyddy, while I churn or what not. If she gets to cryin' haller 'n I'll come.' Of course she bawled quick's a cat could wink its eye. Puffickly nat'ral. Ma always suspected a pin, and never failed to find it.

"Another trick o' mine was giving her a chunk o' meat on a string and pulling it away when she got it half swallered. The pore little thing was just crazy for meat vittles, I s'pose on 'count o' being born in November, just before killin' time and a good eight month from when the last roast o' pork n' quarter beef was eat in spring.

"So she growed, always nine year behind me, and forever a-tryin' her level best to catch up. Everythin' I had she hankered after, everythin'. I did she'd try to do, everywhere I went 'twas tag, tag, tag. She was kind o' pretty complected, but she had tow hair—the kind that is always all over her head. Dretful easy to cry, she was, 'n I took special delight in hectoring of her. They didn't have any special school age then, but nobody's young ones ever come much under five, she, 'course, had to tag me there when she was only three and couldn't unbutton herself. Mortified me terrible before the sixth Reader class.

"I will say she was smart as a steel trap at book learnin'. No sooner knowed her abc than she could do real hard g'ogerfy and spell words o' five syllables, jest from hearin' 'em recited. Examples do, that is she always knowed what the answer was, but more often than not couldn't tell how she knowed, and I'd tease her about that till she was ready to fly off the handle. This was when she was eight or nine and I was through school 'n helping ma 'n braidin' palm lead for my clo's.

"Though she was such a cute one for books, she didn't seem to have no sense a-tall for some things. Over 'n over again I arsk her `Which you druther—a roaster or a pullet?' She wouldn't recall 'ever hearin' it before. So she'd say 'Pullet, sister, for eggs'—and I'd pull her ear till it cracked. Then I'd show her Ma's monkey in the glass when we was fixin' for bed, and other tricks. That one about Adam 'n Eve 'n Pinch me going swimming—Adam 'n Eve fell in, who was left? She'd get catched every single time.

"Meaner 'n fer'sley, but she never seemed to think so, even when I made her bawl a dozen times a day. Peart enough to other folks, but when I spoke she'd stand thredding her fingers 'n fairly tremblin', she was so anxious to please me. And yet she couldn't cure herself o' telling lies. As matter o' fact, pore little Elsie was a liar from the minute she begun to talk. F' instance, she'd come runnin' into the house claimin' she'd seen a crazy man in the clearin' back o' the barn when 't wa'n't no such thing; she'd walk along talkin' to herself and then try to make out some little gal from the village was with her. Even give the made-up gal a name, 'n tell what color delaine she was wearin'. Once they was a great to-do 'cause she came late to school, tellin' how a carriage with four horses was on the road, and a man in a plug hat 'n coat 'n trousers accordin', with a lady in a silk gownd all flounces, tried to make her go away with 'em, said they offered her a cross-bar muslin, 'n gold rings, 'n bronze slippers. Well, she was so faithful to her book that the teacher excused her bein' a 'leven o'clock scholar, but as for the story, there wasn't a word o'truth in it.

"Sometimes she'd be real pop'lar, yarnin' during the noonin' to other young ones on dinner rock, but they'd generally break up in a komtouse, 'cause she would insist that 't wan't no story, but a really truly a'count of somethin; that'd happened to her. Puttin' of herself into all of 'em just nat'rally sickened others, like it did me. 'Specially after she'd turned fourteen and knowed better.

"But she kep' right on, only she was cuter, and didn't tell taradiddles beyond belief. 'N she'd figgered out how to hitch 'em onto somethin' that act'ly was hap'ning, too.

"Wal, it come along the time when she'd have to leave school, see'n 's the teacher'd l'arned her all she knowed herself. I rec'lect the day she come home at the end o' the term, 'n said some committee men was over from the Turner neighborhood 'n had offered her the summer school there. It wan't strange, her bein' such an applicant, 'n Chris—I was goin' with him then, 'n fixin' f'r the event—told me he'd heard they wanted a teacher there the worst way. The summer schools then w's only small children, 'n young gals allus teached 'em.

"So we stopped workin' on my grenadine, 'n made her up a lilac gingham 'n turned a cashmere skirt o ma's sendin' her off lookin' real comf'table 'n slick.

"Makes me laugh ev'ry time I think on't," Lydia would say, and so laughing would make up a horrible face, while big round tears would course down her leathery cheeks and often fall between her thin lips and toothless jaws, to be swallowed in bitterness. Whatever cat or cats were being addressed would change from Lydia's apron to a chair cushion, or back again, adjusting themselves with wondrous nicety so that tail warmed more and paws were cozily bestowed in space between; other cats would show anxious furry faces at the stoop window, begging to be admitted, and still others would as imperatively demand exit. And Lydia would continue, "Her school let out last o' September, after she'd been gone about three months, 'n one day she walked in remarkin' she'd got an unexpected lift 'n didn't wait to be sent after. Wal, I still didn't care a hate for her, somehow my gorge riz right up when she was round, trying always to pattern a'ter me 'n tellin' hifalutin stuff you had to take 'th more'n a grain o' salt.

"But I had to admit she looked pernickity. She'd put up her hair before she went to take the school, but now she wore a blue chenille net that was mighty becomin'. Had a new dress, too, and that was mazarine blue, 'n on her arm was a amber bracelet. A new bonnet hung the strings down her back—a real boughten one—'n when her boots hit the kitchen floor with a queer sound she lifted her feet 'n showed us a silver quarter glued on to each heel.

"This was kinder sorter s'prizing, the Turner neighborhood never bein' much for style f'r all we'd heerd; but pretty soon she let it all out. One the Turner boys was beavin' her round, 'n he'd made her a present o' all the fancy fixin's. Well, we believed it. 'S ma said, 'Tain't one of Elsie's stretchers, 'cause there's the clo's to prove it.'

"The first sat' day night she dressed all up, 'n kep' runnin' down to th' gate, expectin of him. I'll never forget how her pettic'ts crackled—they w's all starched, clear to th' waist, 'n seven yards round, 'n she wore three. I looked kinder skimpy beside her, 'cause I was savin' my best f'r the weddin', 'n 'pearin' out. W'l, the harvest moon come up 'n me 'n Chris went to a apple cut over to Young Bull's—he was livin' with his f'rst wife then—'n Elsie said mebbe she'd come later 'n fetch her beau. But it got along f'r 'leven o'clock, 'n she hadn't 'peared, so I hunted up Chris 'n we put f'r home. I'd been in the kitchen, peelin', with the other girls, 'n hadn't seen Chris once. He always wanted to be off with the men folks 't such times.

"When we got home, pa 'n ma w's in the bed room snorin', like they had been since sundown, 'n there sat Elsie, swingin' in a rocker, 'n hummin' to herself,

I see thee not, I hear thee not
I stand not at thy side,

IX. A Petticoat That Rustled

Weekdays Lydia was no more draggled-tailed than her neighbors, but come Sunday one noticed a difference. Eleanora Burnside drove by to church behind the old racker and just to see her made Lydia mad. From Monday to Saturday Eleanora encased her feet in her husband's cast-off shoes and her legs in his overalls on their second week. Language to match. Eleanora could rip out a damn just as easily as if she lived in New York City, wickedest place in the world, where lots of people never went to bed till eleven o'clock at night. Sundays, silk stockings, and a mouth butter wouldn't melt in. "An edifying discourse" was what she had heard from the pulpit, and that was "the cow's husband" deviling round out in the clearing!

Other women most as bad, though no one accompanied Eleanora the limit in the matter of overalls. A skimpy calico with a section of black oilcoth table cover stretched round one's torso was the favorite female working rig. The Rev. Dunlop was quite reconciled. He had to be, and knew well enough why the sittings were sparsely attended on the off year for apples. If, as was rumored, he sent his wife to spy out who were having bonnets altered over at the milliner's, beginning of each season, it wasn't any more than a sensible business precaution. Slow millinery and he wasted no time composing new sermons. Instead, he planted a bigger garden and dipped deeper into the barrel.

Rev. Dunlop did not omit Lydia in his semi-annual calling tour of the mountain, but she had never sat under his preaching, and he never expected she would. He did not insult her by an invitation to do so; he knew well enough that the checked gingham in which she apologized to him for being "catched" was probably her best, hastily donned as she saw him emerging from the Burnsides'. Rev. Dunlop was popular with the women, if for no other reason than because he always paused between houses to tell the birds from the wild flowers. The next woman could be sure of time to clear the last baking of pies off the parlor sofa, rescue the Bible from the kitchen, where it made a high chair for the next to the youngest, and either wash the family skeleton (Grandfather) or get him safely out of the way upstairs.

The year silk petticoats were in style (rustling ones) about every woman on the mountain got to go to church, and Lydia complained that she felt like "the last buffaler" every Sunday.

"It's dretful handsome," she said to Mrs. Burnside, who was exhibiting hers, which owned the added aggravation of being plaid. "I bet it swishes something grand when you walk down the aisle."

"Wal, I guess they know I'm there," replied Eleanora, with proper modesty. "I've took a seat up front this year. He's liable to be hard o'hearing most any time—his mother was before she reached his age— 'n so I keep telling him, though of course he won't own up to it."

A petticoat that rustled—Lydia felt ambition beyond the bounds of possibility.

"Oh, M's Burnside," she breathed, deliriously, "what wouldn't I give—if th' place wa'n't mortgaged a'ready—'n the cow gone dry—"

Eleanora should not be blamed for her endeavor to rouse Lydia's spirit. As chief sufferer in the result she will not be blamed.

"Lyd Dutton," she began, "why on earth don't you wake up 'n earn the money to buy yourself some fixings? No sense your living up here like a heathen all your life, when they's the best church privileges only three mile away."

"I wonder—" Lydia murmured, but Mrs. Burnside kept right on.

"All we women have to do for ourselves nowadays. Why, how fur towards reg'lar attendance to meeting d'ye s'pose I'd get if I depended on him?" with a gesture toward the pigpen, atop of which sat Wash Burnside nibbling a straw. "Not a dratted step beyont my own dooryard. But I have some gumption, 'n get the rest when he's asleep, 'n there you are!"

"Wal," said Lydia, rising to go, "I'll see what I c'n do." She realized that Eleanora's source of supply, in the pockets of a slumbering husband, would never be hers. Chris Dutton never slept until he had spent all there was to spend.

Eleanora sped her on her way with a copy of a woman's magazine that was designed (in the twentieth story of a Manhattan office building) to be of great aid to tired housewives five miles from a yeastcake. The only similitude was the fact that the editor was tired, too.

Perhaps this was why he recommended women like Lydia to mend their neighbor's stockings for "three cents an aperture," and to provide "creamcheese a la pimento" for "their neighbors' functions." (What the blazes was a pimento, and how long since bonny-clabber became "cream"?)

The sole appealing suggestion in all the long sixteen columns, started in the front part amongst the pictures and carried from page 104 on among the big type pieces about automobiles, was the one that said "make doughnuts." Lydia didn't know but she could make doughnuts, provided, of course, she had some milk and sugar and grease to fry 'em in.

The cow being dry, there was, to begin with, no milk, either sweet or sour.

"Gerald!" she rudely aroused her son from manufacture of a "ticktack" which placed against the window of some lonely and ancient woman on the eve of April Fool day would presumably have the pleasant result of driving her into "hystrikes" until dawn.

"Y—Yes, ma."

"Take this pail right straight over to M's Burnsides, 'n tell her I need sour milk the worst way. Tell her whole milk, not skim. 'N hurry, 'cause then you got to go somewhere's else 'n borrow me some sugar 'n lard. I'm aiming to fry a mess o'doughnuts," she added, seeing he was slow to start.

"Oh, goodey!" he shouted, and went.

He was dreadfully disappointed when she later confessed her intention to sell the doughnuts for fifteen cents a dozen.

"Oh, ma," he droned, "what you want to go to meeting for? Will I have to eat a cole dinner? Oh, ma!" as a horrible suspicion crept over him. "You won't make me go too?"

Lydia shook her head, and such was his relief that he went out peddling doughnuts almost willingly. Sometimes he was hounded to Sunday School, because that was possible at the beginning of the school year, when school pants hadn't come to patching. But no boys went to church, except the minister's son, and he couldn't be blamed. Oh, and Willy Dunster, who got religion one revival; but there was always something queer about Willy. After he tried it and found it made him violently sick he even claimed he didn't like to chew tobacco!

"What luck son?" Lydia asked on his return, though she knew it must be pretty fair because he wore the basket upside down over his head.

"Oh—M's Burnside took all they was left. I went there last, like you tole me to. Mr. Burnside said they was a crock full nutcakes in the pantry, but she shut him up pretty lively. He had to get the money for 'em out the clock. He didn't have enough in his pocket. M's Fanning took six 'n give me one to eat myself. She's pretty nice, ain't she? 'N M's Buell would have some, though he said not to. He said her kind was better."

Lydia nodded understandingly. Mr. Young Buell had been noted eighty out of his eighty-four years on account of a peculiar taste for doughnuts that soaked fat.

She turned Gerald's pockets inside out and found herself seventy-five cents rich. She had provided her own flour (from the half barrel Father Dutton had grudgingly sent her) and a grating of her own nutmeg. A plaid petticoat seemed to rustle only just out of sight.

Before $5 was attained Lydia certainly became a pest to her neighbors. The Burnside pig would have suffered from superfluity of water in his swill, had not lacking nutriment been made up with extra meal. All the men folks complained that the last dollar's worth of sugar wasn't lasting any time at all. Empty lard pails were common as corn cobs in every house except Lydia Dutton's, and she had had the lard. As for doughnuts, Mr. Young Buell expressed the general sentiment when he told his woman, "I don't never want to see another nutcake if I live to the age of Methuselum's gre't granther."

The day she attained five dollars and ten cents all supplies of such (except home made) were shut off. Lydia's thought flew to Eastfield where in some store as yet unknowing there hung a plaid silk petticoat that would rustle. She had turned her cashmere dress, and mended the moth holes; she had decided how to sidle in and where to sit so the breadth that didn't match wouldn't show. Mother Dutton had almost promised her a light complected straw that would look real good done over with shoe blacking. Besides, who would notice what one wore—if only one rustled.

"Ma," said Gerald, "what you aimin' to bring me when you go to the city tomorrow with M's Burnside?"

Lydia realized in a jump that with a petticoat rustling in her ears she had turned selfish. The petticoat would be $4.98, which left 12 cents for Gerald. Only 12 cents for Gerald. And she had hankered for a 10-cent meal in an eating house. However, she could put some cookeys in her pocket and buy him something.

"I got to be brang something nice," he went on, "'cause all the folks where I peddled do'nuts 'spects I will be."

"Gerald Christopher Dutton, you ain't been telling the neighbors nothing—nor braggin'?"

"No, ma. They tole me. Mr. Buell said not to buy none no time, but she said 'twas to help a likely boy. Then she tole me wa'n't it so, 'n I said 'Yes'm. So she got a dozen 'n a half 'n he took the ones of the time before 'n throwed 'em to the hens. 'N M's Fanning, she said, I deserved something pretty good for coming so reg'lar, rainy days 'n all. Oh, ma, I'm lotting on it, too. Jest say yes, ma, 'n I'll keep the hawks from the chickens 'n not go no place till you get back."

Lydia's heart sought lowest depth. What could it be? A velocipede? That would take all her store. Or at least the baseball mask and glove, which would pretty well spoil the petticoat.

"Out with it, son," she murmured, faintly.

"A spin top 'n an All-day Sucker."

So she breathed again.

It was most inconvenient for Eleanora Burnside to go to town just then, and she had been obliged to sing small in order to get the horse when her husband most needed it in farm work, but having started Lydia Eleanora felt obliged to complete the job.

She chuckled as the racker racked them over the Plains which stretched a sandy ten miles between the Mountain and Eastfield.

"Big surprise due," she remarked. "When you go to meetin' next Sunday it'll be about 's if you was 'pearing out after getting married. They all think you worked your fingers to the bone with the idea o' rigging up the boy. Gawsh, Lydia Dutton, you did fool 'em good. Tickles me right down to the ground to think about it. As if we women didn't have no interest in life that didn't wear pants."

Lydia said she felt that way too.

They put the team up at Collins' stable, and as they emerged from its odorous darkness into the sunbaked alley by which one reached the glories of Main Street, Eleanora completed the day by saying, "Now you go your way 'n I'll go mine. 'Tain't no fun tagging round watching other folks spend money. I'll meet you—say at three o'clock over to that rest'rant where the feller is frying flapjacks in the winder. 'N then I'll stand treat. Only not there, but next door, where we can have some ice cream 'n tonic to drink. I always hanker after something that sort after six months o' fried pork for breakfast 'n pork fried for dinner."

She was good as her word, and they started home feeling pretty kerflip, just as the shadows lengthened.

"Get a good bargain?" asked Eleanora, when—at length convinced that his head really was turned homeward—the racker ceased to need tickling with the whip.

Lydia nodded.

"Makes a pretty big bundle, but I s'pose you had it done up loose so's not to wrinkle it too much."

Lydia nodded again. She dared not, while so far from the mountain, confess what the package contained. Eleanora Burnside had an awful temper, she was quite capable of making anyone she took a mad on get out and walk.

Not a plaid petticoat, but a suit complete (with extra pants) for a boy about the size of Gerald. Also stockings, collar, red necktie and a funny hat that would fold into the pocket. Yes, Gerald would be mad, too, because it would mean that he had to be the one to get religion and attend church regular.

"Still, he's most nine," she ruminated. "Perhaps it's as well not be dawdlin' any longer. I don't want him to grow up into a frequenter of taverns."

It had been a hard day on the city pavements. Lydia closed her eyes to as fair a view of field and forest as ever delighted a summer visitor. Plaid silk, tortured into flounces, danced before her eyes. From afar came the wood notes of a Veery. Lydia heard only a petticoat that rustled—only just out of sight. She guessed likely that was where it always would rustle. She guessed likely she'd known it all the time.

X. Prodigious Beebes

Schools are the hotbeds of tradition: even the district school, the "old red school-house" of the cross roads, has its legends.

The Mountain School, which Gerald attended, and which Lydia Dutton his mother had attended in her girlhood, boasted a standard, most difficult of attainment. In the far-off days, when there was a winter school taught by incipient clergymen and embryo lawyers from the Academy, a most prodigious couple had sat on its benches, had carved their initials on its desks, and left a memory be-cursed of today's youth.

"Oh, dear! oh, dear!" moaned Lydia, when her son banged his slate on the table at seven p.m.; "you can't see head nor tail to

I happen'd one Evening with a Tinker to fit
(Whose tongue ran a great deal too fast for his Wit;
He talk'd of his Art with Abundance of Mettle;
Then I ask'd him to make me a flat bottom'd Kettle,
The Top and the Bottom Diameter to be
In such just Proportion as five is to three;

Wal, now, that wa'n't nothing but ABC to Gaius Beebe and his brother Decius."

"Maybe," said Gerald, "if I had a piece of pie I could do it better. A whole half, ma. Mince."

Lydia produced the pie, being proud of her art, but while it was going down in gulps observed that she hoped he at least had his spelling.

And then proceeded to set the task.

"Land o' Goshen," she was soon exclaiming, "don't you know diphtheria is spelled with a haitch? An' diaphragm ain't with a 'f'? Why, Gaius Beebe spelt down the whole entire school once on schism an' his little brother Decius done the same thing two year after on feoffment."

"What's that, ma?" asked Gerald, more with an idea of delaying bed time ('tis to be feared) than of acquiring knowledge.

His mother answered the question with another (being a Yankee). She wanted the latest concerning his composition. There was to be a prize for the best, and every clever child in school was laboring to find something to say about "The Seasons." It would seem as if there should have been plenty to say. All the Mountain was at the mercy of the seasons. Did the Groundhog show himself on February 2nd in a blaze of sunshine (and the prophecy come true), many a barn ran short of fodder, many a good cow was sacrificed, and many a boy went to work the next fall, becoming a tiller of the soil rather than a preacher of the gospel. If the spring was bright and cheery was not a girl's fate settled in May Walks—be the summer drouthy it meant small profit at Harvest Home—and there was no need to point out the difference between the autumns of good apple year and the opposite.

Yet all Gerald had been able to accomplish, on the very eve of handing in, was the not absolutely original sentence:

"The seasons consist of four times of year, spring, summer, autumn or fall, and winter."

Lydia gave him no peace, dinging into his ears reminiscences of the marvelous compositions of Gaius Beebe and his little brother Decius. She had been a wee girl at school in the pristine days of Gaius. She remembered him as a great big boy, thin and pale, as was becoming a scholar, with a great deal of forehead and eyes that seemed to be always viewing that unseen by others. Indeed he was a prodigy, he sucked all bits of unique information from the instructor of the moment, and between studies fattened on books. By no means a poor lad, it was rumored that he studied geography from the globes in his father's house, and knew which way to turn 'em, too. His attire was of superfine broadcloth; and what joy on a Friday afternoon to see him mount the rostrum (teacher's platform), toss back a lock of wavy hair, and with appropriate gesture remark:

"Sir— The atrocious crime of being a young man, which the honourable gentleman has, with such spirit and decency, charged upon me, I shall neither attempt to palliate nor deny."

Gaius Beebe had passed onward and upward from District No. 9, always attended with glory. He shone at the Academy, it was understood that he had shone at Harvard College. Once there came a rumor that his name was not found in the catalogue among graduates of the proper year, but this disturbed tradition not at all. If Gaius was refused a diploma it was probably for the same reason that James Russell Lowell was refused a diploma. Gaius, also, was somewhat inclined to frolics. Lowell had become a great man in spite of his Alma Mater. The Mountain presumed the same fate attended Gaius.

Decius, ten years junior, was likewise fitted into a niche of fame's temple by those who had known his school days. He did everything Gaius did—including the problem beginning "There is a certain number consisting of 2 figures, and it is equal to 4 times the sum of its digits, and if you add 18 to the number, the Digits will be inverted, viz., the first figure will stand last, and the last first; I demand the number?" (You know, the one the committeemen spring on the applicants for schools, and generally floor 'em with, flat.)

And, besides, Decius did a lot more. He could find a false syntax in Addison. He could parse "Paradise Lost"—read it, too. He knew who wrote Johnson and who Jonson. He had pieces printed in the Eastfield Republican. Once, when the candidate failed to show up he went right into the pulpit and delivered a thrilling discourse from the seemingly dry text, "Old shoes and closeted on their feet."

Public opinion rang with no doubtful note regarding the Beebe boys. If Gaius was governor somewhere, of something, (and very likely too), then Decius was whatever man is the governor's boss. They had never returned to the Mountain because they were so very, very great. Great people seldom did come to the Mountain. And they had no folks to visit because Hunting Hill (once Beebe property) was all cut off; their father's house had burned down.

Gerald wished their heads had been cut off and their bodies burned at a stake (this sanguinary and fiery desire was the sole residuum from a term of English history). He entertained no doubt as to their mental attainments—hadn't his own mother seen Gaius sweep a page of Lindlay Murray with his eye (with her eye) and then apply it in a manner that amazed and entranced every ear? But such examples were darned discouraging to a boy who wasn't always sure of the difference between syntax and surtax, or why a fussy teacher held such an insuperable objection to leaving Mary ("harsh and tyrannical in character and an inveterate foe to the Protestant religion") the wife of William III.

Gerald liked going to school. It was a pleasant walk in the summer, along a road shaded by head-high brakes; in winter one could coast the whole distance. He pleasured recess and nooning, they were his principle chances to enjoy the society of his kind. Even coming home wasn't so bad, nibbling at the left overs in a dinner pail and "last tagging" some nice little girl. Lickings, too, were entertaining, especially if some other fellow was being licked. It was fun to see him and the master come in from the entry, and notice was his shirt torn round the neck band, or was the Master flushed and panting for breath and the pulpit consequently swaggering.

Only for such useless performances as reading out the second reader, spelling from the middle to back pages, writing from a set copy, and figuring on either blackboard or slate, did Gerald despise school.

"I do' want to go to school, ma," he whined most Monday mornings. Sometimes he added that he would "rather go braking." To go braking represented the lowest depths of youthful (masculine) despair on the Mountain. Other boys, hounded with school and Saturday baths, ran away. Back o' the Mountain youths went braking. It was supposed, by mothers and grandmothers, to be tantamount to suicide. If a brakeman wasn't ground to death coupling cars, he was swept into eternity passing a low bridge. There was no escaping his fate. Thousands of brakemen were killed annually on the two trains which stopped at Holly Depot, five miles from the Mountain. That was why there was always an opening for a likely boy.

Lydia, by frequent harping on the undoubted advantage of education to Gaius and Decius, kept her lad at school until he was going on eleven. He came home one day in June bearing all his books strapped atop of his slate. Last day and examination had come and gone. Lydia, lacking a proper bonnet, had failed to attend.

Besides, the peas had required brushing, and there were the beans to pole. She had been tempted, even to keep Gerald home the week previous, for thinning the onions, but had finally decided an education would be worth more to him in the end than plenty of food to eat the coming winter. So she had spared him all the spring, had spaded and planted what of the tillable ground she conveniently could, and had let the rest go. Had spared him most off the chores, also, though she found herself about beat out at sundown, after combined household and farm labor since 4 a.m. still it was "See if you can't have all your examples by the time I've milked Mooley," and "if I feed 'n shut up the chickens, you sartainly can c'mit to mem'ry `Ruin seek thou ruthless king'."

Vacation impended, but it held small hope for Gerald. He was about to perform the feat known as skipping a grade. His teacher said he could—with application. His mother determined he would—even though it had to be with application of another sort. Gerald groaned as he slung his books on the old lounge, and sneaked into the butt'ry.

"Now, Gerald, don't you go clogging up your brain with pie nor nothin' indigestible, I will remember M's Beebe tellin' how Gaius took his meals always with a book in front of him, and you could give him dry bread in place of fresh or even a cold griddlecake, which there ain't nothin' much wuss, and he'd never mind so he was readin'."

"Ma," said Gerald, emerging with currant pie in one hand and custard in the other, "they was a whole busload of big bugs out to last day today. They was the Mayor o' Eastfield, 'n two bankers, 'n a feller they called Sheriff, 'n two come from a c'mmission education in Boston. They all had plug hats but the sheriff 'n he had a cap with brass braid. The man who drove the bus had lost a front tooth 'n he could spit terbacker..."

"There, there," cried Lydia, "that'll do about him, son. I guess he wa'n't of much quinseconce in that schoolhouse. But th' mayor 'n th' c'mission—did they ask questions?"

"Ya-as. They didn't want to, but teacher made 'em. So the Mayor wanted to know who was vaccinated, 'n then one the c'mmissioners asked who was the biggest dunce."

"Land o' Goshen—what an idea? 'N what did school ma'am reply?"

"Oh, she hemmed 'n hawed, 'n finally said they was a whole lot o' dunces. Said one was a dunce in 'rithmetic, 'n somebody else didn't know nothing about parsing. 'N she said I was as good as any when it come to `words of different meaning pronounced alike.' And they made me stand up and tell which was whoa to feel like you'd like to bawl and woe to stop a hoss. And they all laughed."

Lydia showing signs of weeping he went on hurriedly, "And the biggest c'missioner—he had a awful shiny hat, an' his overcoat was lined with stuff that shined, too—he patted me on the head, an' said, `That's good, boy,. Just keep on being a dunce an' you'll maybe stand in my shoes some day. Who was your ma? Lydia Luther. Ask her does she recall John Kingman, who went to this school along of her'."

Then Lydia did sit down hard and raise her hands in holy horror. John Kingman, always at the bottom of every class because no deeper depth of scholastic infamy existed. Forever being "kept in" with no obvious result as to improvement. A boy who spent his study hour wriggling his scalp for the amusement of his companions, or seeing how long dead flies would stick to his eyelids, for his own amusement. A boy who was "sarsey," and rough, who stuck his foot out in the aisle for little girls to trip over as they went to the blackboard, who cut all of Europe and part of Asia from his geography the better to hide a dime novel between its covers.

"And, oh, Ma," Gerald went on, taking advantage of her amazement to send a chunk of gingerbread seeking the two pieces of pie, "that wasn't quite all they was to last day, either. After the bus got there, 'n unloaded, they was a quiet lookin' man walked in 'n set down along with us boys. They was a vacant chair on the platform, but nobody asked him to come up there, 'n anyhow the Mayor seemed to want it to put his hat in. He was kind o' dusty—I mean the quiet man was—'cause he'd walked. They was a patch on one side his shoe, and his collar had some ragged pieces sticking out against his neck. He sat right side me, so's I could see. And he didn't have no plug hat. It was a straw an' awful sunburned. I don't b'lieve there's been hot weather enough this year to burn a straw up so."

"Wal, what'd he want?" asked Lydia, in so careless a tone that it was evident she felt little interest in the answer, and indeed was putting the question only out of love for Gerald's voice.

"Oh, nothing particular, I guess. He jest listened to us reciting 'n smiled when Lucy Jones, saying her piece, made 'bosom' into 'baison'— he shall carry his lambs there, you know! The folks on the platform just hawhawed. When we had sung "Goodbye to School" and been let out, he was going too, on'y just then the c'missioner spied him, and jumped right over the chair with the mayor's hat, and grabbed him by the hand 'n hollered, "'Gaius Beebe, y'r darn ole fraud, y'r needn't think you can get by me 'f you are some bald. Now tell me where you're living 'n what profession you've took up'."

"Gaius Beebe!" all the marks of exclamation in the spelling book were in Lydia's tone; she fairly trembled as she gasped out her query, "Wal, what'd he say he was doing'?"

"He said he was a printer, ma; over to Eastfield. He's always been there. He come out today because he was loafing. He got fired from his job last week."

Lydia had only sufficient breath to murmur something about the other one—Decius.

"Oh, the c'missioner didn't forget him."

"'What about Decius?' he arsked."

"'N the quiet man answered, quick's lightening, 'Oh, Decius s' workin'. He's a telegraph operator on the Squagus Branch. Three trains a day each way; he gets $40 a month'."

"Gerald Christopher Dutton," shouted his mother in a voice for calling home the cows, "stop daudlin' round those books this instant. Put on your overalls 'n ghet into that p'tato patch 's quick's the Lord'll let you. If you work fast you c'n bug two rows before it's dark under the table."

Gerald obeyed, with no reference to braking as an alternative. Bugging potatoes was hard, but not a circumstance to fractions.

He was hugely disgusted when his mother—having considered that after all printing was an honorable trade and $40 a month a sum not to be despised—called him back to his books at the end of the first row.

XI. A New Front Door

Ed Caswell possessed a collection of souvenir postals and a wood colored house which had long needed a new front door. Ed didn't dare make and hang such a door because if he did everyone Back o' the Mountain would say he was going to get married. It was the way such events were announced thereabouts. Ed was infernally proud because he had lived to be forty-eight and never been catched.

Lydia Dutton, a matchmaker when she could find time, hated to see such wilful waste.

"Mr. Caswell," she would say, while purposely raspb'ring where he was plowing, "don't you want to drop in a little while this ev'ning?"

And he'd very likely say he would. Then Lydia would plax round and get Flory Brewer—or at least her sister Emogene. Their father had never allowed them to have beaux, so they too were waste products. The entertainment, furnished by whichever Brewer girl came over, was chiefly doughnuts, of which Mr. Caswell was inordinately fond. So also was Gerald, Lyddy's boy, who sat up till 7.30 and always took some every time they were passed. Lyddy seldom cooked them on account of expense and keeping no steady pig.

Flory Brewer was worth considering, if she did stutter. She had a neat ankle and at forty-five still wore Oxfords. Her sister Emogene, with no stutter, had taken up side elastics at thirty and was quite hopeless. (But she made the better doughnuts.)

At 6 o'clock Lydia, working away at her matchmaking, would set the couple looking over state capitals for the hundredth time, and then find something of absorbing interest in the henyard. There they'd sit, Eddie's lank blonde head no more than a yard and two feet from Flory's fat brunetteness and the grizzled hair she'd lately begun to touch up and friz.

Their conversation was well worth listening to. Lydia listened without making any bones about it.

"Ain't it queer, Miss Brewer, what a lot capitals has pillars like the one to Boston? I say, ain't it queer, Miss Brewer?"

Flory would simper and say it was queer. Awful queer.

"And ain't it queer, Miss Brewer, they call it a Bulfinch front? I say, ain't it queer, Miss Brewer?"

Flory, who was lost in guessing what kind of kisses Mr. Caswell's prim lips would make (for, though a spinster, she had attended the district school up to fifteen, and so did not lack connoisseurship in kisses) said it was queer, awful queer.

"Because, you know, it might just's well be Bulfinch back. He must 'a made the backsides too. Eh! eh! Miss Brewer."

Flory, scenting something skittish and thus compromising to her admirer, laughed heartily.

Eddie, rather scared, grabbed the last doughnut and fled.

But he came again. He came many times, so Lyddy, and Flory, and all the female neighborhood, thought he "meant something."

They were reckoning, however, with a tough proposition. Ed Caswell hadn't lived single forty-eight years in order to be easily caught. The doughnuts were luscious (Emogene made the better ones) but Eddie refrained from "popping" and in winter mince pies appeared. The Brewer recipe for mincemeat is worth appending:

24 cupfuls top round minced.

12 cupfuls Bancroft apples scanted.

Raisins, currants, citron, candied lemon and orange peel, quince jelly, crabapple marmalade, all sorts canned fruit juice.

Boiled down cider, brandy, rum cherries, and the rum, cherry brandy, peach brandy, and wine made from wild grapes.

Put 6 whole plums in every quarter, add brown sugar, white sugar, and molasses, black pepper, cinnamon, clove, nutmeg and alspice.

Bake in two crusts, rolled thrice with layers of lard, dab with butter.

They were very good pies.

Flory presented them as her own, but it was Emogene who made them. Emogene had the face of a put-upon sheep. Emogene walked as if something protruded at the knees (nothing did). Even when dressed up she wore a calico with large patches under the arms of pieces that hadn't faded. Her hair, the color of ashes, was yanked back and coiled in a tight pug on top. It made her look like a scared rabbit. It made her look like the devil Eddie Caswell said to himself when he had attained the solitude of his own house and locked the old front door.

Flory, nowadays, was all diddled up in fibre silk stockings and shoes which, if old, had been treated to bronze dressing. Her shirt waists looked almost like the pictures on the pattern sheets. Emogene wore the old cotton stockings, conscientiously darned. The darnings meandered down the legs, they showed in "V's" at the ankle. One imagined what they might be higher up. And those shapeless, bepatched leg-garments and upper body garments seen on the clothesline a-Mondays must be hers (no intimacy can be much of a surprise to the swain who lives in the neighborhood; this accounts for the common practice of falling in love with perfect strangers.)

Flory's were the coquettish things. Sometimes pink with lace edgings and funny tabs that made skirt things into bifurcated things.

(Yet Emogene's were the better doughnuts.)

Ed Caswell looked about his house, kept pretty much to his liking since ma died, and decided he better run away.

"Flory's fussy," he told himself. "Flory's darn fussy. I seen her glare at the Dutton boy when he wiggled doin' his 'rithmetic and tipped her glass sweet cider over. No boy can't do 'rithmetic 'thout wigglin'. Wiggle some myself addin' up wages."

He suspected Flory wouldn't stand for a table always set, on a cover of Eastfield *Republicans*, with brush, comb and razor handy to the plate. She had once remarked he spent too much swapping postals with other swappers.

So he went and told Wash Burnside he guessed he wouldn't stay through haying, and agreed (on a duplicate Bulfinch front card) to accept an offer from a former employer in Vermont. Ed Caswell never lacked a job, being famed in all places of former residence as that phenomenon, a hired hand always ab-so-lute-ly sober. Mr. Burnside sent him to Mrs. Burnside for the three months' pay due—lacking a few advances for finecut.

"She's handlin' the cash now," remarked Wash.

"Ya-as," responded Eddie, "I noticed she was wearin' the overalls most the time."

The remark made Wash mad enough to discharge Ed. Then he realized that he couldn't, Ed having discharged himself two minutes before, so he went into the barn and took it out on an old cow he kept for that purpose, she being too tough to turn for beef. Ed strolled over to his own place and meditated on the sights of freedom, and how nearly they had been lost. Never before had he sparked a whole winter—but they were such all-fired good doughnuts. If he wanted to marry any woman Flory Brewer would probably be the woman. All women were cranky about keeping house and spending money. In fact, one rather liked 'em to be that way.

While Eddie re-established his independence, women-folk at Lydia Dutton's plotted against it.

"F-f-four inches off," Flory was saying, from the kitchen table where she reworked the skirt of her very best a-top of a gingham.

"It'll be halfway to your knees," remonstrated Lydia, through a mouthful of pins. "Climb on a trolly car and you'll show all you got."

"What of it? They all do! F-f-four inches off—I'm determined on it. Jerushy Squire's took off three and she's eighty if she's a day."

Just then Eleanora Burnside walked in. Not speaking, being busy reading Eddie Caswell's postal. That, at least, she felt her due for hastening it thus far on its way to the Green Mountains.

"Don't chop off nuthin'," she advised. "Mebbe they'll be puttin' ruffles on 'em next summer."

"Go ahead," retorted Flory. "It'll be all strung out before fall. Circus, and Methodist picnic, and cattle show."

"Coming," remarked Eleanora. "But he's going."

Lydia, startled, jabbed the scissors into Flory's leg. Flory instantly stepped on the rickety leaf and for five minutes there was a regular catawumpus. Then they all settled down to read the postal.

"It's gospel truth," said Lydia. "He's walkin' off cool's a cucumber."

"Set by steady all winter," commented Eleanora. "S'pose, tho', he never laid his tongue to nothin' you could hold on to?"

"N-n-no," sobbed Flory. "On'y once he did ask what I'd do 'f he left town."

"What'd you say to that?"

"Said I sh'd cry my eyes out. 'N ain't I?"

"You pore dumb idgit," ejaculated both matrons, and added that she deserved to die and suffer, being an old maid all her life. Then both of them, being pretty miserably married, put their heads together in an endeavor to throw the spinster into the arms of a reluctant bridegroom. It was Lydia who finally evolved the plan which Eleanora was to execute.

"Hold up his wages," said Lydia. "He ain't got nary red cent. Hearn him say so night afore last, settin' right in that comb-back rocker eatin' do'nuts. He can't fly th' coop, 'n he can't even get a meal, 'cause he won't be workin' for you 'n Mist' Burnside no more. Let him go hungry, two-three hours, 'n then I'll ask him over here."

"Good work," exclaimed Eleanora, with animation. "'N after he's chockful of victuals it'll be up to Flory. Git back onto that table. Here, I'll give you a boost. How much was it you wanted took off?"

"F-f-four inches."

"Make it five. 'N when you're goin' anywhere from now on make it your way to go by his house.

"You know, M's Dutton," she added, after Flory had been properly shortened and sent home to have Emogene hem it up, "Flory don't stutter a bit in her laigs."

"Sure enough she don't," Lydia agreed, "but I put rather more dependence on victuals 'n drink. Hope she don't forget to have Emogene make one her strawb'ry shortcakes."

She didn't and it made a great hit with Eddie, avid from a half day's fast. Still ("Drat him!" snarled Lydia) he didn't fail to ask Mrs. Burnside for what was coming to him. Not getting it he accepted an invite to Sunday breakfast and made way with exactly twenty-nine griddle cakes, fried by Emogene in the Brewer kitchen and secretly relayed to Lydia's by Flory and Gerald Dutton. At noon there was roast chicken with the famous dressing which Emogene constructed from piping hot soda biscuits sent straight from the oven to the chopping tray. After which he lounged and smoked till sundown brought a light supper of cold beans and pie. At nine p.m., following a snack of three sorts of cake, he went directly to his own domicile and slammed the (old) front door.

Flory and Lydia fell on each other's elbows.

"He ain't been near Burnside's a-tall," murmured the rapturous maiden. But Lydia was more wary. "Don't holler till you're out the woods," she advised. "Mebbe he knows bills ain't legal paid on the Sabba'. Hyper along 'n tell Emogene to stir up a johnnycake in the mornin'."

The feeding of Eddie went on for six weeks, until even the gifted Emogene was obliged to repeat herself. After a time he stopped reminding the Burnsides of their debt, except for chalking the sum total on the barn door whereby all who drove past might read and chuckle. He had plenty of chalk because he was carpentering. At first the noise of nailing got Eleanora and Lydia and even Flory all worked up, but by and by it seemed as if he was just doing it to be vexatious.

"Land o' Gideon," snorted Eleanora, one afternoon at about the end of the sixth week, "seems if he'd done everythin' could be done to a ole house now. He's shingled, 'n puttied up th' winders, 'n tightened ev'ry clapboard, 'n painted the underpinnin', 'n made bran' new steps."

"Inside, too," chorused Lydia. "Pink flowered paper in the bedroom 'n trellis work with nestin' birds in th' parlor. Rural free brunged the stuff from Hamson 'n I see th' bill. Resayted. You ain't been fool enough to go lendin' him no money, Flory?"

Flory shook her head. "Ain't n-n-none to lend," she remarked, dolefully. "Mine's all spent. Had to borry two dollars off Emogene yest'day to pay for my new hat. 'N I guess I'll have to git some more for lard 'n sugar pretty soon, 'f somethin' don't happen. Pa's a good provider, but he's beginning to notice how often we're out."

"Beats all," said Lydia, peering down the road, "how he goes round 'n round that old door with paint 'n varnish, 'n won't tetch it no more'n 's if 't was p'isin."

"Well," queried Eleanora, "what's the answer? How much longer you goin' to stick it out, Flory? Got to stop some time soon, 'cause even Wash is gettin' tired o' washing chalk off 'n the barn ev'ry mornin'."

Flory's way of solving any problem being to sit down and cry about it, she was proceeding so to do when Lydia chirked her up by an order to make a last try with the famous doughnuts.

"He always did seem to favor 'em, 'n said somethin' t'other night about they're bein' better'n fruit cake, after all. Fry a good batch," she added, remembering with a mother's heart that Gerald loved nutcakes, too. Flory did as she was bid. Thus it happened that when Eddie sat that evening in the Dutton sitting room, looking at the capitals of the states for the two hundredth time, Eddie held a doughnut in his other hand, while his right cheek bulged.

Their conversation was well worth listening to. Lydia—who had absented herself on the plea of a skunk in the henyard, listened without making any bones about it.

"Ain't it queer, Miss Brewer, what a lot folks make doughnuts round with holes in 'em. I say, ain't it queer, Miss Brewer?"

Flory simpered and said it was queer, awful queer.

"And ain't it queer, Miss Brewer, what a lot other folks make do'nuts twisty, 'thout no holes in 'em. I say, ain't it queer, Miss Brewer?"

Flory, who still hadn't the slightest inkling as to whether Mr. Caswell was the kind who kissed with a smack or kind o'quiet, said it was queer, awful queer.

The talk then went wild, adrift from the pattern.

"'N others five fingered, Miss Brewer. 'N yet I s'pose all do'nut dough's about the same, ain't it?"

Flory nodded. Cup o' sugar to two eggs always, but it seemed a waste of breath to tell a mere man.

"'N yet, Miss Brewer, no more taste alike than they is shaped alike when fried. Now, f'r instance, Miss Brewer, you 'n your sister—"

"Ma's reseep," put in Flory, shortly. She was tired and sleepy; it was most nine o'clock. If he was going to pop that night she wished he'd hurry up and be done with it.

"Thought like enough," returned Eddie. "But the do'nuts—now, see here, Miss Brewer, I bet yer I can tell 'em with my eyes shut. These I've jest put my teeth into—"

He took the last and a good half disappeared in a bite.

"Well, guess," coquetted Flory, thoroughly awake again, and with a heart going twice the necessary thumps to the minute.

"Yours, Flory, yours!" he shouted, as he grabbed his hat and went out of the house as if he was shot.

Such a determined mark of affection was not lost on Flory. She fairly teetered home and went to sleep trying to decide whether they had better take a wedding trip or put the money into a young pig.

The morning sun rises pretty early in June, but not so early that it did not find a new front door at Eddie Caswell's. Evidently he had made it in secret and kept it ready to be hung when he was ready to hang it. There it gleamed, gay with pink panels on a substratum of blue. In the centre was a polished plate bearing the name of "Caswell" in such flourishy letters that you'd never have guessed. Beneath was one of those bell handles which, turned, give a rasping noise warranted to scare dumb creatures out of a year's growth.

The neighborhood was agog, only Flory Brewer took it with calmness.

"I never expected nothin' less," she remarked, as she sat enthroned in Lydia Dutton's best chair.

"Did he say it—in so many words?" inquired Eleanora Burnside, who always was nosey and wanted to know.

Flory shook her head in luxurious reminiscence. "I guess he ain't that kind, M's Burnside," she observed. " He was partic'lar—very special p-p-partic'lar. We don't have to have ev'rything said straight out. W--w-we understand each other."

"Well, I'm glad on't. I'm darn tired havin' all that money in the house 'n recollectin' where it's hid days 'n puttin' it under my pillar nights. But where's he gone? I stopped 's I came by 'n it's locked up over there tighter 'n a drum."

"I do' know," murmured Flory. "M-m-mebbe to buy me a ring. I always did think g-g-garnets was g-g-grand."

Lydia shook her sensible head. Not a ring, but very likely the license. Rings were silly things, and—though she did not say so to Flory—Lydia could not imagine Ed Caswell spending money on anything not eatable.

But they were both right. He was buying a ring—a plain gold one for the third finger of the left hand. Also a marriage license. The one fitted the other bore the name of Emogene Brewer. Flory, Lydia and Eleanora got the news next day, on three souvenir postals, exactly alike. They bore pictures of the Bulfinch front and were dated "Statehouse Steps." Anyone who read this story even to the halfway point will remember that Emogene made the better doughnuts. Also, she did not buy fancy fixings and so had money when Flory had none.

It was six months before Lydia Dutton stopped running out her tongue every time she passed Ed Caswell's new front door!

XII. A Great American Poet

Even houses in which nothing was read but *Old Farmer's Almanac* dates telling when the red cow was expected to "come in" could produce a copy of Aaron Drake Sherborn's poetry. Aaron meandered about selling his poems, bound in red, with a badly printed halftone of his own face as a frontispiece.

"Howdydo, M's Burnside," he'd say some Monday, when she was suds to the elbows. "Don't you want to put your name in my little book? I got already the autographs of the Representative to the Gen'ral

Court, Joe Jefferson actor and Agnes and Sam Villa ditto in 10, 20 and 30, also Ella Wheeler Wilcox Sweet Singer of Michigan."

Then she'd write her name in the book, which was the kind given away to advertise a patent medicine, and he'd go out in the barn and collect a dollar from Mr. Burnside.

Aaron Drake Sherborn's *Everyday Rhymes* figured on the parlor table ever after, illustrating the story of the poet's cuteness in getting real money where the victim supposed she was only giving an autograph to figure among those of the great and famous. Aaron would have been despised as a poet had he not been so admired as a peddlar.

His eyes were pop and his manner silly. He was supposed to have become a poet in order to avoid work. By and by there came a time when his market had absorbed all the poetry it could possibly assimilate, he then took to going about declaiming unprinted verses, also composing on those who had disturbed the hearse from its between funerals slumber.

At this stage he approached Lydia Dutton's screen door and discovered her son Gerald in the throes of expression.

"Great American poets of America," Gerald was transcribing from a slate to everlasting characters in soft lead pencil on a school tablet, "was Whittier who wrote 'Snow Bound,' Ralph Walden Longfellow and Miss Hemans whose poetry 'Pilgrim Fathers' will never be forgot."

"My Gawd," remarked Aaron, who had perhaps been sampling somebody's hard cider, "dost mean to say, boy, thou'st never heard of Poe?"

"It's poets he's writing of," said Lydia, from the sitting room window behind the screen, where she was at one and the same time repairing her son's trousers (seat) and preparing him for a firmer (same) on Pegasus.

"Poe by name and Poet by nature," declaimed Mr. Sherborn, his eye in a fine frenzy rolling. "Didst never hear—

It was night in the lonesome October
Of my most immemorial year;
It was hard by the dim lake of Auber,
In the misty, mid region of Weir—
It was down by the dark tarn of Auber,
In the ghoul-haunted Woodland of Weir?"

"Well, no," said Lydia, turning the trousers outside out and attempting to get an idea of their effect, as patched, on her son's plump form, by super-stretched left hand, "I can't say as I ever did. Weare village is over beyond Three Rivers, I know. Was the gent a friend of yourn, Mr. Sherborn?"

"My dear lady," said Aaron, "out of a single production of that marvelous intellect I was inspired to write a book which to date has fetched me in seven hunder dollars and seventy-six cents—pennies accounted for by postage to outertownites. There ain't nobody like him. I only wisht he might of been a friend of mine. F'r instance—

And I said, she is warmer than Dian;...
Come up, in despite of the Lion
To shine on us with her bright eyes,—
Come up through the lair of the Lion,
With love in her luminous eyes."

"Ain't that grand, M's Dutton? Ain't that inspirational? I perused it one Sunday evening on my return from Christian Endeavor meeting, and before I hit the hay, M's Dutton, I wrote that handsome poem which starts off my book:

"At Love's Door"

At the door of love I stood with bated breath,
A great strong passion flooding all my soul;
I fancied I could almost cope with death;
Should I meet up with love I never would grow old.
Methought that life would be a eternal dream,
I hoisted castles whilst I pulled the bell,
Ah! What is life that we must always scheme,
Ah! What is love that we so frequent tell?
And as I waited, anxious for a sign,
The door was opened and I seen a grin
Upon the butler's face as he seen mine,
I asked for Love, he said Love wa'n't not in."

Gerald was gazing in open-mouthed admiration at a Great American poet making Great American poetry in the dooryard, but Lydia was perfectly cool.

"I like yourn full as well as t'other," she observed, "but his seems to run more slick."

Aaron Drake Sherborn cast himself on the piazza floor, and his battered straw hat to the pebbly walk.

"There you have it, M's Dutton, in a nutshell," he groaned. "A peanut shell, as it were, which is the easiest cracked and the most difficult to put together again, of any in the wide wide world. I can get inspired and I can write 'em off, but when I get through they's something lacking. It ain't feeling. I'm chock full o' feeling. Just two or three lines o' that immortal master o' verse and I've feeling sufficient to make love to the entire female side o' the Academy to the village.

Then I pacified Psyche and kissed her,
And tempted her out of her gloom,—
And conquered her scruples and gloom;

There's a picture, now, to think about. I imagine that girl Sykey was a corking good looker, though one of the quiet kind, not a trainer at all. She got the glooms over something, and she had scruples, too. Well, you know, M's Dutton, some girls have. Some the very best girls have. You go to a whole lot o' trouble to see 'em home and—Here, listen! I wrote a pome about that sort. It's called

"The Girl I Didn't Kiss"

I overlooked her in the crowd
Of lads and lassies gay,
The prettiest little girl I deem
That ever came my way.

Again I seen her upturned face,
But I was vain and proud,
And left her with a passing look
Amid the passing crowd.

Again I seen her little basque,
And overskirt of red;
Maybe the wearer is alive,
And maybe she is dead.

I often wonder at her gate,
Amid the world's cold din,
Whether she kept her record bright,
Or tarnished it by sin.

'Twas years ago, but yet tonight
My heart with grief is filled;
I might have kissed her, but I know
'Twas as the angels willed.

'Tis ever thus, I find in life,
Our dreams of earthly bliss
Are sadened by the memory
Of the girl we didn't kiss."

"Shucks," was the comment of Lydia, who never seemed to lose her head. "That gal didn't have no scruples. She wanted you to smack her the worst way. I know what 'tis to have scruples. I useded to have 'em myself."

Gerald gazed pridefully on his mother; Mr. Sherborn swept his eye over Lydia's slab sided form, toothless jaws, leathern cheek, haggard eye and grizzled hair, and then remarked so conversationally that she never dreamed he was quoting

"What is written, sweet sister,
On the door of this legended tomb?"

And when Lydia suddenly replied she didn't have the slightest idea, he went on

"She replied—'Ulalume, Ulalume,
'Tis the vault of thy lost Ulalume'."

After which he proceeded to give her the verses which had been thus inspired:

"Bessie"

I don't know none that's neater,
More fair to look upon;
She cannot read our meter,
Nor laugh our words to scorn.

She don't care none for candy,
Or caramels, or gum;
She loves no fickle dandy,
Nor flirts with anyone.

They is a look pathetic
Within her dreamy eyes,
Though she's not so aesthetic
As some might wish, or wise.

She don't care none for dresses,
As you must soon allow,
Who is she then? Who guesses?
Why, Bessie is a cow.

Lydia liked that. Lydia saw some sense in that. She even went into the butt'ry and got Aaron Drake Sherborn a section of apple pie and a trifle less than a quarter of a pound of cheese, which disappeared into the poetical maw in about thirty seconds—because she liked that and saw some sense in it. After it Mr. Sherborn waxed extremely confidential.

"I do' want to depreciate myself, M's Dutton," he observed, "seein's I've made some seventeen hunder dollars and sixty-seven cents outo *Everyday Rhymes* (the pennies accounted for by folks sending stamps not knowing the exact amount). But I admit that while Poe's inspirational he ain't always quite inspirational enough. I seen it that way myself a long time. Yes, a very long time I seen it that way. Then, M's Dutton, because I never don't spare myself nothing, I set up one night till eleven o'clock perusing the life o' Poe, and I learn what was the trouble. I was too good, M's Dutton. I was too respectable behaved for a true poet. He often got tanked up, the great poet Poe, and when under the influence his productions was something the world has not let die."

"You orter both be ashamed yourselves," exclaimed Lydia, but it was parrot talk, and she drank in the tale of the poet's reprehensible performances very much as one imagines the innocent Desdemona swallowed Othello's tall yarns.

"Well—it's all in the interest o' art. For art's sake, you know."

"Was Art," inquired Lydia, "the Poe feller's first name?"

Mr. Sherborn laughed a laugh like a bark, and plunged into his story.

"B'lieve it or not, as you like, M's Dutton, but I went right out and got How-Come-You-So. Tell about seeing two of everything. I seen a whole meetinghouse of folks 'n 'twas only the Dankster twins. Then I got somebody to put a pen into my hand and when I'd sobered off this was what I done. Can you beat it?

> There ain't no any nicer stunt
> As sit us in a closeup far
> And see the background at the front
> Oh lovely blonde with curls of tar.
>
> Sure any stunt ain't nicer not
> As closeup in a double reel
> And in the big dark of a spot
> The silence of her eyes to feel.

I dedicate it, M's Dutton, to Mary Pickford. And what I suffer when I learn she's going to get married again goes beyond sayin'. I could stood it all pretty well, only f'r that, again! And she wouldn't buy a copy. Her maid said her private secretary never bothered her with nothing like that. Oh, M's Dutton, 'twas hard. I knew just exactly how Mr. Poe felt when he seen Helen in that garden. On'y I didn't write nothin' more to Mary seeing's I'd already done so."

He wandered down the road, in the direction of the Burnsides. It was getting on to dinner time. Gerald returned breathless from running after the poet with the poet's bad hat. His mother was about to improve the occasion by a warning against ever growing up and being a poet (she always issued warnings after calls from tramps, shiftless persons, and those who had come upon the town), when Gerald cut her off by shouting for his quarter of pie and declaring he was going to write his compo. all over again. So he commenced by applying a very red and exceedingly moist tongue to the slate, destroying at one fell lick the chances for fame as Great American poets of Whittier, author of "Snowbound," Ralph Walden Longfellow, and "Miss" Hemans whose "Pilgrim Fathers" the world was henceforth quite at liberty to forget.

The compo. was finally completed, though not before all the pie was eaten and the cookie jar levied upon. It was a long compo. and Lydia presumed would attract considerable notice on last day. It did.

Imagine the scene. The schoolhouse floor scrubbed, also the desks. Walls hung with princess piny and garlands of oak leaves. A complimentary(?) sentiment on the blackboard, written backhanded by Lordknowswho:

Goodbye schoolmates, goodbye school,
Goodbye teacher, you darn ole fool.

Teacher smirking on the platform because she had earned sufficient for her wedding clothes, and she wasn't ever coming back. In the audience, prominent among smug mothers and sheepfaced fathers, Aaron Drake Sherborn, who certainly had been sampling somebody's hard cider. On the platform Gerald Christopher Dutton, reading the essay that won the prize (a copy of a stupid book called *Ann Lively and Her Bible*). Gerald would care nothing for it as a story, but Lydia would gloat over it as a prize. He begins:

"A Great American poet who is not always nown to be great but who ought to be because he put in his whole time at it, is the subject of this piece. He is a Great American poet we ought to all know because he wrote some of the Greatest American poems. The true spirit of Great American poems is in all these poems, and so we are glad to hail him as a Great American Poet. A Great American poet would be of course very different from a Great Poet of Roosia, Proosia, France, Brazil, Korea or any other Great Country where Great Poets live. This Great American is free and equal and so the Great American poets write very different from Great Poets of any other Great country.

Aaron Drake Sherborn leaned back in his chair, an unsafe proceeding the chair being kitchen and rickety, borrowed from old Pall Hackett acrost the road. He threw out his chest, because he believed he had been instrumental in introducing the boy to the Great American Poet of whom he was writing. His chest was not covered with a real shirt, but a dirty dickey; the throwing out process made an uncomfortable revelation of gray flannel beneath. Next he shot his cuffs. As he had none that too was disillusionizing when one considered Mr. Sherborn as a poet. His coat was greasy, the lapels scarred with pins and drops of bygone fluids. His waistcoat would doubtless have looked likewise only he had no waistcoat. His trousers needed pressing. They had apparently needed it for several years. His shoes, which were oxfords, were held on by white strings. Seen from the rear it became evident that Aaron Drake Sherborn had no one to mend his stockings.

One wonders if Edgar Allan Poe ever looked thus disreputable. His wife, to be sure, lay dying on straw, her only coverlet her husband's great coat, her sole comfort a tortoiseshell cat. "The coat and the cat were the sufferer's only means of warmth, except as her husband held her hands, and her mother her feet." And in the Poe biography one finds the story of the poet's leaping. "It was Poe who was expert in the exercise, two or three gentlemen agreed to leap with him, Poe still distanced them all. But, alas! his gaiters, long worn and carefully kept, were both burst, in the grand leap that made him victor."

Very possibly all this was embalmed in the memory of Aaron Drake Sherborn, gazing thoughtfully at his own poor shoes. Aaron was a simpleton and a faker, the Greatest of American Great Poets could inspire him to nothing better than bosh. But he beamed happily (and hazily) on Gerald Dutton. He was joyous because he had introduced the boy to "Ulalume" without any trite mention of "The Raven."

The boy was going on:

"The poet writer to which I alude is the well nown Mr. Aaron Drake Sherborn. We all now Mr. Sherborn, and have bought a copy of his poet writings. In them he tells us the good advice,

One thing remains immortal,
The world cannot disguise;
Amid the change unchanging,
A good name never dies."

A disturbance took place at this moment, compelling the impassioned reader to cease reading. Aaron Drake Sherborn, having reduced his kitchen (and rickety) chair to kindling wood, was quitting the assemblage. In doing so he walked over numerous large taxpayers and several of their promising offspring. The taxpayers approved. They thought Mr. Sherborn "felt mortified" at being thus publicly brought into notice.

After a time Gerald completed his presentation of the local G.A. poet, which bristled with quotations of a moral and edifying character.

"Better some narrow path to tread
Than a highway ending in shame and dread."

came at the close of a noble peroration. A few feeble handclaps broke the silence. Yes, district nine forgot decorum, and actually applauded. In the yard Aaron Drake Sherborn shed tears. Standing at first base he reflected on Poe, receiving $10 for "The Raven" but feeling better repaid (with no food in the house) by a letter from Elizabeth Barrett Browning.

With the mission ever before him of that rare creature—"proud and beautiful head erect, dark eyes flashing with the electric light of feeling and of thought, a peculiar, an imitable blending of sweetness and of hauteur in this expression and manner," Aaron Drake Sherborn, knew himself to be meaching and quite unequal to the production of aught the world would not let die. He might recite his own verses to Lydia Duttons, with enthusiasm, yet know them all the while for specious nonsense.

So he thought he'd go out in the woods and drown himself at "Peggy's Dipping Hole." Only just then the benediction was asked and everyone came trooping out, including Gerald with his copy of *Ann Lively and Her Bible*, suitably inscribed, and various large taxpayers.

Instinct conquered temperament. Aaron whipped out his little book, which had still several blank pages. He mentioned casually the fact that he had the autographs Yours Truly of John L. Sullivan and Laura Jean Libby. And would like that of the one to whom he spoke. He secured $17 in cash and the promise of $9 additional ere the last buggy was driven down the road. His way home led directly past Peggy's Dipping Hole. He considered it casually as a pool of dirty water, not in the least worthy the attention of a Great American Poet.

XIII. Those Hellion Students

Princes probably no longer have whipping boys, but duties appertaining to such shriek for performance in Republican environs. The town of Holly blamed everything on "students."To hear people in Lydia Dutton's neighborhood talk you'd think that noble red brick academy in the village harbored as wild a set of roysterers as Newstead Abbey in the legended days of the young Byron. The catalogue declared students were expected to attend divine service twice each Sunday, to bring from home a silver plated knife, fork, spoon and napkin ring, and to meet the other sex only at promenades under espionage of professors' wives. Yet stories floating about convinced one that the young men were occupied exclusively in robbing hen roosts, draining cider barrels (whilest owners slept), and making love to farmers' daughters.

Nothing was too wild to believe about a student. A student was only disbelieved when he tried to say he was working his way into the ministry, and that he wrote every Saturday night to his widowed mother.

So when two eager-eyed youths approached Lydia one autumn morning with the abrupt question, "What's the one thing you want most, ma'am, that we can do for you?" Lydia saw in it only concealed devilment. She was not even reminded of that famous three-wish fairy in the old tale, her infancy having been mentally nourished on *The Child's Guide* with at least half of each story worn away by previous owners.

"I want nothin', thank ye, young sirs," she replied, promptly, but coldly, industriously continuing to "tat." She was seated in her favorite place for relaxation and fancy work, on the front doorstep which had long ago got itself made and become weatherbeaten, though the door had never been cut. The neighbors were all used to this, and indeed saw nothing strange in it; Lydia's husband being what he was (and a carpenter); her husband's father being a carpenter also. But the youths ventured a couple of questions.

"Did there use to be a door there once, ma'am?" asked the taller one, in the choice diction of a well-educated boy temporarily debarred from slang.

"Not's I ever hearn tell," Lydia responded.

"Then there's going to be one made by and bye?" the litle lad broke in, with the air of discovering something.

"Sure-ly," said Lydia, all the more stoutly from her own conviction that "he" never would get round to it.

For an instant each boy gazed into the other's face; then wildly got into action.

"She'll want a flagstone," cried the little chap.

"You mean a gravel walk," shouted the other.

"Goodie!" yelled both in unison. "Bullie! So much interestinger than chopping wood."

While Lydia sat in a maze they secured the sickle, goodness only knew where, since it had been lost for months even to Christopher Dutton, the last seen to have it in his hand. They stretched strings from step to road, and mowed an even swarth in the space between. Then they got forks and tore away the turf, spades and dug to a considerable distance. They tamped down the earth, they put in wood ashes and bound them tightly with several buckets of water, they made a border of fairly large stones which they lugged from the crumbling wall back of the barn; then they tipped their hats and went away ruefully reminding one another that they "had a date to mind a baby." Lydia pinched herself, rose and went the rounds. Were they real boys? Every implement was scrupulously returned to the place where it was found (even the sickle successfully lost again). That wasn't boylike; and the walk was almost too well made for the work of human hands.

Each morning for a week Lydia rushed round from the very minute she had her clothes on, to see if it had faded away. It was always there.

She called her neighbors to help her look, they assured her the boys were actualities. They had tended a baby that day, at M's Randolph's— M's William Randolph, she that was a Slade, not M's Henry, she hadn't got her baby—yet—while M's William went to the village and bought six yards of calico, spry colored, and without no up nor down to it, so 't would cut to advantage. They had made Eleanora Burnside the same offer they made Lydia.

"Got the woodbox filled and four pails water drawed," Eleanora exulted.

"Don't let no boys sarse me 'thout gettin' th' wu'st on't."

It was the general opinion that such offers of assistance were plain "sarss." Only M's William Randolph had credited them with their avowed determination to do "one helpful deed a day, ma'am; and seeing's we're at school we have to perform seven for the week all on a Saturday." Hence the baby tending. Most places drove them off with hoots of derision. At Mrs. Young Buell's they had peremptorily torn clothespins from between Mrs. Buell's lips, dumped her into an elbow chair (she was very old, was Mrs. Young Buell) and finished putting out the things. They then apologized, saying, "Excuse, please, but we just had to. We were a help behind, the 'all in' bell rings in half an hour and there's two miles to go."

"'N they scooted," said Mrs. Buell, "'s if the very Old Harry was after 'em."

Lydia Dutton prided herself on being always "to home," but the following Saturday she dined out. Against her will, but Father Dutton had loaned his best gun to Lute because Lute was sixteen and had been teasing for it every since he was six, and Lute had killed a wild goose which flew low "going over," and Mother Dutton had roasted it, and "I didn't never eat no wild goose no time ma," wailed Gerald.

They went. As Mother Dutton's idea of a roast goose dinner included fricasseed chicken, stewed oysters, seven sorts of vegetables besides potatoes, three of pickles and four of jelly, with both pies and pudding, fruit and 'lection cake to top off with,—they were late getting home. Gerald did the chores by lantern light. It was not until next day that Lydia found the flagstone.

Placed just right, plumb up against the lowest step, stretching half way to the road.

"Reg'lar whale of a stone," Wash Burnside expressed it (before the arrival of his wife. When she was present she established the family opinions.) He had loaned the stone boat and horse. Yes, the same two boys and a gang more. They offered pay, but he said, "No, not s'long's 't was for a help to some poor body." He never supposed 'twas anything like that!

Then he went away hoping he'd put Lyd Dutton all out of conceit with her front walk. Lyd Dutton and a front walk—the idea! and one better than the Burnside walk; since they hadn't any flagstone.

Perhaps Lydia did put on too many airs. At any rate there was a desire born, in the neighborhood, to take her down a peg. It didn't attain the dimensions of a plan or a scheme; but it was an understanding. Mrs. Jim Fleming started things moving by a discovery that there was something funny in the shape of the stone.

"Of course it's a dandy walk, 'n all that, but ain't it funny shaped? Seems to me I never seen such a funny shaped stone."

Then Eleanora Burnside and Mrs. Bugbee, who were helping in the looking on, decided they never had, either. Mrs. Bugbee wondered where on earth those boys found such a funny stone. Eleanora said it was white, well, pretty white-like marble that had been weatherbeaten more or less. There was no such funny stone in the outcroppings round that town.

"Must have come a considerable distance, I sh'd say," she remarked gloomily, "and some time ago."

Lydia found herself shivering as her erstwhile friends flounced off. It didn't need the return of the Bugbee woman to eject a venomous whisper, "Looks—exactly—like a—gravestone!" But that was not lacking.

Next day the story flew right over the mountain and settled five miles away in the village "Street." A woman who lived "Back o' the Bushes," ('twas said) had a gravestone for a doorstep. This differed one degree from accusing godless farmers' wives of stealing gravestones for ignoble uses. In proof thereof a stone was missing over in the Dell.

"True as Gospel," the Bugbee woman burbled out, and acting as if she expected Lydia's thanks for fetching the news. "There's sots the underpinnin; solid's the Rock o' Gibraltar, 'n the footstone, but that tall headstone's clean gone."

Lydia, who was getting ready to make pies, ceased caring economically at this moment, since exasperation must have some vent.

"Marble, that was, I guess," her tormenter continued. "White but sort o' yaller in spots. Just exactly like—it, 's near's I c'n make out."

She paused for comment, but Lydia had wickedly chopped her finger, and was sucking the blood as an excuse for silence.

"It matches up pretty good with what Jim Fleming's wife tole me her step mother's sister-in-law heard from a friend of a friend of her'n. Name o' Jones or Boynton or somethin' like that. She's been watching at that fambly's livin' in the old Sanger place—you know, way up the mountain. Lighthouse they call it. She come by here just about sunup Sunday morning, 'n they was a whip-poor-will follered along the whole way. Made her terrible nervous—the dratted things allus seems possessed to hang round when they's sickness. Wal, as I git the story, she come right by here, 'n jest as she got in sight o' that step stone see that bird stop and settle on it. Now I ain't one bit superstitious, M's Dutton, or given to gossip. But when I get a story straight; wal, no smoke 'thout some fire, sez I."

Perhaps the taste of blood helped Lydia to see red and snap out, "Looks likely! I don't b'lieve she went by here a-tall, I'm allus up and stirring 's soon's it's light, and I never set eyes on such a woman."

"Not credit the story!" exclaimed the Bugbee woman, "my land, Lyd Dutton, do you mean to tell me I've got a duty to go and tell M's Jim Fleming you called her a liar?"

Lydia rose up in her wrath and was fully primed (in her mind) to smite the Bugbee woman. Perhaps Mrs. Bugbee felt thunder in the air, at any rate she took hasty leave, and repeated the tale of the two whip-poor-wills at Eleanora Burnside's. By the time it got to the Silvers' the whip-poor-wills numbered a dozen, all whip-poor-willing fit to beat the band. Mabel Silver related it to numerous callers on her father's cider barrel and increased the birds into a flock. Some were crows, because the crow is also of evil omen.

The Bugbee woman, indefatigable in annoying attentions, traipsed all the way to the Dell and ascertained that the missing gravestone appertained to Mr. Young Buell's first wife. There was something in this, because the first Mrs. Young Buell had lived her short life and died her unduly gruesome death on the mountain. She was the only one of Mr.

Young Buell's wives buried in the Dell. Had never seemed contented down there, either. Everybody remembered one version or another of how her husband spied her walking along natural as life t'other side of the graveyard wall and looking reproachfully just after he'd married the second woman.

Lydia saw what was coming. She told the cats and Gerald she saw what was coming.

"It won't be two days," she told them, "before they'll have Mrs. Young Buell herself standin' round on that flagstone."

Lydia never let a chance slip by for calling the stone a flagstone; the neighbors let none pass for mentioning it as "the gravestone," or even "the first M's Buell's stone—she that was a Howe."

The ghost appeared on a moonlight night to Henry Burr, as he came from sitting up with the youngest Pease girl. He didn't know it was a ghost, probably because his eyes saw nothing much but the youngest Pease girl. He reported a white fog something the shape of as woman, but Mrs. Bugbee soon told the world. What he had seen was Mrs. Buell in a shroud, what Mrs. Buell in her shroud wanted was the return of her gravestone.

Soon it became no trick at all to see Mrs. Buell. Frightened children, rushing past the house with their eyes shut tight, said they saw her. Eleanora Burnside, generally sane and sensible, "saw something queer from the kitchen window betwixt sundown and moonrise." Oldest inhabitants were called upon to give evidence as to life and death of the first Mrs. Buell. There wasn't much to the life, she lasted only twenty-three years. Her taking away, now attention was called to it, had been such as should precede a haunt. A woodtick was heard in the wall right over her head. Neighbor women who went in to bake up a batch of bread she'd left rising before she quit said every loaf broke across the top before it was out of the oven. The dog howled regular under her bedroom window—folks didn't like to watch with her for that reason. She's brush up and say 't was because she always fed Tige and like enough he was hungry, but 't was no such thing. 'T was a plain sign.

Besides, there were those who knew, when she was a bride, that she wasn't cut out for a long life. Didn't she make her own wedding dress?

"What a dod-rotted mess o' nonsense," said Lydia—(but then, she must be considered a prejudiced party).

"Why, M's Dutton, don't you b'lieve in nothin'?" asked Mrs. Bugbee, who was hanging round as she always hung around scenes of possible excitement, whether welcome or not.

"W'l, if they is anything' a-tall in signs," Lydia continued, "there is all contrary to any idee of the first M's Buell bein' a ghost at this time an' place. Dog howlin's 'n cracked loaves may have signified she was a-goin' to pass on, an' she did. That's all over an' done with years an' years ago."

"Did you know," Mrs. Bugbee went on, undaunted, "th't her corpse lay over Sunday 'n rain fell into her open grave?"

"I've heard somethin' o' th't sort," Lydia replied.

"W'l don't them mean somethin'?"

"Mean another death in th' same fambly. Didn't Young Buell lose another his wives?"

"Two on 'em," Mrs. Bugbee broke in, eagerly.

Lydia shook her head. "One. Loretta Drew. Buried with her folks over in Sodom. Her baby with her."

"Nance Bullock. He married Nance Bullock."

"He did," cried Lydia, in a tone of exasperation. "Courted her two year and she lived with him two weeks. Nance vamoosed the minute she set eyes on the big washin' he'd been savin' up. You can't make a spook out o' her 'f you try from now till the cows come home, M's Bugbee."

The pest went away angry, the anger increasing the venom of her tongue. Presently everyone excepting Mr. Young Buell knew that the first Mrs. Buell was haunting the neighborhood. Naturally, Mr. Young Buell remained in ignorance, because if a thousand people know anything about a man's wife, the husband's number is figure one and three ciphers.

Lydia continued to grow more and more in love with the stone. She got up early and scrubbed it with soft soap. She lay in wait when there was "passing," hoping some one would say, "What a beautiful flagstone." She often stood ten minutes at a time craning her neck from a front window admiring the stone and not doing another identical thing. What wonder, when it stood for the first gratified ideal in a long life!

Of course Lydia didn't think, for a minute, that it was the first Mrs. Buell's gravestone. Or, even letting on that it might be, that those hellions from the Academy had gone and stolen a gravestone. Lydia didn't believe there was anything in the hauntings. One thing probably led to another, and fogs were very deceiving. As for Wash Burnside, didn't he see a queer man riding a horse, always keeping just so far in front of him going through the woods? And it turned out to be a hayseed in the front of his hat.

Then rappings began! Now it seemed impossible to explain rappings. For one thing, Lydia heard them herself. They weren't boys with tictacs, because she proved they weren't. Nor were they the wind shaking shutters because Christopher Dutton had never blinded the house.

There was an old book at Father Dutton's about ghosts. Lydia slipped down and borrowed it without bothering to ask permission. She ramped through it, hastily securing all it had to say concerning rappings. There were the Rochester rappings, and the rappings in Epsworth parsonage, which came after Mrs. Wesley's determination to bear her husband no more than ten (or possibly twelve) children until he ceased to pray for what she considered the wrong king.

Most important information was that showing how by asking questions one got raps meaning "yes" or "no," and so discovered what the rapper was rapping about. Lydia determined, alone and unaided, to thus solve her own mystery.

Trembling, but with her jaw set firm, Lydia sat all by herself in her own house one November night. She had disposed of Gerald by allowing him, as a treat, to go to his grandfather's and sleep with his big brother Lute, who would tease and pester till both fell asleep from exhaustion, and probably kick him out of bed before morning.

It was an ideal night for ghost seeing. A big wind twisted the tallest trees and wailed in the chimney. Clouds scudded past an old moon, and from time to time rain fell in torrents. It was a night when loneliness ate into the soul, when the regrets of a lifetime came forth from nooks of hiding; when the best tended of kerosene lamps seemed to burn but dimly. If anybody in a person's ken had died during the past ten years that person thought, on such a night, of the grave, of sodden earth pressing a once beloved body, of brown leaves drifting and white worms creeping. Death bed scenes came to mind, and shadowy forms of girls whom villains got "in trouble," and who made way with themselves after creeping into old homes and leaving beautiful infants in long empty cradles.

The rain ceased, the wind went down, the moon lay low in a cloudless sky, the temperature dropped to zero.

Lydia paused in the act of reaching for a hug-me-tight.

She heard a rap!

There was no denying the noise. She pinched herself, she counted the cracks in the ceiling, she shelled a chestnut and tried to swallow it. Yes, she was wake. It was an actual rap. It was soon followed by another.

Now was the time to try the formula. In a hollow and sepulchral tone ("quiet and expressing confidence" read the rule), Lydia asked, "Have you a message? Answer `yes' or `no'."

After a little came the answer—"Yes."

"Air you—air you a woman?"

"Yes."

"Be you—dead?"

"Yes."

"Long time dead?"

"Yes."

"Be you—be you the first Mrs. Young Buell?"

"Yes."

Lydia stopped, fear and disappointment using her for a battlefield. She was scared half out of her wits to be alone with this queer thing, yet she rejoiced that no one was with her. As for the natural next question, as to whether or not the socalled flagstone was a gravestone, Lydia determined not to ask it. The raps were coming in perfect positives, something must be done, she cast about for other questions, and proved beyond dispute that Mrs. Young Buell (if 't was she) could rap "no" as well as "yes." She was not concerned about her husband—no; nor about her children nor about their children. She had not left a secret hoard in a sugar bowl which had gone fifty-five years unwashed. She did not even know of any ten dollar bill in the Bible at a place where nobody ever read, not even when the minister came to call.

With the first hint of sunrise Lydia rose and proceeded to kindle a fire. It was Thanksgiving Day and she had to go to the big dinner at Father Dutton's, whether or no. Christopher wasn't home from the turkey shoot of the night before at Hamson. Just as like as not he wouldn't even show up when his mother had the victuals on the table. Then his folks would say something about her needing to do more to keep him straight, and she'd think as she'd thought many times before, that no good ever come of marrying a man who hadn't been brung up right.

It was early when Lydia and Gerald went home, lugging a full basket of goodies for the prodigal's supper. Lydia strode along dreading the evening and the future. This getting messages from another world was not what 't was cracked up to be. She didn't wonder "mejums" expected to be well paid. Then her thoughts (as ever thoughts of unhappy minds in that town) flew to students. It all began with the two who offered her what she wished that day she was sitting on the steps not wishing for anything in particular. It would not have been well for any boy with a good deed to perform, had he crossed Lydia's path just then. She would certainly have slapped him in the face, quick as that, though she had been obliged to sacrifice one of Mother Dutton's best mince pies as a missile.

"Ma!" yelled Gerald. "It's gone. Old woman's gravestone's gone!"

Never before had he dared so to miscall it. He now went unrebuked, for it was gone. Vanished; lock, stock and barrel. Only a slight oblong depression remained to show that it had once lain on the ash-paved walk.

Lydia's heart stood still. Some dratted neighbor had it in a barn, all the others in there priming themselves to taunt her forever and ever. Gerald propounded a theory more comforting, less probable.

"Guess the old woman," he observed, "picked it up her own self 'n lugged it back to the graveyard. Ghosts can," he added in polite explanation. "Rocks ain't nothin' to them."

Lydia had time for but a single pang at this evidence of long existing sedition in her own household, before Eleanora Burnside bustled over to tell the truth. She was evidently trying to be real kind, because she supposed Lydia would feel dreadfully over it.

"Your man n' Ed Silver," she whispered low (as bad news should be whispered). "They had Ed's stoneboat. Went by lickety larrup, so I sent 'him' on the run cross lots. Caught 'em at the State Road, where the stone crusher was workin'. Money passed, but 'he' didn't sense how much."

"Oh!" wailed Lydia. "That lovely—flagstone?"

Apprehension made the apparently grief-stricken cry a question, which Eleanora answered.

"Mebbe so. Too bad! It's all gone to pot now—machine chewed it right up."

"Didn't nobody a-tall see what was on t'other side?" Lydia just managed to gasp.

"Worse luck, no! Your man 'n Ed had been celebratin'. They couldn't a read a circus poster. He stuck round 'n asked the man tendin' the machine, but the feller only knowed dago."

"Glory hallelujah!" thought Lydia, and pranced into the house. She guessed she was well cured of wanting things. She guessed she's stop wishing for store teeth and a good cashmere dress. And she was sure that never again would she try communicating with spirits. So, when the nights grew chilly, and Gerald said, "Ma, 't sounds as if someone was knocking," she'd carefully explain that it was only the frost driving nails out of the clapboards.

"Some folks go all over their houses with hammers makin' em tight before cold weather sets in," she would explain.

Gerald, nodding solemnly, would add, "Pa never does." He knew why. It was because his pa had been a carpenter before he became a drunkard.

The fetch of Mrs. Young Buell ceased to haunt the mountain. Nor was it observed hanging round the stone crusher though it should have done so if there had been any connection betwixt spirit and stone. For the "flagstone" had in truth been a memorial to the first Mrs. Buell, and Lydia Dutton knew it. The words "Sacred to the Memory" and "Consort of Mr. Young Buell Esq." had been as plain as print on the moist ashes. She smoothed them out with her foot before Eleanora Burnside got there.

They had stolen a gravestone—those hellion students!

XIV. Craziness Better'n T'Other

In the spring Lydia Dutton sat and considered next year's winter. Even if there should be potatoes enough to carry them through, Christopher could be depended on to sell half. The shed would of course be empty, and fencerails had long ago given out, this being a land of stonewalls. Then—Gerald's pants! Somehow, Gerald never had a sufficiency of pants. Probably boys didn't anyway, because his legs were the same as common.

A woman, who had come crosslots, entered the kitchen. She was young rather than old, better looking than was necessary, and not a resident of the neighborhood.

"I guess craziness better 'n t'other," said she.

"Celestial Angel, sit," said Lydia.

"I jus' like being called Celestial Angel," said she. "You take notice I've growed. Few 'members my whole name 'ceptin' you. Lil' Ann's what them I live with make it. Hear you callin' me it, feel's if 'twas still pantalet time."

"You act like pantalet time," said Lydia, "a-sayin' craziness better 'n t'other." She did not consider, very much, what she was saying. She was wondering if it would be a long, cold winter. She'd recollect, at killing time, to ask Father Dutton was the heft of the lard backward or forward. Though, come to think of it, finding out wouldn't do much good. One could be just as cold in December as in March. And early chilblains did hang on. What was it Celestial Angel was saying?

"My blood is sweet today, for I heard good news. Guess I will throw back my bunnet 'n make myself to home. Shades o' Betsey, how this chair squeaks! I jus' admire to rock whack-o'-t'-whack! Them syrinzas smell nice. Some says the flowers on p'tato plants is more like real orange blossoms. I d' know."

Sensing that she had been brought to a halt in her pretty constant task of cleaning up dirt, Lydia produced three strips of rag, affixed them to the back of a chair, and started to braid. A rug, completed, sometimes brought a dollar—that is, providing you could find anyone to buy it.

"What's your good news?" she inquired, rather grimly. "Anything that'll stand repeatin'?"

She really thought it was going to turn out that Celestial Angel had a beau:

"Tilly Webster's come on the town."

Lydia stopped thinking about herself and Gerald, to shiver for poor old Tilly. She even spoke about what she was doing—shivering for poor old Tilly. With it she combined reproach for Celestial Angel.

"Of course, you wa'n't sprouted here," she remarked, severely. "Nor even come up here sence you was knee high to a grasshopper. You've always been a sort o' stranger sat in our midst, tho' I don't hold it agin you. You ain't real Back o' the Mountain."

Celestial Angel took this in good part and went right on with oak leaf edging.

"That's why," she said, "I say I've hearn good news. If I was Back o' th' Mountain I s'pose my lot 'd be cast somewheres round, so's I could make a stab at lookin' after her. As 'tis, I send M's Buell some flannen nighties for her when what she needs is a good warm petticut, all for want o' bein' on the spot. To be sure, the neighbors has been liberal in the way o' yaller kittens with O's on 'em, which the Websters always was partial to; also pies 'n caraway cookies. But what's a caraway cookie—or a jar full—when a person needs constant care? Many a night last winter I woke up in a wash o' sweat 'n after I'd kicked the soapstone out onto the floor I'd like awake quite a while worryin' for fear Tilly didn't have bedclothes enough."

Lydia kept her eyes on her braid. She could not raise them, they being filled with bitter tears of self pity. Who lay awake fretting because she and Gerald were short of bed clothes? Possibly craziness was better 'n t'other.

"My mind'll be real easy now," Celestial Angel continued. "The s'lectmen 'll get some proper person to stay 'long o' Tilly 'n see she eats her three meals reg'lar."

"Goin' on the town don't sound very nice," observed Lydia, making an attempt to rally her own pride.

* * *

"It don't," agreed Celestial Angel promptly. "that's what makes me say craziness better 'n t'other. She don't hear it, and she wouldn't take it in if she did."

The conversation had come to an end, but only temporarily. Celestial Angel was on her way to the Webster place—would Lydia go with her? She had come in the cars to the Depot, she had hired a half-Yankeed Irishman to drive her, but he was one of the sort who given two roads would take the wrong one—given but one, could be depended on to turn in the opposite direction.

"I told him Top o' th' Mountain, and it being so pushed in since I was here last I didn't notice much after we left 16 acres. So we fetched up in Silver Street. I give him half a dollar 'n told him to go right back to the stable for a great farmin' fool. You 'n me can make it together, can't we?"

Celestial Angel spoke as if a distance was diminished by sharing. Possibly she confounded it with sorrow, so considered in poetry. Lydia seemed to think the same.

"I ain't been there in a month o' Sundays," she remarked. "It's dretful fur off 'n up hill all the way. I'd never think o' goin' all by myself."

But she put on a slat sunbonnet and went with Celestial Angel. Even this was proof of craziness better 'n t'other since a rag carpet requires conscious superiority before it associates with ingrain.

Being New England women they preferred not to talk about that which was uppermost in their minds.

Lydia looked at the blue sky and said it was a good day, but likely enough a weather breeder, and Celestial Angel improved on that and said very likely we were in for a good spell o' weather. Lydia meant it was likely to rain tomorrow, so she guessed she wouldn't enjoy today. Celestial Angel meant to be polite.

Then they passed Mr. Young Buell running his eighty odd years on the stoop, and swapped a few yarns of how he lived in his comparative youth, after his first wife was dead and his second run away.

"Used to lay down his stove handle 'n lose it, so he went over t' Eastfield 'n buyed him a bushel o' stove handles to set handy back o' the stove. Tight's the bark on a tree, tho', wouldn't hire no woman to do his washin', used to tie his dirty clo's to a string 'n hitch that to his ole flat bottomed boat, 'n let 'em foller him down stream. Finally the string broke 'n he lost 'em all. Guess that's one thing sent him settin' up with Geo. Parsons' widder for his third."

While Celestial Angel was dutifully giggling, though she has probably heard it before, Lydia was quite busy thinking hate for Young

Buell's broad acres, already ploughed and planted, with a fourth wife to benefit. And not a scratch on Christopher Dutton land as yet.

Buell land ended, Webster holdings began. At least this was the bound in Tilly Webster's grandfather's time. Probably Buell owned this also now, because he had got along in the world by always being forehanded and having money to lend on mortgage. Still it was called Webster land; it probably would be called Webster land for another half century, this being the country in which greetings to a new king drown out death rattles of an old one.

Lydia did not know just why she must think, at this moment, of her worst year, but she did so think. When there had been no money in the house to buy salt, when she had stolen an old salt bag from Mother Dutton and boiled that with parsley greens to flavor 'em.

Well, perhaps she had come way up on Webster land to pick the greens. She wandered far in those days, and nearer home would be pretty dry picking by May.

Celestial Angel was panting out a remark.

"Seems to get lonesomer ev'ry time I come up on this mountain. I tell you, Lyddy Dutton, craziness is better 'n t'other 'f you got to live here, 'thout even neighbors to talk about."

"There's the house!" both exclaimed, a moment later. Celestial Angel suggested they sit down before going any further and meeting with nobody knew who as keeper of town's poor. She's walked her frizzes most out and her hair was all over her head.

"I s'pose I look some like a wild woman," remarked Lydia, "but I do' know's I care a tite. My market's made. Proper still up here, ain't it?"

"Yes. 'N I'm proper thirsty. Wish't I could get over t' the well 'thout bein' seen. Water allus tasted so good from the Webster well. A cocoanut dipper to drink from—the same old one wasn't lost nor busted last time I was here."

"Gre't hand for such things—the Websters," said Lydia, making another grievance to herself of that. "They even had a fambly board for layin' out such of 'em as died, I've hearn tell."

And considered raspingly, that if she ever got such a board she'd be obliged to use it to iron on!

Celestial Angel rose heavily to her feet.

"Feel's they was a blister on my heel," she observed.

"You'd ought to soaped the inside your stockin' down to my house," replied Lydia. She was hot and tired out herself, and almost ready to remind Celestial Angel that the job was none of her seeking.

The door stood hospitably open. So did a door at the opposite end of the narrow hall which numerous bumblebees were using as a short cut to wherever bumblebees go to. No one answered their knockings.

"I s'pose she's gone away," said Celestial Angel.

"Land sakes!" said Lydia. "They don't let her roam?"

"She never wanted to. When I say gone away I mean—well, completely out. Never that for long, but once in a while it comes on her. And such kind of a day as this most gen'rally."

Lydia nodded. She understood. Tilly Webster's wedding day had been a day like this. Another grievance. When Lydia got married to Christopher it rained. Her bonnet and dress were never quite the same.

"There she is," said Celestial Angel. "In the parlor. I know 't was a day she'd be out."

The parlor was well furnished and nothing was worn out or shabby because Tilly had no husband to break the chairs or sit them out in long lazy hours of pipe smoking. There was a marble top table with a stereoscope on it and an attendant pile of pictures, none of them smudged from being handled by dirty fingers. Over the mirror hung pink cut paper for defence against flies; and the mirror differed from Lydia's in not being cracked. Every chair was set slantwise from the wall, and a nice looking woman with an unwrinkled face was waving very white fingers in the direction of each, while addressing them in dulcet tones.

"Thinks they're folks come to call," whispered Celestial Angel. "Le's us go right in 'n set down in some. And answer up whatever she calls you."

While Celestial was being spoken to as Mrs. Deacon Bowers, and asked after her several children—poor Celestial, not even beaued yet—Lydia's roving eye took in more of the scene with disapproval. Tilly Webster wore a pink dress, and it was clean. No other woman of her age could keep a light colored calico decent after the first half hour of an afternoon. But Tilly had no chickens to look after, no night's wood to fetch in. Her hair was still yellow in the sunlight, and she evidently had plenty of time to do it up slick.

"Fact truth," thought the disgruntled Lydia, "she don't look more'n a year or so older—'n the room don't look a day older—than that day—"

Then she realized with a jerk that everything was so intended. Up here time had stood still for Tilly Webster, while down below it was busy pulling others out of comfortable ruts, and jouncing them over "Thank—you—ma'ams," and occasionally running away with them and throwing them out with tragic results.

And yet anyone with half an eye would have supposed Tilly Webster was marked by fate for a life of woe. Everybody gathered in that same parlor for her wedding, thirty odd years before, did think so after they'd waited two hours and the bridegroom didn't come. Lydia had been there, a little girl, just beginning to take notice of love making and such goings on. Lydia remembered it all perfectly. There sat Parson Bowers, all ready to perform the ceremony when he could get any two to perform it on. There was Tilly's father, with a black stock so high and grand one was obliged to take his collar on faith. Fifty other people were there, crowding parlor and hall and jiggling the table in the kitchen where stood the tray of glasses ready for the currant wine. The cake was in the butt'ry, Tilly's mother had been days making it, the only wetting for the sugar and flour was brandy and sherry, the frosting was two inches deep top and sides. Tilly herself wore a flowered silk, pink, a good deal like the calico she was wearing now. There was a wreath on her head of real orange blossoms. Nobody knew, but she said they were. And she had been over to Eastfield working at a real dressmaker's, cutting and fitting according to pictures, not the pin on kind. Real worked up, Tilly seemed to get, as the day wore away, shading her eyes and looking down the road; not crying, but her under lip trembling and her chin working sorrowful.

So that presently, without anyone saying much, every woman at the wedding took Tilly's worry as her worry, and reared her head scornful like as saying, "If Tilly Webster's been mittened I been mittened."

And each man began to act as if he was the brother Tilly never had, or—if along in years—the father she needed then, rather than the stock-imprisoned old beau who was her father. There was Cyrus Thornton, who held that strong language wasn't necessary and spluttered only, "Shucks!" when driving a hog. What did he do but double his fists and roar out, "Gee Whitaker!" and add, "Good riddance! She'd never been happy with such a mean skunk."

Now Lydia thought of it, Cy must have been touched some himself. How else did an old hard headed fellow such as he come to say, a year or so later, that when Tilly went plumb out of her head she landed right into all the Back o' th' Mountainer's hearts? That wasn't any sort of way to look on a girl who'd been deserted. Lydia was reasonably well acquainted with the ways of the love cracked, she had read the New York *Ledger* stories for years. Girls were frequently left at the altar, either intentionally by the villain, or through inadvertence by the hero. In any case the immediate result was the same, they peaked and pined, their beauty faded. Frequently, both in tales and in real life, they became objects of ridicule.

After speaking kindly to both her guests and all her chairs, Tilly wafted herself out of the room with a tea tray. It was a real one, Lydia hoped she would return with real tea. Celestial Angel began to talk about her the moment she was shut of the room, just as if she had been a real hostess.

"You see—she's clean forgot there's any fur off. Sometimes she's here's much 's you'n I, but I guess everyone likes her best when she's gone away. She's all sunniness, like we jest see her, and conjures out she's got on anythin' heart can wish. I wish she'd cut loose 'n sing. I come up here one night, long 'bout sundown, 'n she was a-settin' in the middle o' the kitchen with a candle lit on the table an' a-lookin' out the back winder, an a-singin' a sort o' loose jointed tune, the sort th' words seem to cut right through.

One, two, three, four,
A face at ev'ry pane;
One, two, three, four,
An' ev'ry face his face—

Somethin' like that. Ain't it jes beautiful? 'Tis real true love allus t' see one person 'n everywheres you look to see that same person. Oh, more'n half the time Tilly thinks she's a real bride an' happy as the day is long. D'you ever hear what she done with that pink flowery silk she set out to be married in?"

Lydia shook her head, and drew her lips in at the corners. Her wedding dress had been only cashmere and she'd made it over till there wasn't so much as a shred left.

"Wal, she cut it up into strings, an' she hung the pieces in front o' the back door, an' for years 'n years they wasn't a bird's nest anywheres 'round that hadn't got a strip wove into it. Parson Bowers said that w's poetry jes as much as any that Miss Ella Wheeler Wilcox ever wrote. And Tilly's that quick motioned she'd go out under the trees, 'n catch at the lowest branches, 'n then she'd dance up'n down—"

"She's a-doin' it now," snarled Lydia, whose stomach yearned after a cup of tea.

Both women looked into what had been the Webster apple orchard. The trees were old and scraggly, the limbs and trunk bark bound. Of course it produced poor apples, but the blossoms were good as the best. Pink and white they clustered just above Tilly, who was also pink and white. Up and down she danced, even as they danced in the south wind. Better than they, she sang:

Matilda, when these lines you sing
Attend the one who love doth bring,
Thine I am and only thine,
In my heart your heart entwine,
Love I have for thee alone
Due all others only stone
All for thee, for thee alone.

"'Tain't much of a chune," said Lydia. "Sounds as doleful as th' one th' ole cow died on."

"Oh—well, 't was writ for her special. Spells out her name—don't you see? It needed to be lyin' round here somewheres on a piece of paper with a lace edge. 'Twas s'posed her feller wrote it when he was sparkin' her over in Eastfield. Cy Thornton thought mebbe he'd see it 'n do somethin' 'f 't was printed, so he put it into the Poet's Corner o' the Hampson *Chronotype*. It looked real good, but nothin' come on 't."

"Wal, I guess I'll move home-along," said Lydia. "I can't do no good here, 'n I feel 's if th' pit o' my stomick 'd fell through. You goin' to wait a while longer—on the chance o' seein' the town's woman?"

"I be," said Celestial Angel. "I sense that laylock speck way off in the pastur 's prob'ly her. Diggin' dand'lion greens most likely."

"Yah," said Lydia. "I'd like a mess. But I have to dig my own!"

Celestial Angel tilted back in another rocker and laughed comfortably.

"Didn't I say craziness better 'n t'other?" she inquired.

Lydia clattered down the hill all out of sorts. Eighteen years of poverty, freezing winters, working her fingers off summers; neglect, hard words, sometimes blows from Christopher. Oh, yes; craziness was much better 'n t' other. Neighbors teasing, sneering, grasping, purse proud. His folks always thinking she hadn't managed right. Her folks remarking that she'd made her bed and now she could lie on it. Nobody in all the world to think for her, or do for her, or even be sorry for her.

Craziness better 'n t'other. She wished she had gone crazy. She might, even now, try to go crazy. If only she knew how to go about going crazy. But no, even for that remedy 't was too late. She'd never again be pink cheeked and soft handed. She's be only old looney Lyd; they'd pack her off to an asylum where she'd be strung up by the thumbs and fed on mush made from musty corn meal.

Lydia flounced up to her own house. It was way past milking time, but of course Christopher hadn't come home. Probably over to Silvers', drinking hard cider (for which he paid well, generally from the result of Lydia's labor), and holding eyes with Mabel Silver. The pig, too, squealed like all possessed. And all those chickens to count and shut up. If only she might be sure of the reward for these chores. But Christopher would doubtless sell the pig and trade the cows for a new buggy to drive himself round in, while most of the eggs found their way to combination with Silvers' cider, to the result of flip.

"I swan to man," she said, in a voice loud enough to be heard a quarter of a mile to Burnsides', "craziness is better 'n t'other."

She entered the kitchen. Gerald sat by the table, wriggling his fat legs and of course wearing out his school pants something terrible. Somebody had played ball with his new straw hat that Lydia had pinched herself to buy, it was laid, a muddy ruin, on the clean table cloth. Gerald's face was all over the canned blueberry pie she had meant to save for Sunday. Much had dripped, too, on the floor, freshly scrubbed just before the arrival of Celestial Angel.

"Ma," said Gerald in a hectoring tone, "I want a red necktie. If you don't get me a red necktie I'll run away."

Lydia looked well at him—her boy. All over freckles, dirty, hard to manage, a lazy little tyke, sassy, had to be driven to mind his book. Didn't like Sunday School. Wanted something that cost money constantly.

His mother went over and tried to smoothe the hair from his grimy forehead. He scrooged to avoid a kiss. She beamed on him. Craziness better 'n t'other! No such thing. Celestial Angel was a cock-eyed liar.

APPENDIX

(Later Contents Page)

I - Where Lydia Lived - [check]
II - Lydia Puts a Hen On - 0
III - Both Ways Across the Board - 0
IV - Helping God Out - 0
V - Just Exactly Like Her - 0
VI - As Three Comforted Job - 0
VII - Poor Fish (XIV) - [check]
VIII - The Little Girl Who Died (XII) - [check]
IX - A Petticoat That Rustled (VIII) - [check]
X - Prodigious Beebes (VII) - [check]
XI - A New Front Door (IX) - [check]
XII - A Great American Poet (X) - [check]
XIII - Those Hellion Students (XI) - [check]
XIV - Craziness Better than T'other (XIII)

(First Contents Page)

I - Where Lydia Lived —
I - Lydia Puts a Hen On —
III Both Ways Across the Board [comedy]
IV - Helping God Out —
V - Just Exactly Like Her —
VI - As Three Comforted Job —
VII — Prodigious Beebes [comedy]
VIII - A Petticoat That Rustled [dress]
IX - A New Front Door [comedy]
X - A Great American Poet [literary]
XI - Those Hellion Students [weird]
XII - The Little Girl Who Died [tragedy]
XIII - Craziness Bettern T'other [comedy]
XIV Poor Fishes [summer talk]
XV Comedy
XVI - Plot begins
XVII - Halts
XVIII - Plot
XIX - Sorrow Starts
XX - Parting
XXI - Sadness
XXII - Ending

[the summer visitor who gives us all opinions. Lydia accepts in silence &
then home.
* * *

[the admirer of Poe.
* * *

[I'll go braking Gerald]
* * *

[The brilliant couple & Cora - oh - Cora's. I'm a day laborer telephone
operator.]
* * *

Takes a State Kid & adopts it because it yells.
* * *

Operation. People's List
* * *

[The little Girl That Died]
* * *

Boarding the Dog
* * *

[Comes on the Town]

THE VILLAGE GREEN

The time is 1923.

PERSONAE (*compiled by the editors*)

Blodgett, Belinda (Mrs. John). Daughter of a man adopted by Great Aunt Lury's parents. A member of the literary society "The Club." (Possible model: Laurie Sawyer.)

Calista (surname not provided). Elderly boarder in Flora Hancock's house.

Comyns, Amelia (Aimé). Unfaithful wife of Arthur Comyns, who has Mr. Posie and Jim Jeffreys Hazelwonda as lovers. (Possible model: Elise Dorothy (Grant) McLaughlin Houtain (1889-1980).)

Comyns, Arthur. Flora Hancock's beau during her Chicago days. He has returned East and become the husband of Amelia (Aimé) by the time of the story.

Dennis, Elsa. Secretary of local literary society "The Club." Boards in the home of Clarence Miller. Afflicted with a chronic cough which keeps Flora Hancock awake of nights.

Drake, G. C. A. (or S. G. A.). Village Green undertaker; conducts funeral for Great Aunt Lury.

Ellis, Ed. Husband of Betty Hepburn and son-in-law of Great Aunt Lury. Father of Harry, who changes his name to Harry Emerson.

Emerson, Belle. Wife of Ben Emerson (brother of Clark?). Meets Flora Hancock in a Boston restaurant, later shares a bed with her following Aunt Lury's funeral.

Emerson, Clark. Banker, third husband of Great Aunt Lury.

Emerson, Harry (Ellis). Son of Ed Ellis and Betty Hepburn, grandson of Great Aunt Lury. He changes his name to Emerson in respect of Great Aunt Lury's third husband Clark Emerson.

Etta (surname not provided). Man-hating tenant in Great Aunt Lury's home, continued by Flora after her inheritance.

Hancock, Flora (b. 1893). Daughter of the brother of Aunt Lury's second husband Mr. Hancock. Inherits home on the Village Green from Aunt Lury.

Hazelwonda, Jim Jeffreys. Well-groomed lover of Amelia Comyns who urges her to elope with him to New York City. (Possible model: George Julian Houtain (1884-1945).)

Hepburn, Betty. Only daughter of Great Aunt Lury, by her first husband Mr. Hepburn. Deceased by the time of the story.

Hepburn, Catalpa. Sister-in-law of Great Aunt Lury. Sister of Aluria's second husband Mr. Hepburn.

Hollister, Mrs. Hostess for meeting of "The Club" attended by Flora Hancock. Lives in a hard-to-find European-style house on Sachem Hill. Has "Gibson Girl" daughter Gwendoline Hollister.

Howe-Hepburn-Hancock-Emerson, Aluria. "Great Aunt Lury." Deceased aunt of Flora Hancock. Born a Howe, she marries (1) Mr. Hepburn, (2) Mr. Hancock, (3) Clark Emerson (the local banker).

Miller, Clarence (Clare). Next-door neighbor of Great Aunt Lury and Flora Hancock. Has wife, daughters Nancy, Rachel and Annie, son, and coughing boarder Elsa Dennis.

Posie, Mr. Middle-aged and salaried lover of Amelia Comyns. Commits adultery (a felony in Massachusetts at the time) with her in a room of Flora Hancock's house.

Sullivan, Florence (Flo). President of the local literary club, known for his singing of Irish songs. (Possible model: Joseph Bernard Lynch, 1879-1952.)

Theobald Jr., H. "The man with the long chin," a member of "The Club," who considers ordinary conversation an interruption to philosophic discourse. (Model: H. P. Lovecraft.)

Trinkett, Herbert. Attorney for Great Aunt Lury and Flora Hancock. (Possible model: Walter H. Thorpe.)

It was allowed to be as green as it liked. Flowers trimmed it—daisies, Black-eyed Susans, the plantain that so frankly claims to be "white man's footstep," and, in August, suggestive remains of what had been spring dandelions. As for paths, as many had been beaten as encircling doorsteps invited. The doorsteps were all alike of the local red sandstone. Such uniformity stood for economy. There was no reason, however, for expecting a Hepburn to keep to the path of a Hancock, and the Hepburns did not. Individual paths had been trodden time out of mind, and continued to be clear and plain in this summer of 1923.

It was shaded by a considerable number of elm trees, sufficiently far apart for each to enjoy the true vase shape of the unhampered elm. Though a trifle sallow, along toward midsummer, from reminiscent elmnutling, they were still pretty good trees. They swayed in the sultry wind, casting dappled shadows upon the turf that was allowed to be as green as it liked; and also on the exceedingly dusty though so numerous paths.

Flora Hancock called it the Village Green. For her it centralized a homecoming to which she believed her steps had tended in all the twenty-five years since she had been removed from its neighborhood at the age of five. Chicago had been her dwelling place, but not, she told herself, her home. Chicago was too busy selling itself to epitomize home for anyone. Chicago's shamelessness was well represented by those inhabitants who undressed at the house, then hailed a street car and rode miles and miles to the beaches in bathing suits.

Because Chicago never seemed to have any message for her, Flora Hancock believed one was ready written for her in New England. Which was quite as snug to the truth as the common remark that "James must be in love with Mary because he does not like Clara."

When Flora returned to the Green, in her thirtieth year, it was affectively decorated with hoppers and flutterers—robin redbreasts and butterflies. It also wore, on its north margin, the town hearse. That, indeed, was the real reason for Flora's coming back. Yet she brought with her no burden of sorrow, only a slight irritation that circumstances did not permit showing the joy she felt. One could not really grieve over the death of a great aunt, though decorum had prompted a stop over in Boston for the purchase of a back frock and a discreet mourning hat and veil. Black silk gloves completed the picture. Flora had never worn such raiment before; she rather fancied herself in it.

The Villagers (who did not call themselves Villagers any more than they called the Common the Village Green) universally held that Flora was to be congratulated on having timed her arrival so that it did not tamely take place before something of importance was going on. Such a funeral as Lury Howe-Hepburn-Hancock-Emerson's was worth attending from more than as far off as that wicked City Chicago.

Flora would not have understood this point of view. She had started jauntily enough on her Eastern journey, a journey she would have taken long before had she felt that she could afford it. Life interest in Hancock property which great Aunt Lury had held because of her second marriage to a Hancock would now revert to Flora. The substantial buoyancy lent by assurance of financial security sustained Flora until she was about to board a train which would land her near the Village Green two hours before the time scheduled for the obsequies to start. Suddenly she became conscious of a shrinking from too exhaustive observance of death. Two hours to kill—and with whom? Some sadfaced women, and they would talk exclusively of the deceased. She knew almost nothing of the deceased, whose only notice of her grandniece had been an occasional disagreeable letter saying that the property needed shingling, or painting on the underpinning, and Flora should pay for it because it was to be hers in the end, and the writer was only an old woman who'd never see the snow fly or the peonies blossom, or the hay cut or the hogs killed, according to season, again. When she kept right on living, rolling in riches left by her third husband, Deacon Emerson, and meanwhile Flora banged at her typewriter overtime without leisure to find out what painting was in reference to underpinnings.

Another train got in exactly at two. She would risk it. After all, the sensible thing was to eat lunch in Boston. There might be no inns or cafes where she was going. She could scarcely rush into her inheritance at once, and that G. C. A. Drake, who had signed the summoning telegram, was probably some lawyer. Why should he invite her to his home? This was today in America, not the time of Wilkie Collins and an English novel.

Flora was partly right about him. Though not a lawyer, he had no intention of inviting funeral guests into his home. He was the undertaker.

A taxi was justified by new clothes and a sense of opulence. Flora took a taxi for the restaurant which she had been given to understand was more a state of mind than Boston itself. Ignoring the tiny reception room because she didn't see it was there, she went up a long flight of stairs not in the least alienated by turn or landing. A highly starched head waitress waved her to the one vacant seat at a large round table. The eight occupants of mahogany arm chairs were prosperous looking men. Each was engaged in eating a large cooked dessert with two kinds of sauce, hard and sloshy. While eating cases were discussed—court cases, but not criminal.

Flora laid aside the twelve-page menu. She did not need to consult it. She had always planned to go into this restaurant and order clams. She ordered them, then looked about idly while waiting for them to come. The walls of the room were covered with Linvusta Walton, and hung with pictures. Huge steel engravings of royal deathbeds and Congressional Prayings alternated with oils of the heroic type. Opposite the stairways was a banjo clock. It was exactly as Flora remembered it when she had lunched here with her mother. Flora was four, and they were going to Chicago. The mother would never return, Flora was just coming back. They had had clams!

The waitress returned and placed before Flora a bowl of crackers, an egg-shaped cup of melted butter, a pitcher that steamed and a huge dish covered with a napkin. Whipping off the napkin the clams were displayed. There was a trifle less than half a peck of them, each shut in a double shell.

Not being void of a sense of humor, Flora smiled at herself too broadly for consonance with her black dress. She thought of the beautiful little barrel of oysters which Dora Copperfield bought for the dinner David gave Traddles. How did the author put it? "As we hadn't any oyster knives, and couldn't have used them if we had, we ate the mutton and looked at the oysters."

"Shall I order a chop?" she asked herself.

"How do you do?" said a voice from the next chair, which a dessert eater had just vacated. It was a feminine voice, yet not so very feminine. The same description applied to the user. She was tall and bony rather than thin. What was visible of her face and hands made Flora wonder why that old governor of Massachusetts bothered to tan the shins of deceased inhabitants. From this observation it is obvious that Flora took a keen dislike to her neighbor before she so much as answered her question.

The ugly woman—so hideous as to be distinguished, just like a gargoyle, pushed higher the heavy veil that was draped on the bridge of her nose, and went on, "Of course we know each other. You are Flora Hancock. Etta wrote me that you were expected to the funeral, and I remembered you had red hair, when we were both of us five. I was getting on to that eleven o'clock train when I saw you get off. Well, I said to myself—cinnamon toast and tea, bring a large pitcher of hot water and leave the teabag in the pot—if she is waiting till the 1.28 I might as well do the same, because they can't very well have it unless she is there. So I got in the car and came straight here. I think I never lost sight of your taxi until Adams Square. My eyesight is pretty good. And then your folks always did come here so I guessed you would. Why don't you eat your lunch? There's not any too much time, unless you intend to taxi back. That's why I've only ordered toast and tea. It seems foolish to get a great big expensive lunch when perhaps one can't eat it all."

The tea and toast arrived; the woman poured two spoonfuls of liquid from the pot into her cup, filled the space with hot water and sent the pitcher to be replenished.

"I cannot drink it strong," she remarked. "A cup full strength even this hour of the day and I'd never close my eyes! I believe I'll have to stay over. Everyone will have to stay over except those with cars. There's no train out after 5.30 and we will hardly be back from the grave by then. Which husband are they going to bury her with? Do you know? Why don't you begin on your lunch."

"I'm not hungry," returned Flora in a tone calculated to put an end to grewsome curiosity concerning her great aunt. It was a tone that had been very efficacious in stopping foolish questions from fellow filing clerks after prolonged and unexplained noonday absence. It had absolutely no effect on the possessor of those great brown hands glittering with diamonds in platinum settings; those feet like ends of legs turned up, encased in comfortable yet smart patent leather sandals.

"Well, you will be. I shall be. Nothing gives me such an appetite as a funeral. The smell of flowers, and sitting still, and then I always cry. The last time I saw Aunt Lury she said to me, `Well, Belle, if you come to my funeral I'm sure of somebody crying.' Only a week ago Sunday. I wanted Ben to go out with me, because I thought very likely she wouldn't get well, but the roast was so large it wouldn't go into the fireless without cutting and so he had to stay at home. Flora, why don't you eat your lunch?"

"I ordered clams," said Flora, exasperated beyond argument by hearing her name so carelessly used. "I don't care for them."

It was asinine, but so was the adventure.

"Clams? Clams! Why, they are delicious. Clams are delicious. Now Margaret, she cannot abide shellfish in any form, but as for me..!" Reaching forth dark yet artfully manicured thumb and forefinger, grabbed a clam, whipped off the top shell, and lifted the other to a pair of thin lips in which the juice was tilted. The other hand then grabbed the blacky-white morsel, dipped it into the still steaming clam water, then into the melted butter, and then into that gash in the face. "Delicious!" the process was repeated. "Why won't you have some of my tea? I'm afraid there isn't a great deal left, but we can squeeze down the leaves and send the girl for more hot water. I don't care for this piece of toast, either. I think it's been scraped. They will do it, when the bread is burned, and it often must be after it's warmed over the third or fourth day. Do have it!"

She continued to shuck and eat, stopping after every half dozen to butter a cracker or nibble a pickle. Disgust and bitterness struggled for supremacy with Flora; it was petty to be disillusioned by anything so petty, but she could have wept for pity at the tumbling ruins of her romantic first meal in Boston. Sudden rage determined her not to be utterly done. She snatched a clam for herself, denuded it of the upper shell, drank the juice, thought it as palatable as salted lake water; washed and buttered the clam according to pattern and then—felt her courage oozing.

She supposed that she made a rather ridiculous figure sitting there in her beautiful black holding an innocent, repulsive, half-mourning clam. It was such a little bite, and her abhorrence was so enormous.

The woman, of whom Flora as yet knew nothing beyond an equal abhorrence, that her name was Belle, her husband's Ben, and an Etta and a Margaret were somewhere in the scheme, ate the last clam and dipped into the finger bowl. Then she turned abruptly.

"Afraid!" she said. "I thought so all along. Eat it quick. We're late and will have to taxi."

Flora ate it and anger at obeying so unreasonable a command lasted while she paid the check for two, indeed lapped over till she settled the entire taxi fare while her companion obligingly bustled into the station to consult the track diagram.

There was no time to buy tickets, and Flora drew out a bill in readiness for the conductor. She was not, however, supported in such extravagance.

Choosing—apparently at random—the first passenger with a trip ticket, Belle bent to a whispered conference which resulted in two extra punches. Their benefactor was a cool blonde youth who read *The Outlook* industriously and never once glanced across the aisle at the ladies he was assisting.

"Nice, isn't he?"

Flora, in an agony of shame, managed her first direction question to the other. "I suppose," she said, "his mother is a friend of yours?"

"I wish she were! He looks good, doesn't he? There was a girl I played with one afternoon at Aunt Lury's twenty-eight—no, let me see!—thirty-two years ago. She was that blonde type. But she was only a visitor, and probably didn't marry anyone around this locality. The New England blonde is rapidly dying out, you know. He may very likely be a Swede. I remember her name perfectly. Fiducia Anne Grahame. With an "e" on both. I might ask him if his mother was a Grahame."

"Oh please!" ejaculated Flora, struggling to reach the aisle over those gaunt knees.

"The money? Oh, it's of no consequence. Eleven cents, no one ever has change. The regular fare is twenty-two, and thirty-four if the conductor takes it. Well, here we are."

A station beside the village green bore no visible sign, but had its name grown in cannas. Flora inconsequently wondered what they did in the winter, as she followed her companion's dignified stalk to the door. The man to whom she owed eleven cents had escaped at the first hint of slowing down.

Exactly opposite the station was a large and shabby wooden house, set on a bank faced with pudding stone slightly out of plumb. Unpainted steps crumbling on the edges from rot, led directly to a door in the exact middle of the front. This stood open. It was flanked by side lights and had a fanshaped glass overhead. Two long windows on either side were draped with lace curtains, one set immaculate and costly; the others of a coffee-colored dinginess. On each side of the steps stood a man wearing black clothes and gloves.

Every path crossing the green was in use; women—even a few men— were approaching the house of grief, where a couple of petrified palms tied with a wisp of purple gauze depended from the knob of the door bell. This knob was made of a dark brown material, marbled with yellow. The insignia of death was so arranged that the knob seemed a part of the scheme. Flora was afraid she would always see it thus decorated.

The people approaching, as well as those already thronging the steps, carefully and most obviously abstained from looking at Flora. Flora fancied this might be because she was companioned as she was, a delusion which gave small credit to etiquette. If she had noticed she might have seen that no one of them seemed to know any other one. Even the husbands who had shut up the post office, the branch bank and the meat market and grocery, slunk into position beside their wives without recognizing them as human beings. There is something about a funeral, in some parts of the world, that makes it seem desirable to attend as surreptitiously as possible. This was one of those parts of the world. The reason, of course, is that grand old Anglo-Saxon ambition— to seem above all display of emotion. To "give way" is hardly forgivable and never forgettable.

Of course it wasn't likely anyone would give way at Aunt Lury's, for a more cantankerous, tight-fisted, gossipy, suspicious and eccentric character never existed. Still one never could tell who would come off victorious in the duel between cultivated phlegm and the officiating clergyman.

Belle pulled down her veil with a view to practicing pulling it up, and securing a large and clean handkerchief, she tucked it into the tops of her glove.

"Have one handy," she admonished Flora. "There are sure to be reminders. When did your mother pass on?"

"In 1916," said Flora, stiff with anger.

"And you still wear mourning? Chicago style? Two years is the custom here. I kept mine on two years for mother, except for the second summer. I went to Philadelphia to see friends, and as I knew it would be warm I had some colored muslins made up and a light hat with some rose trimming. They had a good many parties, and I didn't think it would be considerate to cast a gloom... Aunt Lury made a peculiar remark when I came to see her after I had got home and put on the black to finish the year. 'I see your mother's dead again,' said she. How nice yours has worn. It looks good as new."

"My God!" exclaimed Flora. "It is new. I bought it in Boston."

Belle was astounded at nothing but the fact.

"I hope," she said, "you'll find the property worth it."

She extricated her heel from a hole in the top step, while Flora stubbed her toe on a piece of new wood covering what appeared to be a still larger hole in the threshold.

Belle's observation was disagreeable, catty, and exactly what Flora herself had been thinking. A second example of successful mind reading that day.

Fear that they would sit together, possibly weep together, was dispelled by the undertaker. Ascertaining just who they were he consulted a note book, crossed two lines off, directed Belle to the front room with the soiled curtains, and put Flora into a back parlor on the other side of the hall. The old fashioned lounge and a great many comfortable chairs had been placed in rows against three of the walls. All were occupied with people elaborately employed in not seeing the last comer. Two women had a thin man between them on the lounge, but nobody moved up and the timid attempt of the man to arise brought a severe look from the younger of the females, as if she said, "You forget yourself. This is not a street car."

The undertaker could be heard out in the hall wrestling with a mass of conglomerated folding chairs. Finally one unloosed itself and was brought for Flora. She sank into it at once, notwithstanding the prominence of its position, near the wide open door which occupied practically the whole of one wall.

When she could ignore the creaking and raise her eyes she found herself staring directly at her great aunt.

Aluria Howe-Hepburn-Hancock-Emerson had the entire best room to herself and the numerous floral pieces that came despite—or perhaps because of a reminder conveyed in the words "Please omit flowers." The casket was of the open variety and Aunt Lury's appearance in death was at least ninety-five percent better than it had been during the last forty years of her life. Flora was startled to remember what a very old woman she had been remembering. Then she realized that Aunt Lury was beautifully made up. Her face had all the lines painted out, all the wrinkles filled in and all the proper tints laid on. Her lips were what they had probably never been, a perfect Cupid's bow. For hair, at least $75 worth, in purest white, waved, in addition to her own. Garbed in a handsomer satin gown than she had ever allowed herself, and on her bosom rested a more stunning bunch of violets than anyone had thought appropriate for a jaundiced old woman.

All other furnishings had been removed from the room, she was the only furnishing. Above her hung a marvelous crystal chandelier; the walls were covered with a shining and obviously expensive paper that successfully imitated brocade; there were handsome rugs on the waxed floor. The few pictures were large oils in brilliant colorings; every one had won a prize in some art exhibit and bore testimony to such distinction on the bottom of the gilded frame. Over the marble mantel was a portrait of a gentleman. He had white hair parted in the middle, and Burnside whiskers as symmetrically disposed. So well done was a Masonic charm on a background of fancy vesting that it seemed the picture, and all the rest simply perspective.

Uncle Emerson. That room, was furnished for Aunt Lury by her third husband, the bank president. So much Flora knew without any cousinly aid. He had been a friend and backer of Uncle Hancock, had loaned the money to Uncle Hancock when this house was built. It was when calling round, in the interest of his bank's interest, that Clark Emerson had fallen in love with Aunt Lury. He married her despite her double widowhood; thus his mortgage had never been foreclosed.

Under her eyelashes Flora ventured a glance at the back parlor, now nearly filled with folding chairs, unfolded and bearing human burdens. Yes, this was the Hancock room. A crayon enlargement of Uncle Hancock stood on an easel, the walnut frame partly obscured by an embroidered drape. Furniture, of course, upholstered in black haircloth. Uncle Hancock had provided a carpet in body Brussels. Flora's feet were resting thereon. As a final refinement, an enlargement of Aunt Lury, as a Hancock hung between the front windows. Was there a Hepburn room, sacred to the marriage of her youth, the only one that resulted in offspring? There must be, how else had Flora a memory of straightbacked chairs and daguerreotypes?

Seemliness and sleepiness were now interrupted by a sound strange indeed in a house of mourning. Weeping, loud and unrestrained, like that of Rachel of her children. In spite of the undertaker's "Madam—madam—please don't go in here—an opportunity will be afforded for all to view the remains after the services"—the sacred best parlor had been invaded by a female in a tipsy bonnet and a mangy plush coat fastened down the front by safety pins.

A few "Ulalus" and crossings and she allowed herself to be led away, remarking in an extremely audible tone, "Eight 'n' forty years I've washed her, poor soul. It's she gave me this very coat, all but the buttons..."

The voice of a young clergyman now filled the house. By the craning of a neck or so one judged that the appearance of this particular man was a surprise. He spoke extremely at length, without saying anything. The Holy Christian Church, he observed, influenced many people, but he did not say it had had any influence on Aunt Lury. A noble life, he declared, was not lived in vain, yet of reference to the life of Aunt Lury, whether noble or no, there was none. He expatiated at length on funeral customs of the past, mentioned the grave of Moses, the fact that David slept with his fathers; and Lazarus; did not mention Aunt Lury.

A choir then rendered Rodenheaver's touching "I Walked with the Lord in My Garden," and everybody arose and formed in line for the agonizing last look. It was a long look, that is, it took a long time. The house had been thronged. Hepburns, Hancocks, Emersons and more than a few Howes. Easy to guess which was which by solicitude over the cards on the gauze ribbons attached to floral tributes.

The Village Green was entirely surrounded with limousines. Even the usually self-absorbed children going home from school were stirred into staring. Years hence they would remember this as an historic occasion.

The first four cars were filled with tottering old people; Flora was assisted into the fifth, where she was companioned by a hooked nose woman who gave an impression of being entirely clothed in beads and earrings; a stout man; and a dainty little old lady engaged in clawing at her lace veil.

"For God's sake, Catalpa," said the hooked nose woman, "let it alone. It'll be a ruin."

"I want it to be. Damned old fool that I am paid seventy-five cents for it. She hasn't left me one red cent to rub against another. Yards and yards of tatting! Every bit of the edge and insertion for the parlor curtains. She said I would get a hundred dollars. There!"

The veil, in shreds, was cast to the floor.

"Well, by George, Catalpa," said the man, "you haven't got a thing on me. She hasn't left me a single penny, either. Me—married to her only daughter! But you bet you I'll have Betty's engagement ring, if I rob the old shebang: my wife's ring! The girl I kept single for fourteen years!"

"You consoled yourself, didn't you, Ed?" asked the woman with the hooked nose and the earrings.

Aunt Lury's son-in-law bestowed on her a hard look, and changed the conversation.

"Sixty-three limousines back of us," he declared. "Some funeral the old girl's having. But it does gall me to be fifth in line. Harry's father and four cars in front of Harry's father. If Harry was here I'd be his side partner, right smack up to the hearse."

"Harry ought to be here," said Catalpa in the same ladylike whine with which she had apostrophized the veil. "It's a devilish shame he isn't at his own grandmother's funeral. Where in blazes did he run away to?"

"He did not run away," returned Harry's father, stiffly. Turning to Flora he jerked two fingers in the direction of his hat brim. "Miss Hancock, I suppose? You get the house. Emerson personal was supposed to go back to the Emersons, but the old lady was pretty fond of her grandson, my boy Harry, and I understand she sneaked considerable out of the income every year, for him to feather his nest."

"If he didn't run away," persisted Catalpa, "why ain't he here now? Why'd he come two months ago and leave just five days before she passed on?"

"How'd the boy know she was a-going to die so sudden? Harry consulted me and I told him no use sticking round all summer and like as not nothing worth staying for. He's right on the way to Hollywood now."

"I thought he was in Californy," said Catalpa.

"O.K. So's Hollywood. He's what they call a chance man—taken all the chances the big boys are too cowardly to take. Good money. Charlie Chaplin he's going to be this time. Back up to the audience and be slammed by custard pies."

"What a liar you are, Ed," observed the woman of the earrings. "We ought to tell Miss Hancock who we are so she can sort us out from the sixty or seventy limousines of relations that may fall on her later. Catalpa, you first."

"Miss Catalpa Hepburn," said the neat old party, putting out her hand. "My brother was that old hypocrite's first husband. He left her poor as a church mouse, with Betty to fetch up. I worked out then, in a factory down east, and boarded in a nice place. I was a hauled mealer. But in order to help her I gave up the ride and walked. Boarded myself, too. And she hasn't left me one red cent..."

"Well, I married Betty," interposed the man. "Betty picked me for a husband. My name's Ed Ellis, but when Betty died having Harry, I let the old one take the boy and name him what she was a mind to. So he's Harry Emerson though I don't believe she done anything to make it legal. Anyhow, he never forgets he's my son."

"Never give him a chance, do you, Ed?" asked his special tormenter. "I don't know just how to introduce myself. You're united by being Aunt Lury's kin, but I'm not even that. Her folks adopted my father, so I count as a Howe and called her aunt. I know I'm not in the will, but if Etta sells any furniture, I wish I could bid on the what-not in the hall. That's Howe, too."

"You haven't told Miss Hancock who you be, Belinda," remarked Catalpa.

"Oh—well. You know my rotten memory. I'm married. When my husband was born the doctor said to his mother, 'It favors Blodgett.' He's been 'it' ever since. So I'm not fussy about being Mrs. John Blodgett, or even Belinda Blodgett. I like folks to call me Little Lindy."

"Haw-haw!" hollered Ed Ellis. "I don't have to lug you upstairs like Sappho was. Weigh along toward 175 pounds don't you now?"

At this moment the limousine suddenly turned off the highway. Representatives of the Howe and Hepburn families nodded solemnly at one another and then triumphantly at the one Hancock.

"Emerson!" they exclaimed in absolute unanimity.

"I don't blame her," said Belinda Blodgett. "Any of us would choose an aristocratic grave if we had any choice. There are people in this town would willingly die ten years ahead of time if by so doing they could get into Mt. Hope and a lot like Uncle Emerson's."

"Snobs!" bleated Ed Ellis. "Well, some women'll stand for anything! With Betty's pa—or even with the Hancocks"—he bowed toward Flora—"there'd be no first wife. Le's see, B'linda Blodgett's lot's over in the annex, ain't it? Come judgment day you 'n my mother-in-law can rise up and make snoots at the inferior puck kicking off the dirt down the line. So much for your democracy!"

"No grave in Mt. Hope for me," she answered. "I belong to the Society for the Promotion of Cremation. But a couple of months ago I sold my cadaver to the Harvard Medical School."

Everybody jumped. Flora had an idea this was exactly what the lady had banked upon. An instant later Ed rose undaunted.

"Rats! All they want is remains that are eat up with some queer diseases. What good would you be?"

"My disease may be queer as Dick's hat—" here she winked at Flora—"and one may always be useful as a skeleton. Of course I only did it for the money. With Blodgett tight as the bark of a tree, I have to scratch round when I want a fur coat. Well, I've spent the fifty, so now all I have to do is pass out. Blodgett don't know, as I'll have a full-sized funeral, only saving him the gravedigger's fee. That's rotten, but can't be helped."

Luckily the graveside was reached at this moment. Ed Ellis jumped the ladies out and hustled them over the hemlock boughs so they might miss nothing of the patented grave vault.

"Some invention! Same's a tumbler turned upside down in water. A lid fits tight over the casket. They used to serve brandy floats like it in the good ole days. Here, Miss Hancock, I'll give you this circular. I got it off Drake."

* * *

Flora felt the impropriety of reading advertising literature by the side of an open grave, but Ed Ellis would not allow her to hide his gift under a handkerchief. Brazenly he pointed to the heading:

How Nature tries to Comfort

This was catchily if not appropriately illustrated by a cut of a Noah's Ark, a doll-in-a-cradle and another in a poke bonnet, a ball and a toy horse evidently feeling his stuffing. Below one sentence stood out in black face:

"So certain and uncompromising is this Grave Vault that is guaranteed for 50 years."

For fifty years Aunt Lury would lie on those white satin puffs with painted Cupid's bow lips intact.

Fifty years, thought Flora. She'd be eighty by that time. Probably dead. And what would her funeral have been like? Not an imaginative person, this was the first time she'd ever wondered about that ceremony. So much had the Village Green done for her already.

The return to house, where a collation was supposed to be in waiting, was quickly over.

Belinda Blodgett talked about her husband's all night poker sittings at which he invariably was a loser; Belle Emerson who had pushed right into Aunt Lury's family circles when she didn't belong, being only married to Ben and doubtless not allowed to come lest he lose a day's pay; Blodgett's fondness for servant girls, but the comforting fact that he never spent money on them or on anybody else; etc., etc., also about an unidentified party named Etta.

Ed Ellis talked entirely of the funeral, which began to impress him as something big now it was nearly over. He had caught a few jiff's conversation with S. G. A. Drake while the limousines were unloading. The casket which Etta had ordered would let the estate in for One Thousand Dollars. Aunt Lury's hair "and the rest" had been fixed according to Etta's specifications by that manicure girl who'd opened a place in the Knight Block. Darn good ad. for the little minx, and she knew it, too. Came up every morning since Aunt Lury was laid out to be sure nothing had happened to muss her. Etc. Etc. Subjects all funereal. Authority, invariably Etta.

Catalpa Hepburn spoke once, wondering audibly which would vex the deceased party (and Etta) most—for her to stay and partake of refreshments, or to shake the dust of the place from off her feet. Belinda gave terse advice. "Don't be a fool, Catalpa. Etta's got Elliott roasting one hundred pounds of chicken over at the hotel. You haven't anything half as good at home."

"I haven't anything at all," whispered Catalpa, as she trembled to the curbstone. "How you do get onto everything, Lindy. Gosh, I wouldn't know I was not out of the will if it hadn't been for you."

Most of the mere neighbors had the decency to go to their own abodes; so the paths were in considerable requisition, but some forty people sat down at the table which had been prepared in the hall and two back parlors. As before Hepburn, Hancock and Emerson families were carefully sequestrated; the few Howes being thrust into corners wherever they chanced to fit. It was a good meal, beginning with a cup of tomato bouillon at each cover.

Luckily Belinda was at the Hancock table, so Flora found out all about everything. The bouillon cups were from Elliott's Hotel. Aunt Lury never had any, her sets dating back of soup drinking. All the rest of the services, though, came from her stock. Emerson Haviland, this gold banded from the Hancocks; and there was quite a lot of plain white stone china with which she had married a Hepburn. Silver, too; the Emerson silver all solid, even to after dinner coffees.

Chicken, currant jelly, finger rolls. Nothing hot...Etta had considered hot dishes not exactly the thing, though nothing saved in cost by chilling the digestive apparatus. A Waldorf salad rich with mayonnaise. As a tender bit of sentiment Etta had had this made from Aunt Lury's own recipe, which used condensed milk and eggs beaten together, but no oil. Dessert: French pastry and coffee. Silver pitchers of thick cream and bowls of cut sugar were pushed genially about. At the ends and centre of each table were huge baskets of fruit—the kind that comes from the coast wrapped in tissue paper and refrigerated. Ben Davis apples of such exquisite color and firm texture that one was presumed not to miss flavor. Peaches ditto. Plums that started from the Santa Clara Valley as prunes, but changed their name over the Great Divide. Cherries, appearing petrified and varnished as the millinery ones. No local contribution?

Yes, there was a local contribution, and a very popular one. Out of season strawberries. On Dresden saucers, wearing their hulls, grouped about powdered sugar and Marshall berries. Marshall berries!

Ed Ellis endorsed the feature as he stood at the door dispensing farewell handshakes to Emersons, Hancocks, Hepburns and a few Howes.

"By George, won't forget this in a hurry. Marshall berries and Aunt Lury's funeral on the same day and that the twenty-twoth of August. Etta's some manager. I'll say so!"

As the Arabs their tents the undertakers—chief and assistants—silently folded their chairs and stole away. Only trestles and odds and ends on the first trip, chairs having been left for the collation, account of packing closer round the table than those that went with the house. Flora wondered what had better be done with herself. Baggage had been checked, and was presumably at the station. Her handbag had been seized as she entered the house. Should one have taken a night gown container to a house of mourning? And from whom hope for its return?

Flora was not exactly dumb, though she had done very little talking at Aunt Lury's funeral. Caution had been strongly developed in her school of regular work at small pay. Also, her looks had helped develop it. She was mighty good looking if one liked the type—of middle height, plump. A mass of reddish gold hair covered her head. It was disposed, from eyebrows to nape, in artfully arranged swirls. Her eyes were blue, the blue of the turquoise rather than of the forget-me-not.

She was not happy. She had been so long unhappy that she believed it was always. Most of her life she had looked to the Village Green for altering all that. New England must have a message for her; she had determined to go there in a receptive mood. There would be a "type"; it would bear no resemblance to the type shown in moving pictures, in novels of Mary E. Wilkins-Freeman, or plays of Percy Merkye. In Chicago she was supposed to be of that type, probably because she was precise in manner, tenacious of sorrow; in music largo, in literature Austenish, in art a drypoint etching. Those seeing her often without knowing her at all—as the men she met in business offices—made mistakes, because they judged her by the red hair and the perfect red lips. One of these misjudgments caused the ten-year sorrow of Flora's life.

At twenty she emerged from a cheap "college" a good typewriter but a bad speller, or the reverse, according to where the blame lay for putting an "h" in sugar. There was a man—about five years her senior. He wrote good poetry and gave it away, but received a rather splendid salary for turning out advertising booklets. He fell in love with Flora, honestly and thoroughly fell in love. He loved her for her youth, and because she was young supposed he could mould her to his will. He loved her because she was the grand niece of rich old Aluria Howe-Hepburn-Hancock-Emerson and heir to a splendid family mansion fronting the Village Green in a New England town where had been born and whence he had been borne away at the age of two. His mother used to tell him all about it whenever she felt especially disgruntled with her second marriage and its consequence of life in the Middle West. Above all, he loved Flora for the passionate promise of her golden hair and poppy-red lips.

Flora adored him with a single heartedness that made her a bore to all the rest of the world. She told her love in foolish ways over which it was impossible not to blush even ten years afterward. Brought him to her boarding house so that the waitress might say "sure" when asked if Mr. Comyns hadn't a "Byronic profile." (Poor Swede, she thought Lord Byron was a ten-cent cigar.)

The love affair of Arthur and Flora was very usual. At first they met every day for dinners and theatres. Then they met every day and took long walks—over bridges and through parks. They were saving for a home. He took her to the museum to see a picture of a Dutch interior—it was a window beside a fireplace, and a window seat so arranged that you might look out of the one while warming your feet at the other. Conscience told her she should tell him it wouldn't be practicable. She loved him, however, and so couldn't bear to see him disappointed. She peered closely, in order not to seem unappreciative, whereupon an attendant came up and said, "Don't be putting yer fingers on the pitchers."

Arthur Comyns lectured her on the way home. With her hair and her coloring she must be very careful not to make herself conspicuous!

He still thought her other than what she was, which was piano. Indeed pianissimo, after that.

The sentimental dermgolende was of the commonest order, but Flora did not know it was the common order. When her lover found that constancy brought from her no thrill inviting matrimony, he tried neglect, but she did her weeping on her pillow instead of in his arms, and he never dreamed that she wept at all. So, the engagement came to a natural end, he disappointed, she desolated. That she had failed she knew, how she could not guess. With doglike fidelity she lingered round the grave of her hopes, surreptitiously keeping anniversaries, fetching forth rags and tags of mementoes on Christmases and Thanksgivings, dressing inconspicuously because of that museum-inspired lecture.

He was a good fellow, he even gave her one more trial. Two years after they had parted he began seeing her again. He was going East, he said; he and his mother were going East. His step-father was dead, there was a considerable fortune for the education of his stepsisters. They were all going East to obtain the best for the girls. He and his mother were going to take the little old buggy and drive all the way without entering a hotel or a garage. No repairs except what he made with his own hands. It would establish a record, and after the book was out, which he planned to write about it, no further need would exist for producing advertising junk. Very likely he would become a magazine editor. His mother had known T. W. Higginson in her youth.

A good deal of this extraordinary programme was actually carried out, for Arthur Comyns possessed ability as well as determination. Failure, however, still poisoned his lovemaking. Flora noted sickeningly that he said nothing about coming back and getting married. He seemed only interested in getting her into his arms. It was Flora's idea that one proposed first and kissed afterward. So they parted once more, and she remained permanently puzzling why. Of the actual Arthur Comyns she heard once or twice—that he was not a magazine editor, but had started something called "Comyns' Syndicated Sensations." That he had been a year bedridden with paralysis, but finally recovered. That he was married. In making the name of Arthur Comyns stand for Romance, Flora soon found memory growing dim. Her concern was with an easily controlled manufactured sham. They were forever meeting and when they went out on moonlight nights walked as closely as to "only cast one shade." During her actual courtship Flora had been superstitiously fearful of thinking ahead of fact in imagining love-scenes.

Years of absence happily killed this apprehension that disaster would surely follow forwardness. The greatest possible disaster had overtaken her, she had lost Arthur and forever. Whereupon she let herself go, never realizing that if she'd had done it earlier he might not have gone. It was now over three years since he had been admitted to her meager room in the Chicago boarding house, where he had admired the pincushion, had read the backs of her extremely miscellaneous library with the good-natured derision properly expected from a literary lover; had addressed her night and morning with a fairly chaste salute.

Of course this female Jobiness of sitting amid ashes had its result. Flora was melancholy, she was unhappy in a purely defensive way, she had dug herself into—quite ready to repel any such approach of joy. This hour after Aunt Lury's funeral found her longing for her common diurnal tryst. It had been lacking that morning, owing to the necessity of instantly getting out of her Boston hotel and buying mourning. The possibility that Arthur might be at the funeral had made it seem unseemly to think of him in another creaking camp chair by her side. She wished he might be spoken of, but if the entire funeral could have been reassembled she would not have been able to look for his face or ask for him. This, she told herself, was a direct result of her indulgence in fond dreams. Her mother, books, everyone, her own good taste, told her they were bad. Here she was, now, bound to a habit which made her feel that speaking a man's name was quite like publicly exposing one's toilet subterfuges; like telling the world secret and shameful tricks, like biting off the right hand nails when one couldn't afford a manicure.

Change of residence easily suggesting change in hair dressing, dressing and character, Flora decided that this was the time and place to cut loose from her private hasheesh. It should be simple enough in this new life. She had always contemplated such a reformation. Now she had only to fill her life with interests of and about the Village Green. There certainly would be interests, sympathetic, vivid—despite the rather arid promise of her own and allied families.

The versatile Etta came downstairs and told Flora who she was. Otherwise Flora would have taken her for a servant girl, not realizing that hardly anyone in town had such a thing in the house. Etta's plainly disposed brown and brick-red hair, her high cheek bones, surmounted by small steel-colored eyes, her neat, upstanding figure and her brisk step, combined to express her principal characteristics. She was smart, that is, she was smart as the Village Green read the word. She could estimate the quantity of oysters needed for a church stew, and how much coke would carry a furnace through the winter as compared to coal. She loved economy so much that she practiced it for other people. Not a trained nurse, she was able to carry out doctor's orders with absolute fidelity, and had done so in the case of Aunt Lury's rather unique jaundice. Making a virtue of the fact that she never read books—that not one was written which would keep her awake—she was lost without her 88-page *Saturday Transcript*.

"Real pretty sundown," she remarked, moving her thumb in the direction of a sky done off in strips of cerise, mauve, elephant's breath, mouse's ear, back of some hemlock trees over the way.

Flora smiled and looked. She had not been used to considering sundowns. She had been considering the home-seeking commuters and wondering who of them might be the husbands of friends. Flora did not know Etta was smart, because Flora used the word as did the salesperson in Ye Specialtie Shoppe. Etta wore a perfectly clean green and white gingham dress with long sleeves. This was partly obscured by a full skirted and honest-to-goodness bibbed apron of brown gingham in a different check. The cameo fastening her collar was worth all Flora had on.

"I guess we're all pretty tired," said Etta. "I thought I'd toast some bread and make a pot of tea. Then I'd feed the cats and go to bed. You and Belle sit up long as you like."

"Oh," said Flora, wishing these people weren't all so casual and unexplanatory. "I thought shouldn't I go to a hotel?"

"Isn't customary when you have a home of your own. I put your bag in the front room to the right upstairs. It's been aired and fumigated and the mattress is a new one. I'll call when supper's ready."

She walked off. Twilight was gathering over the Green. The sky was that dove-gray peculiar to late August; a sharp reminder that winter was merely biding a time. A train of fifteen old-fashioned wooden cars stopped, exuded and moved off. Instantly a flock of sparrows, thousands of them, fell, as it were, from the upper air, and took possession of the station for the night. The track tender closed his hut by the gates, and crossed the Green. He carried a basket and walked on club feet. A boy wearing overalls, but so well shod and shirted that he seemed to be doing it for a joke, drove eighteen cows from back of the station, over the track and over one corner of the Green, then off R.U. Lights twinkled from a great many houses, but not from fanlights over street doors. Evening visiting was apparently not expected. All the village appeared to be at supper. Dozens of bells tinkled, whereat children "Last Tagged" and scampered. The clashing of many plates rose as the clashing of a single plate; clattering forks and butter spreaders made rhythms as the new poetry should.

"Come and eat your victuals," said Calista from a door at the end far end of the hall.

"My word," thought Flora, in an adopted slang bit which had achieved popularity in her special Chicago. "If this is my house...if this is my party!"

She followed the jerky Calista into a kitchen. A soft pine table, hacked and splintered by generations addicted to steak pounding, was set with odds and ends of a half dozen china "sets." Clean but ragged towels served as table cloths. The table was pushed against the wall, under the fluttering remains of what had been a patent gas mantle. There were seven chairs, in one of them Belle was already seated. Three were occupied by cats. One, a sleek maltese, slumbered in a trustful attitude, forepaws falling limp and kitten-like on a breast adorned with a single diamond-shaped patch of white. A second, huge and white, was immaculate except for his nose. This loomed, a literal embracing of dirt, beneath and between a pair of extremely handsome amber eyes. The third, a nervous black kitten, appeared to be frightfully afraid he might escape notice. Therefore he banged himself, on anything handy, while husky gasps of anxiety issued from a pretty red mouth. Etta lifted an agate-ware dish from the gas stove and plumped it into the centre of the table. Flora did not wonder what was in it, because she saw plainly enough that it was an oyster stew made economically with water. She wondered if the oysters were hers to pay for.

"There's plenty of oysts from this afternoon," observed Etta, "but I thought we'd all prefer something we hadn't seen before."

"Even though there's no 'r' in August," said Belle, helping herself.

"I'm tickled to death to see boughten pickles," contributed Calista. "She always skimped on sugar. It takes plenty of sugar to make a pickle set on my stomach."

Rejecting the fork with which she had vainly tried to spear a little cucumber she rose, dashed abruptly into a dark closet, and emerged with a pair of scissors and a nutpick!

Etta conscientiously fed the cats, giving the white one broth, the maltese two oysters and the kitten a saucer of milk. She then pushed the dish toward Flora. "Have some?" she asked. Flora said she would and did.

Belle then approved of the crackers. "Delicious," she murmured, inserting her hand in the waxpaper that lined the carton. Whoever had designed the label caused it to read "We recommend that these crackers be served from the box," and for that or some other reason they were. "The ones that come in bulk are never quite so good."

"Couldn't make her see it," grumbled Calista.

To the oysters succeeded a salad composed of cucumbers, boiled beets, tomatoes and sliced peppers on lettuce. With it a mayonnaise in a fancy bottle so adorned with curlicues that the most exploring spoon missed half the crevices.

"Ah ha!" said Calista, growing darker every minute, "you got this at the grocer's, too. It ain't that dreadful mess she was always giving the receipt for. Aunt Lury's Salad Dressing made with condensed milk. Ach!"

Cal gave an excellent imitation of one suffering with acute mal de mer.

"The green stuff was sent in by the neighbors," said Etta.

"And darn queer stuff for the occasion, I call it," remarked Calista, shoveling it back of her rattling teeth as if afraid it would melt underwater in haste.

It now appearing that the maltese would not eat oysters, Etta presented them to the white, who disposed of both in a couple of gulps. The kitten, having tipped over the milk, sat upon the edge of the mess and huskily demanded something to eat. "That feller's fussy, ain't he?"

said Calista, referring to the maltese. "He'd ought to have his victuals marrowed for him."

"Sometimes he'll eat salmon," said Etta. "I'd open a can, only the smell drives the kitten crazy. He has to have his mixed with bread crumbs and a pinch of sulphur. The vet said so. Well, I guess I will open one. Can you reach it, Calista? Right behind you in the cupboard?" Owing to this and subsequent excitement Flora got no salad, and when the subsequent pie appeared, it with clean plates, but no forks.

"Blueberry!" exclaimed Calista and Belle in one voice. Belle said she would advise wiping the salad forks on the table cloth, seeing that it was really a dish towel. She wiped her own, also obligingly wiped Flora's. Calista preferred a spoon on account of the juice.

"Pretty good pie," said Belle. "You make it, Etta?"

"I did not. B'linda Blodgett fetched it along. She said she bet most anything I hadn't been able to get a pie ahead."

"That accounts for it," said Calista. "Linda's mother always was a master hand at pies. I guess I'll have another piece."

"Anybody want any tea?" asked Etta. "I didn't make none. How about you, Flora? You don't seem to have made out much of a meal."

"Everything is very nice," said Flora, rather breathless from trying to follow the pacemakers. "I don't really care for tea..."

"I do," said Calista. "Strong. Strong enough to bear up an egg. The slops she used to pour out and call tea! Dishwater!"

While it was being drawn she and Belle swept the doughnut plate bare, and Calista insisted that somewhere in the house were the black walnut doughnuts which their departed relative had coated with batter and fried, mixing 'em with the real thing and sending 'em to swell her contribution at church fairs.

"Nonsense!" said Etta, now engaged in making a lap for the maltese and fending off the kitten from a table raid.

"Oh, it's quite true. That's why the Reverend gave her such a poor laying out today. He swore he wouldn't speak her name, because one can't say what one wants to about those that've passed on. Got to speak well or not at all. So he made it not at all. Cream, Etta."

"Down by Flora, Calista. She'll pass it if you can't reach."

"Oh, I guess I can reach anything on this table," returned Calista, sharply.

The white puss, as if to take her at her word, made one graceful leap to the breadplate and settled in a beautifully purring circle.

Flora couldn't avoid a startled jump, and Belle puckered her face into an excellent imitation of a gargoyle feeling extreme disgust, but Calista remained calm, stirred her tea and swallowed it in three long gulps.

"There," she observed, wiping her lips on a corner of the towel-table-cloth. "I guess I'll last till breakfast. And now I'll just put my head where I can find it in the morning."

"G'long up then," said Etta. "I left a light turned down in your regular room."

"Good enough. I rather expect Red Jacket'll be around. He's pretty apt to come after a funeral. And he does like that old desk my brother made out of butt'nut when they was first married, and she was ashamed to show it downstairs with the Emerson stuff."

Calista disappeared. There was a long silence, then Belle rose and wanted to know, "Isn't Calista the queer old thing, with her Red Jackets? It's a wonder she didn't have us tipping the table. I suppose spiritualism seems funny to you, Flora. But it's only old Calista."

Flora opened her lips, but was forcibly silenced by a swift under-the-table kick from Etta.

"Go right up the back way, Belle. I left a light for you, too."

"Not in that room with the set bowl? You know how I feel about germs, Etta. You know, Flora—or rather you probably don't know—but Aunt Lury never entered the sewer."

As she stalked off Flora found herself viewing Aunt Lury as she survived in childish memory, a sternly defiant female Jean Valjean, who would not enter the sewer. What things that great and good man had seen in the sewers of Paris—rats, a fragment of a ballet girl's dress wrapped round the bleeding flesh that might have been human...Etta was speaking.

"Excuse my leg. Sometimes, y'know, there's no safety unless in keeping a close mouth. You like cats?"

"I—I really don't know. I was never where they were at the table before."

"You mean on the table. Well, Aunt Lury didn't encourage it all the time. Only when certain relatives outstayed their welcome. Belle will put for home tomorrow. Belle says a cat ought to have his own dish and never eat from nothing else. She can't abide cats. Ben sets great store by 'em. They had a dog once but it run away and never came back for all their advertising. Always been my opinion Ben knew more'n he told."

"Were these all Aunt Lury's pets?" asked Flora. The white one had advanced to her side of the table and was fawning with loud purrs and much working of paws.

"All? Oh, this ain't no real keeping cats. We had to dispose of the heft of 'em, when it begun to seem probable Aunt Lury'd got her never get over. There was several females, and all their kittens. One litter had the hind feet put on wrong, they was like an extra set of front feet, if you know what I mean. She wanted 'em brought up for some museum, but I had too much else to do to be cosseting cats. Another cute little thing that its mother took a dislike to, so we raised it by hand, and a doll's nursing bottle, turned out it should be called Victoria after we'd named it Victor. So the Animal Rescue called and Aunt Lury gave 'em. I thought she hated to most dreadful."

Flora, who had thought three cats a rather goodly supply, gazed in silence while she wondered how many there had been with the heft added. Almost absolute silence seemed to have settled over the old house. In fact all she could hear, when Etta stopped talking, was a dry cough from what seemed next door. She rather thought she had been hearing it all the evening. Somehow it reminded her of herself as a child.

The gray cat now created a diversion. Fitting his nose to that of the white animal he put up his back, established the hair of his head in a shoebrush pompadour and that of his spine in the fashionable monkey for border effect. Then opening his mouth he emitted the most blood-curdling cries of wails. In rhythm with the noises he twisted his body until the rear set of legs were wellnigh at right angles with chest and head. Thus, in Etta's very lap, he transferred himself from a sleek pet to a fiend incarnate.

"Look at that!" exclaimed Etta, in a voice of disgust. "Just like all of his sex. Waits till he gets his belly full and starts to complain. Open that door, will you, please?"

Flora flung open the door indicated, disclosing a butler's pantry as it looked with no butler and after a collation. Recollections of a hurried glance were made up entirely of roast chickens lacking drumsticks and white meat. Etta deposited spitfire in the midst and shut the door firmly.

"There, he's fixed for the night. Won't touch a thing, neither. Too fussy to think any victuals is worth eating 'less it's handed to him a piece at a time."

Another silence ensued, broken as before, by the cough.

"You want to sit up?" asked Etta.

Thus interrogated, Flora didn't, though she felt thousands of questions surging through her brain.

"All right. I'll leave my table in the floor this once." With a prodigious yawn Etta shoved Flora into the front hall. "Front room where there's a light. I'm not going to muss up another bed for myself. I'll slump down on the sitting-room lounge."

Flora was half way up when a sibilant "s-say" brought her down again. Etta had the black kitten on her shoulder and the white cat draped over one arm. Thus hampered she was trying to screw up her front hair on pins.

"Looky here," she said, "you musn't be prejudiced against Aunt Lury by what Belle says. The old lady got kind o'cranky when she thought folks was doing her. You'd think, to hear Belle, she hadn't a good streak in her. Really, she was the most conscientious person I ever knew. Why, according to the life interest in this house she could use all the gas she wanted, and the company'd never send her a bill. Her second husband got it fixed that way when he was vice president of the company. Instead of putting it on the minute it got dark under the table, as most folks would, she didn't even burn it in the hall unless there was company. So, whether she entered the sewer or not's neither here nor there. I say Aunt Lury had a conscience!"

Her duty done, thus, Etta clumped out of sight. Flora intended to go into the room allotted her and have a good laugh, but when she had emphatically shut the door and reached to the button of gas she turned it out instead of up. The shades being drawn, black darkness enveloped her, and from where the light had been came first a sound of falling and then the crash of broken glass. What had Etta said, quite early in the evening?

"It's been aired and fumigated and the mattress is a new one"?

She understood. This was the room Aunt Lury had died in. Death ticks had been in these walls (Flora's acquaintance with these objects of honor was purely literary) which had further reverberated to dying rattles and admonitions. Nobody had told her, yet, that Aunt Lury departed from the world hurriedly, in the midst of an acid remark. "If you numskulls feel you got to stand round watching me die I should think some of you might fix my legs so I could die in comfort."

Ridiculous to think of Great Aunt Lury hovering round her own bed and breaking lamp shades to show that her conscience still worked in the interests of economy. Idea worthy of poor old Calista. Nevertheless Flora did think it, did shiver, did wish she knew the exact position of the problematical match safe. Wearily feeling beyond the bracket she found a narrow, high and very chilly marble mantel, which seemed to be entirely adorned with metal objects of rectangular shape. There were any number of them—at least there were a dozen. There was engraved matter on each, and all but one stood up to show it. That one laid flat on the end nearest the door, just as if recently brought into the room.

In fact, it had been placed there that very afternoon. It was the silver coffinplate from off Aunt Lury's coffin. The undertaker had pried it off in response to a request from Etta, who said—Yes, she knew they didn't keep them nowadays, but all the husbands' and some others had been where she could see them whenever she did up her hair, and it might be just as well to put hers with them.

The third journey up and down that shelf was too much for Flora. She turned precipitately in the direction where she supposed she had left the door, banged her head against solid wood, and was caught in the grasp of a human being. She yelled.

The human being said, "Have you got any matches? Calista 'n I both forgot to look before we turned out our lights."

Flora clutched Belle's bony arm as if its covering of outing flannel was the pinion of an angel.

"I've been pawing that mantel—with the graveyard doorplates—for fifteen minutes but there's nothing else there. And there's a flashlight in my bag, only I wouldn't dare try to find that."

Belle giggled. "If Etta's on her good ear, as she probably is, we could holler from now to breakfast and she'd be the last of the neighborhood to get wise. Can't you sleep in your shimmy this once? You better come and get into bed with me. It's right across the hall and nobody's died in it recently."

Flora surprised herself by obeying the suggestion and gladly. After Belle had told her why it was so dark—because there was a moon in the almanac and the town burned no street lights when that was the case—and had complained bitterly of Aunt Lury's never having had the house wired for electricity; silence ensued. A silence broken by a cough. Familiar sound, and Flora knew why.

"It's five and twenty years ago," she told herself in the book-made language she dared to use only in such hearing. "I'm here, a roundfaced solemn child, put to bed a full hour before the time because an angular old woman says I ought to be. I won't go to sleep. I determine I won't. I determine to prick the palms of my hands with my finger nails before I go to sleep. And then I can't go to sleep because some one in the next house coughs. Coughs every five minutes, for at least a minute. Just like that. All night long, just like that. And when I screamed after an hour or two, and made them rush up with crumbs on their lips and slices of cheese in their hands, Aunt Lury shook me and said a great girl of five should know better than to say 'make it stop—make it stop!' The very best doctor from Boston couldn't make it stop. And then she promised me—she promised me that something called God was going to make it stop before very long. 'Next time you come to see your old Aunt, Florry, it'll be stopped.' And she and mother had looked at one another and nodded as if they were in the secrets of the universe. They said something, too, not meant for her ears, about 'a wasting disease' and 'belly no bigger 'n a bowl.' This last made the wrong impression, because the child thought of a washbowl.

"Then she and mother had gone to Chicago and five and twenty years had passed. This was the next time she had come to see her old aunt, but the cough was not stopped. In a woebegone dream, with Belle's exquisitely sharp knees pressed against her spine, she said to Aunt Lury, "You're a liar and God isn't on to his job."

* * *

Some time in the middle of the night an incubus in the back of the bed was removed and Flora slipped into beatific slumber. In other words Belle rose early and took the first train out. She troubled Etta with a request for a cup of coffee and a demand that she listen to the usual anecdote of Ben, invariably bringing a bowl of cocoa to his wife's bedside before he got his own breakfast and went in town for the day.

When Flora came down the hall was obstructed by all her trunks and the crated rocking chair which represented the accumulations of thirty years.

"How'd you sleep?" asked Calista who was twittering round with a feather duster, doing nothing, like the soubrette in a nineteenth century melodrama. "You look as though you'd been poorly staid with," she added.

"I've got a good breakfast in the dining room," called Etta, "if only I had somebody to eat it."

It was a good breakfast, and served excellently, with butter spreaders, damask napkins and finger bowls, after the cantaloupes. Like most of the rooms in Flora's inheritance the dining room was made such by name only. Its principal articles of furniture were a brussels carpeted lounge, a golden oak bureau, a bona fide Martha Washington sewing table in mahogany and well-worn silk, a whatnot which Flora dimly associated with Belinda Blodgett, and several chairs upholstered in gray haircloth on which little wreaths of gay colored flowers had been done in worsted cross-stitch.

Calista took the rocker and lolled luxuriously, her chin on a level with her saucer. Somewhere between the scrambled eggs and the marmalade Etta told Flora that Herbert Trinkett would see her that forenoon in his office. For twenty-five years Flora hadn't realized that a day had a forenoon, but infantile breeding asserted itself and she knew he did not want her before ten nor after twelve. Herbert Trinkett legally advised Aunt Lury, that is he had done so for perhaps twenty years. He was not an old person, though much older than Flora. There was a memory of him as well as of "forenoon." A boy with very long legs always falling off a high bicycle.

"Is Mr. Trinkett a bicyclist?" she unthinkingly asked Etta.

"Mercy—no! But he did ride an ordinary a good deal when he was in high school." Etta spoke as if this had been last year. "I heard him say once that these low-hanging safeties made the sport too tame for him."

"He walks," sputtered Calista. "I see him last Fourth o' July just at sun-up striding along like a good un. Had on one those dinguses, tells how many times your right foot goes ahead the left before you get there. Said he aimed to make Providence. Hotter than Hell's Kitchen right then. But he felt like nothing but a grease spot before he got to Needham."

"He didn't stop—that is, for good—till he got to that place just out-side Providence. Pawtucket. Or perhaps Pawtuxet."

"I never can tell t'other from which, neither," observed Calista, en-couragingly. Etta instantly froze.

"It's a pity you wouldn't read something once in a while," said she, jerking open one of the drawers in the Martha Washington table and unearthing a mass of newspaper clippings. "It was all in the *Review and Rekkid* and a picture of Mr. Trinkett looking off toward Provi-dence and reciting `Carcassone'."

"Oh, I've heard him recite that piece—" interposed Calista, but was at once put in her place by Etta.

"If you have it's been very lately. He didn't know a word of it when Arthur wrote the article and put the words into his mouth. At least he told me so. Anyway, one or the other is a liar, like the rest of their sex."

Flora, fearfully begoggled over Etta's surprising acquaintance with subtle verse, and the abrupt introduction of Arthur's name, sat in a blur while Etta collected the dishes in pyramids, and Calista opened a worn old handbag and took therefrom a few small coins.

"That right?" she inquired. "I had two eggs, but only one slice of bacon. I suppose you trade at the chain stores. She did."

"I guess it's about square," returned Etta. "I collected from Belle last night. That's why she didn't stop for breakfast, probably. She was wish-ing for new cords, new cars. But she had another wish coming."

A pretty Japanese saucer, containing about two dollars in coin of the realm, was placed before Flora, with a casual explanation that those of kin using the house as a convenience had been in the habit of pay-ing scot and lot and would continue to do so. Quite in vain to protest, or to invoke the gods of hospitality. Flora found herself faced by her own pettish reflections of the night before, to effect that she who gave a party should have the right to name the guests.

"Aunt Lury didn't ask all the relations to come," Etta explained, "and when you get into regular living you may not want any of us. It's for you to decide who you'll give houseroom to. First place, slip along down to Bert Trinkett's office and see what you got to do with. You aim to go home today, Calista?"

"Yes," said Calista, rather reluctantly. "That is, if you can call it home."

"Well, hyper along, then, and show Flora the way. It's only down t'other end of the Common but there's a bad crossing in front of Jackson's meat market and a person from Chicago will be pretty apt to find the traffic bewildering."

"Etta aint' half such a fool as she appears," said Calista, benignantly, as their feet scuffed the leaves on one of the Green's diagonal paths. "She's sore because she never had an education or got married. That's why she hates highbrows and men folks. And yet I've known lots of times when she went out of her way to be just as nice..."

Flora wondered if every New England woman burst forth in criticism instantly after parting with a friend. Was the fabled Sewing Society real, in which no reputation could be left behind and live? Or was such right of candid comment peculiar to the kin of Great Aunt Lury?

Beautiful mansions clustered along the opposite side of the Green, where it turned away from the railroad. Some had pillars supporting a pediment of grace, both Grecian and Roman, even though actually a projection of the attic floor. Others were of red brick with panes of purplish window glass. Brass knockers polished to a brightness that winked at the sun were in use, Flora saw a young girl in a pair of pink tinted knickerbockers jump out of an electric coupe, trip up the steps and knock a "Rat-a-tat-tat" in the most matter of fact manner. There were not many of these houses, but such was their magnificence that they gave an impression of dominating the square. Gazing rather wistfully at the signs of opulence—huge masses of gladioli, zinnias, asters, in which gardeners were working; two saddle horses waiting with a neat groom at that elsewhere obsolete accommodation, a carved carriage block, frilly curtains evidently just "done up," Flora hopefully anticipated acquaintanceships where one might forget the shame of haggling with breakfast guests over a rasher.

* * *

After the mansion trade abruptly introduced itself. Free air was promised, and a youth clad principally in grease was chalking up the day's rise in gasoline at one of those cute "Colonial" filling stations. A chain grocery with a green front decreed "Pancake week" and proved it by a window of self raising flour. A very large window glared with pyramids of oranges and grapefruit, strings of plump figs, dangling bunches of hamburg grapes, and bunches of red and yellow bananas labelled

"No, We Got 'Em Today."

Another chain store, with a yellow front, declared soap at reduced rates week, but made an unattractive showing compared with the red fronted chain store next door, which boldly appealed on behalf of apple week with a bushel box of Mackintosh Reds. A chain dairy, all virgin white, was celebrating cracker week. Of the three drug stores one had its show window devoted to a stack of stationery and one had no show windows at all, having blocked them with matched boarding, as if quite oblivious to any need for the public lure. A Mr. Upsty kept the most elegant shop, apparently devoted to tennis rackets, golf balls, paper patterns, cards of sympathy and cheer, Stetson hats, magazines but not newspapers, walking sticks, playing cards, Mah Jong sets from $12.75 up and orders taken for one-day laundry. His door was locked, but several customers stood patiently on the steps. Flora thought they looked as if they had taken advantage of the laundry and were now out after Mah Jong. Feeling this to be rather clever she did not waste it on Calista, who was very busy nodding to everybody, even a couple of delivery boys who were doing a brisk race with a couple of hand power express wagons.

"Come in here a minute," said Calista, suddenly turning into a small shop, the door of which opened with an iron latch, the two windows of which were filled, respectively, with an obsolete line of toys, and some bolts of percale and flannel half unrolled but not in the least displayed.

The store, once entered, proved to be so full of stock that the attendant—and she was a tall woman—was visible only for the eyes and top of the head. Indeed, she was not that visible where the ribbon showcase and the drawers of spool cotton and silk were set. Calista asked twice for a certain number in tattling thread and it was quite exciting to note the woman's complete disappearance for a moment, then her reappearance in a (comparatively) distant part of the establishment. While Flora took note of a lending library in the rear, also a table of toys firmly defended by a fine meshed net, Calista was being told that there was no such cotton in the store, and no knowledge if there ever would be. She was also advised to try mercerized and after pettishly refusing she flounced out, nearly running into two women and a bunch of children on a recess who were entering.

"Drat her," said Calista, "that's the fourteenth time she's tried to make me take something else. Seems if she keeps store just for the sake of saying she ain't got it."

"Why not go to another store?" asked Flora, innocently appraising two devoted to dry goods and located across the street. At one a man lay in wait for trade, furtively peering through the screen door; at the other a stout man and woman on camp stools sat guarding the entrance in a bower of swinging house dresses. Neither shop seemed to be doing any business.

"Jews!" Calista dismissed them with the word. "Here's the Trinkett block," she added, directing Flora into a good-looking mosaic and tile entrance. "He's one flight up. I guess you better walk, because the elevator don't generally have anyone to run it unless you want to wait an hour or so. Well, meet you in church!"

With this farewell, which Flora would presently learn was inevitable, Calista twittered away. Flora watched her headgear, which was like a child's hat with the visor of a jockey's cap added, until it disappeared around a corner, thus proving there was at least a street as well as a Village Green to the town.

Then she went into the block, which had its ground front occupied by an insurance and real estate office the copper meshed blind of which announced that it was open Tuesday and Friday evenings after 7:30.

As Flora climbed the broad, shallow and fairly clean marble steps, she inspected herself as to hang of skirt and fastening of gloves, for now she was sure of being observed. The inhabitants of her native place had hitherto been strangely lacking in that inquisitiveness which the west attributes to the east and the city to the village. Not one of Calista's numerous acquaintances had given her companion a second glance, still Flora was not ready to abandon her ready made resolve not to be pertly annoyed at the annoyance of being stared at. What had these people to think about, they who lived pitifully lean lives clustered about the Village Green—if not the occasional stranger?

The Dentist on the second floor of the Trinkett block had the lettering on his door to think of—he was doing it over the blurred remains of an earlier lettering, very neatly and skillfully. Standing back he reviewed the effect, and not Flora. He was applauded by Maude-Hats, Dr. Dow, Jr., who was quite baldheaded; and the New Thought Reading Room. They all remained at their doors, which was considerate, because Flora had no trouble finding Herbert Trinkett. He had a waiting lobby, with a stenographer at a machine. She was not typewriting, however, but reading a book called *Kimono*. Flora, who had never heard of it, presumed it had something to do with clothes and had probably come out as a serial in a woman's magazine.

"He's in conference," said the young lady confidentially, but he says you'll please walk in."

Herbert Trinkett's private office was very small and had a cheerful outlook into a graveyard. The description applied with truth, for that graveyard grass was very green, its trees exceedingly crimson and golden on that autumn day, its many birds quite twittery, while its exclusively slate stones bespoke it as a scene of burial at no time in the present and probably at few times in the immediately passed century. There was an old fashioned roll top desk before which Trinkett sat. He was a man of bulk, some two hundred pounds or more, his legs were so long they lay all over the place, but he had no neck at all. Flora seemed to remember that when he was a boy atop a high wheel he had had no neck. The head that rested on his high and narrow shoulders was small, and surmounted by a small amount of black hair. He wore a mustache of the walrus type, but his chin was carefully shaven. His black clothing shone with newness and was evidently the artwork of a tailor determined to turn out a difficult customer looking as well as possible under the circumstances. Not a fleck of dust marred the splendor of a super excellent shine, though dust laid thickly on the window sill and other projections of ledgy variety in the place. One corner of the room harbored a sagging pile of small, dog eared books, in the opposite corner was a broader pile of some small paged newspaper. In a revolving case was a collection of Mass. Gen. Rets. in calf, and a copy of Wm. De Morgan's *Alice for Short* in red cloth.

Mr. Trinkett was in conference with a young lady, whose elegance and beauty transcended anything seen by Flora since arriving in the village. Her dress was of the refined neutral tinted character suited to her delicacy of form and feature; her hat and hair combined to make a perfect setting for her face; there were no jewels in her ears, the lobes of which were visible in despite of fashion, no string of vulgar beads marred the perfect fitting of a modest white blouse adorned, for the few inches where it rested on her neck, with the merest edge of obviously valuable lace.

She rose as Flora entered and put out a graceful hand, saying archly, "Now I am real pleased to see you, because you are someone new to me—but to you I'm only another of those connections. You think they are all over the place! And didn't you snub me nicely yesterday, just because I sat in the Emerson room with the dirty curtains and no real view of the corpse at all. In revenge I'll go right away and have Bertie to disappoint you as he has me. A perfect lady shopping for a divorce, and he claims he hasn't any in stock! What's the use of having a legal adviser if he can't supply your wants? Suppose a doctor told you he had no drugs—or a dentist said he never kept false teeth."

"Take a seat, Miss Hancock," said Mr. Trinkett, with a heavy gallantry that accorded with his avoirdupois. Her smiled a trifle grimly at his former visitor, and his eyes matched those of Flora in following the pretty creature down the hall before he shut the door.

"Pooty little woman, isn't she?" he inquired, with exactly that pronunciation.

"She doesn't really want a divorce?"

"Oh, yes she does. She's been wanting one for ten years, ever since she got married. She's married to a perfect brute."

"How horrible!" exclaimed Flora, finding this an unimpeachable explanation for beauty's flippancy.

"Ya-as. Subtle about it, too. Never fails to kiss her when he comes home or when he goes away, but they're not the right kind of kisses. I have the little lady's own word for it. Gives her a satisfactory allowance, but if she don't spend it instanter he borrys it back the next week. Pays the rent, but always has some reason for not moving where she'd rather live. Always remembers the anniversaries with gifts of candies, but eats most himself. Last two years has been staying out nights and spending his money taking Masonic degrees as fast as the traffic laws allow. And when she objects to being left alone every evening he tells her he's doing it so she may stand a chance of a being a rich widow some day. Or he gives her the price of a seat at a movie and tells her to go to our local show shop with some female. Not into the city, because she's so pulchritudinous some one might annoy her with attentions! He kind o' complicates matters, too, by giving a home to her mother, who otherwise would have to go to work or give a seat on the Common as her address. Just now she's specially vexed because it's her birthday next week and he had the nerve to tell her to buy a nice raincoat out of the house money and say 'twas from him.

"Pardon my garrulity. It's one of the direct signs of growing old." He passed a well cared for hand over his thinning hair and nodded at Flora with a prime smile, assured that she would understand. "You came in to learn exactly what chance you have for making your inheritance something beside a white elephant. I'm real sorry, Miss Hancock, but you haven't a chance in the world—not a chance!"

* * *

In good plain words, Flora learned exactly why she inherited the former home of her Great Aunt Lury. The house had been built by Aunt Lury's second husband, the brother of Flora's father. He had killed himself building it, toiling with his own hands nights after long houred days filled with building houses for other people. He had introduced into the planning and the finishing all the fads of his era. The house had been too large for him to furnish, too splendid for him to support. He could not afford coal to heat it. He was obliged to mortgage it for a thousand dollars to avoid defaulting on payments to his workmen. This money he obtained easily and on fair terms from the local bank, then under control of the man named Emerson who was destined to be his successor in the house and in the affections of his wife. The debt irked him, the last efforts of a feverish existence were devoted to paying it off. On his deathbed he burned the torn mortgage note, a dramatic performance commonly associated only with pastors of orthodox meetinghouses.

His will gave "Aluria, beloved wife" a mere life interest in case she married again. This was a nasty slap at one who had broken a widowhood to marry him. Popular opinion declared that Mrs. Hancock got her dander right up and set her cap for rich old Emerson. At any rate, she became Mrs. Emerson within a twelve-month. Emerson money furnished the principal rooms in gorgeous style, and kept the mansion in the list of show ones of the town for many years.

Mr. Emerson was the most generous of men, he left his wife the independent use of a large income; but Aunt Lury had seemed averse to spending anything on the house. It was then she brought down the old Hepburn and Hancock furniture, and fitted up the back parlors as shrines. She had been sparing of paint and chary of repairs, she had hoarded and had willed everything willable to her grandson, whose mother, long dead, was her only child, fruit of her first union.

"In short, Miss Hancock," said Mr. Trinkett, "you have a fine old family mansion with not a brick but needs mortar, not a shingle but needs renewal, not a clapboard that isn't suffering for paint. I'm scarrit to go up the front steps, which is why I generally sneak round through the kitchen; and the women folks who hang out there more or less—you've met 'em!—assure me that the window glass rattles so it can't be washed safely; and the plumbers come so often to patch the lead pipes that they don't nail the bath room floor down at all."

The furniture, it appeared, was all Flora's, but only because he had personally gone to the chief Hepburns and Emersons and told 'em it wouldn't give a gal from Chicago—yes, he said gal—a very good idea of Massachusetts to leave her with probably no table to eat her dinner on or knife and fork to eat it with. Of course if she started selling off things he might interfere, because it was only a verbal agreement. Hancock stuff was hers—but who could be quite sure at this date which dynasty a coal shovel or a spider—spider was his word—hailed from.

For instance, Belinda Blodgett claimed a whatnot was Aunt Lury's before she married anyone at all! For his part, he didn't know in the least what a whatnot was. What good Belinda's explanation—"It's not the *etagere*. That's Emerson."

* * *

Spanish castles fall silently. The Village Green was not in the least disturbed by the smash of Flora's, which was that of the woman who goes out to business most everywhere—a life devoid of economic problems.

* * *

Flora was not a fool, though at present appearing rather dumb. She had not expected riches. She had looked for a house wherein life could be organized with elegance and ease, after what she supposed was the New England fashion. She had vaguely presumed there would be some sort of an income attached. She could live on very little. She had done so for ten years, in hall rooms, stewing breakfast cocoa over gas jets, augmented by surreptitiously introduced "volcanoes." She had dined on delicatessen with the table laid on anything—a trunk, corner of a dresser, a mantel shelf. She had shivered when "heat from the hall" proved little but the smell of onions. She had made a budget and stuck to it, though shoes intended to last three months proved to have card-paper soles in a week. She had washed vests and bloomers in a hand basin and dried them on the footrail of her bed; she had dried her handkerchiefs on the mirror and the window panes. She had done over her last summer's hat with shoe polish, she had given an old blouse a new color with crepe paper and hot water. Withal she was lucky; many girls practiced these subterfuges and merely got a living. She had saved a thousand dollars.

She had made no friends, friendships with women meant spending money, keeping up one's own end in the matters of sodas, luncheons, birthday gifts, matinee tickets which cost like the deuce though second balcony. Two women who elected to spend Saturday afternoon or an evening together could hardly sit in a hall room and talk. They must "go some place." Even if the time was summer, and they managed to grab off a park bench, chocolates were required.

Flora had been admired as a daily bather, an efficient worker, a good looker, and a New England heiress. Without bragging, she had let the story leak out. There was property coming to her in the east. She would go East and live. The mere fact that she was saving, in spite of being an heiress, proved her New England bent. Then, too, she had a sense of detail. Did not put one item under head of "Salesmanship" and two under "Selling Points," and have "Miscellany" stuffed to the bursting point. She didn't care for split pea soup, so she must like baked beans. Her clothes were good rather than two bead chains ahead of the style. She thought "nude" stockings a perfectly useless extravagance. Flora had lived long in Chicago believing herself a more perfect New Englander than she was now turning out to be.

Herbert Trinkett now seemed to her an absolute stranger. During the first part of the interview he had been interesting, as the man should be who took annual walks to Providence. Now he was fat and alien, he retired behind his half inch thickness of eye glass as if immensely weary of Flora's affairs. It was all of a piece. She walked the Village Green and no one seemed aware of her existence. Her inheritance was a ruin, she was reminded that begrudging charity alone left her the use of tables and chairs.

She dropped her veil and standing up began nervously pulling at her gloves.

"I must think things over," she said, rather sullenly.

"Well!" Herbert Trinkett ceremoniously shook hands. When her fingers laid in his well cushioned palm he took a step forward and seemed about to say something more. Disagreeable, of course. Perhaps remind her that taxes were overdue. Flora got away without any more colloquy. At another word she would have burst into tears.

* * *

Absently crossing the street, under the very nose of a miniature truck with something under the hood rattling to match the tin stovepipe in the load, she skirted the Green on its opposite side. Evidently enough the other had been the shilling one. The chain store, a soiled yellow as if pelted in the past with eggs that the next day would be very bad indeed, announced no day at all, but said by a sign that it would be opened at two o'clock. That a store was ever closed during a working day seemed to city wise Flora, in her present mood, like a final truckling before succumbing to utter despair. Yet it would have been a naïve village custom had she noticed it on the way to Herbert Trinkett's office.

The ancient mansions, with twisted French roofs were topped by useless observatories from which assuredly nothing was visible that was worth the climb. These houses had square front yards where un-clipped grass grew in raggedly. They were enclosed by bushy hedges that in their turn were confined by fences of chicken wire. The privacy at which this hinted was damaged by gates so long opened that gold-enrod and wild asters climbed in front of the hinges. Beyond these, jutting out to the sidewalk, last outpost of "business" was the neat little ten footer housing the weekly paper *Chronotype*. "Chronotype" twice in gold on the neat wire screens, once again over the door. Three men came exuberantly forth, and Flora's heart stood still. But no one could be Arthur, even allowing for ten years of change. They poked one an-other in the waistcoat buttons and departed by different paths for pre-sumable noon dinners. This was Arthur's shop, the place where he was to be found daily. All the time she had been gliding in swift elevators or wearily climbing stairs that started marble and ended in ragged oilcloth, he had been pressing those two steps with his feet, and lifting that old-fashioned latch with his hands, and looking out of those side windows against which next door's lilac bushes must scrape ghostly like in bad weather. Trite enough, all this, about hands, and feet, and eyes; but Flora was thrilled as she had never been thrilled before. The everlasting power of oldtime love was real, it seemed; it did not dimin-ish; it grew. She had omitted her morning orgy of sentiment for two days, these qualms were the result. She hurried on, past the house with the small yard and the locked gate flanked by post with bell and speak-ing tube fit for a ten-acre estate; past the house with the peacocks, past the one with the exotic fig tree by the piazza.

She went into her shabby inheritance, and came upon Etta blacking the stove. The kitchen had been scrubbed during her absence, starched sash curtains put up, and the brass faucets polished.

"I guess I've earned my lunch," said Etta, pulling down her sleeves. "I thought I'd fry a few onions in pork scraps and pour 'em over the mashed potatoes. You like them that way? There isn't any meat. I've stirred up some bran muffins, tho; and put dates in 'em." While she talked she scalded the blue and white Japanese teapot and measured the tea from a pink lustre caddy that belonged in a museum, Flora sat down, looking and feeling as gloomy as her new dress. "I don't see as I have any right o expect you to work for me," she remarked. She did not intend to be offensive, but she probably was.

"You have not," returned Etta, setting her lips grimly in a straight line. "Only I thought, being green, you might consider my company better'n my room. 'Tain't any great stunt for me to pick up and go any time. You only got to say the word."

"Mr. Trinkett tells me," said Flora, "that what I have here is nothing. I can't live in it, and I can't sell it."

Etta jumped and slopped the tea over the potato.

"If he told you such yarns he must be out of his head. Of course the house is sort of rickety and would be the better for a few boards and a lick of paint, but anyone could manage to live in it a while, same's Aunt Lury did."

"Oh—well. She had something to live on."

While believing she could not touch food, Flora was doing wonders at clearing the well-piled plate Etta had put before her. It was the vigorous Etta who drooped somewhat. "There be folks in this town," said she, "who'd think they was pretty well fixed to have a house handed 'em free and clear."

Flora shook her head slowly. No slightest idea for capitalizing an old shack had come out of a well paid filing job and traveled East with her.

"As for—selling," Etta brought out the word with a gasp, "Are you sure he said you couldn't?"

Flora, transfixed, glared at the clove nailheads in her sweet pickled peach. When and where had Herbert Trinkett told her she could not sell the house? At no time. Yet the impression that it was unsalable had made a dent in her mind. If the impression was wrong, no reason for upset remained. She would instruct Etta to remain, under wages, and clear everything off. The Emersons and Hepburns and the rest might take what they claimed, all else should be sold with the house. She would go back to Chicago, a little better off financially, much the worse for her lost illusions. But it was doubtful if she ever could live contentedly in this cold and inhospitable town. She had been left to the offscourings of her great aunt's circle, to old Calista, whom the will had forgotten, to Etta, who was probably a servant. And everyone was so casual. Mr. Trinkett had not even introduced to her the pretty girl in his office.

A confessed thirty was as good as a round middle age in the office where Flora had worked; she had felt as one approaching a safe harbor for the remainder of life, when she drew nigh the Village Green. It was her hope; practically her belief, that she would become a sort of local Queen Victoria, social dictator, source of impeccable advice, a finger in every pie because having no personal interest in any. A large part of the respect due a super-grandmother would come because she had so long dwelt in the metropolis of the middle west.

Flora put Chicago on the pinnacle where it naturally belonged when one visited in Galesburg, Illinois. Inhabitants of that town had seen it, had experienced its winds, had gasped with awe at its lake front estates. Some of the people who crossed the Village Green occasionally spoke of Chicago, but the Chicago of which they spoke had wooden sidewalks elevated six feet above the mud, and talked only about pigs, of which everything was utilized but the squeal. Arthur had not aided anything in understanding when he ate peanuts and popped corn from his coat pockets, explaining that 'Gene Field and Finley Peter Dunne always did so. He was only too easily credited.

"I'm going to see Mr. Trinkett," said Flora, "about selling."

It was the next day. She had spent the previous night in the room wherein she and Belle had heard the cough. The cough was heard again; all night at short intervals it was heard. Again it brought Flora's childhood back, and Great Aunt Lury's promise that the cougher was bound for the heavenly kingdom.

"I want to be an angel,
And with the angels stand,
A crown upon my forehead,
A harp within my hand."

Even after adolescence had eliminated from the cast line any connection with a popular monthly magazine, Flora had felt no doubt that the cougher was slated for immediate location "on" heaven. She was going to be quite amazed when Etta would tell her it was the same old cough from the same old cougher.

"Old-fashioned consumption or asthma may be. It's always something else carries them off."

And that was New England. Lake Front winds could carry the weak lunged off in three months.

"I'm going to give Mr. Trinkett instructions to sell the house," Flora vouchsafed to Etta as she prepared to leave on the next afternoon. Etta waited until the front door was safely shut, and then sniffed for the benefit of the cats, "Folks used to buy sight unseen," she observed, "and there's a gump of a girl selling the same way. Hasn't so much as looked into a clothes press. Well, there's only one cure for red hair and obstinacy—the same one.

Mr. Trinkett was in and alone. While the stenographer was enjoying a good read he was writing what appeared to be business letters by hand. The book propped on the girl's machine was called *Laddie* and seemed to be the adventures of a dog.

"Am I allowed to sell my house?" Flora wanted to know.

Herbert Trinkett said that she was. Her mother would not have been, which was probably why Flora had inherited a doubt. The Hancock who had married Aunt Lury and died in fear of his successor had tied up the property as tightly as the law allowed. It was his evident wish that it should ever remain in Hancock hands. But there is a limit to the generations who can be compelled to retain life interest only in an estate.

"I have even got a customer for you," said the lawyer. "A letter came this morning. Evidently inspired by perusal of an obituary."

The writer in an exceedingly neat hand opened negotiations by a statement of age as twelve and one-half years; grade 8B and would have been 8A only "the she devil of a teacher put me back." Papa and "ooncle" were anxious to buy the house of the "nice lady who died Friday in the paper." They had "lots money on the bank," also "beeg farm with man to by it." The name signed to this epistle was "STANLEY SWANSON" and across the back, as an endorsement, was written in another hand, "14 children."

"It's all right," said Mr. Trinkett, "and quite in the mode of today. These Polanders pile up the jack while their kids are in school learning to write. Papa and ooncle are desirous of starting a grocery store and think one of those large front parlors would be excellently adapted. Not that the town hasn't groceries and to spare, but papa and ooncle don't think they're sufficiently scattered. Bundle wood and bags of coke displayed between premises and sidewalk. The money is as good as in your reticule"—yes, he said reticule—"Miss Hancock. Ask a fancy price. Ten thousand—or even twelve."

Flora was caught without an answer. She sat and thought of the fourteen children, while Herbert Trinkett wrote six lines in picturesque script, signed his name, blew on it for want of a blotter, and licked the envelope and stamp quite as if mechanical assistants to such performances were unpardonable. Then he continued, "Of course it's all one to you who buys. You want your money. Someone sometime will be responsible for introducing these new citizens to our midst. If this deal should fall through I can get you some perfectly solvent Africans. Dey's jes' been a-homin' t' get into some ole Mass. quarters since ever so long. An' good money to pay for that same is what they ain't got nothin' else but. Got their hopes all elevated once when next door to Belinda Blodgett got in a squabble over a hencoop and hung out a sign `For Sale To Colored People Only.' but as Belinda very sensibly refused to go up in the air the label came down in a few weeks. So the customers are still in the market."

"You are—you are spoofing me, Mr. Trinkett. Surely I am not obliged to leave such bad reputation with the—family—as sales like these will mean?"

Mr. Trinkett grinned. "What has the family—what have the families—done for you that you should consider it—or them?"

Flora flushed painfully, for of course he had touched the raw place.

"They have not even called to see if I am worth knowing," she said, bitterly.

"Of course they haven't. And you think it is because you were a stenographer—beg pardon, filing clerk—in Chicago. Or because you have only an old house with no money for repairs. Or because they have discussed you at length and somehow found you wanting. Now let me assure you, Miss Hancock, you are wrong in every particular. Holding down a good job injures no woman nowadays, unless in one small section of the Back Bay in Boston where the inhabitants raise Maltese cats and read the *Transcript*. As for old houses and nothing to keep them on, most of us have inherited legacies as crippled as yours.

And you have not been discussed. You haven't made yourself of sufficient importance."

With a jolt, Flora made herself believe this last brutal revelation. It was supported by so much performance. People had not avoided looking at her from either politeness or aversion; they simply did not notice her. They were not agog to see the new owner of Aunt Lury's house, most of them had known for years that it would be hers; in fact, they know all about her. While she had been considering the effect of her black dress, of her red hair, they had found their lives no more crowded with detail after her arrival than before.

She needed everything, her life had been empty but for her work, here she had not even that. However long she might wait, nothing would be given her except in return for an offering. And what gift did she possess; to be prized by those who had already the Village Green?

"I'm afraid I've been mistaken," she murmured, "I did not know any small town was like this. I thought—there were aristocrats—and a great many gossips—and respect for cities—and people trying to be like other people—and eagerness in reaching for new ideas—"

"It's a very great pity," said Herbert Trinkett, "that you didn't write to me before coming East at all. Then I could have saved you the journey. Only I suppose you would have stuck to your picture of a village, and not believed me at all. There are such places in books, and booty enough to read about. We read about 'em right here, but they don't describe us. This town suits us as it is, if we saw anything we liked better in any city we'd go there. We have as many hard wood floors and bath rooms as we need for comfort or health, and if every mother's son of us hasn't hooked up or tuned in it's because we have the original Uncle Wiggley for a neighbor and he can tell better stories than the bedtime ones from W2G. Aristocrats are received if they are aristocrats and we know the place where codfish belongs. Both kinds are living beside our chief thoroughfare.

"As for the work of the world, a place in the sun, what're you doing for Democracy, we don't care a hoorah for cheap talk about Pore Ole New England, one hundred years in the same rut, reg'lar stick in the mud, wouldn't support an up-to-date notion if 'twould bring us in a million dollars in a year; worshipping the graves of our ancestors like the Chinese, don't know anything's happened since the Civil War. That's mostly mouth. If we do things the same way it's because we've finished experimenting and found out the best. If we think a house or even a graveyard that's been a century on the ground, with trees and grass and vines according, more bootiful than a gash in the earth made last week, I guess the finest art critics and architects will support us. And how we make our money it ain't always necessary to explain. That we make it is pretty plain from the folks from all over expecting us to finance their new contraptions. New England and such towns as this—regular old feeders, always. Young hot bloods running west since before the time when it was no further than Pennsylvany where you lived underground, and killed off three-four wives with consumption doing it. The quieter ones stayed here, and made the money to irrigate the mines and dig the ranches. Today we got the schools, we got the slums because we got the immigrants that make 'em, we even got the styles—or so the women folks tell me."

By this time he was haranguing Flora as if she were a recalcitrant Master in Chancery. This meant that he had risen to his feet, even to his toes, every other half minute, raising himself with his fingers in his trouser pockets, in possible emulation of his ancestor Eliphalet Trinkett, who was supposed to do the like with the straps of his boots. Herbert Trinkett laughed and sat down. "I give you $45 worth of good Rotary luncheon stuff every time you call on me," he remarked, "and I wager you didn't appreciate it in the least. After which I suggest we go out and get some pie."

Yes, he said pie. He took Flora into a Tea Room at the back end of the hall, where the chic white haired attendant with a sweet, patient yet patently humorous smile told them to ask for anything at all that they seemed to fancy.

"The order will have not the slightest effect on what I have," she remarked, "as I haven't anything except tea dust and an already sliced lemon."

"Rush of business?" asked Trinkett.

"Well, you needn't be too sarcastic. My last freezer of ice cream only had to be repacked twice. And I have only to fry a mess of doughnuts or mix up some bran muffins with dates, and telephone a few people, and there are perfect crowds. But I was darning stockings today and didn't have time to cook a thing. Belinda's husband's. She read about a woman who forced her husband to pay three cents each for all the holes stopped in his hose, and she wants to try it on hers."

About six dozen pairs of men's socks reposed in a gaudy heap on the other table.

The tea room was a pretty enough place, if not exactly novel to one from large centres. It bore sign "Ye T Wagon" and displayed a whole one over the door. Chintz covers had been tied over very wooden chairs, and sketchy embroideries indicating tea wagons in delightful places—as in tops of trees, or on Fujihama—adorned the natural linen doilies and napkins. When Mrs. Russell had been introduced she put away the socks and put on a black sateen apron which had a teawagon on it, in yellow.

"Now, Mrs. Russell, you go downstairs into the One Arm lunch, and you fetch up two pieces of that luscious lemon pie with the goo-goo on top. And two cup coffee. Also, if they got any green stuff in the meat shop can't you slice it in a bun and slosh it round with vinegar an' ile? Bread, of course. And should you meet up with a can army beef, did you know, Miss Hancock—were you aware—that the most delicious hash is constructed therefrom? You mince it with a cold potater, and fry in butter..."

Mrs. Russell made a pass at him with the percolator which she had hitched to a socket and filled with water.

"Back before you can say Jack Robinson," she remarked and fled.

"Pooty little woman," said Herbert Trinkett, "and plucky. Takes care of a loony husband, a darter with T.B., and a devil of a darter's child who can't ride a bike up the street without straining a tendon. Oh, yes, and a blind sister. Mrs. Blodgett got her this joint to run because it needed money."

"And there isn't any." Flora thought this contribution bright, but Trinkett knocked that idea out immediately. "Oh, yes, there is. Eat here myself enough to more'n pay the rent. Lotta other fellers do the same. Reg'lar breakfast trade. Mrs. Russell is some cook! Only woman left on airth can make the real ole yeller meal Johnny cake. When us fellers come up here to lunch two-three times a week—Fred Hutchins and Ed Seanerus, good feller, runs the garage; and Art Comyns our local representative of the metropolitan press. Mrs. Russell cooks us a whale of a steak and several pots coffee. To be sure we have to wait while she goes and buys the steak and trimmin's, but as Comyns says, the married guys would do the same if they went home. An' perchance and more have to cook it themselves also."

She had heard his name again, and shown no sign. Then imagination, with its usual trickiness, showed Flora long wedded to her Arthur, and coming to lunch with him in this back room. He sat where Herbert Trinkett sat, his Byronic profile—he must still retain his Byronic profile—was outlined against the window glass, in place of Trinkett's tilted eyeglass, bulgeous nose and luxuriant mustache. But, no—not here would she and Arthur foregather. Arthur came here because his wife did not perform her wifely duties. There were no whales of steaks in his home.

For ten years Flora had mused, each time she sozzled her own handkerchiefs in a set bowl, "I must be in love with Arthur, because I would wash this just as eagerly if it were his dirty shirt!" Of course she believed herself intended for the perfect wife, immaculate house, meals at all hours, favorite pudding never too much work; at the same time his intellectual equal, social adjunct, and better dressed than the sirens of the city on practically nothing at all. Therefore Flora pictured herself preparing delicious luncheons of consommés, salads, stuffed peppers. She would do her own salted nuts, in olive oil; there should always be quaint little jars of preserved ginger and dishes of home made candies...

A regular old maid's paradise! She recognized it herself as such, and began to laugh. Herbert Trinkett thought she was laughing with him, because he had been talking all the while. He told Flora he usually sat mumchance, but she seemed somehow to set him going. As for Flora, she was not entirely an over reckoner. She could actually do many of these things. She could turn a shabby frock into a handsome blouse, having ingenuity and beads. She read the "new" literature by fits and starts, and understood more than half of what she read. She even researched. When she found "parkin" featured in an Arnold Bennett novel she did not rest content until she had proved what she suspected from the first, that it was gingerbread. She gurgled over the heroine who got in bad with an admirer because she thought Madame Bovary an author instead of a book. As had already been noted around the Village Green, that Flora Hancock was not a talker. So she had never given herself away during the years she supposed Oscar Wilde was so called while his real name was forbidden to the world.

* * *

As for selling the house, Herbert Trinkett packed her off from the door of the block in rather cavalier manner. "Think it over," he counseled. Just as if she hadn't. Then he said, of course, she must come to his office again. Flora wondered if he might be holding her back because he enjoyed those calls. She wondered thus without coquetry, she was rather sorry for the heavy old bachelor. He seemed to have no business—at least she met no clients and there were evidently long, unproductive luncheon parties.

The evening being mild and lovely Flora strolled the length of the Green—without looking at her own door. Thus she missed her first caller, the pretty girl who had shopped for a divorce.

"She's gone out," said Etta. "She's gone up to Trinkett's office to dispose of the house. And what the deuce to do with these cats I don't know!"

Etta bore grey in her arms and was holding his jaws so that opinions of the black and of the white should not interrupt general conversation. Those sinners were enjoying life in the parlor, which had not been refurnished since the removal of Aunt Lury.

"Send 'em over to my house," laughed unlikely Amelia, who was trying to make her relations stop 'Melia and start 'Aimé' which it is not surprising they wouldn't.

"Get out!" said Etta. "You wouldn't stay home to feed a cat. Don't even stay home to feed your man."

Beauty grinned. "He's so darn fussy! If I happen to burn the toast twice pretends his barber says his hair's getting curly. Putting such silly stuff; just does it to make me uncomfortable; because I always make the toast as well as I can."

"Narsty. Like all his sex!"

"Thanks, Etta, for them kind words. But speaking of cats as I was before being interrupted, my husband will be grateful for one or more ere long. He's going to lose me!"

Etta began to respond, "Poh! I've heard that before, or something similar," but Amelia caught sight of Flora progressing along the Green and with a charming and eminently ladylike imitation of a whoop galloped in pursuit. She was dressed in pale lavender and carried a parasol; rather useless at the hour, but fittingly completing the millinery scheme.

"Hullo, Flora," she bawled, "park on that bench and wait for me."

* * * *

"So you went out and sold your house?" she told rather than asked Flora. "Good work. There's nothing ties anybody like owning a house. Now my husband—if it isn't the lawn mower it's the heater. No weekends or wild parties for him. So I have to go with other people. And he kicks at that! It's just as easy to have a good time with your husband as some other woman's. I know. I've tried it. We went to B'linda Blodgett's over the 4th and were having a noble time. She's made a program where all went to bed at noon and slept till evening and then we had breakfast and did forenoon things till lunch—midnight, you know—and afternoon stuff from then on, and a big seven course dinner just as the sun rose, and got a little bit lit up from then on. Well, we were having obstacle races and jumping over lighted kerosene lamps, and he was as busy and as happy as anyone, mixing up those near-Bronxy cocktails out of orange juice and synthetic gin, when all of a sudden he says we must go home. Linda'd put a record on—"And the Green Grass Grew All Around"—and it reminded him he must cut it. I just hope you got a whale of a price."

"I'm not as far along as that," said Flora. "But Mr. Trinkett has given me permission to sell."

"Mercy, do you have to have a permit? I don't know a darn thing about business and I don't want to."

"I was a filing clerk," said Flora, not without an air of condescension to young butterflies. "Ten years in one office."

"How perfectly awful! Ten offices in one year would have been more fun. I never did so much, but I've had five and six jobs in a single place. I was a filing clerk, too, a few minutes. But my really regular professions are switch-boards and proof-reading and assistant book-keeping, and on the tube and secretarial without stenography. Did you take shorthand?"

Flora shook her head.

"Whatever they say, not a bit necessary. A personal interview beats it every time."

* * *

Flora found Etta grimly sitting among the cats in the Emerson parlor, her long fingers twitching at a beautiful and intricate design in smocking on a child's dress of filmy material and amethyst rose color.

"Bert Trinkett just handed a note in at the window on the end of his walking stick," she remarked. "Claims he's afraid to come up the steps. There 'tis on the mantel."

"Dear Miss Hancock

In the capacity of legal adviser I neglected an important matter of council. This I propose to rectify.

In your natural reflections pro and con advantages of

(a) selling

(b) retaining

the property taken by direct claim from your great aunt recently deceased I trust you will be actuated by none but considerations of practical benefit. Pay no slightest attention to

(a) family pride

(b) souvenirs—portraits of ancestors, contents of china closets, samplers, junk found up attic

(c) nature, such as sunsets

(d) art, especially the old southernwood bush, the Baltimore Pride my grandmother's grandmother fetched on a pillion, et al.

Very sincerely yours
Hebt. Trinkett.

Simply, cut out the slush.

"What's a Baltimore Pride?" exclaimed Flora. "What's a pillion?"

"It's 'the' Baltimore Pride," returned Etta, glib as if she had read the note for herself. "A rose bush the old timers set a lot of store by. Grows over against the fence. Town hist'ry has it that it's the first rose bush in town, brung in by the first Hancocks. He was a minister and she rode pillion behind him. Horseback, of course. Your own sense might tell you there was a time sometime when no wheeled vehicles had got over from t'other side. She was supposed to have put some rose in her pocket and planted them beside the door. "Not this house. Your great uncle wasn't born or thought of then. Some ole shanty the sort they lived in those times."

Flora gazed at the letter while Etta went on to state she didn't, for her part, believe a word of it. Practical folks, like anybody's ancestors, wouldn't be apt to start out for a new home in the wilderness with a rose bush. They'd bring something worth while....

Flora questioned herself if Herbert Trinkett's plea against sentiment was not really an adroit plea that its powers be given a chance? She was fully convinced that he did not want her to go away. This conviction was intensely pleasing to one who had exerted no influence on either man or woman for a decade. It was a direct tribute to her personality.

Then easy tears welled up and Etta and Etta's work became a rose-colored blur while Flora dwelt fondly on the time when she did matter to some one, this being one of the memories which left her believing that Arthur had loved while he loved. The memory was of a kiss—no, not of a kiss, but of the gentle yet deliciously awkward manner in which her lover had pulled down her veil after the kiss. Close her eyes—hiding the tears as well—and she felt once more his great clumsy hand trying to manipulate the fragile lace, tearing it, yet somehow shutting in her quivering chin as he thought he ought to do, and patting the job at last as if pleased with his ability.

Flora was obliged to rise hurriedly and go to bed, unless she wanted Etta to catch her crying.

"Don't be scared if you hear me moving round for an hour or so," Etta called up. "This thing ain't half nor quarter done, cuss it."

The dress was for one of the girls next door, to wear at a garden party. Etta did not believe in young children going to garden—or any other—parties, except doll parties such as of her youth. She did not hold with dressing young ones in anything more expensive than percale, now that was a quarter since the war. There was no money in this, she was finishing it because the girl had tried to make it for herself and got begoggled.

"Poor old maid," thought Flora, and considered it well enough that Etta should cultivate vicarious pleasures. Then she laid her head on Arthur Comyns' (vicarious) shoulder and slumbered.

Advice or suggestion quite unconsidered, it was impossible to live even three days beside the Village Green and amid Great Aunt Lury's furniture, books and pictures, without feeling influences. Flora was particularly susceptible because she had lived for years with the furniture of whoever happened to be her landlady. Her pictures had been those in magazines, Sunday Supplements, and art museums, because you were not allowed to make pin holes, nor even push pin holes, in the walls. And the books were in libraries, because a person who lived in a trunk was crazy if she bought books.

Aunt Lury's furniture has been partly described. The rest was like unto that. It probably needed weeding out and rearranging. Flora caught herself in imaginary assemblies of all the good mahogany pieces in one or two rooms. Aside from the flamboyant collections of a trip to Europe in the Emerson parlor, the pictures were nightmares. Yards of cats, roses and children, given away with household monthlies. Evangeline, hair done up nicely and a "circular" on, waiting for Gabriel. Lady Butler's distressing "Roll Call" with the glass broken. "The Horse Fair," "The Dead Bird," "Queen Victoria in the Highlands," pony led by John Brown. These were engravings. "U. S. Grant and Family" was a print. The general apparently wore full uniform in the homeside, if not while accepting the surrender of Lee. Mrs. Grant engaged in needlework the width of a large table from her liege lord. Little Nellie in abundant crinoline. Intermixed with these many chromoes, also hair wreathes and mottoes worked in shaded worsteds on perforated cardboard. One, evidently a wedding present, still bore an inscription: "The Future Mrs. Hancock," and hoped delicately, in every red obtainable, "May All Your Woes Be Little Ones." Crayon enlargements—Aunt Lury had been addicted to crayon enlargements. Even those of the family whom she could not have liked, as Ed Ellis her son-in-law, she had not been able to have unenlarged.

Aunt Lury had been a hoarder and a keeper. Cupboards, bureaus, secretaries, desks, tables with drawers, all a-jingle with things. The sole attempt at assorting had been based on the marriage epochs; and then one wondered if all that box of faded auburn "combings" had come out during the lifetime of Great Uncle Hancock; at the connection of the wealthy and powerful banker Emerson with a great many rounds of patch work complete but with no hint as to how they were ever to be put together.

The yard, too, had its power. Flora had enjoyed no green grass but that in public parks, attainable after long walks or short car rides. This turf, however mangy, was her own. That was her barbary bush, just reddening as to berries; that was her Virginia creeper up which the Gray and the Black of the cats sometimes climbed spectacularly to the second story, watched by walking parties from the nearby kindergarten whose teachers led them thither and then delivered lectures inspired by the picture. There was a wisteria on the front which Etta said needed only ruthless cutting back and a rope to the peak of the ridgepole for climbing on, to likewise be a sight. There were pear trees, just becoming so lavish with fruit that raids were more than welcome.

"Though where in tunket they come from I do 'no," fumed Etta. "Every yard in this town has pear trees. Some agent must have been through here twenty-five year ago and every dratted prop'ty owner bought pears and Norway spruces."

Great Uncle Hancock had fenced in his place, and Great Uncle by marriage Emerson had kept the fence repaired, but original pickets and new ones were now equally decrepit. Soon this yard would be open to all the others down which there was a vista to the first chain store at the bend. A vegetable and flower garden with hen house and rabbit hutch—a wired pen where a small child in overalls was sunned daily—a yard where crab apple trees grew—a yard where linen whitened on the grass—one laid out to zinnias and gladioli, evidently for commercial purposes—one devoted to a queer old fashioned game played with striped balls and half hoop crickets—croquet, Flora had read about that.

Flora did enjoy sitting at an upstairs window, idly appraising her neighborhood. Her rooms had so generally looked into light shafts, and she had been so long without a neighborhood. She had kept on sleeping in the small room where Belle had taken her to the comfort of company, if no other comfort, on that first night. It was a very nondescript room, probably furnished by Great Aunt Lury in a hurry for a sudden influx of relations on a paying-visitor basis. The straw matting had been well worn since laid in place, but it was nowhere nailed down. The painted bureau did not match the old maple bed, nor did the washbowl "go" with the pitcher. There was a strange rug, made from carpet remnants seamed, with humps, on a machine. The one comfortable chair had been sat through and only a few newspapers kept the two cushions and the occupant of the chair from falling to the floor. Flora usually perched on the edge of the bed, partly because of this and partly because some cat was generally ahead of her with the chair.

* * *

Great Aunt Lury had held on to all printed matter with the tenacity of a log hut dweller who glimpses but a few poor books in a lifetime. She had preserved the quaint architectural books of Robert Hancock, the Barnes' Notes on Everything Religious peculiar to Banker Emerson, Young's Night Thoughts and Various Poetical Glooms dating to her first husband; also the Toy Libraries of her own childhood; and nondescripts—*Way Bills of an Expressman—Eliza Wharton the Coquette—Directory of Boston* with Coloured People listed separately.

The bound *Peterson's* and *Godey's Ladies' Book* were delightful. Flora opened a volume for 1863 at random, and vastly enjoyed a tale by "The Author of 'Susy S—'s Diary'," "Agnes Marshall of Dummer Court." Agnes found a sum of money and returned it to the owner, thus abruptly introduced. "(His name was Callamore. He did a large business on Nassau Street.)" In return he promised her a rose. Also advice.

"Would she promise not to do one sentimental thing, or think one sentimental thought, before the rose, if he would bring it?—or send it, more likely he would send it."

It made Flora think of Herbert Trinkett and his letter. Were men always afraid women would prove sentimental?

Looking toward the end she discovered that Agnes was duly rewarded.

". . .No sooner were they within the room, which the loveliness and perfume of the rose seemed to fill, than he turned to her with his arms outspread. `My child—my Agnes—my little wife!' he said. And she, poor thing!, was glad to be taken into them, and to the wide, firm breast, where she might not only hide the happiness and the blushes a little, but feel herself at rest, now and forevermore."

All this because Agnes left off wearing some "fine bits of lace and velvet for a head-dress" which she had purchased when the first visit of the money loser impended, and worn daily (referred to by the author as "duds"). After he had "looked with contempt on the finery," and made the before-quoted remark about being sentimental, Agnes had "stuffed her head-dress away in a corner, as a poor worthless thing, and put her abundant, soft hair back in plaited bands."

And there was one delicious touch, prelude to the final clench, when Agnes had begged the great Mr. Callamore to leave her to her poverty, because, forsooth, the neighbors said such as he never meant well by such as she:

"I guess not. I mean, I guess I won't leave you. I guess I'll go home with you."

Had there ever been such men? Were not such men the kind produced only by authoresses of the Victorian age, of whom critics wrote, "Her men are all old governesses in pants"?

* * *

Flora decided to call it a vacation. Her stay without decision as to the future. She was paying out no money, except for the food which she actually consumed. Etta had remained, at Flora's request, cooking and dishwashing in return for her room. As matter of fact, Flora often washed the dishes. She did not cook, partly because she had very little knack for it, largely because cooking brought Arthur Comyns so forcibly to mind. She had learned cooking for his sake. She had made fudge and rarebits, also that other nourishing dish, shrimp wiggle. A bitter memory pictured Flora, in a delightfully dotted Swiss apron, standing beside Arthur. She stirred the—whatever it was in a chafing dish—he put his arm about her—not waist, lower down—and as he drew her as closely as the chair allowed, whispered amorously, "Don't you like to cook for me?" She felt that she did—she did. She had longed to clasp him close, in her turn, and say so. She still thrilled with the thrill that might have been, had she cut prudence adrift. She still blushed with the shame that might have been had all things turned out afterward as they did turn out. Instinct had saved her from any unmaidenly behavior. Thanking instinct, she did not wish to cook.

* * *

The days went by with wonderful rapidity. Knowing how days of idleness dragged in the city, where one did not spend money, Flora sat amazed at their easy departure beside the Village Green. She and Etta had very little in common, yet they managed to consume several quarter hours in conversation. And not tell the stories of their lives, either. Etta knew the public portions of Flora's; all Flora learned about Etta was that her mother (long dead) could make delicious soup and frequently employed the child Etta in conveying it to sick folk; that her father (also dead) was like all the rest of his sex; that her brother (living, but estranged) was like his father, and had hogged most of the family funds; that her sister thought she was happily married and would like to have Etta live with her, but "I can't stand the way he treats her even though she does like it!"

Flora did not grow fond of Etta. Etta's blunt and uncouth remarks infuriated Flora several times a day. Flora also knew herself as cold, unsympathetic, given to repression of feelings. She couldn't cut loose and roar at ancient wheezes, as Etta did under the influence of strong tea or even a genial afternoon. As for trailing an old song all over the place, tune wrong and words largely unknown, Flora longed to smite Etta when she heard

Cann't git away
T' marry' day
My—wife—won't—let—me.

Etta lived on a diet, and Flora had always distrusted people who lived on diets. They were inconsistent, morbid, and, of course, affected. Etta's diet seemed especially lacking in consistency. It was presumed to be simple, yet it allowed consumption of pies, cookies, elaborate layer cakes. Nothing fried—but doughnuts. Of all things, doughnuts! No fruit, not even the plain, unadorned apple. Jams and marmalades of the richest character! Strong tea three times daily, hot buttered toast, every fish that swam in the sea; no sensible beefsteak, no roast beef medium. But boiled onions. The environs of the kitchen were never free from their odor.

Yet spite of mealtime irritations Flora had numerous real good times with Etta. They would run to the front door mornings, eager to see what of the blossoming things in the vicinity had survived the night; it was a year when the frost held off unusually well. The tress on the Green were interesting, the grapes and pears in all the yards in sight; the smells of piccalil. Flora found novelty in the scrapings she made of things, being long used to Big City ways of scamping this season for next, of wearing velvet hats in August and eating cucumbers at any time, but the one in which they attained full growth in gardens.

Despite herself Flora was drawn to people. It was all very well to despise Etta for being an old maid and taking a vicarious interest; Flora's honesty would assert the fact that she also was an unappropriated female, as the male fussbudget who had been her Chicago boss nicely phrased it. With Arthur Comyns in ideal proportions still dominating any room in which she remained long alone, she was obliged to feel direct envy of any long wedded couple not engaged in obvious combat.

There was a couple next door, parents of the girl for whom Etta had made the frock, also parents of other children. They came into their extensive back yard and built a hencoop. It was built of old lumber and tar paper, also of new lumber which they ordered piece meal, a few scantlings at a time, and which a huge truck made terrible fusses about delivering. Tar paper partly covered it; there was a window over which the man tacked a piece of netting, boasting that it had been around the cellar seven years and just found useful. Where it fell short of covering the opening he pieced it out with one side of Baby Boy's wheelbarrow. Then he made a patent lock for the door, of the back of a kitchen chair wedged under a practicable door knob, the other sided one, being white, unscreened for a nest egg. His wife, a large woman whose hair was not dressed or even done, but merely pushed out of the way, came and argued every post, nail and shingle. So also did the older children, while dogs, cats, rabbits and guinea pigs acted natural, and the cocks and hens inspected gravely. There was everything in that backyard! Tomatoes and carrots, flowers—even roses and an Easter lily astonishingly blooming in the back of the year; trees, tools, toys, clothes always drying. If anything alive, as a rooster or a rabbit, appeared sick or unhappy, it was instantly taken into the house. One could only imagine what the house was like.

The family retired therein when they felt impelled to making a superior noise. Loud cries of "Ouch!" "Ma-ma, make him stop!" "Oh, ain't you the devil!" issued at apparent mealtimes, and were explained by Etta, "The mister is a-tickling of the children. Regular hector, just like all his sex."

When he went up the street he was seen to be slender, with an intellectual face and immaculate clothing of excellent material in quiet colors.

"She made that overcoat," Etta would offer. "She's making him some pants now, that loud hollering we heard last night was they laughing when he tried them on." The oldest girl, the one so blonde that she was frequently (to her own disgust) taken for a Swede, further explained the pants episode. "He took the money for some and went to Boston. Well, first before he goes anywhere he goes to Cornhill. And they were selling a set of *Elsie Dinsmore* for the money. So he bought that instead." Nancy didn't think much of them, preferring modern series—*Helen Redmond Freshman*, *Helen Redmond Sophomore*, etc. The second girl, Rachel, she of the long ashblond curls and the innocence that made her terrifying company, tried to form the family on the Dinsmore standard.

"You did spit on the floor," she told the small brother, in smashing accents. "I saw you with my own two eyes. You'd have been sent to bed without your supper and made to stand in the corner a week at the Dinsmore's for doing such a Rotten Thing." Then she wondered audibly why there were no bathrooms mentioned in the Dinsmore mansions, and where Elsie went when she wanted to do what we do in them.

There was another girl, younger than these; remarkably pretty, with black curls. Care set upon her tiny brow, she was forever feeding the chickens or feeling the clothes to see were they dry enough to fetch in, or running to the grocery store end of the Green. She was frequently called "Here, you, Orphan from the Alms House," and seemed to like the name, which was peculiar, she being actually an alien, child of divorced parents, boarded in a neutral land.

One of the town's prettiest sights was Rachel and Annie, with hair bows which they themselves had damped and fussily pressed since school, sitting on the steps of Mondays waiting for their music master. They took off a man, which was not generally the custom. Yes, they said "took off," though in a year and four months Rachel would be in high school. Presently he would come, on the 4.26, and the sounds of duets mixed with the sounds of tears would penetrate the air. "My Gawd, can't you ever remember anything!" the man would be saying, and the small boy would explain, "At's Annie. Nex' time he give my sis'r Rachel duet to p'ay all herse'f." This child used Annie as a whipping boy, and beat her with his fists whenever he had a grievance against anyone else. He was exceedingly fond of blood, and in the course of a day had generally punched out the eyes of all human beings with whom he came in contact, cut the arms and legs off icemen, deliverers of pasteurized milk and the letter carrier; had killed the cats and throwed a stone at 'em too. Then he was put to bed as curfew rang, and wanted the window shut because of gypsies.

"Dont make the mistake of getting acquainted with her," warned Amelia, who dropped in one morning wearing a chintz gown and a market basket. "Domesticity's her second name. I mean Mrs. Miller. She may be smart and able to paint and paper a house all by herself, but who in blazes wants a woman to paint and paper a house all by herself? Her hair's a mess and she don't know the first thing about making a complexion."

"Neither do you," retorted Etta viciously. "Yours is quite natural. You don't dare say it ain't!"

Amelia blushed a real blush. She wanted to retort that not for always would she be guilty of offensive fact in an era of fancy, but Etta didn't give her time. "The Millers strike me," she observed, "as all right. Otherwise how could they buy a place for not one red cent, asking price ten thousand?"

"Good gracious!" exclaimed Flora.

Etta nodded. "Character. Character did it. And reputation."

"Good five dollar words," said Amelia, "but you know, Ettie, they don't mean a darn thing. His reputation never got Clare Miller above a $25 a week job. But what's odds I didn't call round to talk about the neighbors, 'cause I'm not normal anyhow. I called to give Flora the glad news that she's coming to The Club Tuesday night."

"What is it?" asked Flora, "and who invites me?"

"You don't have to be invited. You're just let to come. You may join, too, if you want to squander twenty-five cents per annum."

On hearing the economical terms Flora unwisely turned to Etta and said, "I suppose I can go with you?"

"You can not," returned Etta, with a face redder than Flora's hair. "The family fool isn't considered eligible."

The door registered a first class wooden damn.

"'S all right," said Amelia. "She doesn't write. We're all writers. It's a club of writers."

"Oh, but..." said Flora, depreciation of self battling with respectful understanding why it called itself "The" Club.

"Faissey nos. Anybody can. Everybody does. When you write a letter describing some old trip or dress or impression you're doing it. The club makes you one. We can make a writer of anybody at all. We bring out the latent talent—or maybe it's the innate. I didn't know I could write until Linda made me join. This year I got three different $5 bills in newspaper contests...for a slogan, and for getting Xmas gifts for a family of seven out of $2, and for why a coat of so-and-so's paint beat repairs."

"Is Mrs. Blodgett a writer, too?"

"Rather. I think she's quite the cleverest gink among us. She takes famous misters out of literature and makes Misseses of them—and writes their thoughts and things. Dialect if possible. She's professional, too. Sold one to a real magazine, though she never got her check because it failed right after."

* * *

"What will they wear?" Flora inquired of Etta on the evening of Tuesday. By dint of anticipating the ridiculous Etta had not only made peace, but offered to loan her diamond earrings. Being rich in furs and jewels Etta ostentatiously never wore anything better than cloth and a single cameo. When winter came she remarked that sealskin was warm, but above her station. It cost her $25 every summer to have it stored and insured.

"Oh—well, Amelia will wear her white broadcloth suit. She wears it generally, ever since one of her dear friend members outened the remark 'I do hate dirty white,' when she first bought it. Linda Blodgett will have some new bead chains and a set of earbobs like bugs or reptiles. That oldest girl next door will wear a bran' new lilac-colored cotton pongee with drawn work if her ma can get it done in time. She's running the machine lickety-larrup this minute while some the others pull threads and hem the skirt by hand. It wasn't cut out till most 5."

"Do they go?"

"They do. Mr. Miller has written a book. It's up in the library here, but of course I never read it. You better get ready and go along with them, Flora. Sachem Hill, where the house is they're to meet at, is the hardest place to find!"

* * *

Even at half past nine all the members hadn't found it; several were locating themselves by 'phone and asking that they be looked up and rescued. Amelia bustled in last, representing herself as having gone round and round the house without being able to get into the house, program only varied by sitting on strange doorsteps to weep. Owing to a vow she had not asked the way. The house was a tiny chalet let into the hillside in such a manner that approaching in one way it was difficult to avoid stepping into the third-story windows. Rumor said it had once been a "lodge" and imported entire from Switzerland. The only door was so narrow that Herbert Trinkett sidled in. The passage, also a tight squeeze, suddenly debouched into a room big as a 12-cow barn. There was everything in it—everything. Like the Miller's backyard. Only a different everything. Magnificent engravings, but slightly mildewed. A steel piano, an organ, a melodion. Hundreds of books, displayed in undisguised soap boxes. A small table set with exquisite Haviland; a great many chairs worn perfectly comfortable; on the unpainted floor a threadbare drugget. Over the more obvious holes Mrs. Hollister, the hostess, roguishly tossed small rugs on learning who had 'phoned for directions—as Herbert Trinkett, or a man called Joralemon Hickox. Which performance was good for a laugh.

Mrs. Hollister was quite beautiful, with snow-white hair and pink cheeks; she was modishly dressed and evidently did not consider sparkling rings above her station. She frankly referred, however, to the poverty of her home. It appeared that the house was not her property, though it had been inhabited by her ancestors for many generations. At some remote period a lord of the Big House—long dust and ashes— had bestowed it on a farm hand together with permanent doles of as much butter, milk n' eggs as you want. The dole continued even unto that day. "Which is why we always serve chocolate."

The refreshments were indeed touchingly simple—merely the frothing chocolate and hard biscuits. It was the best chocolate.... One end of the room was filled with the only window, huge, diamond paned, with dull red glass. Beneath it was a window seat which Mrs. Hollister confessed was her bed by night. Gwenn was so huge she had to have the only real bed. Mrs. Hollister mischievously confessed to rheumatiz in the side next the window, resulting from draughts, and in the impromptu dance which closed the evening (yes, they had a phonograph, too, and oodles of records) all and sundry endeavored vainly to guess which side that might be.

"Gwendoline was indeed a magnificent young beauty, a regular Gibson girl. Before Flora had been in the house ten minutes she had been told by six people that Gwendoline Hollister was a regular Gibson Girl. She had blue eyes and light hair done in braids which ever and anon burst into tiny wriggling curls. The girl herself was somewhat likewise. She was demurely knitting an object which started in war time as a soldier's wristlet, but had lately been deflected into a baby's sock, since the married Hollister girl threatened to make mamma into granny. She was talking intelligently about the Normal and her chances for a school. And she gave a whoop when Herbert Trinkett entered and claimed that he had lost their wager (he called it waigger) over Saturday's football game. She had other whoops and much loud toned animation in describing several Big Games of the previous summer; and after consultation with mamma whooped particularly loud in acceptance of an invitation to bowl with a stout young man who was called Waldo, not because Waldo was his name, but because Emerson was his surname.

At 9.45 the president, a sleek and good-looking man who, to Flora's amazement, bore the name of Flo Sullivan, rapped for order and asked for the minutes of the previous meeting. They were then read, rather inaudibly, to the accompaniment of a cough which Flora could not mistake. Shut her eyes, and she was in her room in the house by the Green, vainly courting sleep. Good heavens, the woman not only had lived twenty years beyond the day of her death, but she went out nights.

There was nothing offensively invalidish about the woman, who was middle-aged and wore clothes twenty-five years her junior, like everyone else. The closing sentences of the report made such a terrific hit that they were repeated:

....a move was made to the piazza where refreshments were served by candle light.... the only moving features were the bad action of a Paul Revere lantern, which after some century's service decided to strike and did so, setting its own candle into so fierce a blaze that it would probably have been a matter for the local F. D. only for the large number of brave men present. Several of them supported Mr. F. Sullivan on the piazza railing and he succeeded in grabbing the flaming lantern in his bare hands and flinging it unaided on to the lawn, where it was finally put out by a shovelful of dirt which Mrs. Miller thoughtfully fetched from the extreme back garden, utterly ignoring the several tons directly in front of the conflagration. The chief sufferer was Mr. Akron, whose new summer suit was shot full of lead drippings and looked as if it had just returned from three years' hard service in the Forest of Argonne. We were all extremely sorry about this, but like a good sport he made light of the affair, and departed with, we understand, good hope of a service badge. The other regret came from the fact that 25 beautiful coconut macaroons were overlooked in setting the tables, but Mr. Sullivan, host of this occasion, found them just the same—in the bill. —Elsa Dennis, Sec'y.

Wildest enthusiasm followed this composition. Several men pounded their own or another fellow's knee, in delight, and Herbert Trinkett bawled out, "That's literature, that is!" while Akron—a dapper schoolboy—moved, seconded and carried through a vote to get out a magazine and print it.

Was it so funny? Or were they spoofing the lady with the cough? No flush of chagrin was in her cheek, she smiled a little with one corner of her mouth and shoved the book into a handbag as though the episode was over. Probably it was. The treasurer then seized eagerly upon a brief pause and opening a large book made an impassioned plea for "authority" to collect two years and eight months back dues from a recalcitrant member named Elbridge Wood, and who appeared to be absent. A lively debate followed, in which there was so much to say that the president ruled two or more were allowed to talk simultaneously, in order to avoid delay. Then ensued arguments—it isn't as if he couldn't afford to pay, you know....When he's at college I doubt if his mail is forwarded....he's no intention of paying, he wants to get Flo's goat....who has the floor?....it's not a trifle. 58 1/3 cents is not a trifle. It will pay the secretary's bill two months and leave....Just what I've always contended. The dues are quite high enough, if only the members would pay 'em....and above all the superior bellow of Herbert Trinkett, "Ladies and others: Did the honorable member resign when he left us two years and eight months ago or was his departure informal as that of the Arabs? Therein lies the crux...."

As the clock struck ten the secretary lifted her hand and by not using any voice obtained silence. She then proposed employing Mr. Trinkett in collection of the bill and Mr. Trinkett eagerly accepting the case, was seen thereafter in conference with the treasurer, filling a capacious notebook with data.

Instantly the evening was handed over to a stout lady whose official title seemed to be "Entertainment Committee," and who rose and complacently announced the topic of the evening—

My Favorite City and Why

"Delicious!" murmured Amelia. "Nothing could be better."

"Unless `The Seasons'," muttered Linda Blodgett, who shared Amelia's chair, directly behind Flora. Whereat both sibilantly intoned, "Spring, Summer, Autumn or Fall, and Winter."

One by one favorite cities were named and why. General offerings were in the ironic spirit of the evening; then Clarence Miller recited a few stanzas of delicate beauty, of extreme simplicity—"Boytown—Girltown"—shimmering in the mist of Never-Never-Land. It was understood, appreciated, anybody who desired to shed a tear or two did so unashamed. Flora thrilled and told herself it was a literary club, after all.

There was laughter later, of course. The entertainment committee herself was the cause of much, as she solemnly and in good faith accounted for her own love of Boston—

"The city of Boston employs 0000 minions of the law who arrest 00000 human beings yearly, of whom 60 per cent. are found guilty. Of these 0000 are sent to penal institutions in the harbor, 000 are transferred to the various state prisons and 00 executed.

"The number of insane supported by the city of Boston are (laughter).

"Automobile accidents (fatal) inside the city limits number (laughter).

"Paupers cared for by the city total (laughter, followed by look of amazement from lady reading paper).

"We now pass to consideration of hospitals, of which no city has a larger number in proportion to inhabitants, so many indeed that in summer several are floating. All more than filled to repletion, so that...."

"She stirs—she moves—she seems to feel—," breathed Amelia.

All ended beatifically in gales of mutual glee.

"Well, well," said the Entertainment Committee, "that was quite a joke on me. I was so absorbed in considering the wonderful size and efficiency of Boston's institutions that I never noticed the inferences. Quite a joke on me!"

She was one of those who enunciate "wonderful" as if it tasted good.

* * *

The "social hour" was well along. Gwendoline Hollister had sung "Just a Song at Twilight" and "The End of a Perfect Day." She only sang the old songs, her mother remarked. And she had never been taught. Flora believed they had formed themselves on stories of "The Old Fashioned Girl" type. Therein the fashionable titles mechanically banged the box and banded in imitation of Grand Opera, to general disgust. Then followed the miss from the country, and she moved all hearts with artless art in "Bonny Doon." Gwendoline wore white, too, just as those heroines used to wear. All the glory was not hers, however. Flo Sullivan was called for, and sang his own song. It was so excessively Irish that it left nothing that was Irish for any other song. The shamrock was there; a lovely colleen; fairies flitted and over all enfilading starshine. It seemed rather amazing to Flora, why had it not been published and made into records?

"It's quite as fascinating as anything...." she caught herself telling the author after he had grinned over a second encore and sat down.

"To be sure it is," he observed with no false pride. "But it's got to be better 'n that before a publisher will spend money. Never mind. I got song in a show about 20 years ago. Sheet music with handsome soprano on cover n' everything. That ought to be about all for me. Suffering cats, let the other fellows have a chance!"

"You're too darn modest," drawled Herbert Trinkett. "Contented to be known as Man of One Song as well as Man of One Story."

"Right you are. Did I tell you folks that I've just sold Canadian rights to 'Pep'?"

Congratulations, more or less facetious, followed; and Amelia sketchily informed Flora that seven years before Flo had sold a short story to a popular magazine. The check had been for $500, when that was spent he got the copyright and started squeezing the yarn. He had sold it to small magazines and to Sunday supplements. He had syndicated it. He had put it into boiler plate. Now—"I say, Flo," piped up Amelia, "there isn't anything more you can do, is there? You'll really have to go to work?"

...He threatened her with a hairy fist. "Young lady, you forget there are places on the map like Australia and Virgin Islands."

"How long since you were in the street car business, Sullivan?" asked Herbert Trinkett.

"Before the One Man car was invented. That wheeze has been pulled for me before now."

"He was a real motorman—or at least a conductor," said Amelia, in her character of chorus. "I guess likely he's starved in a garret and pawned his other suit. Oh, our prexy is a regular author, he is!"

It appeared further that he was about to start a magazine. That is, he was one of several present that evening who were about to start magazines. Flora, listening, was obliged to hastily revise her idea of a publisher as a man with a backing of wealth who bought a city block and a spruce forest and cornered the popular authors by increasing royalties. Mr. Sullivan, true to his One Man principle, had induced a One Man Printshop to move into half his office, and to pay the rent by printing a magazine that should appeal to the manicure and marcel-waving trade.

"There'll be a lot about therapy and electroanalysis in it too," he went on. "I think of calling it *Keeping Fit*."

"Keeping yourself out of jail, eh?"

"I suppose so. Advertising stunts seldom bear repetition. Excuse me while I explain to Miss Hancock. I once had a magazine of romance coming along fine. Ten good paid up subscribers who looked anxiously for its coming every month. Couldn't keep house without it. Felt so lost when I happened to skip an issue that some of 'em complained to the P.O. authorities and I was finished for obtaining money under false pretenses. Lost my second class rates so *Romance* was no more reality."

Then he started about collecting a few manuscripts for *Keeping Fit*, and one woman promised a poem about Beauty Culture, "which will be writ special, because I'm concentrating on vers libre now—nothing else sells"—and Gwendoline Hollister said she'd make a stab at a story and anyway, mamma reminded her there was the one about the hairdresser who quarreled with her lover and was sent for to dress the hair of her rival and felt tempted to put the wrong stuff on it and turn it green or purple, but she nobly forbore and somehow got him in the end. That would bear reprinting; it had only won fifth prize in one of the *Sunday World*'s contests.

In the meantime the project of Mr. Clarence Miller, the man next door, came to the fore. Mr. Miller reminded Flora of pictures of Edgar Allan Poe and E. H. Southern as Hamlet, though it was difficult to explain exactly why. He was a trifle lame, and made very picturesque use of a cane in connection with a long and loose overcoat which he quite declined to remove during the evening. The lame foot brought Byron to mind, of course, and the "atmosphere" was not disturbed though his daughter remarked that papa didn't always limp, only he had tummy ache one day and fell down and there wasn't room to stretch his foot so he wrenched it against the coalhod.

Mr. Miller pooh-poohed the extravagant notions of Mr. Sullivan. He was issuing an all poetry magazine with over 100 bona fide subscriptions and it didn't cost him $15 an issue. He'd some type and a press in his cellar, with a stove that burned waste paper and a real good kerosene lamp with a chimney made by Mr. Macbeth. The thing was noticed the country over, he had a scrap book full of notices. As for poetry...he could run two years on what he had now in stock. Good stuff, good as any in the *Dial* or *Broom* or even the *Century*. The very same authors. His only method of payment was 50 copies to each contributor. They were satisfied, they distributed the copies to their friends many of whom sent subscriptions, so he was also satisfied. The circulation helped in the securing of advertisements of "dignity."

When the listeners yodelled "What?" he replied, instantly *Keeping Fit* as an organ of therapy, but not of Hair Dressing."

The Committee on Entertainment had, it appeared, brought to the meeting advance notice of a prize contest to be started the next week by a Boston paper. She most generously begged everyone present to try for it. From general comment Flora learned that the lady herself seldom failed to win, she said, weekly that she had taken $72 and a barrel of flour since September 1. This was a slogan contest, the paper supplied five letters of the alphabet—or rather five duplicates of the same letter. She had a tip the first was to be "G"—G—G—G—G—G—. She was prepared to offer "Good Giggling Girls Grin Gushingly." She thought that was as well as she could do.

"Is that a slogan?" the question was jarred out of Flora in spite of her vow to listen and say nothing. "Why, I thought a slogan was—"

"It is!" snickered Amelia. "But she'll get the 50 dollars. Her limericks are always famous."

* * *

A group that didn't feel interested in jaunty publications talked just as jauntily about literature, and not entirely their own. Indeed the large man with the long chin, who had received a letter from "Bob" Davis containing the startling words: "It (The Bats in the Belfry) is splendidly written, but it exceeds the speed limit....I have been some time coming to a conclusion about this story, but I didn't want to push the matter hastily. Even now I may be wrong...." took the confession in a nonchalant manner that shocked his confreres. When he tried to introduce the Elizabethan Dramatists he was drowned by outcries, "Man, you don't know your luck. An editor owning up that he may be wrong! Ye Gods and little walruses. Send him a weird one not quite as weird."

But the temperamental author dismissed his chances with an airy wave.

"'Tis plain," he remarked, "that this good fellow wants nothing save prattle of lacteal mildness. I shall trouble him no more."

Many authors looked grieved at this waste of opportunity. To sell oneself first; to write briefly and to the point, yet never neglected the slightest excuse for writing; to flatter yet always affect not to flatter; to keep this side of the horizon yet not be a blot on the landscape; these seemed to be common customs. Flo Sullivan spoke further regarding "Pep." It had been declined a good many times, on each new journey it bore the letters which had accompanied its previous refusals. He didn't know if the device was absolutely new or not. At any rate, it finally fetched home the bacon. A humorist repeated the missive which had not been successful in selling a joke.

"This yarn," he had written, "is as funny as I can make it, but it will be funnier yet if you buy it." To which had come the crushing reply, "Sorry, but this is just as funny as it ever will be."

Theobald—the man with the long chin—opined that this retort had been ancient in the 18th century. At this arose a fusillade of comments. Theobald did not really try to live in the 18th century, though he might date letters 1723 and refer to Colonies. Had he actually asked for a typewriter with a long "s"? Did he smoke the pipes of that period—did he read the newspapers of that day? "I hate to say it, but you're nothing better than an anachronism, Theobald," observed Trinkett.

Theobald calmed the tumult with an upraised hand—the too white hand of an invalid. "'Tis plain," he said, "that my character is receiving a Dickensonian or 19th century distortion to the grotesque, which well conceals the quiet manners of a gentleman of Geo. the II's reign. You must know that in my time 'twas thought monstrous vulgar to excite remark in publick assemblies; and that no matter how humorsome a queer old fellow might be he would save his odd humors for the coffee-house, nor seek to drag them into a rout of any sort of mixt genteel company."

There had been a general subsidence into chairs, several turning to rest their chins on back rails and face the speaker, who talked with intense rapidity as if stuffed with words. At cries of "Go on!" he continued: "In 1746-7 my Lord Chesterfield writ to his son that a well bred man...if he is a stranger...observes with care the manners and ways of the people the most esteem'd at that place, and conforms to them with complaisance."

"Thus you perceive that in my natural character as a survivor of the 18th century I am very careful to avoid any assemblage in which I can not sufficiently conform to the prevailing manners to remain modestly unobserved, even if I share but little in the merriment. I am studious never to smack a church warden where the other old gentlemen do not set me an example, nor do I call for any sort of rum, toddy, or family prayers, which I observe to be foreign to the company in whose midst I am situate.

"And as to a parade of my favorite paper, which you rightly guess to be the *Spectator*, why, sirs, and ma'ams, I must protest I am ever mindful of what this same Chesterfield said to his son in 1748 upon a like matter.

"If you happen to have an Elzevir classick in your pocket neither shew it or mention it."

"So when I am in a company, I hold it an honour not be seen or markt at all; or at most to be noticed only in a geographical way, in the pointing out of some one else; as when (for example) Sir Clarence Miller might wish to shew to a stranger the Hon. Florence Sullivan, and in so doing say—"Why, Mr. Sullivan is that fair handsome fellow next the door, over against that stout, ill-dresst old country gentleman with the long chin."

* * *

"Yes," Flora told herself, "these people are all happy. I have never been in a room with so many happy people. They are playing giddy goats and showing off, and everybody understands everybody and there's not an ounce of bitterness in the place. The old ones aren't morose at this moment, and the young don't condescend to them. No one is respectful or calculating and I think all are quite truthful. Nor has next week's lunch money been mortgaged." She could not have made anything like it in Chicago. Probably any city had materials, the difficulty would have been assembling. This had evidently grown. And perhaps all the meetings were not of a like character. This little old world house, half sunk in the hillside, was in itself worthy of being made into a delightful woodcut and used to illustrate the place where a famous coterie met. Only this coterie didn't care a hang about being made into a woodcut—she felt sure of that, in spite of the viciously commercial talk. They were careless and wasteful of wit.

The one lamp made a small circle of pale yellow light, from the open door of the funny little stove gleams of red appropriately touched Mary Queen of Scots about to be beheaded, Louis XIV about to die, Grace Darling about to perform deeds of valor, changing the engravings to pictures in warmest colors. Exquisite comfort lapped the company. It was time to go home.

* * *

Considering a few dozen cows those who lived near the Green crossed a farmyard, fell over or crawled under a set of bars, scrambled down some ledges and yelled goodnights to Gwen Hollister, who held a hand shielded candle exactly as it is held in every third picture of a pretty girl answering a ring on a windy evening. Flora found herself walking with Amelia and a portly middle aged person who answered to the name of "Posie" because of having signed a story of Pirates with the dainty title of PansyBloom. They were trying to animate the bunch into singing. Years before someone had composed a club song, Amelia declared it ought to be sung. Like Pansy-Bloom's name, it was charmingly out of focus.

> This is a tendher theme,
> A tendher, touchin' dream,.
> The Night that Father wore his Boots in Bed—

Having started a chorus Amelia whispered to Flora, "Etta home?"
"Of course. She isn't ever out evenings."
"I mean, going to be home tomorrow?"
"For all I know. Oh, yes; she said was going to clean paint."
"Well—oh, wait a jiff. They've forgot the words—

> He came home with a howl,
> Well, bless my modest soul,
> I cannot find the key-hole, dammitall!
> So many thieves is pokin' round
> The blamed old ranch will leave the pound;
> They gone and stole the key-hole from the wall.

If it's too rowdy, let's try "We All Know Who They Are."
Another genius, it appeared, had also written a club song.It rested upon a legend, to effect that a female member had asked for a male

150

member, describing him as the ugliest man among them all, and hastily naming three male members who it was not. The ditty was composed by the third of this trio, the chorus explaining:

> We all know who these gentlemen are
> We all know who they are—
> She meant three men in particular
> I wasn't the first but the third ha ha
> And we all know they are!

Mr. Posie used his privilege as a rather new member to inquire who they were and Amelia said nobody had ever found out. Then she harked back to Etta. "Ask her if she'll go round to Belinda's Thursday and help with some sewing. Will you, please? You don't mind? You won't forget?"

"Of course—of course," said Flora, surprised that the usually volatile Amelia should be so earnest in delivery a pretty message.

The party now debouched on the edge of the Green, and broke into fragments. Amelia suddenly detached herself from the arm of Mr. Posie, on which she had been hanging, and butted him betwixt the shoulders to the detriment of her chic hat.

"See who that is just crossing under the light? Harry, you can catch him. Arthur."

"Arthur?"

"Arthur Comyns. Shake a leg!"

Mr. Posie obeyed, loping down the street without a word of farewell. Amelia quitted Flora's side, also; she joined Belinda Blodgett and they started over the Green. It was as well, for Flora was beyond speech. Though but the rear view of a black overcoat and a derby hat it was Arthur Comyns that the fog obliterated; had five minutes been cut from the farewells on the hill and they would have met face to face. Flora had been picturing such a meeting; in the pictures the two met as it were on a desert island, or in the very middle of those woods still found in poetical prose by Wm. Butler Yeats. That is, no one else mattered. Possibly he would call at the house and Flora would open the door, eye would meet eye...or maybe Etta would answer the ring, he would be put into the Emerson parlor, Flora, coming down the stairs (Beatrice-stuff) would see his face reflected in the great mirror...or they might all but pass one another, unnoticed, on the Green, quickly he would half turn and cry, "Flora!"

The setting of night, mist, herself quiet among the group of chatterers and singers, would have been sufficiently interesting. Flora felt queerly desolate as she stood watching the bit of luminous mist that represented the last seen of the two men. With absolute lack of reason, she wanted to run after them, crying out to Arthur in her own name. Time's healing power! Time had no healing power. She was where he had left her 10 years back; just as ready to iron her bed with a body made red hot by fever; to hear the striking of each hour, to watch the slow dawn, to be first at the breakfast table yet unable to eat; to walk miles and return home unwearied; to watch patiently for hours at some spot where, quoth hope, there is a possibility of his passing. Yes, and to continue thus until her eyelids were dry for want of sleep, until every shred of her body ached and ached and still would not cease throbbing, until she felt afraid that she was going mad, and wondered if others thought likewise.

Oh, she had lived through these storms; she had supposed she had lived through them forever. Not so. Old sorrows, for years unremembered, rose and demanded attention. The days when her longing for an affectionate letter had been met by a facetious postal card; later days when she would have been glad of a card and nothing came. She had been living in a small hotel, coming in at late afternoon she would invent excuses for not going to the desk for her key, putting off the inevitable moment of disappointment. Or she would invent portents on the way home, counting the people met, telling herself that more men than women meant a letter; when the sign failed telling herself she had cheated because there were always more men than women on the streets at that hour.

* * *

"Too bad to keep you waiting, Miss Hancock, but I simply can't walk. I crawl!" It was the coughing woman, being dragged along by Mr. Miller and his daughter. Flora was obliged to join the cortege, in a few moments they were at the Millers' door, which stood open, disclosing the plump and blond Mrs. Miller, evidently newly awakened from a nap, tho with evidences of crochet work in hand.

"Come right in," she said, "the coffee is a-boiling."

"Oh, no!" gasped Flora. But no one heard her, and she was borne into a warm room where lights blazed and cups and saucers were set out on a small table.

Impatient to get away with her misery Flora drank two cups of black coffee. She said "yes" when the coughing woman asked if she was a disturbing element next door.

"I don't know what you're laughing at," said Flora, and felt bewildered when they laughed the more.

"Are you a sound sleeper?" asked the coughing woman. "Does any excitement—like this evening's—keep you awake? There's a look in your eyes. . ."

"I do not sleep," said poor Flora, feeling as if these overkind folk had driven her into a corner and were pestering her with badgers and things. "I shall not sleep tonight."

The first statement was horribly ungrateful, because Flora had polished off eight hours pretty nicely ever since the night after Aunt Lury's funeral. But she was living 10 years back at that moment, she thought. She had again forgotten what sleep might be.

"Run upstairs, Rachel, please. Go into my room and lift up the lid of the lower part of the desk. Open the right hand drawer and in a small round wooden box you will find a blue glass bottle. There are some pills in it. Very small pills, and eight-sided. Fetch one for Miss Hancock."

The woman had force of mind, else she would not have lived all these years after the time for her death. She made Flora take the pill. The Millers went into the house next door with her, so that she shouldn't feel lonesome. Etta was lying on her good ear, presumably, she made no sound. Flora took off her clothes, screwed half her hair in pins, and suddenly desisted from further preparations for a night of misery.

"Here's some coffee," said Etta. "It was, fustrate at 9 o'clock, but that was an hour ago. I'm going over to Belinda Blodgett's. She sent a message by 'Melia's husband; she telephoned it to Amelia and the man just stopped a minute on the way to his office. Suppose he thought he was doing an awful favor. . ."

* * *

The pill had spared Flora from her sleepless night. She did not give it particular thanks. Interest in living had departed, a deep melancholy lapped her round. She sat by the kitchen window, inertly watching the bad coffee, when the back door opened gently and Amelia entered. Sweet and innocent she looked, and 10 years less than her age. Dear little white stockings—not silk, nothing so sophisticated as silk—made a background for slipper ties of black ribbon, as the girls wore before the Civil War. Her gown was of percale, pink and white, with muslin pockets on which some person who could not embroider had embroidered pink children carrying yellow nosegays, processing into red schoolhouses where stood green schoolma'ams ringing bluebells. Amelia's hair was all in little doughnuts; that lace which hung below her skirt was probably petticoat, but it gave an impression of pantalettes.

"Flora," said Amelia, in a conspirator's tone, "would you be willing to let your house?"

She went on to explain that she didn't mean permanently, or even for weeks or days. Just for that afternoon. Amelia wanted to use it for a farewell. She was bidding goodbye forever to one who loved her too well. They had met, they had been too happy not to be miserable. Parting was necessary. But when one loved—and was about to lose—one couldn't say "so long" just like that.

"In fact," she confided, with a few dainty tears, "the poor fellow doesn't know yet that it is goodbye. When I tell him—and I intend to be firm—he is liable to do anything. So I cannot invite him home. Suppose he fainted and my husband came in. This isn't a Decameron story, where the ladies always had trunks. And I simply couldn't kick him under the davenport like in 'The Lady of Quality.' They're made different nowadays. Lower hung models. At Belinda's there's an ancient aunt and an ancient ma. Unsympathetic as anything. So I told Belinda I was going to ask you. I told her I was sure Flora would understand. You're not even out of the running yourself. Now, you know very well you're not! And you're not shocked because ages and eons ago other people married us. Poor fellow. His wife's a cormorant and his daughters pirates!"

"Have it your own way," said Flora. The little fool was a little fool, yet Flora did sympathize. How dared she quibble—she with an unspeakable mental attitude toward Arthur Comyns; of whose wife she knew nothing. Immediately Amelia was galvanized into quick action. Jamming her own hat on Flora's head and thrusting into Flora's hand a "store" milk bottle she cried, "Buy a quart of the A.&P., then, please, dear, skip round the square till you come to the station. He's waiting. Tell him to come to this door. I'll let him in."

Such is the compelling force of any organized plan that it is sure to be followed. Flora could see no use for the milk bottle, as an instrument of romance or duplicity. As for the rear entrance, it appeared more than likely that the neighbors would be surprised to see any beauteous young man risking his head in the grove of clothes baskets and garden rakes which Etta kept dangling from the porch roof. Still, she bought the milk, and rounded the Green looking for the object of Amelia's affection with curiosity.

At first she thought no one was waiting, then she saw it was no one but the middle-aged Mr. Posie. He took the milk, looking just about half foolish. He told Flora he hoped she would enjoy her walk, and that she must be back by five, as he and "Amy" would look for her then. And he hastened, as a lover should, to the tryst.

Poor, poor Mr. Posie! Of course he saw everything that was desirable in youthful Amelia—what the dickens did Amelia see in him? Not much, evidently, as she was breaking with him forever. Flora approved of that; she was glad to loan her house for that, he did not mind feeling she had been made a catspaw in getting Etta out of the way for that. Mr. Posie possessed physical evidence of prosperity in a "corporation." His waistcoat evidenced personal property in the shape of fountain pens, shape of pencils and eyeglass case and a watch of the thickness indicating inheritance; each telltale shape bulging between horizontal wrinkles. Not only was he old—a bald pate showed as he lifted his hat—he was guilty of neglecting himself. A cormorant and any number of pirates in his home could not prevent a man from asking the Jew on the corner who pressed pants while customers waited. As for a necktie stripped with cotton wool and that leaking...condemnation failed! And his face was the face of a man who wouldn't care if he was condemned. Tallowy, pasty, unhealthy; great pop eyes of pale blue; a smirk of self satisfaction; the shape of his head like the shape of a big pear; heavy jowls, like those of the pig ready for killing.

* * *

155

Mr. Posie was not so bad as all that. Flora was prejudiced, her mind's eye being filled with Arthur Comyns at twenty-five, Byronic profile, flush of early and ardent manhood, luxuriant hair, lithe figure, neat blue serge and black cheviot suits of that era. By and by Amelia would gush to Flora about Mr. Posie as a wonderful lover. His intensely affectionate nature would be present as his most admirable trait. Amelia could not live without affection. She would explain to Flora that she had been started for many years; her father had deserted his family, her mother and sister had made her the Cinderella. Her husband had proved a disappointment. She longed, oh so utterly, to be in love with him—because after all one might just as well be in love with one's husband as with any other man—but he didn't care for "that sort of thing." Those everlasting kisses whenever he went out of an evening or down cellar to look at the heater, were perfunctory, purely perfunctory. He expected her to be grateful when he snared ten pounds of sugar during the war shortage; when he sent home waterglass and a jar for putting down eggs; when he fixed a battery on the garbage box that worked automatically as you lifted the lid to dump swill.

Mr. Posie held her as the one and only love of a drab life; he devoted to her all his thoughts—waking and often dreamed of her—all for love and the world well lost expressed him. If they ever got caught they were going to run away, go to Mexico or Saskatchewan or some such country. He would lose a corking job (his salary was between five and six thousand, the cormorants and the pirates made way with it all) but he was skillful in electricity and could make wages any place at all. Amelia would work, too. Amelia would declare herself more than willing to work in such necessity. Out of her last salary she had bought and nearly paid for that splendid ring he was wearing—and he had given her that orange blossom wedding ring all properly inscribed with initials and dates that meant everything to them.

"My husband? Oh, he doesn't suspect anything. He's too stupid to suspect. I told him I had the old ring made over up-to-date. He thought it a whale of an idea."

As all this was to come, Flora simply wandered out to the graveyard, sat on an iron bench which printed designs of grape bunches and vine leaves in yellow rust on her frock, and mused over the scene being enacted beneath Aunty Lury's third husband's portrait. Would the man grovel on his knees? Flora fancied she saw him groveling on his knees. He didn't seem to have any dignity at all! A man with any sense of proportion would never consent to creep in at a back door, carrying a quart of milk. He was a poor creature, and for that reason the loss of Amelia would be a tragedy of terrible character.

Beyond the tiny burying ground wherein most of the gravestones were of that dismal black slate which tradition says was brought to New England in the seventeenth and eighteenth centuries as ballast, Flora could glimpse a pool as black. She was beyond the Green, on a road which was a continuance of the one bordering the Green; she was out of sight of shops and even houses. A few shabby oak trees grew in the swamp surrounding the pool, the gentle wind rustled their leaves; the sound was of skeletons in silken shrouds walking. Flora told herself so and was rather proud of the telling. She lingered in this unwholesome spot until the shadows were exceedingly long, then turned back and walked rather quickly toward the lights of the first chain store.

The clock on the engine house struck five as she ascended her own doorstep. The house was well lit up—much brighter than Etta allowed, with Aunt Lury's memory in mind. The piano was being played. Etta had told Flora that the piano belonged to the Emersons and she wouldn't be responsible for considering it anything more'n a thing to dust. Mr. Posie opened the door. He was not haggard or wan; his red nose was probably not the result of tears. A bottle that confessed gin, and three glasses, rested on the white onyx and gold gilt table which commonly bore a panel photograph of Aunt Lury in trained reception costume leaning over the back of a chair and dangling in one hand a magnificent feather fan; framed in red plush with a spray of hand painted flowers on the upper n.w. corner. The picture lay face downward on the tete-a-tete.

"Welcome to our city, fair Flora, goddess of flowers!" quoth Mr. Posie, catching her to his bosom and imprinting a loud kiss on her forehead.

"Have a lil' drink," said Amelia. "We've been waiting for you to have a lil' drink. Try it with orange juice. You hardly taste the turpentine at all!"

They swept her into the dining room, where there was tea. Also cinnamon toast and French pastry, neither having the slightest connection with the pantry. In a few moments Etta came in and was greeted cheerily, though not as Flora had been greeted.

"Have some tea, Etta?" cried Amelia. "It's damn good and strong, way you like it."

"Don't care 'f I do." She let herself drop into the chair Mr. Posie solicitously drew out for her. She grimly made an observation about absent cats and playful mice. No one gave a guilty start save Flora, at whose teaparty it was indeed directed. From conversation it then appeared that the man had called on Flora to tell her how long insurance on the house had to run; that Amelia had just dropped in. "Oh, what a tangled web we weave"! . . .We do not. Etta scarcely listened, being anxious to tell of her own day, during which she had absolutely refused to manufacture for Belinda Blodgett a corn colored overblouse, Chinese cheap labor pattern, when she found it was to be beaded with red bugles.

Mr. Posie went gleefully away to catch the 5.53. Amelia asked Etta how long to cook those little cabbages. Sprouts? Yes, sprouts. That man had sent home a couple of quarts, she wasn't familiar with the things. Neither was he, for that matter, but he had dined with his sister and she had them. He's been raving ever since. Darn these in-laws. Well, she must fly.

She did, merely pausing an instant in the hall to whisper Flora, "Upstairs—front room—ahead of Etta."

A $5 bill was hitched, by the largest of safety pins, to a pink lingerie ribbon dependent from the chandelier. The bed spread was wrong side out; the pillows that had stood up now laid flat.

No broken glass. Aunt Lury's fetch was laid.

Flora had compounded a felony.

* * *

Etta gave Flora another jump by asking in Amelia's own words, "Say, do you want to let the house?"

Flora still vaguely supposed she was about to sell the house.

"Oh, well, I didn't mean permanently—or the whole of it. You might's well be making the worth of your board while you do keep it. I'm thinking of that poor old soul Calista. She isn't contented where she is, they put upon her, expect her to stay home evenings with the young ones when it's about all she lives for, going to psychic lectures that don't let out till half past ten. Now she can afford to pay $3 a week for a room, but there ain't no such room these times. Still, it's all that back room upstairs is worth, when you consider no bathroom. What d'ye say?"

Flora was certainly falling under the economic influence of her surroundings. She no longer thought in dollars. She had learned what a meal was. It was not a check for $75, which included "overhead," starch in the busboy's apron, and wave in the golden haired cashier's hair. It was two lamb chops—fifteen cents and very expensive, instead of 35 for one off the shoulder. A slice of bread was a small part of an 11-cent loaf, not "Bread-extra." Coffee might be 48 cents a pound and cream 22 cents a jar with a nickel back on the glass; at that no cup of coffee was worth ten cents.

"Let her come," she told Etta of Calista.

"All right. And you let her put the third quarter in the meter; and buy her own food. She'll be in clover."

* * *

Flora woke up laughing. It was night. From next door came a cough, a flash of light (candle), a drift of incense (asthma powder wastefully burned with the window up), an easier cough, silence. Flora saw herself emulating one of those persistently cheerful old maids in a novel for young people by A.D.S. Whitney or L.A. who "had a bee hive and went up and down it." She let rooms to real nice old folks who couldn't pay much, and got their own frugal meals on gasplates.

Flora wondered if Calista would neutralize the felony?

* * *

Calista appeared to be a pretty liberal minded old party. She couldn't for the life of her see why that sister of hers way down east, who had nothing but an old shack of a house to support herself with, wouldn't take the rich old codger who wanted a home for the rest of his days. What if he did throw out hints that a few wifely attentions must be included. Lord knew Lucretia was old enough so there'd be no town scandal. But Lucrece would rather starve.

Then Calista told a story of her youth, when she was doing factory work down east and helping support Aunt Lury in her first widowhood. A real nice man who traveled for a cheese factory used to take her out buggy riding every time he came to town, but you just bet your gizzard she didn't go without having her time paid for. A dollar and 75 cents a day was what she averaged, and if he wanted her company of an afternoon it stood him 87 1/2 cents. He was free-handed with his cash; he used to say 'twas worth all it cost.

Amelia laughed immoderately when she heard that Calista had moved in; then she came to spend the afternoon, bringing her work. Her husband's B.V.D.s which she was meticulously patching with neatly sewed little patches cut from B.V.D.s beyond patching. Amelia had been reading a novel with Greenwich Village orgies, she thought it would be lovely if she and Flora could go to New York when Flora sold the house.

"You'll have a lot of money, and we might as well go. I'm bound to leave home sometime; Belinda took me to a medium in Boston last summer and she saw me with a suitcase all packed. You believe those things, Calista; you see I've got to make a break."

"I never had the slightest idea of going to New York," said Flora, laughing.

"That's the best of it. We will arrive on the Fall River boat and check our grips while we look for lodgings. And we'll see a sign 'Down the Rabbit Hole' and you'll pop down. A tall woman dressed crazy and smoking in a big jade holder will say 'There's nothing but ice cream on hash today, have some?' and we say we will so she brings us some tea in cups that don't match their saucers. The cups are cracked, too. In the back room a lot of wild students are playing ukeleles and pretty soon one comes out and reads his poetry to us. And we grab each others hands hard and say 'So this is Greenwich Village'."

"Bah," said Etta, "I see you lasting just one night in that locality. Bugs! Washington Square and all around it! I know. I helped a woman close out a private hotel in 8th Street last year. And you had your whole house fumigated last year because Mister fetched home a flea from going hunting."

After Amelia had gone she became a subject of conversation.

"Good looking, but not quite all there," said Calista. "She tried to learn to tat, but hadn't the mind for 't. I don't think she was very well brought up. Her mother's queer as Dick's hat. Had a 6-months baby in alcohol on a shelf in the clothes press for years. Give it a name and said it seemed just as much one of the family as Elmira or Amelia."

"Gabby," said Etta, "That's her failing. She's no more real idea of quitting her comfortable home than I have of flying to the moon. She's have a fit if that man of hers heard what she's been saying round town and took her at her word."

"She really must like him better'n most ten-year wives," said Calista. "All them little scantling patches on where he sets down. Turn my stomach. But then I never even got married."

"Well, I must say she's got a man better 'n most," was Etta's grudging tribute to the one who put up with Amelia's whimseys. "Of course he has the faults of his sex, but for a man he's a real good sort of man."

* * *

They were both wrong. Amelia would fetch up in New York. Flora would stay at home beside the Village Green.

* * *

Flora kept right on living half unpacked, and feeling as if on the move. Etta was bound she would clean the paint, she must do something beside wash dishes for her room; and everybody knew she'd no money to speak of. Flora found it difficult to understand these jocund maiden women with no anchor for old age who lived so gleefully from hand to mouth. Etta, to be sure, was not quite destitute. She'd always been a regular attendant at church, and her denomination maintained a splendid home for its destitute women. You had a room to yourself and your own furniture if you wanted. The matron was a tartar, but maybe she'd be gone before Etta's entry. They wouldn't have anyone under sixty-five. It sounded bleak, even as Etta told it. But there was always a chance of Etta's getting some justice and her share of the family fortune. Her never to be sufficiently cussed brother might see the light, or she might spunk up and have the law on him.

"Bert Trinkett says I got a good case."

"Like enough," commented Calista, "only it's hard as the hubs o' hell to bu'st a mile in Massychusetts."

Poor old Calista had nothing but her earnings at tatting, and a mysterious "state aid" of $50 a quarter as the spinster descendant of a person connected with some war—not Civil. Calista's age was a mystery; Belinda Blodgett declared Calista would never see 75 again, but that seemed impossible considering her good eyesight and her limp foot. Tatting made her fame. She reeled off yards for curtains; she took orders for babies' bonnets; once in a while she created large piece and "sold chances." Belinda Blodgett made the book, she knew everybody and Calista wasted no time, but kept on tatting something else.

Etta considered that Calista spent far too much of her money on improving herself. Three dollars for a course of lectures by the pastor of a Spiritualist Church on Developing Oneself. They didn't do a thing but soak poor old Calista at her church. Spiritualism was a silly doctrine, anyway. Etta herself was not, however, above listening to lectures on mystical subjects. She particularly fancied men who came from far away—Texas or Europe—and who claimed one might attain mental poise and perfect digestion by combining a certain diet with subscribing to and regularly reading a magazine under their editorial guidance.

Where, Flora queried, were the thrifty New Englanders with their feet firmly planted on provision and plans for a century? Amelia continued to talk Greenwich Village. Next it was stale stuff, that the real Villagers were quitting, only gave her keener liking for the idea. Everybody had tried it, found nothing in it, got over it, now she wanted to try it. Millions had looked at the tomb of Napoleon, but when Pershing got there he said a mouthful. Or was it the Unknown Soldier? Nobody seemed inclined to stay put. Belinda Blodgett was considering going to California for the winter. Belle Tupper had actually gone to China. Not China, Maine, but China, China. She hadn't intended going to that part of the world especially, but a chance to have her fare paid by calling herself nurse to a Naval Officer's child was too good to be missed. Etta pitied the child!

These were descendants of the people who stayed back when their ancestors pushed to the Gold Coast in '49, when the middle west was opened up in the '60s and '70s, when Oklahoma land was won in a race in '89, when gold was discovered in the Klondike in '98. Two hundred and some odd years back their people had embarked in cockle shells and started Plymouth and Boston. After a few years these congeries could not hold them all. They trod the Bay Path to wildernesses that later became Springfield, Northampton, Deerfield. Kidnappings and scalpings could not protect the Indians in their pet tobacco fields.

There were no more Puritans. Flora had expected to find a few, but old Calista's conversation convinced her of their final passing. The vaunted individualism of church government seemed to have grown into absolute individualism. Each woman—probably each man—did what seemed right in her or his own eyes. It was apparently unnecessary to do anything or be anything for the sake of public opinion. Or even have anything. Poor old Calista had nothing, yet she seemed to be of consequence in town. There was the drinking fountain for dogs and human beings, at the lower end of the Green. She had decided for it, and had taken round the subscription paper. No one had turned her down. The calling list of Flora's establishment grew immediately after Calista's installation. Not all who came were after tatting, either.

* * *

It was awful, though, to think that year after year passed, and Calista was in no way advanced toward fame or independence. She just worked to get strength to work some more. Oh, hum! Flora had done better than that in the city. She had saved a thousand dollars. As a result she had a thousand dollars. She had no recollections (save for a few bitter ones mixed with Arthur Comyns) of excursions, lake trips, theatre parties, gallery seats at Grand Opera, table d'hote dinners with "the bunch," dances, Dutch treats. The girls with such memories were actually, at each year-end, just about even with old Calista. They had earned "good" money, had spent it in keeping themselves fit and well dressed, so as to keep right on earning "good" money. They had no more feet on firmness than Etta or Calista. Somebody might marry them, though it was not very likely. Their Great Uncle in Australia that they never had might ignore nearer and dearer claims, and give them fortunes. Nothing was assured. Even school teachers were defrauded of their pensions; were forced to resign a year or so before that reward for long service became due.

* * *

Flora rather plumed herself on being safe; preened and plumed herself as if fancying she had so arranged it. Suppose she sold the house for $10,000; and returned to a job in some city. At ordinary investment her cash would increase at the rate of a thousand every two years. In ten years it would double; she might retire, she might build a bungalow—she supposed they would still be building bungalows—she might even keep on working. Women often worked until sixty.

The objections to such day dreams was their inevitable end in a burst of self pity for the lonely and unfriended Flora of sixty, fifty or even forty. She would never love any but the lost Arthur Comyns; she had never been able to make a woman friend. In fact, she had never met with a woman whom she wanted for a friend. Women were like the flippant felon Amelia, willing to talk but never to listen. You bought their companionship by pretending an interest in their affairs which you could not possibly feel.

"Suppose," thought Flora, "I were insane enough to suddenly rave to that little fool about my heart aches and my sentimental sorrows: would she sympathize or would she, more likely, snicker? Suppose, just as a matter of supposition, that Arthur Comyns did meet me, and did remember the past, and wasn't happy with his wife—and once I did hear he was not—and he wanted to talk just once and nevermore, would Amelia invite us to her home?—why, she's never so much as asked me to come and see her. Beyond understanding it's somewhere beyond the Green at the opposite end from the Trinkett Block, I don't even know where she lives."

From time to time, in all her ten sorrowful years, Flora had of course given thought to Arthur Comyns' wife. When news had drifted west of his marriage it had been some time accomplished. She had heard that he selected his wife in his native town and that in writing about her existence he humorously referred to her as "The Squaw." He added that she was not literary; she liked stories in the magazines, especially those by Fannie Hurst, and privately believed they were not made up, but just things the author saw happening and wrote down. Out of nothing Flora had evolved a large woman, very blonde, with much color and high cheek bones. She was not good looking, though her description would sound like that of a goodlooking woman. Her blue eyes were hard, she lacked fascination in manner, lacked grace of movement.

Once Flora had dreamed of their home. She seemed to have driven there in a hearse. A thunder storm was going on, Flora and her hearse took refuge under an open shed. The sheets of rain came between her and a large damp yard, quite like nature. In the far corner of the yard was a well and sweep, like the pictures on that piece of music, "The Old Oaken Bucket With Variations." Arthur Comyns came into the shed, lithe, handsome as of yore. Sternly he informed Flora that she must go, and at once.

"But I want to see your wife," implored Flora—in the dream.

He was unmoved and unmovable. The thing could not be.

"Cannot you," asked Flora, "give her a pail and tell her to draw water from the well?"

No-no! He was most unreasonable, he would not enter into the plot. And then he uttered the memorable words, "And if I could—of what use to see a fat woman cross a yard?"

Upon this evidence Flora believed Mrs. Arthur Comyns was fat. A fat, middle-aged woman, who neglected his home and was heedless of his comfort; a stout, ungainly, elderly woman, by no means his equal intellectually; an awkward old woman, neither a good housekeeper or good company—what more satisfactory supplanter could a discarded sweetheart discover in the place should be hers? When he discovered, as some time he must, that Flora was in the same town...

"That's a cute notice of you, Flory, in the 'It Is Said' column of the *Chronotype*, bawled Calista up the back stairs on Saturday at dusk. "Arthur Comyns wrote it, I presume, but I guess Bert Trinkett gave him the info'mation."

It Is Said—

That—Ed Nichols made a nice profit on his last year's hay in Taunton.

That—Cora Wilworth received a genuine autograph from Pres. Harding shortly before his death.

That—Miss Flora Hancock is still at home in the old Emerson place on Elm Street.

That—There is no truth in the rumor that this landmark is to be put on sale.

"He knows I am here, then—he knows, he knows!"

Flora fled to her room and a night of suffering. No alleviation by pill.

* * *

Yet was there not some slight alleviation due to circumstance, or time, or disgust that the Hancock place should be so mislabeled. What if Aunt Lury had lived in it forty years? A Hancock built the house and a Hancock was now living therein. Flora was not unacquainted with that Eastern trick of calling a place after a former owner, so that the DeCourceys lived and died in the old Smith place without hitching their own name to it, or even something neutral as The Pines or Meadowbrook. But she had believed that Aunt Lury lived forty years in the Hancock house, quite in accord with the fashion. Whatever the extent to which tears soaked her pillow that night, Flora rose next morning with a stern determination to remain long enough beside the Village Green to make Great Aunt Lury look like what she had been after she married an Emerson—a squatter. In other words, the fire of anger dried up the tears of sentiment—she thought of that herself.

Process of the performance seemed indefinite, Flora thought dismantling the Emerson parlor might help. She consulted Etta.

"If you want a suggestion," said Etta, "I'd put a notice written out in that Gift Shop window. Let the room. Some folks'll pay all out of proportion for most anything nowadays, and there's a good furnace even if there ain't no bathroom. Also coal, because she bought it early in the summer, having had to piece out all last winter with soft and coak and Welsh and pea that leaked through the grate before it even came through."

"Shucks," said Calista, "Flory don't need to advertise. I know a feller wants a room to teach music in. Teaches those Miller kids now. Ask him $2 a day, because them learners make a devilish noise, but Etta's got one deaf ear, and I go out considerable. So will you, Flory, now you got chummy with 'Melia. Her folks always was great for running street yarn."

* * *

Flora amazed herself at this meek descent into a landlady. She guessed likely it was because filling the house meant no more compounding of felonies. But Amelia suggested no more. Mr. Posie was eliminated from conversation. Conversation was now principally concerned with a party which Belinda Blodgett intended to give. Flora was urged, by Amelia, to come on over and help get it up. Getting it up was considered more fun than the party.

"Why should I go to Mrs. Blodgett's?" asked Flora sharply, in her character of the reigning Hancock. "She hasn't troubled herself to come to me."

166

"Well—don't be so techy. She hardly ever calls on anybody, unless they're terribly poor, and going to a hospital for an operation. She's awfully good then. Only last week she got wind of a girl who had a ulcer on her tummy and had to lie flat on her back with nobody only a young man to feed her, and he didn't know any better than to pour soup out of a pitcher and half choke the critter. Belinda got her a glass feeding tube and a doctor and went all round town collecting flannel nighties and sat up all night making them over into bloomers so she shouldn't freeze from cold legs in the taxi. Getting along O.K. now, so Linda's concentrating on the party."

This story of philanthropic action had its effect. Flora descended her high horse and consented to visit the woman who was merely the daughter of the man adopted by Great Aunt Lury's folks.

They found her in bed, or rather on bed. She had her head wrapped in a Turkish towel, having, she explained, contracted neuralgia while out collecting nightgowns. The heating apparatus of her house seemed to be working well, as the temperature was nearer ninety degrees than eighty, but Belinda dashed down cellar twice an hour to stoke the heater, each time complaining of her husband's inability. Her bed was covered with a breakfast tray, pen, ink, scissors, fancy paper, a cat; aids to manufacture of "unique" invitations; menus with "the personal touch"; epigrammatic insults to be baked in cakes. Such preparations seemed childish to Flora, like the Queen she was not amused. Belinda and Amelia—who achieved Cumé-hood in this congenial atmosphere— rolled all over the furniture in spasms of hilarity. They had all sorts of catchwords based on past performances. These, too, were to be laughed at. Flora was politely made acquainted with these. For instance, "they don't like beans," had been perpetrated by Aimé on an occasion when a "very special" friend of hers had hinted he didn't. "Eleven others did, but still 'they' don't like beans," moaned Belinda. Aimé snickered her hair down, and while readjusting her net observed that it had been a New York man who didn't like them, and that they would never see the creature again. And "Thank God for that." Flora judged that he had preceded Mr. Posie into the discord. Mr. Posie rather haunted Flora, now he was so finally lost. She had a picture of him, lolling in one of Aunt Lury's few lollable chairs, beaming fatuously at his lithe love, who perched on the chair arm, her adorable cheek nestling against his balding head. It had been a pretty sight—something like Little Nell and her Grandfather.

The guests were finally decided on and written in two columns on a large sheet of paper:

Herbert Trinkett	Flora Hancock
H. Theobald, Jr.	Elsa Dennis
Florence Sullivan	Aimé
Little 'Linda	

Elsa Dennis, it appeared, was the coughing woman from the upstairs of the Millers! She was nice at a party, because she never slept nights anyway, and so wasn't one of those killjoys who expected to go to bed when it got to be 3 or 4 a.m. Of course she coughed if you got her to laughing, but that wasn't any more annoying than other people's habits. There was Flo Sullivan, he would sing. These were to be the house guests; they were to stay over the week end; on Hallowe'en others would be asked...

"I've thought of the funniest stunt," exclaimed Belinda, suddenly putting her feet on the floor and beginning to embroider an owl on a bit of unbleached cotton cloth which later turned out to be one of a set of souvenir napkins. "I'm going to let Henry come to this party. In fact, he's already invited. And I've told him to bring any friends of his that he wants. Isn't that clever of me? You see I'll find out just who he's with when he don't come home."

"He won't bring her, whoever she is," said Aimé, "no man would be that easy."

The plan continued to develop into real devilishness. Everybody was to have a character-name, out of Mother Goose or a weird book; these were to be given by Belinda and mentioned in the invitations. They, right on top, this character person would assume to be somebody else; would be rigged up like this other person. When Flora blinked Belinda instantly informed her that she was Eleanor Glynn and that it was time for tea.

While Belinda was in the kitchen clattering dishes Aimé and Flora drifted into the parlor; the walls of which were covered with pictures of most varied character—agonizing Christs with crowns of thorns, madonnas with children, roads to Calvary, in juxtaposition to a large blue-green Annabel Lee, a vivid scarlet and orange Sands of the Desert, leggy fencing and dancing girls. On a fine old fashioned etagere was a collection of objects sometimes art and sometimes junk; in book cases *Molly Brown* by The Duchess and *Ishmael or Out of the Depths* by Mrs. E. D. E. N. Southworth jostled a great deal of W. H. Hudson.

The dining room was a pleasanter apartment; there was a built-in china closet packed with beautiful china; and a wide window filled with fairly successful house plants which are something quite different from potted plants and nowadays hardly ever found. On the sideboard was a great deal of tarnished silver, and whoever did the room seemed to have had no idea of the extent to which chair rounds accumulated dust. The tea table, as set out, was charming. The china bore cherry blossoms, black on white, with green centres; the doilies had been embroidered with the same design; the cosey matched; and Flora understood why Belinda Blodgett had set up Mrs. in a TeaRoom.

In the warm corner by the radiator, sat two old ladies, one square, the other oblong. Belinda's mother and aunt, nearing fourscore and ten. They had put their widowhoods together and made society. Interfering not at all with the tea party they talked—

"Sister, Belinda says when she gets the next pair of shoes she's going to be measured and have them custom made."

"Oh, like the inmates of the penitentiary in Thomaston!"

The aunt had a caustic tongue. The conversation of the pair was principally located in Maine, their native state.

When Flora discovered that each room in the Blodgett house was of the same size, and absolutely four square with no jogs or extra angles, she thought she understood why Belinda felt the necessity of being bizarre.

The tea was wonderfully stimulating to the woman who had made it. She decided that Herbert Trinkett should be Frankenstein, and that the first hour of the party should pass in the parlor, absolutely dark. Also that people would be given paper bags for their hands, so if they shook 'em there's be no guessing of identities. After Aimé had been reminded of a husband due on the 6:28 and had dashed away at 6:15 to become Amelia, Belinda confessed an additional bright thought.

"Did you notice Aimé speaking about a New York man? Calling him creature?"

Flora admitted it.

"Well, I think I'll invite him. To the week end part, of course."

There was nothing for Flora to say. Amelia—Aimé was Belinda's friend—if she wanted to ruin the party for her best friend—

"I really think he is the one person meant by fate to settle Aimé" Belinda spoke as if the pretty thing was a pot of coffee. "She's been all roiled up ever since she was fourteen. Some darn fool gave her the suggestion that a man was necessary to her peace of mind and she's been running round with her tongue out ever since. Four years ago she saw this man—his name is Jim Jeffreys Hazelwonda, he's a lawyer, deals in real estate, also coal and wood—and thought she had to chase him. He fell strong, but there was nothing to it because they were both married and his wife had just presented him with a case of cholic called Junior. So he proposed a purely platonic affair, no visits, no letters, no not'ing. Also he gave her a new suggestion, that she wasn't nearly so strong for the passion stuff as she had thought she was. It worked, too. I never knew Aimé to have a year so contented as the one which followed."

"What ended it?" Flora wanted to know, breathlessly. She was always fitting experience of other women to her own; she not only imagined herself being true to unrewarded memory—she had been true.

"Oh, he spoiled things, of course. He could talk platonics to her, but when he was tempted he fell. One of his clients, a beautiful goose married to an old man and getting divorced because she couldn't think of anything else to do, decided she wanted Jim to help her spend her alimony. Well, when Aimé discovered that he had been leading a life of vice in limousines while she was sending him sweet messages by the moon she was madder'n Matthew Mears, who wound his clock faithful every day for forty years and then discovered 'twas an eight-day one."

"What makes you think," asked Flora, still breathless, "that he will come—or be welcome when he comes, or—"

"I've a hunch. Besides, I heard indirectly that the limousine lady, is extravagant, treats her alimony like pocket money—I say, that's clever, wait till I got it down—and springs amazing 'phone and gas bills on Jim, considering them trifles. He won't like that, he wants what he can get for himself. As for Aimé she's at loose ends now. In fact, I really think I'll have them get married. His wife's already divorced him, and she's been longing to leave home for years. You may have heard what her husband is? Tells her to take a few dollars out of the household allowance and buy herself a raincoat for his Christmas present."

"I've heard it before," murmured Flora.

Belinda did not listen. She was saying, "I will do it. I will! I've always wanted a place to visit in New York."

* * *

For a time they lived upon letters. Even Flora, affecting indifference, came to live upon them. Their contents were communicated to her by other letters, by verses, by rebuses. Belinda's rebuses were famous as far as the other end of the Village Green and round the corner. Scorning the common form she used one of her own, in which each letter had a symbol, and a picture of a bird, of such a human eye as Barty the Martian drew on Sunday mornings, and of the 'em of a garment, spelled the name of the hoped-for guest.

"Tell the truth, Miss Flora Hancock. Ain't we got fun?" Belinda wanted to know. Flora supposed they had, but wasn't it childish?

"Of course it's childish. Why should the High Schoolers have all the good times?"

After all, why should the High Schoolers have all the good times? Or the Kindergartners!

The first responses of the New York creature were intensely unsympathetic, tho'; Belinda had employed the wisdom of the serpent, and sent him a regular blurb, torn out on the typewriter and sent with all its transgressions intact, thus looking like a product purely of the heart. Jim was tied up for all weekends and hers truly J. Jeffreys Hazelewonda dictated but not read Mr. Hazelwonda left the office without signing this, which was done in blue pencil by a presumed stenographer. Presently the great man became more intimate with his rural acquaintances, and there were no more letters because, as was carefully explained to Flora, when Jim liked you he telegraphed and when he loved you he 'phoned. His wires were cryptic beyond any of Belinda's own. One reading "Hair cut n' everything" was repeated, at her request, twice, before she could credit such nonsense; and "Rain prevents wearing flannel trousers" from Providence was welcome only as showing he'd gotten that far.

Flora began to anticipate ructions when the rival jesters met. Aimé was supposed to be dead to this preparation for her future. Perhaps that was why Flora had been temporarily elevated to Mrs. Blodgett's right hand.

"Very intimate," said Etta, carrying messages with a conscientiousness that accented their idiocy. Yes, Flora was intimate, without caring to be. Belinda Blodgett's nervous energy, expended on trifles, was tiring. Her funniest cracks were continually split asunder by veritable hard blows. Belinda's husband was, naturally, chief sufferer. Flora got used to meeting the man, who stole into his own house with the air of a schoolboy guilty of playing hookey from school, and by no means sure of any supper. He was lank, with a death's head face, but splendidly dressed because haberdashery by wholesale was his line. His stories were supposed to be drummers' samples and Belinda never allowed him to finish one in the presence of her guests. Nevertheless she had a good stock of yarns Rabelaisian in her own poke.

Henry Blodgett's chief offense, as reported, was tight waddedness. Belinda was supposed to have existed for years without so much as carfare. When she had demanded a new dress he had told her of his mother, who for fifty years was satisfied with a cotton poplin at twelve and one half cents the yard once a year. It was related of him that nights as he entered the house he lowered each gas jet, and then, consulting the grocery slips, looked in the pots on the stove to assure himself that what he would have to pay for was actually being cooked. Flora did not see him do these things. She did, however, hear him say "they managed to run up considerable of an ice bill while I was down East on my vacation." She learned, also, that Belinda never accompanied him on his vacation trips, that he took in Big Games, that he played poker until early morning several nights a week, and that he knew the cast of every musical show in Boston while Belinda knew none.

As for the house, he hadn't so much as a dollar in it. Belinda told him so often, in presence of Flora, for she was soon so intimate that they didn't notice her scarcely at all when they felt quarrelsome.

They had lived together over thirty years, occupied the same sleeping room, and had a son who exhibited such signs of atavism as attending a Baptist Sunday School and marrying a good twelve months before becoming a father.

(The baby died. Flora got another side of Belinda when she discovered a shelf of Fairy Tales, Three Bears and Mother Gooses, inscribed "To My Grandchild, N. or M.")

Belinda was not jealous in friendship, she positively forced her friends to be friends of one another, bringing them together in a violence of concussion that made any other form of melding unnecessary. Flora having shown lack of understanding for Mrs. Dennis, was thrown at the head of Mrs. Dennis continually. Belinda sent rebuses for the two to guess; she sent notes in alternate lines, so they had to meet to read them. Flora found Mrs. Dennis not in the least like an automaton distinguished only by a cough. Her rooms in the upstairs of the Miller house were filled with beautiful old china, miscellaneous books and the kind of furniture that illustrates stories. Mrs. Dennis was generally found at table, in the sunshine of her backroom; she rose at noon, after one dainty meal blended into another. Various Millers drifted in and out, between whiles Mrs. Dennis read *Middlemarch* propped by *Main Street*—sometimes it was the other way round. Mrs. Dennis was alone in the world, she had not a cousin within a hundred miles. Her husband was long gone, whether or not he had been a good one was for thirty-five years no matter. She never railed at any memories of him, or at fate for depriving her of his love and protection. She railed only at radio and movies, sometimes she thought there might be something done with those.

* * *

Jim Jeffreys Hazelwonda arrived on the evening of October 30th. Rain preventing wearing flannel trousers he wore a soiled and badly creased suit of black and white check. It was unbecoming because he was stout. His linen was beyond criticism, however, and his necktie smart. He bathed twice daily and put on everything spanky clean except suit and shoes. Belinda learned this to her disgust; he was forever imploring her to light the tank, or sozzle out a pair of socks dearest darling little Linda please. He shaved all over the house and shook powder wherever powder could be shaken, which was everywhere but the dooryard.

He brought joyousness to the house, he was literally the life of the party. Etta might say always, after a chance inspection on the Green, "that man with the dreadful laugh"—the laugh was mirth compelling, boyish, spontaneous. Flora liked him, albeit she could not understand why Aimé so instantly loved him. He seemed to her untrustworthy.

Flora had lived to a considerable age, and had suffered, but she had still to learn the undeniable fact, that women do not love men for their virtues; any more than men love the women of whom other women-folk say "she has the makings of such a good housekeeper."

Aimé's attentions to her husband prevented her being present on the 30th. The husband—whose directions for a Christmas gift were here repeated—was starting next morning on a hunting trip. Then...

Jim joined forces with Henry Blodgett. The two made toast for the ladies. They made it on a gas stove which boasted a pilot light. Jim affected never to have seen a pilot light—he was the funniest creature! Henry Blodgett's death's head was rent asunder by grins. The rest of the party howled. Belinda went to bed beaming. It was all coming out fine.

Next morning Flora, waiting the call to breakfast, had her room invaded by Aimé. Exquisitely dressed, blushing, palpitating, she twiddled from foot to foot—poor Mr. Posie quite forgot. In time word came that the conquering hero was bathed and dressed. She went forth, and in ten minutes Belinda brought the glad news that everything was fixed up. Indeed, she had been obliged to invade their privacy and remind them that it were unwise to be caught holding hands by the two ancient Sisters.

"They're in the state now," said Linda gloomily, "that they just want to show the world. Mother and Aunt, of course, haven't the slightest idea that she isn't a most respectable married woman. Well, my work is cut out for me!"

* * *

The party was pretty wild. It would call Herbert Trinkett Frank N. Stein and ask Mr. Stein how was the trade in wooden pants. Henry Blodgett's contributions were a neutral man and two women. One resembled Mme. nothing so much as Mme. Patience out of a 10-20-30 "Camille" company of the old days, the other was smart but not pretty. They produced flasks, they evidently considered the affair more in the line of rough stuff than it had set out to be. They added unconsciously to hilarity, however, by insisting that Aimé was Mrs. Blodgett, because she brought in the pies. They also fell afoul of Flora, believing her the wife of Herbert Trinkett, and attempting to rouse her jealousy.

The entire party remained at the table from ten to four; it was a most beautiful table, gay with pumpkin colored candles and every sort of black cat lantern and a weird figure procurable in the five and tens of Boston. After the three unknowns had gone in a taxi of Henry Blodgett's ordering, and Henry himself had subsided into bed, the die-hards went into the damp air of early morning, strolled laughing the length of the Green, and disturbed the deliverers of milk at the One Armed Lunch. There was plenty of coffee and cream in the Blodgett kitchen, but this eating with the hoi polloi was so much more skittish. Bernard Sullivan reminded himself of his lowly beginnings, and asked for 100 on a plate; Herbert Trinkett laboriously tried to wait on the females with paper napkins and glasses of water; Theobald took this as he took all life, as an interruption to philosophic discourse and greeted with a pale smile. Jim hovered over Aimé as a big fat hen hovers over a darling little white chicken just after pecking a couple of black ones to death. He performed miracles, investing with romance the covering of a plate of hash with tomato catsup.

To Flora's relief, the party was not all racket. She had pleasant talks with Mrs. Dennis, with Trinkett and Theobald. One evening was spent in playing with Planchette; another, which ended only at dawn, in discussion of Marriage. Belinda Blodgett uttered a great deal of revolutionary stuff, dated at about the time of Pinero's peak. No mumbled words of a minister could truly unite any couple, she observed, and for a couple not truly united to live together was nothing but prostitution.

A few moments later Henry, who never took part in anything "highbrow," yelled for his wife to close the session and come to bed. Meekly, she obeyed.

* * *

Time passed. An entire week passed. Belinda Blodgett's cleaning woman, the one who had wept so violently at Aunt Lury's funeral, had wiped much of the powder from the bathroom floor. Jim's toothbrush had been discovered where he left it, in the parlor, and forwarded to him by parcel post. Flora also had the cleaning woman, and prepared the Emerson parlor for the music teacher. The carpet was taken up, he painted and waxed the floor with his own hands. It was a barbarous old floor made of wide boards and cracks in the days when carpets were nailed to baseboards and lifted once or twice in a lifetime. He filled the cracks with soaked paper; the result was good. A baby grand entered through a window, in full sight of a mob of three-two children under schoolage and a grocer's boy trying not to hurry in delivering two cans of peas and a yeastcake. Flora reflected on the thousands who would stand open mouthed when a safe was engineered to a tenth floor. And she had supposed idle curiosity to be a small town vice!

Then came telegrams. Everyone had a telegram, even Mrs. Dennis, even Flora. Signed "Jim," asking them to meet "first train Sunday." Now the first and only Sunday train on this branch was the paper train—4 a.m.

"Gosh," said Belinda, who had been religiously brought up and knew much Bible as well as the naughty story about deacons being equipped with can openers the year tin underclothing was introduced for female wear at any meetings, "whatever I asked for, I've evoked a whirlwind."

Funk-stricken she induced Aimé to go away. As Aimé had no place to go Belinda provided a cousin of her own for the pursued heroine to visit down East. Thus Aimé's cruel husband was kept serene while the plotters wished him that way, and Belinda was saved one week's extra housecleaning. Jim, provided with unobstructed chances, did pursue the heroine, and judging from the souvenir post cards sent all and sundry from the Congress Square Hotel in Portland they had gone there to get everything fixed up and obtain, almost free, means of announcing the good news.

"Your booful bumptious beehive grows," said Aimé, dropping in on Flora from the 3.20, before she had approached her own home. "Jim says the quicker I cut loose the better. So you will have to let me have a room."

"I'd much rather not," murmured Flora, frightened at the rapidity with which a fantastic dream was realizing itself. She wanted to tell Aimé to reflect, to stop and think, to take advice. All she dared was a faint, "If you were just leaving I'd be glad to help—"

"Of course," interrupted Aimé, "any right-minded woman would be. I've given him ten years, and if I was asked to go to a really first class dance tonight I wouldn't have a darn thing to wear. Why, any Judge in his senses—Belinda knows a girl went to China with her husband and came back after five years wearing the same dress she went out in. There was lots more evidence, but the Judge said that was enough. To be sure, he was a Reno judge, but. . ."

"I mean if you were going to be independent—to live your own life for a while," Flora blundered on. "It's so dreadfully sudden. How can you be quite sure Mr. Hazelwonda is the right one?"

"Oh, he's carried me off my feet. I admit it. I didn't think any man could, but he has. Everybody else seems like a shadow... You haven't any 'phone?"

Flora shook her head. "Or bath room," she added.

"Bath room be darned. If I want to wash, I can go over to 'Linda's. But you must have a 'phone. Jim will call me at least once every day."

"From New York? But that will cost..."

"Cost be darned, too. Thank heaven I shan't be bothered much longer with such things. Will $3.50 be enough for a room, Flora? I don't much care which room."

"I cannot have you," said Flora, at last asserting herself. "Think. I've Etta and Calista and the music man now. Why don't you go to Mrs. Blodgett's?"

"Oh," said Aimé, "I get you. This isn't any afternoon interview. Jim and I are going to get married. Belinda thinks getting married is old fashioned, but Jim says that as he's a lawyer he has to respect the law. So we will be actually hitch-em-up, like our pas and mas. Presbyterian minister 'n everything. A regular honeymoon, Niagara Falls and so on, the bridal chamber in some hotel, and if any boob friend spies out our hiding place and send us a parcel with a nursing bottle in it I shall die of embarrassment. If he should call at your house for me he'll just wait downstairs and gas Etta and Calista. Get me, Flora?"

Flora supposed she did.

"All I have to do is just what Jim has laid out for me. First, I tell my husband I'm going to leave him. Because he neglects me, and I've had about enough. He'll think I'm going to 'Linda's and he'll plan to go right over and bawl 'Linda out for influencing me. But he won't be able to bawl you out, not knowing you from a hole in the ground. After I'm safely out with my personal property I shall send him word I want a divorce. Jim says I can get one in this state for cruel and abusive treatment if I and 'Linda both swear he threw a knotted towel at me. Then I'm going to take a course in stenography. Jim says it will come in useful. After which we shall get married. I'm going to have a diamond set in platinum worth about two automobiles. . ."

Did things happen like that? Flora liked Aimé and thoroughly disliked what she knew of Aimé's careless husband. Yet she almost hoped everything would not be so cut and dried. Could a man, even a careless one, let his wife be lost so easily?

No, he could not. Yet Aimé rated her home worth so low as to be surprised. She told him of a Monday morning, while they were breakfasting. He had been sarcastic about the burnt bacon, too; just as he had been on all the bacon mornings for ten years. He implored her to think it over. During the forenoon he sent her a dozen carnations and some green stuff—the sort they throw in—reminding her that their wedding anniversary was somewhere about this time.

("Two weeks ago and he was dead from the feet up," commented his wife.) On top of this came another sentimental appeal. One single ticket—but orchestra—for "The Love Nest." Wouldn't she go and let that picture of home convince her of cruelty in breaking up theirs?

The ticket was for the Wednesday matinee, whereat Aimé and Belinda waxed very merry. Wednesday matinees were cut price.

One Tuesday, however, complications developed. The about to be deserted husband went to his office a crushed and broken being, met his brother-in-law, to whom he confided his domestic miseries; then rushed home, grabbed what Aimé described as the old family pistol from its hiding place, and boarded the 8:34 for Boston. He was going to kill a co-respondent.

"What co-respondent?" 'Linda wanted to know. She and Aimé had met at Flora's because they thought it best not to be seen at each other's houses. Jim's counsel.

"Well," Aimé confessed, opening her pretty mouth exceedingly wide and mouthing her words, "if you must know, his darn old brother-in-law snooped up on me when I was doing a night trick at the switchboard the time of the telephone strike. You recollect, 'Linda, I worked six weeks last summer and got a few new clothes out of it. Well, 'twas dull after midnight, you-know-who, and I got to fooling

... And he said—his brother-in-law said he'd hold his jaw because he wanted his wife's brother to keep on being happy, but that if he ever got wind of my planning to leave he'd squeal. So this morning he did so, and my ex-husband's gone after revenge.

"Oh," said Linda, as one who saw light. "He thinks you're quitting for..."

"Posie. Yes!"

"But will he shoot Mr. Posie?" gasped Flora, visualizing that corporationed figure weltering in blood on the smooth floor of some office building, while pale faced men disarmed an excited husband and a brother-in-law stood in the background reflecting as he bit his nails that this was entirely his work.

"Hurry!" cried Aimé. "I hope not. Jim wants no publicity."

She was quite nervous for the rest of the morning. So was Flora, who had never been so near real first-page people.

* * *

He did not shoot Mr. Posie. According to Aimé he tried to make her believe he would have done so had the revolver been loaded for action, but she and 'Linda were skeptical. Because he had met with the brother-in-law at the door of the telephone exchange, where Aimé's and Posie's romance had started in the midnight watches, and where Posie and the brother-in-law were both superintendents of something.

"So they planned a nice sort of thing," said Aimé. "They are going to get Posie fired. And I guess they can do it. They are Masons, and the High Muckymuck is a Mason, and Posie is a Mason. That was why I wanted him in the first place, you remember my telling you, 'Linda, that that was why I wanted him in the first place? I never believed that respect for a Bro. Mason's wife had anything in it. They expect to get him out of the Lodge, too!"

"Then there is more than a little in it," grumbled 'Linda. "How the dickens do you know all this, Aimé?"

"Oh, Posie told me. He got me on the 'phone and whined till central cut us off. He wants me to confess that he isn't the man."

"By chowder!" exclaimed 'Linda, "if you do—"

"Don't worry. I shan't. I might," murmured the heroine, with the prettiest imaginable blush, "only all he cares about is keeping his darn old job. That was the whole of his argument—that I'd fix things so he'd not lose his job. Well, I guess that's all any of 'em really care about. Their jobs!"

She burst into tears and sobbed violently the length of time needed for fine sobs. This, so far as Flora knew, was all the emotion roused by the affair. She had no reason to believe anything was hidden from her. 'Linda and Aimé continued to find her house both neutral and handy as a meeting place. As the interviews were held in Flora's bedroom, on account of Etta pervading the first floor, Flora felt obliged to dress that chamber with marsailles quilts, cretonne cushions and drawnwork bureau scarves, also to finally unpack her toilet requisites, polish the silver ones, wash the ivory and generally get settled. Suit case and trunk went up attic, so that Belinda would have no excuse for lounging on the bed, there now being room for an extra chair.

"Thick as three-in-a-bed," Calista was overheard saying to Etta. After this 'Linda made a point of running in on Calista, often with a bag of fruit, or a pie of Mrs. x; Aimé let nothing interrupt her stream of confidences.

Devastation being nature's easiest performance, Amelia's home and Amelia's marital union, of ten years' growth and standing, were ruined in a week. Three days sufficed to jar Mr. Posie from a line of promotion in which he had been mounting steadily all an adult lifetime. Once only did Aimé soften toward her former leman, when for a moment he ceased regretting his lost job and mentioned regret at losing his lost Aimé. Luckily, and by a most amazing coincidence (just one of those things nobody would believe in a book) that very evening provided Belinda Blodgett with a means of stopping any such weakening.

Belinda and Flora took the seven o'clock train in for dinner at the Athens Café. It was a sudden affair; Belinda just had to have some artichokes and Flora was her guest. As they hurried across Concord street in a pouring rain Belinda suddenly squeezed Flora's umbrella arm and ejaculated, "Quick—who's the man getting into the auto?"

A stout man, accompanied by a woman, was emerging from the Haymarket, was following the woman into a car. The woman at the wheel, they drove away.

"Posie!" said Linda, in absolute amazement. "You recognized him! Just wait till I tell Aimé."

When Aimé was told she at once surmised who the woman was. Not his wife. Oh, nothing like that. A very rich woman from out Stoneham way, who had always been crazy about Posie. She owned a car and drove herself. She would doubtless lend him money. Oh, the immorality of men! And the untruthfulness. Claiming he had been absolutely faithful to his memories.

Much was made of the fact that Flora recognized him, too. Flora wondered if she had recognized him. She had no doubt the man was Posie, but in the blur of rain she had only seen a stoutish man under an umbrella. At any rate, his fate was fixed. Aimé ceased to hold communication with the victim; like passionate dames in medieval tales she allowed him to be given the sack.

Her attention turned to the practical details of her hegira. Should she take all her "things," or be like the eloping ladies, burdened only with a change of linen and all her jewels? She giggled, and gave 'Linda her engagement ring to keep for her. It was a decent diamond and she wouldn't risk forgetting herself and leaving it on the little hook under the kitchen clock where she hung it when she washed dishes. Dishes— the china was a wedding present. Jim—and Bert Trinkett as well—said legally a woman was entitled to wedding gifts. Besides, a note had come from the interfering brother-in-law, saying that he was taking her husband away on a hunting trip over the holiday. They hoped on their return to find she had come to her senses, but if she insisted on leaving her good home and trusting herself to a man who now had nothing with which to provide her one (nasty slap, wasn't it? and little did they know they were barking up the wrong tree) why, she could take anything she liked, up to the whole darn shooting match.

"Of course, I wouldn't strip the house," said Aimé "I'm not so selfish! I'm leaving him enough of everything to use in case he wants to hire a housekeeper and keep right on enjoying his selflighting garbage can and his lovely cemented cellar. Four sheets and pillow cases, half the towels, sufficient table linen if he sends the laundry each week, and all the plated silver. The solid is marked with my maiden initial, and Jim hasn't any good flat stuff, he says; his wife looted all that when she left. He has plenty of furniture, good old mahogany that was his mother's. And if I don't like it, he says he will buy just what I want."

Untaught by ten years in that school which Franklin asserted even fools learned in, Aimé luxuriated in visions of a man who was to gratify her every wish. Then she went back to details of the breaking up. What did Belinda and Flora think she better do about a little booze?"

"You know, 'Linda, how the cellar was stocked when prohibition came in? Well, and he bought a case of wine and told me it was mine. Isn't one twenty tonty little bottle have I had, and now I find it's been put under lock and key. But—there's some stronger stuff up in the pantry? Shall I leave it, or..."

"You might be sick," said 'Linda. "You might have the flu!"

"Just what Jim says."

The whiskey was doomed to travel.

* * *

On Friday night a fog drifted inland, Flora's neighbor coughed continually, therefore Flora slept later than usual Saturday morning. She was aroused by Etta. Etta's hair did not wave, it was crimped. Her eyelashes inclined to no-colored bristles; her complexion bore red blotches in places which a skilled artist in rouge would certainly have ignored. Etta was a typical maiden woman; she had been held in scorn and derision from the literary times of *Godey's Lady's Book* to whenever Shaw invented Prossey and put her in *Candida*. Her costume of ginghams not matching added nothing in heroic vein. Yet Flora sat up in something like fear, while her mind ran wildly with dagger-in-hand apparitions from behind bed curtains of French Revolutionists. "There's a woman at the front door with a truck of duds," said the apparition, reproachfully. "What shall I do with her?"

Flora wondered; no decision having ever been reached about the abiding place of the pretty divorcee.

"Who is she?" seemed a foolish question after all the secret conferring, so Flora said frankly, "I suppose it's Aimé. Honestly, Etta, I didn't know she was coming here."

"It is!"

"Does she say what she wants?"

"Your Aunt Lury's room. I wouldn't give it to her. Let her have the room back of Calista's, with the oil cloth on the floor. All she can afford and better 'n she deserves."

Flora was glad to let it go that way, relieved that Etta refrained from exclaiming, "Either that woman leaves the house, or I do!"

* * *

"Perfectly ridiculous," said Etta, "here she's quit her good home and moved and got all settled, and 'tain't noon. Even to her house? I suppose not, seeing as she's been here most of the time since you got within it. Seven as nice rooms as anybody could wish, besides two not done off. Hardwood floors, hot water heat, butler's pantry with swing door opening both ways, refrigerator built in outside so she needn't stay home for the iceman. And she's up in that little two by four smiling as a basket of chips. She's got a pile of cheap novels in each corner, two deep, from floor to ceiling; and there's three good views of that fat chap with the dreadful laugh on the bureau. Says now she's going to wash her hair and be ready for company!"

Flora shivered, but she had not realized the extent to which respect for conventions is cultivated by the unconventional. Jim arrived toward the end of the afternoon, but as an escort to Belinda Blodgett. Aimé was seen for one fleeting moment leaning over the banisters, an ecstatic vision of pink kimono and hair. Then she and Belinda disappeared rearward, where the pink satin negligee was laid aside, and the trumbled blue crepe resumed. Jim remained in conference with Flora.

He was embarrassingly confidential. He told Flora that he knew all about Aimé's "affairs" of the past. He heartily approved, as they gave every promise of a most happy union now she had reached the end of her long quest for the perfect mate; only by such questing could one be quite sure of lasting happiness. Didn't Flora think so?

Flora, conscious of her own omission of questing, even innocent questing, wondered if this fantastic reasoning had anything in it? Had she been happy, clinging to an ideal? She had been wretched, accusing herself of wrong in any sort of clinging. When she saw the contour of her face growing coarser, the expression in her blue eyes bolder, her figure changing gradually from that of an awkward miss to one of an adult more than a little like the blonde chorus girl in the shows Arthur Comyns and she had seen together, she did not blame time, but the effect of her sensuous imaginings. Every law, beginning with the common law of purity, forbade her belonging to another—supposing any other came and she wished to belong to him. Divorce was possible when one was actually married; there could be no divorce and remarriage after an illicit passion. Surely the most illicit of passions had been her own for Arthur Comyns, especially as he knew nothing about it and was married to somebody or other, whether or not resembling Flora's dream.

And Aimé—Mr. Posie only one among many. She would divorce her husband—he would divorce her, poor wretch—those others she could not divorce. They should float between her and Jim Jefffreys Hazelwonda, their eyes looking from his at most ardent moments, their kisses in memory deaden the fire of his.

Oh, Flora, what heroics! Here sits Jim Jefffreys Hazelwonda, discussing with fond particularity the infidelities of his future wife when she belonged to her former husband. He considers them an earnest of bliss, the only fellow he really seems bitter against is that deceived husband. Jim wears spats and a fancy waistcoat, he carries a cane, he has apparently tubbed since he got in on the 8.28, Belinda's bathroom is doubtless a welter of moist towels and talcum powder. He is healthy, handsome, quite normal; he has spent 11.45 to see his Aimé, and she is to him all that is desirable and adorable.

She comes in, hair smooth and shining; slim and sweet in a little new, cheap frock, with stick out pockets of white organdie which she has embroidered, and which accentuate her wee waist. She is cool, kissable only as a child is kissable, an object to stand off and admire. Jim placed his arm about Belinda Blodgett; the two stood off and admired.

"Lend me a penny, Jim, to give Flora for her thoughts," said the dear girl, dimpling. Then, to Flora, "what if we are silly, sympathize a bit. Don't be so stodgy."

* * *

The four drifted along the Village Green, scuffing the brown leaves and sniffing the not unpleasant odor of vegetable decay. The western sky was a riot of cherry and lime, so that Belinda was reminded that this would be a good evening for a party.

"A freedom party," gushed Aimé "I always wanted a freedom party. Like the divorcees have in Newport, with a brazier and you burn your old love letters, and your wedding ring disappears mysteriously and is never seen again. Come on, 'Linda, fix me up a nice freedom party."

Jim laughed the dreadful laugh that offended Etta, and 'Linda asked "what the hotplace you in such a hurry for. You're not divorced yet, milady."

She must do something expressive of her new status. She would walk by her own house and not go in. Flora thought this bad taste, yet she was glad to see the house to which she had never been invited. It was on a side street, the only house on the street; there were dwarf blue cedars guarding the entrance. Arrived, Aimé had a great mind to go in. They might all go in. Perhaps they could pick out some things she should have taken.

A light glared in an upper room.

"Mercy!" she gurgled. "He's come back. He's looking for me to have seen the error of my ways and be ready to stick around and get supper. After which he will get his sword and funny hat and prepare to do duty as the Royal Phush over at the lodge. When I say it's sort of lonely all alone he'll tell me to take myself to the movies, but go in town because I'm too goodlooking. Did I ever tell you, Flora, about my last Christmas present. . ."

The window of the lighted room flew up and a female voice said, "Is that you, Amelia?"

"Yes, mamma."

"Who's with you besides Belinda? How d'ye do, B'linda?"

"Miss Hancock, mamma, and a friend of theirs!"

By a nudge was conveyed the fact of mamma's being unacquainted with Jim.

"Want to come in? If you do, hurry; because a taxi is coming for me in ten minutes. It's you last chance. He was here this afternoon."

"Did he feel bad?" asked Aimé.

"Did he feel mad? I should say he did. He came out of the pantry raging, then he sent for a locksmith and had new locks put on all the doors. So when I go out I can't go back, and you can never get in."

"Whiskey!" gurgled Aimé and fled, hanging to Jim, around the corner, Blodgett-ward.

* * *

185

For an half an hour it was a joke. Then Aimé saw the insult. Insinuating that she would steal any of his property. And she had been so conscientious. Too darn conscientious. Four sheets and four pillow slips and tablecloths and napkins enough for any crowd a grass widower ought to entertain. Some doilies, too, though legally speaking all the doilies were the woman's. Weren't they, Jim?

But she had been like any other woman, too conscientious. The men were all alike, too; they had no real sensibility. Or did she mean sensitiveness? At any rate, they were all alike. Posie worrying about losing his job, not about losing her; and now this! She just took a half dozen bottles of hard stuff in place of the wine he had given her, and he insulted her in this way. The men were all alike.

Jim endeavored to convince her he was an exception. Belinda surmised that the gift of wine might have been forgotten.

"I suppose it was," said Aimé, pettishly. "Injun gift, like my last Christmas one. Did I tell you about it, Flora?"

"No party tonight," said Jim, lighting one of the little black cigars which he affected. "Thanks all the same, 'Linda. Aimé's going to start the divorce rolling at once."

Aimé took the telephone into a room across the hall which was called "Den," and closed the door. It was understood that Jim left her a perfectly free agent, having coached her in exactly what to say.

The other three remained in the parlor. Flora looked at the shelves of Hudson, Herbert Spencer, Mary Jane Holmes, Victor Hugo and Horatio Alger, Jr., at the Christ Crucified and the Artist's Model displaying her wares for a job; Belinda jiggled a crochet needle and a ball of twine from somewhere—probably the atmosphere—and began a boudoir cap. Jim told the ladies condescendingly of the vast difference between New York and New England.

"If you have a thousand dollars, you save it. If we have it, we spend it!"

The only fault he found with his darling Aimé he added, was a tendency to thrift. She thought it unwise of him, when he came over, to pay for a chair when he always rode in the smoker. And when he left at 1 why not get lunch in a Childs' before he started? But he would soon knock these silly ideas out of her dear little head.

She entered the room, distraction in her aspect.

"He says he just won't. He isn't going to let me go into court and claim a divorce on cruel and abusive treatment. He says he thinks too much of his good name."

"Did you tell him that it need be only throwing a towel—a knotted towel—in this state?"

"I did, but he'd hardly listen. He's got a lawyer of his own, it seems, who will 'wait upon mine.' I suppose mine better be Bert Trinkett?"

That was all right.

Flora stopped looking at furniture and looked at the people. She would never have believed it possible. Going to an ordinary 'phone and asking your husband if he would accept your plans for a divorce. Ask him for one, in fact; just as you had probably asked him for car fare ten thousand times in the last ten years. And he had refused!

Aimé went to her new home in a state of despair. Jim escorted her, with third fiddle Flora on his other arm. As Aimé and Jim kissed one another goodnight, Aimé burbled out, "I don't see any hope, unless I go to Reno."

"How much money you got?" asked Jim.

"Forty dollars," she responded, meekly.

"There are plenty of other plans," said he, "Goodnight, gals."

* * *

Calista, Etta and all the cats were cozily arranged in the Hepburn room, where all the chairs wore cushions because they were out at the seat, and all the tables covers because their varnish was ruined with wet flip glasses about the time of the Civil War. Calista tatted; Etta kept the cats from destroying one another.

She peered into the hall. "Are you alone?" she inquired.

"No," said Aimé "we're together. Come into my room a minute, Flora. I want to ask you something."

* * *

Flora was now at a crisis of her life. One might almost say, the crisis of her life. Nature, without providing any shock absorber, had led her to this; now she might take it as she would. Perhaps she would faint, perhaps burst her poor heart with joy. This night her bed must know her not; tomorrow might dawn ordinary November to all the world, but roseate, aglint with hopes also dawning, a day of days.

"Well," said Aimé to Flora, "I want to ask you, do you wear reg'lar old fashioned shimmies and drawers?"

"Unless I get caught short," said Flora, "and have to buy envelopes, I do."

"Here's a trunk full," said Aimé, "that some hussy sent my husband before I ever married him. Take 'em away!"

The trunk was a small steamer trunk. It contained the trousseau Flora had prepared for her proposed union with Arthur Comyns.

* * *

How had it come into possession of Arthur Comyns; husband of Amelia, whom nobody had named as her husband? No mystery there.

Arthur Comyns and his mother, as has been told, journeyed over the road from Illinois to Massachusetts. They wrote a book about the journey, which would have been quite successful with more of the romantic mother in it, and less of the statistical Arthur. This, however, does not affect Flora and her clothes. In arriving in Boston Arthur Comyns would appear to have been overwhelmed by a great wave of love for Flora. He wanted her, and he wanted her immediately. Grabbing a big wad of copy paper—he was a newspaper man, remember—he wrote Flora a letter. It was written in pencil—newspaper men employed pencils then, held between the second and third fingers—in so free a hand that seven words used up a sheet. That letter was some 125 pages long. It was so bulky that it burst the huge manila envelope in which Arthur had endeavored to confine it. It cost Flora four cents beyond the twelve cents' postage, in various denominations of stamps, which her lover had stuck on. Flora had received the letter one rainy Saturday afternoon in her boarding house, where it was brought to her, damp and dilapidated, as she sat forlorn in her room watching drops course down the window pane and lose their identity in pools on the outside sill.

The letter had seemed to her the wail of a sick and sorry man. It yearned, it implored, it stretched out eager hands, it offered tender lips. What of sense there was begged her to take the next train east. An address was given to which she might wire. He would be there to meet her, when the train came in. Whatever the hour, he would be there. Never, never would they part any more.

This cry of the male animal for his mate, trumpeted halfway across the continent, shook Flora. She remembered trying to lift a slice of cold ham to her plate at supper in her boarding house that evening; her hand trembled so that it fell to the floor. She had given the waiter girl a dime for effacing the grease spot. For several nights she no sooner fell asleep than she awoke with a cry, seeming to have heard her name called in piercing accents.

She had not, of course, obeyed his behest, and taken the first train East. That was manifestly impossible. She had her notice to give, her outfit to prepare. She had written almost at once, however, and had given evidence of her good faith by sending a neat steamer trunk in which was packed evidences of her industry to date. She had merely said "house things," because on top there were some glass towels and doilies. A gentleman, he would never think of looking therein.

In the dead years that followed how many distressing blushes had burned Flora whenever she thought about this evidence of undue response to impetuosity. She thought of it as lying in some lumber room, its contents never in the light since she had tricked in the last sachet bag, and covered everything with a pink and white mat marked "Bath." Sometimes, when the chill of white tiling struck Flora's feet as she stepped on a threadbare Turkish towel, she had regretted loss of that lovely woolly mat. Yet it was doubtful if she had ever used it, had Arthur sent her the trunk. That he never did send it encouraged her in thinking he held her always in memory of some fond degree.

The convenience of associating with self centered people was felt by Flora at this time. She might wax red and pale white, Aimé saw nothing. Similarly her voice might tremble, her heart flutter, her breath accumulate in a ball and choking utterance. Aimé went right on shaking out hand made underclothes of long cloth and Fruit of the Loom, fabrics diaphanous in their day, but looking woefully clumsy in this era of chiffon and crepe de chine.

"Your—your husband never told you whose these were?" Flora stammered.

The answer was reassuring, also exonerating the honor of poor Arthur.

"Mercy, no. He doesn't know I have them, or even a key. There's been more keys made for this trunk! First, it came to his mother's house, oh, ages ago. He put it under his bed and was real cross at questions. So his mother and sister got a key and looked in. Well, he told his mother some yarn about keeping the trunk for a man and not knowing at all what was in it, and his mother swallowed hook, line and sinker. So there it set until we went housekeeping out here, when it was brought over with other loot.

"I wouldn't have noticed it at all, only he was so fussy about it. Wouldn't leave it with other old trunks under the eaves, but had it down cellar right by the heater and he used to sit and look at it while he waited for the fire to come through so he could shut the damper. And then he dusted it! So I got his bunch of keys one Sunday when he slept late, but not one would fit!"

(Of course, none would. Arthur Comyns had never owned a key. There had been a limit to trustful Flora's trust.)

Aimé rambled on. "So I asked his sister, because we happened to be on speaking terms then, and after all, I thought, it might turn out to be just loaded with junk and handy to set coal hods full of ashes on. Only why dust it?"

"She was so darned mysterious, and so free with good advice to effect that nice wives never dig into their husband's pasts, that I blew twenty-five cents for a key. There were some house-things in it; wiping towels, real linen, I used those up. Once I put on these pants with the oak leaf knitted edging, and the nigy that matches—it had pink ribbon run in—but when I asked him wasn't it pretty he only grunted as per usual. Either he had himself well in hand, or was like most of 'em, a Dumb Dora.

"Could you use 'em, Flora? Take off your dress and see if they fit."

"I'll take the trunk and everything," said Flora. "All just what I need. You may have the room for them."

"No, no." Aimé waved a deprecating hand. Then "Oh, well, if you insist! Of course I shall be rather short for a time. I've got to buy Jim's ticket back to N.Y. and it will be a few days before he can send a check!"

* * *

Like other heroines, Flora saw it all now. Arthur Comyns had looked on her, from the first, as his wife's relation and close friend.

He had remained in the background, where he evidently supposed they wished him to remain. And now, with Aimé ensconced in her own back bedroom, he could never ring that mottled brown doorbell, stumble over that rotting step, take a seat under the crystal chandelier now so lovely since Etta had wiped each prism with a wet rag, and wait for Flora to descend the stairs in a most becoming costume.

So topsy turvy is life that it was Mrs. Arthur Comyns who descended the stairs ever and anon, while the man waiting was Jim Jeffreys Hazelwonda in a new winter suit, which was still checkered and still too small for his rotund body.

* * *

There were no layers of fat on Jim Hazelwonda's energy. No one could have shown greater vicarious industry than he showed in putting Aimé to work. He suggested, first, that she secure a situation in the city. He consulted Herbert Trinkett, asking him as one lawyer to another, if a divorce didn't have better standing in court if she could prove she was bravely earning her own living.

"She does—if she wants alimony," said Mr. Trinkett. "I understood our little 'Melia like our ancestors in that eighteenth century affair which Theobald won't allow has yet happened, was fighting for freedom only."

Work was decreed by Jim despite Trinkett's hedging. Already thin as the prevailing vogue, Amelia lost several more pounds by rising in time to make an elaborate toilet and catch the 7:55. She had secured a 9 o'clock job, but the office was located some distance from the N. Station. Her breakfast, an affair of doughnut and coffee, was obtained at a drug store.

It was a switchboard job, because Aimé could do only head work; but, still acting on the advice of Jim, she matriculated at an evening school of stenography, and practiced pot hooks and hangers in every interval between laundry work, skirt pressing, darning stockings and answering Jim's daily letter. Etta and Calista spoke in open admiration of this energy.

"Didn't suppose she had as much in her," said Calista. "This round like a hen on a hot griddle."

"Nothing like love for a noble-hearted man to change character," observed Etta.

"Only," Calista cackled on, "I can't for the life of me understand what use all this short handed typewriting is going to be when she gits over to New York and this feller buys her everything she hankers after, as she says he's promised to."

"Ha!" snorted Etta, tossing her head with such vigor that a strong, once japanned hairpin with the japanning worn off flew from her back hair and struck the wall behind her.

"I trust," said Calista, with a slightly malicious grin, "that he ain't deceiving her. I don't think he's going for to do so. I think he's good-natured enough. Sometimes, of course, folks bite off more'n they can chaw. She does her dooty like a little man. Always seems to find time to answer his letters."

"Yah. But she don't always find time to read them. I've heard her tell Flory so."

* * *

Etta took one handle of the little trunk, Flora the other, and carried it to Flora's room. Etta advised shoving it under the bed, otherwise it would be a regular stumbling block. Flora did not like pushing this symbol of sentiment out of the way, but after she had banged her ankles against it a few times she did shove it under the bed. It was difficult to conjure up very much feeling about those wedding clothes, though Flora believed that the difficulty existed because of their various profanations. Had the trunk come to her as never opened since the day she had kissed the top garment, and shut down the lid, all would have been different. Only, of course, she could never wear them.

Flora reflected on a certain ancient maiden lady, long since passed on, who in the childhood of Flora's mother had been in the habit of making a great annual spring wash of the garments she had provided for three prospective weddings, no one of which ever came off. Antonetta's wedding pieces had covered half an acre of green grass, a-bleaching; people drove from all around to see the sight.

"If I stay in this place," Flora reflected, "I shall become such a figure of fun. I shall look in that trunk and note that the things are yellowing. I won't send them to the rough dry. I have to get away. Besides, the roof leaks worse than in August."

A November cold spell filled the gutters with ice. Snow in the gables, melting, provided water to set back and flood the walls. Paper peeled in best bed room and best parlor; brown stains spread over the ceilings, which began to lie down in flakes on the floor. At the same time two actual holes appeared in the front steps, which actually teetered when stepped on.

Etta abruptly stopped cleaning windows because there was no use polishing glass only to have it in pieces out in the yard. She put the matter up to Flora one morning in a succinct sentence. "Be I going to sift your ashes, this coming winter, or ashes for Almira's ex-husband?"

* * *

Now that the wife of Arthur Comyns was no longer a figure in a dream, Flora longed to clutch her by the throat and tear out her innermost secrets. What had been the incidents of their courtship—why had their marriage degenerated into no bargain at all—were there passions of splendor at the first—had the early disillusions affected Aimé with the desolations of sorrow that Flora had felt when her letters went unanswered?

All hope of meeting Arthur Comyns being now set aside, it suddenly occurred to Flora that an entertaining occupation would be collecting opinions as to his life and character. Thus she would build up an Arthur Comyns in continuity; she might come to know the man who had written her the letter of longing; who had forgotten her; who had been able to marry Amelia, to establish a home not in the least like the home he had planned with Flora—yet who had kept the trunk!

It is needless to remark that Flora believed nothing of the story about the new keys and the six bottles of whiskey. Arthur Comyns had come from the cellar in a raging passion. There had been more in the cellar than liquor from preprohibition days.

Etta, interrogated, said as always that aside from his natural handicap as a man, Amelia's husband was a good one. Kind o' stoutish, but nimble. Awful clean, took a bath every day. When 'Melia got married she was some surprised to find he had eighty pairs of socks, thirty black, twenty brown, the rest assorted colors. But so many made the darning easy. Fussy, but sensible about it, too. Rolled up his sleeves in hot weather, but had a special way, so not mussing, and the cuff always on the outside. Bought sugar by the twenty pounds, and put eggs down in waterglass. She guessed 'Melia would wish herself back mor'n once.

Belinda Blodgett was more illuminating. According to Belinda, Arthur Comyns had never intended to marry and settle down at all. He's been one of the boys, as she calculated, he was over sowing oats. He liked taking Aimé places, showing her off to his old bachelor friends. Wasn't any too fussy about chaperones, either. He and another man took Aimé and another girl on week end trips in the Kennebec River boats more than once. Perfectly correct, of course, Two staterooms, a huge suitcase of fruit and canned meats to supplement the dining saloon. This sort of thing might have gone on forever, according to Belinda, if Aimé's mother hadn't interfered. Belinda represented herself as afraid of what Aimé's temperament might lead her to do. There was a young married man in the office where Aimé worked. . . Aimé was quite ready to fall. . . All Belinda could get from her was a promise to let Belinda know if they went anywhere together. . . Once they went up the river, of a Saturday in his canoe. . .

Belinda and Aimé's mother asked Arthur his intentions, like a couple of old Victorian grandmothers. As usual in such tales, the detail of great importance was missing. Arthur either said he intended marriage, or he was made to say so. At any rate, the two were married, after a considerable interval spent in getting ready. The house was bought; it was a new house, quite up to its date. They furnished it, partly on time, but very nicely. The pictures were all on pushpins, no moldings (Belinda's narrative began to resemble Etta's). Aimé arranged to hold her job in town, her mother was to keep house. Flora got an idea, at this point, that Belinda wanted her hearer to think Arthur Comyns a reluctant bridegroom who was yet not unaffected by bribery. The unpaid housekeeper and the office slave had overcome his caution. That was what Belinda meant. Especially when she related what happened on the return from the honeymoon.

That honeymoon! How many hours—evening and midnight hours, that is, for with all her woe Flora had conscientiously held up her end as a filing clerk—had Flora wasted picturing that honeymoon. She sent them most frequently to Niagara, because that customary haunt of the newly married had been mentioned by Arthur when he had been planning a honeymoon with her. Sometimes, though, Flora slightly alleviated her personal sorrow. She imagined the girl suggesting Niagara and he, with a tender memory, electing some other place, equally expensive, as Bermuda.

The honeymoon had been a horrible affair, according to Belinda. He took Aimé to a shack which he and his sister's husband—that same inconvenient brother-in-law and some other masculines, had nailed together with absolute want of skill, for their use in fishing and hunting orgies. Its first rule and regulation had been "No females allowed," but Arthur got the use of it for a honeymoon, and made as big a fuss over allowing Aimé there as if he was getting her into the Masons. It was a teetery shed, on the shore of a lake devoted to producing mosquitoes. Out of the lake you dipped water for household purposes, including drinking. You slept in a bunk made of pine boards overlaid with two or three issues of the *Boston Transcript*.

After a few days he brought down his sister and husband, also the two children. Aimé cooked the meals, over a wood fire in dog days. The outdoor life gave them all great appetites!

"Poor ole Gal! I never shall forget the day they got home and she came over to see me the first thing. I had been feeling apprehensive, and I knew what was the cause when she said, right off, 'Linda, can you lend me twenty-five dollars'?"

While Flora's mind was circling around trying to find something to cling to, Belinda added, "She'd lost her job, of course."

"Oh," said Flora, vacuously, "had she?"

"She hadn't told 'em she was getting married. So they fired her."

"What an awful pity!"

"Wasn't it? But she had a hunch they didn't want 'em married. And she didn't consult me. I should have advised something a little quieter than a full dress evening ceremony with a reception in their own new house and bouquets so heavy that her mother suffered with neuritis in her arm all the next winter from the one she carried. However, it would probably have come anyhow. The young married man in the office would have seen to that."

In asking Belinda Blodgett to talk about Arthur Comyns Flora found she had encouraged Mrs. Blodgett in revelations from which she, the listener, shrank. When and why Aimé sought refuge in "the spare room" (Belinda said it was because Aimé had a romantic affair with a young man in the milk, cream and butter business) was something Flora would rather not have been told. She thought of herself as the reverse of morbid, yet a story such as this crept into memory and stuck there; she found herself rehearsing the scene again and again.

Also other scenes, in which it was the husband who—still according to Belinda—fled from the cute little Aimé. Belinda had made her a pink messaline "nigy" with blue and lavender flowers applique, and that didn't fetch him. Whereat Belinda declared he must be worn out with debauchery in his youth. Indeed, she represented herself as endeavoring to reconcile the pair, as telling Arthur that Aimé required a "great deal of affection," that she "had got to be in love with someone," and it "might as easily be her husband as any other man."

This was sickening; besides Flora didn't believe a word of it. Arthur had not been a "bad" man—she felt a spinster's assurance of that. She went so far as to buy a blank book and make a chronological table proving that he could not have been "bad." She wrote therein:

Arthur & I met...

Arthur & I saw one another seven times a week from... to....

Arthur & I parted... but he returned...

Arthur carefully shut all the doors in Ma Gierstein's (Boarding house) parlor & asked me if I thought anyone could hear or see. Then he proposed. He proposed as men propose in books. According to the girls I afterward talked to, at the office, most men do not propose nowadays. They "go round with you" until it is understood on both sides what he means; he then remarks some evening, at the movies, or in a drug store where you are enjoying banana royals with chopped nuts, "Well, kiddo, what about a gas plate and twin beds for US?"

She was always glad that Arthur had proposed. She might be a bit dense—Flora knew her limitations and that she was by no means swift in the uptake—there was no chance for future woe in thinking she had been one of those fool girls who mistook common courtesy for a "declaration."

(The poor old, old maid, who aired the three separate trousseaux, had been like that. One of the loves for whom she prepared wedding clothes had been her teacher at The Academy. "He didn't speak to me as he did to the other girls," the poor virgin had reported to her stern papa, when he inquired the reason for such bills at the shop where cambric, muslin and frilling were sold. The last trousseau was prepared for the proprietor of this very shop. From the extent of her purchases he considered Miss Emelina Ward a lady worthy of his individual attention.

"How appropriate for a wedding gown," he said, with unfortunate enthusiasm, shaking out a white brocade.

Evalina purchased a dress length, also materials for another dozen of undergarments. Later, when the bewildered merchant was accused of duplicity, he could only beg for one look at the lady who claimed him, and whom he could not distinguish from numerous other customers.)

Flora had never been subjected to such cause for bewilderment. Arthur had proposed in good set terms; after a two-hour exposition of his own part. He had rehearsed his life in full; from his wee boyhood in Boston, a few miles from the Village Green—and no trolley cars or autos to vanquish space in those days. His removal with his mother to a bleak farm where his grandfather had vainly tried to rename him—either after himself or after a son killed in the Civil War, the old mind was never very clear which. Here his mother had evidently tried hard to forget her married life with a man who was acquiring insanity by the sure road of dissipation. They had suffered from absolute poverty; grandfather was too old to run the farm; Arthur remembered being hired out to neighbors for weeding and picking up potatoes and apples; also remembered going with his mother into the woods in fall and hauling out underbrush to make brooms to sell to the neighbors.

His mother had written a wonderful poem about the brooms, afterwards.

From this life of misery they had been partly lifted through his mother's sudden success in writing small stories for Bonner's New York *Ledger*. She did not prove a Fanny Fern; Bonner never came with a spanking pair of horses and a top buggy to carry widow and children to a rose embowered cottage of his providing; but he did send a welcome stream of money orders and pleasant letters asking for more of the pretty tales.

They enabled the lady to buy a silk gown and mingle in village festivities. So she met a well-to-do native son, back from Illinois and in search of a (second) wife. She married him and went west to inspect her future home. Then she sent for Arthur and his little sister. When they arrived—the place was a town fifty miles from Chicago—they found the family augmented by a baby girl. This was the child who grew up the apple of her father's somewhat stern eye. When his will was read it was found that he had left her all his property, subject to the life interest of his wife; with explicit directions that she was to be taken East, at a suitable age, and sent to a New England college.

"Not that he entirely forgot me," Arthur had added. "He left me $1000 in Iowa land, which is now improved, and worth considerable more."

Besides which he had a fair-to-middling job on the *Tribune*, where he saw Peter Finley Dunne and George Ade almost daily, and heard yarns of 'Gene Field first hand whenever he would listen.

He sketched his prospective life with Flora in a manner that evidenced careful thinking out. He said that his mother wanted him to marry; said the sons of a family should marry, though she longed to keep her daughters always with her. He asked Flora if she would agree to take him, and Flora did agree. He held the tips of her fingers in his while this was going on.

After the acceptance Flora had presented her brow for a kiss (she got that out of a book, probably Victorian), and the enraptured lover had remarked casually, "Now—now, none of that."

Immediately afterward he had been obliged to leave, his lodgings being on the west side. Next day he sent her a note, which opened, "My Dear Duchesse." He told her this was what she seemed to him. She had a white chiffon fichu, with ruffles, very expensive and difficult to keep clean, they wore them then. He called it love and told her it made her more duchess-like than before. For a while he used to enthrone her in the biggest and puffiest overstuffed chair of the boarding house parlor, then sat himself on what was called "The Squab" at her side, with his head in her lap. The attitude was patterned after a performance of Hamlet which they had seen together.

Flora, who as an engaged girl had bought new corsets, was forever worrying lest they should creak and destroy the romantic illusion. Never did she take as long a breath as she wished. As shrined in memory being engaged became pure bliss, as do most parts of life so shrined. Actually there were hardships. Arthur was a newspaper man, time meant nothing to him in his hours off. Ten thirty in the evening was an hour in which to commence, not end a call. And Flora with an 8 o'clock job! His manner of entertainment became a perpetual walk, smoking matches, debating on the politics of the editorial office, on the mechanics of selling articles to magazines, on the details of making a single set of statistics provide matter for a dozen manuscripts. The Chicago sewer, the wonderful underground river that came to light somewhere in the vicinity of St. Louis, kept him provisioned with figures. Flora's mind was not the sort to fasten on prosaics. She sat and adored Arthur, but her replies were seldom intelligent. His Byronic profile and his mellifluous voice brought her happiness; she had absolute faith that his ideas were wonderful, that he would land among the Great. After many trials he did land one article on the Chicago sewer. Flora tried not to show disappointment when she read the two scanted pages, in small type, crowded at the very back end of a magazine called *The Cosmopolitan.*

He got $30 for it, which was amazing. Flora benefited by a china pin tray, it was on her bureau while she listened to Belinda Blodgett's revelations. Being oblong in shape, she had used it a good while to hold her tooth brush. The china was very good, and a triumph to masculine taste. He had never given her anything else.

No sooner was Flora inured to the boarding-house jokes about her "late beau," than he ceased to appear, at any hour. Sometimes he wrote heartless notes claiming that he was at work. These would be scribbled on leaves torn from note books, dated in bar rooms, police headquarters, fires. Flora recalled a Thanksgiving Day when she borrowed a flat from two girls in the office who were going home. Here, at expense she could ill afford, she provided a noble dinner, to which she bid Arthur's mother—and Arthur! She had not seen her lover for weeks, he had accounted for his defection on the ground of entertaining his mother in her annual visit to Chicago.

They came. They seemed very glad to come. Arthur's mother was rather beautiful in a prim, over mature way. She kissed Flora, but appeared quite in a fog as to the relationship of the young things. After eating heartily, and assisting in washing the dishes, she said they were all then to go to the theatre that evening, as her guests. She had the tickets, they were for something very appropriate, "Shore Acres." Arthur was overcome with amusement at the idea of a newspaper man sitting at a show in a seat that had been paid for. Any serious "explanation" for which Flora longed, became incongruous. The only moment they had alone was a single one in the narrow hall of the flat. Flora tried to give it meaning, she put out her hand appealingly. Arthur saw, but put up his chin aggressively, refused to be coerced into any reply.

The wall paper of that passage, a grimy fawn color on which unmeaning sprawls of gilding made something in which the eye tried to find a pattern, but never did; stood to Flora a symbol of shame. She had afterward refused a most eligible lodging because it was papered with something similar.

Yet after that she had believed Arthur again, had sent him on his driving trip to the east with palpitations proper only to the Girl Left Behind by travelers of all degree. The summer that ensued was remembered by Flora simply for the evenings in which she tried to follow the course of Arthur and his mother on a road map of her own.

Happy summer, brought to a termination by the call on 52 pages of copy paper. It is a tribute to the really nice way in which Flora had been brought up that she never for an instant considered complying with her lover's demands. Why men made such calls Flora could not imagine. Indeed, she could not believe that men usually did make them. Arthur was a writer, an artist, he had a right to be slightly peculiar. Mark Twain, she had read, was peculiar, but his wife worked hard to make him appear conventional. Flora's sympathies were all with the wife. In her sanguine moments she saw herself reforming Arthur's neckties, which he would call cravats; getting him to abandon red knitted wristers, which seemed to be known in his family circle as pulse warmers. Withal, she was excessively proud that her lover ranked with art rather than business. Her ideal was a great author with the habits of a successful one-man groceryshop keeper.

Certain aspects of Arthur Comyns, as constructed on hearsay evidence, showed that the influence of the East—or of Aimé—had reformed the ties, and turned him from the self-conscious Bohemian to a very dandy. Eighty pairs of socks—or was it a hundred? And the private stock of whiskey! As she remembered Arthur he took an occasional glass of beer. Everyone did that. Even in pretty good society young men spending the evening with young ladies would ask for "The Pitcher," and bring it filled from the Place on the corner, first of course, ascertaining whether the preferences of mamma and the girls ran to light or dark. Arthur did not do this when he called on Flora, and Flora was glad her did not. Perhaps this was because each was uprooted from beside the Village Green in a far off Massachusetts town.

But nice people did not drink liquor or have it in their homes. Everything stronger than beer was called liquor, Flora was at least 20 before she realized liquor as a general term. Up to then, she had supposed the strong drinks of America were brandy, whiskey, rum, gin and liquor!

She listened while Belinda Blodgett called the census of Arthur Comyns' evidently extensive cellerage—a dozen cases of rye; half a dozen Scotch; a cask of bourbon which he would bottle personally; gin, rum, vermouth and other composites of cocktails; the wine so cruelly and unwisely taken from his wife's runaway portion; twenty-five (25) little stone jugs of Irish whiskey; then all sorts of bargains picked up a flask here and another there—G. A. Taylor, Green River, Johnny Walker...

Neither woman was aware that these brands never came in flasks. The word sounded skittish and knowing Flora expressed no doubts, but she wondered how Mrs. Blodgett knew so much. Though always pulling a poor month, Arthur Comyns had locked up over a thousand dollars in the stuff. When his wife remonstrated he had said "we" would benefit; it was all for the benefit of "us." Much Aimé would gain, he begrudged her so much as a half pint when she had a cold. Right after prohibition started he had been crazy over homebrew; had homebrewed until Aimé found the bottoms eaten out of all her stone jars and her grocer bills swelled to enormous proportions by purchases of brown sugar and raisins. The brews were seldom drinkable, either. Since then he had settled down to regular purchases from some regular runner over the Canadian border. A chance to secure a bargain was continually interfering with Aimé's plans for something to wear.

With a feeling that each word spoken by Belinda Blodgett pushed her further from any actual Arthur Comyns Flora said she must be going home. She wanted to hear no more about him; she thought herself just a little disgusted with Belinda, yet it was hard to get out of her exotic atmosphere and face a storm of sleet that sputtered on the storm windows of Belinda's bedroom. Belinda was sitting up today; her thick black and white hair crisply waved, her body neatly clad, but somewhat negligee as to feet and lower legs, which she kept immersed in a tub of steaming water. She was going out that evening and was preparing to wear new shoes. Any kind of shoes nearly killed her, owing to all sorts of corns, bunions, enlarged joints, ingrowing nails, and the callouses that indicate fallen arches. Why did she have these? She didn't know. Nothing that she had ever done called for such punishments. Bum feet ran in the family, just as did bum teeth. Hers had been pulled at fourteen; she fed her son on oatmeal and lime, but his went just the same.

Belinda sat before a beautiful little cabinet of sliding drawers lined with velvet. It had once held spools of thread, and confessed to O.N.L. spool cotton in gilded letters. Each drawer now sparkled with beads. As Belinda demolished Arthur Comyns' character, she made a bead chain, weaving two threads in and out with wondrous skill, using large beads, which she called jewels, to make a pattern that apparently was invented as the work proceeded. On the bed lay literature and the cat, on the bedposts hung fancy garters and caps of various ages. A bamboo case of books was nearly hidden by pink underclothes. In one corner a square sink indicated that the room had once been a kitchenette. An attempt had been made to transform the sink into a dressing table, but it had stopped half heartedly so that the thing remained a simple sink incongruously frilled. The handsome bureau had disappeared. Belinda spoke about that.

"Calista's. One of the few good things she's still kept. Didn't you recognize it in her room at your house? I had her take it away because I felt equal to nagging Henry into buying one. Now I've a spell of neuralgia coming on and don't dare get all worked up. So I've put the things in boxes."

She indicated four boxes which had once held soap, and which now shoved under the bed. Each bore a label as to contents—"Top," "Bottom," and so on. Belinda yanked out "Top" and began to manicure her nails.

Flora pulled herself away. The two old ladies, in the dining room, were loudly discussing their usual subject.

"Now, sister, it is not my intention to contradict, but you certainly gave instruction in the district school at Thomaston for 2.25 each week. I witnessed your signed receipt. It was in a show the Daughters of the American Revolution got up. . . ."

"Well, sister, you are wrong there. I never done nothing the sort. I only got $2, and it's a funny thing to get up a show about, I must say."

Both smiled sweetly at Flora.

"I was just about to observe," said the Aunt of 86, "that Eliza never was obliged to labour. Eliza always occupied the position of the pride of the family!"

Eliza, 88, and so excessively plump that, as she frequently remarked, it was a day's chore to walk round herself, bridled and simpered. It seemed impossible that this placid old woman had once brought into the world the restless and imperious Belinda.

Yet—why not? Why might not her nature have turned as complete a somersault in the years between 35 and 80-odd, as had that of Arthur Comyns in far less time?

* * *

[The following reflective essay on *The Potiphar Papers* (1853) by George William Curtis (1824-1892) occupies the final leaves of the manuscript of *The Village Green* in the Lovecraft Collection at Brown University's John Hay Library. This essay does not seem to belong to *The Village Green* per se.]

The Civil War seems to be a great fence between times that were referred to in the late '60s as "then" and "now"—Just as we let the years 1914-18 divide our time. Wars have a way with them in manners more than physical. They find a few thousand men in scarlet, or bright blue, and leave many hundreds of thousands in muddy brown. When they begin two countries may live, socially, the one by mimicking the other, and t'other by calmly accepting that imitation which is the sincerest flattery. When everything is over but the shouting the two are metaphorically so far apart that it appears as if they never were to be re-united. This was exactly what the Civil War did to this country and England—though it wasn't to be a decade before we would fall for the "Anglomania" of the '90s. However, the Anglomania of the '90s was quite different from the Anglophobia of the '50s.

In 1853 appeared *The Potiphar Papers* which exactly mirrored the feeling of the time, which was an excessive admiration for everything

English, with a most contradictory propensity to poke fun at those who imitated things British. *The Potiphar Papers* aren't fiction, though they deal with fictitious character—Mr. and Mrs. Potiphar, the Rev. Cream Cheese, tame cat of the Potiphar drawing room; Mrs. Geoeans, rival to Mrs. Potiphar as society queen; young Gauche Boosey, who lives up to his name and tips over the punch bowl, remarking anent the ruined carpet, "Well, I've given that such a punch it will want some lemon-aid to recover." There is also a Miss Minerva Tuttle, that perennially humorous character of the last century and some of this, an unmarried female who is not invited to change her name, but who would like to be. Miss Minerva makes "pa" take her to Saratoga, where she hears some English visitors are to be, for whose benefit she held back that last muslin, the yellow one embroidered with the Alps, and a distant view of the Isles of Greece worked on the flowers, until it was impossible to wait longer. I meant, she adds, to wear it at dinner the first day they came, with the pearl necklace and the opal studs, and that heavy ruby recklace (it is a low-necked dress).

It is not made exactly clear whether or not this fine assortment of lapidary's art is presented in irony or as a literal picture of what a wealthy woman did wear in 1850. The picture of a hotel dining room follows:

> The dining room at the United States is so large that is shows off those dresses finely, and if the waiter doesn't let the soup or the gravy slip, and your neighbor doesn't put a leg of his chair through your dress, and if you don't muss it sitting down, why I should like to know a prettier place to wear a low-necked muslin with jewels.

There is another character in the book quite as necessary to development of the slight plot as those for whom it is named. This is Kurz Pasha, the Sennoor minister. He turns up everywhere, drawing comparisons between these United States and his own native land by his naïve humor pointing all the jokes. Thus he speaks anent dinner at the United States—

> When the dinner gong sounds, I am reminded of the martial music of Sumaar. When I seat myself in the midst of such

splendor, of toilette, I recall the taste of the Grim Tartars. When I behold, with astonished eyes, the entrance of that sable society, the measured echo of whose footfalls so properly silences the conversation of all the nobles, I seem to see the regular army of my beloved Sumaar investing a conquered city. This, I cry to myself, with enthusiasm, this is the height of civilization; and I privately hand one of the privates in that grand army, a gold dollar, to bring me a dish of beans.

Quite a galaxy of shams in this, which hits the barbaric flat of the gong, the barbaric colors of the "toilettes," the barbarism of employing negro waiters and the horribly undemocratic custom of tipping. Kurz Pasha serves as hypercritical chorus on every possible occasion—he and Paul Potiphar between them foul the home nest to the author's taste, and presumably, to the taste of readers in the '50s.

Nowhere is the passage of time shown more entirely than in joking. The "fun" of the Potiphar papers is now quite pointless, and one imagines it became so directly after Sumter was fired upon. For instance, all people "in society" were presumed to be extremely ignorant in the lines of arts and letters, yet in no way acquiescing in such ignorance. So when the author "addressing one of the panting Houris who (after dancing) stood melting in a window, one spoke of the Düsseldorf Gallery, "Yes, they are pretty pictures; but la! how long it must have taken Mr. Düsseldorf to paint them all;" was the reply.

Or Minerva Tuttle discovers her poor papa embellishing his conversation with French graces: "We must go to Newport, for they say, Minna, that all the parvenus are going this year, so I suppose we shall have to go along."

Mrs. Potiphar has not the slightest idea what Mr. Potiphar means when he says that, "Rev. Cream Cheese, tho' a very goodgoing man, was addicted to candlesticks tied to the apron strings of the Scarlet Woman," Mrs. Potiphar is quite naïve in her ignorance, supposing the Rev. Cheese's liking for candlesticks is because he has weak eyes, and as for the Scarlet Woman—"Dear Caroline, who is the Scarlet Woman?" And almost thinks her a personage in Mr. Potiphar's *vie de garcon*. Mrs. Potiphar's innocence is stupendous indeed, always, of course, in the interests of humor. When her husband accuses rowdy young dancers of coming to the house just for the sake of his "Margaux, and Lafitte, and Marcobrunner," she wants to know "what kind of dress are those, dear Caroline?" And when in talking (with Rev. Cheese) about servants in livery and Rev. C. asks, "My Dear Mrs. Potiphar, why not have a chasseur?" Mrs. Potiphar thinks it is some kind of French dish for lunch and answers, "I am so sorry but we haven't any in the house." To which he responds, "Oh, you could hire one, you know." And then she thinks it is a musical instrument and remarks, "I'm not very fond of it."

Presumably those who read the Potiphar papers fairly doubled themselves up over the chapter entitled "Our New Livery, etc." Mrs. Potiphar decides to introduce the liveried servant into New York, but finds her way beset with thorns. She "would like to come out with the nig—upon the coachman," but is "sure old Pat wouldn't have it." Rev. Cream Cheese is at hand with advice, saying that "a lady might as well hire a footman with insufficient calves, as a coachman who weighs less than 210." Following which words of wisdom he assists Mrs. Potiphar to arrange her livery thus:

Red plush breeches, with a black cord at the side—white stockings, low shoes with large buckles—a yellow waistcoat with large buttons lappels to the jackets—and a purple coat, very full and fine, bound with gold lace—and the hand banded with a full gold rosette.

Lovely, but the difficulty was to find anyone to wear it in this home of the free. Even Mrs. Potiphar balks at asking prospective footmen about their calves. Mr. Cheese, however, encourages her, saying, "the path of duty is not always smooth, dear Mrs. Potiphar. It is often thickly strewn with thorns." Then, says she, "he sank back in the *fanteuil*, and put down his *petit perre* of Marrasquin." Which seems to show Mrs. Potiphar wasn't so ignorant about fancy drinks, after all. Perhaps she took a *petit perre* also. At any rate she bawled out the first applicant for daring to say his name was Henry when she wished him to be James, and she asked to see his legs quite brazenly. And when he, naturally, asked "What for, mum?" and she mentioned knee-breeches, he asked quite delightfully, "What be they, ma'am?"

Perhaps such things were—75 years ago, 3/4 of a century is "quite some time," as they used to say in New York over on the Jersey side. It was an age of sham—it must have been. Mr. Potiphar has a fine library, all gilt covers to boxes, which are locked into cases, and "the key always lost when anyone wanted to take down a book." This is a fashion that persisted. I have inherited a backgammon board which is covered with leather, properly tooled in reading "History of England" on the back. Even the Widener Library at Harvard has certain beautiful boxes in its "Holy of Holies" where Harry Widener's own wonderful collection is kept. Only in this case the actual first editions are inside, boxes being presumably adopted because Dickens "in parts" and R. L. Stevenson in original and uniform bindings do not lend themselves to beautiful walls.

Some of the Potiphar characteristics survived almost as persistently as have boxed books. "Mrs. Partington's Knitting Work," 15 years later, is homespun where *The Potiphar Papers* would claim to be very fine stuff indeed, yet much of the fun is based on a lack of understanding of foreign phrases. "Will you please to play ABallyon crossing the Alps," said Mrs. P., reaching out of her chamber window, as an organ man was turning his crank with a persistent arm beneath. "*Non entendez,*" said he, looking up, and smiling at her. "Can't you play it in less than 10 days?" replied she, in an elevated tone. "*Non entendez,*" said he, again, still smiling at her, turning away at the crank. "Not in ten days," she mused, "I suppose he means it will take more than 10 days to learn it so as to play it exceptionally." She gave Ike a 5-cent piece to carry down to him.

Mrs. Partington is a vulgar Mrs. Malaprop, always on the point of saying something perfectly awful. Mention is made of the war in the Crimea and the "odor of strife in the perilous deadly breaches." She replies, "And not only the breeches, but the rest of the uniform beside." When "O'Regan" comes into the union (evident Partingtonism for Oregon) "There's room enough," says the good old lady, "and the rear of our institutions should be distended." "Oh, Isaac," she said to the bad boy, coming out of church, "what do you want to act so like the probable son for? Why don't you try to be like David and Deuteronomy, and act in a reprehensible manner?" Some men are more courageous than others, and some an't" said Mrs. Partington, "Some will go to the Chimera to exercise feats of arms, and some will exercise their feats of legs by coming away. It needs more courage to face danger in the dark—to be waked up in the night by the howling savages, or to hear midnight burglars, or like the lady who waked up in the night and found a big nigger man standing right horizontally by the side of her bed."

The good old lady objects to crinoline because "It used to be the remark of Elder Stick that every tub should stand on its own bottom; and though this may have nothing to do with it, I want to see folks jest as they are." Again, "heaven knows when the costiveness of the times will be any better."

LOVE WITHOUT WINGS

The Varied Year, 1902-1910

CHAPTER I

A great red and yellow calendar on the wall opposite the door served as a point of light in the general duskiness and as a reminder that time was fleeting. Otherwise the place was dingy as to ceiling, dirty as to walls, and absolutely pitch dark under cases and behind jutting shelves laden with ten-year-old agricultural reports and tied up pages of type, rapidly disintegrating because of picked letters. It was indeed a gloomy place on such an afternoon as this, with a thunder storm imminent, and nothing coming in at the door save little puffs of dust.

A girl sat on the wide sill of the window, her feet curled under the edge of a scanty frock. She ought to have been sitting at a disordered desk making figures in a large book, but it was a fearful task this, since it entailed putting one's feet in the dark cavity underneath the desk, a cavity fenced in by wood, and as like as not swarming with mice.

So Ellyn sat in the window and looked at as much of herself as was visible. There was her muslin frock, pale pink in color—the paleness induced by a laundress who owned a politician's fancy for soft soap. Still, it was a gay frock, and adorned with many ruffles, sewed on crooked.

A japanese fan was suspended round the girl's neck by a string of beads. The beads had been blue and white before the necklace broke and half of them were lost in the purlieus of this very office. Now they were discreetly picked out with red, and an occasional big pear-shaped roman pearl of dusky smoke color. The pink frock ended abruptly afar up the sunbrowned arms, but was aided in hiding the thin neck by an aggressively stiff and wide enwrapping of scarlet ribbon.

David called it a "sore throat bandage," Ellyn remembered with a curl of the lip—but then, David knew nothing about fashions, never read the *Ladies' Home Journal* when it appeared among the exchanges, as it did about the time premiums and club lists were made for the coming year. Above all, David had no big red and brown scar just above the place where his collar bone began. Indeed, David was so fat one had to take his collar bone on faith. David did not approve of Ellyn's hair, either. It had been the exact color of chopped hay, which he considered fit excuse for glee. Then Ellyn had secretly "swiped" $1 and seven two-cent postage stamps from the money drawer in the disabled counter, and had received in due time a strange bottle wrapped about with a pamphlet printed in four languages and such indistinct phraseology that it took Ellyn a week to learn whether she put the stuff into her stomach, or on her head.

Finally her hair assumed a lovely chestnut hue, except upon the parts newly grown, and then David scolded half a day, and said "Carrots" ever after. The hair was now cut short and curled a great deal. Several deft interweavings of blue ribbons, of differing lengths that failed to match in tint, helped to hide the inch of new growth that was still the color of chopped hay.

A man came into the office while Ellyn was peering out between the limbs of the apple tree that grew close up to the window. He wanted sixteen copies of the June 24 issue, the one which had in it a piece about Sally Ann Fitzhugh's wedding. After much skirmishing in the pigeon holes where back numbers were supposedly placed, there were produced fifteen good numbers and one marked "cut paper" but having, as Ellyn explained, only an advertisement removed. Whereupon the man proceeded to repair the write-up in several places with an exceedingly black lead pencil, which he often wetted on his lips. While he worked at this unusual labor he made a hissing noise as of one soothing a horse. Ellyn stood ready to drop with mortification, for it was she who had written that article, and afterward corrected the proof.

"Well, who'd think he'd know whether wedding clothes was trossu or trowseau," said poor little Ellyn, writing both wordings on the edge of the table, and then feeling not at all sure either was correct.

"Anyhow it hasn't any x at the end," she remarked, still to herself. "I remember the first time I spelled it with an x and David asked me how many set-outs the bride had to one time."

Then she went back to the window. Big drops of rain were now coming down with a pattering sound in the road, a pattering rivalled by the footsteps of people hurrying under shelter.

"I could do much better if David would only send for that Webster's dic," said Ellyn. "I suppose two-thirds cash is an awful lot, but there's a sixth off for getting a hustle on in sending the check, and anyhow he might do like he did with the press, order it on thirty days and keep it sixty. We might use it all the time and I could learn slathers of spelling in two months."

"Maybe it's in here," she continued, lifting down a book as weighty as a dictionary. It was bound in black, and plentifully illustrated, mostly by pictures of old-fashioned ladies having beautifully curling hair. Ellyn dipped into its pages, and forthwith lost all knowledge of the storm and all fear of the mice. An hour went by and she was startled by a sudden blaze of sunshine. It was the last attempt of the setting sun to illumine the world for the day. The shower was only just over, but a break in the clouds allowed the wet town to become irradiated with brightness. Ellyn put out her hands to the sunbeams and drew a long breath. Then she arose and stretched herself.

"No," she said, "Lord Byron didn't write about nobody who was married and had trosseau. But what he says about that storm was just splendid reading with the thunder rolling round old Baldy out there."

Then Ellyn closed the office by the simple process of putting a cardboard easel on the desk nearest the door, after writing in trembling characters, "Gone to supper." The door she left open, as David had taken the key with him when he went over the river collecting that morning. "I'm sick o' climbing in at the window because you lock up so tight," he had remarked.

Old Baldy, a sugar-loaf mountain rising abruptly from the plains on which the town reposed beside a sluggish river, was putting on a night cap of fleecy clouds. As Ellyn went along the streets she heard the tinkle of tea-bells, and saw mothers standing in the doors, pulling down their rolled-up sleeves, and suggesting vaguely the dreadful fate awaiting Harry or Joey if he refused to run into the house directly, "and get washed against pa comes."

Looking at Ellyn the women at the door saw only a skinny girl in a pink frock so entirely ridiculous that one felt assured she had made it herself. Ellyn knew different. Now she was a woman of means, years and avoirdupois—Ellen admired avoirdupois, mainly because David possessed it—slowly strolling homeward to meet someone who loved her very much. They lived in a large air castle which Ellyn had constructed halfway up Old Baldy. Ellyn revenged herself on the High School girls whom she presently met and who snubbed her, by mentally making them do the housework in the air castle. The daughter of the Congregational clergyman, who was especially snippy, was set down as the laundress.

Presently Ellyn passed a couple of boys carrying long sticks on which was elevated property of the village bill poster, squares of board plastered over with brilliant "snipes," reading, "Town Hall Tonight, Uncle Tom's Cabin." Ellyn looked with proprietary interest at the snipes. Sometimes David was called upon to do such. The sight brought present shame, however, for Ellyn remembered the disgrace into which she had gotten over the last lot. More M's had been demanded than the stock of wood type supplied, and she had calmly allowed the work to go out with a W upside down in place of the required letter. Ellyn hastily began to think of something else. So many of her memories ran into pockets full of misery, such as this, that she was past mistress of mental somersaults.

Ellyn was now a great actress—that is, as great as Agnes Wallace Villa, who annually brought the Villa Repertoire Company to town, and herself played such roles as Camille, the governess in East Lynne, and Little Eva, most of the other parts being taken by Mr. Sam Wallace Villa (husband) and by a large number of other Villas (children) ranging in size and ability from the largest boy, dubbed "the humble cat" by David, and only capable of saying, "the carriage waits," down to the smallest girl, called "the wonderful child artiste," who had a role in every play, whether the author had put one there or not. Ellyn knew there were people called Bernhardt, Ellen Terry and even Ada Gray in other parts of the world, but considered it better to tie her ambitions to the known. Neither Bernhardt nor Terry ever played in the town hall, and her principal desire to be an actress was in order to show her talents at home, and with 'em floor her enemies flat.

It would be best, thought Ellyn, to casually write a play, and have it accepted for production. At the last moment the most important actress should fall ill; Ellyn would put on her clothes and make an instantaneous hit. The leading man, she decided, should love her dreadfully, and be extremely jealous of the rest of her admirers, but she would take all her bouquets, and most of her salary home as a present for David. With what was left of the salary she would buy David a new office coat, and hang it in place of the old one. Ellyn was so busy conjuring up the grin with which he would note the difference when next he came in to change, that she almost went by the cottage which bore on its front window the sign "Homemade Bakery."

"I'll have jelly roll for supper," was Ellyn's sudden determination, as she abruptly ceased to be anyone but Ellyn.

CHAPTER II

There was, in this American town, a "dago quarter," inhabited mainly by French Canadians, but called Dago because there were so many Irish in it—at least so David said. It was considerably closer to "Old Baldy" than the main street of the town, and the house Ellyn entered was like most of its kind, built of red brick on the plan of an exaggerated shoe box. She ran lightly up one flight of stairs, and then slowly back again, realizing that she had forgotten something of importance. Down on the doorstep she plumped, and taking a rusty steel purse from her pocket tumbled its contents into her lap. One bill, a large piece of silver, and several small ones interspersed with copper were all.

Ellyn sat an instant wrapped in thought. This was Wednesday. The amount on hand was quite sufficient for liver today, sausages tomorrow, tripe Friday and bacon Saturday, but there was the delightful possibility that David had succeeded in screwing something out of skinflint debtors on the other side, in which case liver would supply a very inadequate menu for a celebration supper. Ellyn was one who liked to get as much eclat as she could for her money. She jumped to her feet just in time to escape inquiry as to the cause of her cogitation from one of those neighbors who hate nothing worse than minding their own business except seeing others mind theirs. Her bee-line was made for a shop which above its doors announced the sale of "Meat, tea, coffee, confectionery, & etc."

David was always imploring some of the last for supper, but Ellyn had been long beyond even smiling at the joke. Housekeeping was to her a solemn proceeding, especially when things didn't turn out well—or turned out too well, like the pie that neatly tipped itself face downward on the floor just as David opened the door and announced himself hungry enough to eat nails.

Twilight was in the corners of the large room into which Ellyn came with her parcels, but the windows were yet patches of light from the roseate afterglow. There was no one in the room, yet it was not exactly quiet, since several flies buzzed sociably on the ceiling, and a few mosquitoes carried on a fugue of their own.

"Bother them screens," muttered Ellyn, "I do b'lieve they keep 'em in 'stead of out."

She was trying to coax a small kerosene lamp to light, but first the match burned out before the chimney was removed, and then the wick refused to remain visible for more than a fraction of a second.

"Shucks," remarked Ellyn, shaking the thing viciously, "I bet the old thing has gone and burned its oil up."

There being no answering swish nor yet swash, Ellyn was probably right. She took the lamp to the window, in order to refill it by the fast dying daylight. When a beam finally shot forth the place was rank with a smell of oil, and Ellyn's frock showed a widening stain in its front breadth.

Ellyn's home was as little genuine as Ellyn. The room pretended to be a parlor, was really a kitchen, got used as a dining room, and had been mentioned by the landlady in her weekly call for the rent as "the attic chamber." Whenever Ellyn took the pillows and slumber quilts from the couch, and turned it into a bed she generally imagined herself pattering round a cool matted bedroom that was never anything else, and getting ready to slip between linen hemstitched sheets that should be spread on a truly brass bedstead. Ellyn had thought so much about this truly brass bedstead that it was sometimes more real than anything she possessed.

The worst of it she considered was the amount of labor necessary to keep it bright! The misnamed room was uncompromisingly square, and little rills of white powder showed where the unpapered plaster was worn from the walls by backs of chairs and sides of tables. The floor shone with the sickly glare of ill-dried varnish. Ellyn had painted it herself, and had been too impatient to wait for proper drying. As a consequence you stuck if you stayed long in one spot, and it was unwise to move the larger pieces of furniture, since the foot of each supporting leg took a large share of the floor covering along with it. This, deposited elsewhere in a superogatory layer, made a "varnish rug" according to David.

It was one of those rooms in which everything pretended to be the thing it was not. The couch was really a clothes chest, the wardrobe was a pantry and bulged flour sacks and apples; the gasoline stove was revealed when Ellyn removed what purported to be the cover of a Smith Premier typewriter, and the trumpery desk—one of the kind thrown in with a box of soap—didn't know whether to call itself a side board or a dressing case, since it held more three-tined forks and crumpled napkins, broken combs and trays of pins, than of articles appertaining to literary pursuits. If Ellyn wrote she went to the office; if David felt the writing fever he stepped over to a case of three nick brevier and composed in his stick.

A nickel clock on the mantel—in a celluloid cover that put up a hollow pretense of being marble—reminded Ellyn of the passing of time by suddenly ceasing its aggressive ticking.

"Gracious," she exclaimed, removing the cover, winding it strenuously, and then turning it face downward as if it were a naughty child; indeed carrying out the pretense of administering several lively slaps. "Seven o'clock and I ain't got supper begun. I must flax round."

The plush covered album and vase of golden rod being removed from the centre table, Ellyn covered it with a somewhat shabby cloth, deftly arranging doilies worked in outline to hide the holes. Plates, cups, saucers and drinking glasses of various patterns were added in such a manner that David was to have the least cracked plate, and the best cup—the one marked "Nassiwano Hotel," while Ellyn was to drink her tea from a mug marked "For a Good Girl," and showing evidence in every crack of having belonged to a bad one.

CHAPTER III

Charlotte Converse looked on the world as a sealed package in which there was probably a prize. Each new friend seemed the agent who was bringing her the lucky ticket. She had been reared by a grandmother with a favorite saying, "Everything is lovely and the goose hangs high." Since being at boarding school Charlotte had ceased using the last five words. The remainder composed a motto as truly hers as those other girls caused to be embossed on their note paper. Charlotte thought it lovely that she had a school to go to in school time, still nicer that home was waiting when school was over. It was nice that grandma had thin hair because she had to wear caps, and the cap splendidly solved the problem: what to give one's grandmother at Christmas and on birthdays. For oneself, it was lovely to be plump and have fat red cheeks, because it was not necessary to work hard in the gym, or tumble out of bed at unholy hours for cold baths and long walks, as must those unlucky beings who were afraid of getting fat. It was lovely to live in the country, because then there was always the town to go to. It was lovely to like to dust the old mahogany in the parlor, and spread the Marseilles quilts on the beds, and wash and wipe the beflowered china; still better that one didn't feel obliged to consider these duties, since Matilda and Sister were capable of performing all the tasks indoors, and grandmother only too glad to welcome any unusual "spell o' work," in order that she might assume some of the briskness of youth for at least the time being.

The girls at boarding school sometimes said "Charlotte Converse has no conversation." It was true that she generally agreed with what you said if it was testimony on the pleasant side. Thus if you remarked of a sunny morning, "Isn't this a nice day?" Charlotte replied beamingly, "Fine!" If, on the contrary, the day was nasty and you said things about the East wind and the fog, Charlotte was certain sure to discover something cheerful—that it was good growing weather for the posy garden, that it was nice to feel cool again after last week's scorching, or at least that it "looked some like clearing." As might have been expected many people liked Charlotte for this, while to others her persistent optimism was exasperating. Some, indeed, gave her small credit.

"She ought to be cheery," said one girl. "An indulgent grandma, a swell old lot of ancestors to get her into patriotic societies when she is grown up, no parents to bother, and a complexion of peaches and cream that doesn't have the least thing in the world to do with a bottle."

The girl speaking, by the way, was the daughter of a half-millionaire, and had a complexion of the clear brunette sort, which many envied her, but lacking contentment she felt that she lacked all things.

In the freshness of the early morning Charlotte knelt before the low window of her room and stretched forth her arms into the dewey mass of jessamine that stopped climbing right there, its superfluous tendrils falling backward in a fragrant cascade, starred with little pale pink blossoms about which the bees buzzed all day long. Early as it was, the sun had been up some time, yet not long enough to dry the heavy dewfall of September. Charlotte's window overlooked the narrow, grass-grown road, and then terrace after terrace of green fields, rising at length to the dignity of hillsides. There was plenty of color in the landscape, for the apples were all turning red—excepting those that turned yellow—and the hilltop was crowned with serrated rows of high huckleberry bushes and sumachs, the first to grow a vivid scarlet in the autumn.

The landscape was likewise dotted with yellow cats, some kitten-sized, others full-grown, all apparently starting on important expeditions, for one with mitten paws walked boldly on the stone wall, in search perhaps of errant chipmunks; a half-grown pair raced gaily down the lane after playful hop-toads; and a sedate old great grandmother cat, the finest mouser of them all, picked her way daintily through the tall wet grass, to a special hunting ground of her own, down in the cornfield. Their industry reminded Charlotte that the day was before her in which to choose occupation. She might take the dogs through the big woods—it would be enchanting among the trees, and if somewhat chilly the sunny spots would be all the more deliciously welcome. It was a good day for repotting the geraniums for winter—grandma always loved to dawdle round the garden, and in such sunshine as this a morning out of doors wouldn't hurt the old dear a bit. The seckel pears were ripe enough to do up in preserves, and it was always fun to mess round the clean kitchen and have Matilda declare one such a help and Sister change it to, "Nonsense, a hindrance, I say," when would ensue a good-natured argument between the two as to whether girls today were what they were when Matilda was just in her teens and Sister just out of them.

"Charlotty Con-verse," called grandmother's sweet quavering voice at the foot of the stairs. "Was you intendin' to eat any breakfast today?"

Charlotte left the window and went down the steep and crooked staircase of the old house with the graceful dawdle that would make her seem to glide rather than walk when she should presently put on long frocks. Grandmother sat chuckling at a little round table that stood, in accordance with a whim of Charlotte's, not in a proper dining room, but at one end of a long hall. Through the open door one saw the garden, and the humming birds that darted about the honeysuckle framing the door at times made a mistake and dashed into the house, getting into no trouble, however, since the open door at the front gave them free egress.

The garden was one of those which resemble nothing so much as a floral crazy quilt, but the nicest in the world from which to cut bouquets. Tawdry marigolds glowed beside pale-tinted asters, currant brush seemed to think itself on par with roses, salvias and scarlet geraniums supplied brilliancy, while heliotrope and mignonette, otherwise inconspicuous, made their presence obvious by persistent sweetness. There were no flowers upon the table, but that was simply because Charlotte had not thought of them this morning. The culinary efforts of Matilda and Sister, however, left little room for aught else, and Charlotte did not see the letter beneath her plate until grandmother cheerfully called her attention to it. Grandmother, since she belonged to Charlotte, was naturally cheerful, indeed she was exactly the fair, fat little old lady one imagined Charlotte might come to be in a half century.

Charlotte tore open the envelope with the handle of a teaspoon and read the brief contents with a smile.

"From David Lombard, gran," she said.

"I ain't a mite surprised," returned the old lady. "When I see a envelop with such bad writin' I can't read it I know he's wrote."

"I wouldn't wonder if he came out this afternoon," Charlotte went on.

"Neither'd I," responded grandma, with another chuckle at her own wit. "He seems to like out here first-rate. Specially moonlight nights," she added.

"Well, there's a moon now," said Charlotte, with a fine smile of her own. Sister, who had just come from the kitchen with a plate of highly ornamental waffles, doubted this. Sister was atall, gaunt handmaiden of the ancient style, now fast passing from even New England country places. She not only cooked for her employers, and scrubbed their floors, but looked after their manners, and reprimanded them when she thought it necessary. Dominated from childhood, however, by the much younger Matilda, she seldom gave offense that lasted. Most of her life had been spent in giving Grandma Converse pieces of her mind, and then apologizing because Matilda said it was better to do so.

Matilda, hurrying up with the coffee-pot, overheard Sister's statement and instantly disproved it by the Old Farmer's Almanac. The interlude over, breakfast continued for a good while, since both Charlotte and her grandmother were deliberate and hearty eaters. Besides, a couple of stout dogs had meandered in and demanded attention. One of these, a Boston terrier, climbed into a chair and fixed his eyes reproachfully on a plate of cookies; the other, a huge white mastiff, rested his chin dolefully on the table and wagged his tail with such good-natured violence that the vines about the door—his length was such that he extended from the table out on the steps—were agitated and the humming birds flew as from a storm.

"Grandma," said Charlotte, meditatively varying her sliced peaches and cream with sips of coffee, in order to get the best possible flavor of all, "You like David Lombard, don't you?"

"Oh, so-so," said the old lady. "'S long's I don't have to read his writing. If I did I should wish't he'd get to get him a typewriter." The she added, "Anyway, Charlotty, 'tain't me that has to like him. Nor you, neither, unless you want to."

"Oh, I like him, grandma, without trying," said Charlotte, blushing only a wee bit, because her cheeks were always as pink as most girl's when they turn red. "He's nice and kind, and smart, and awfully fond of pussy-cats, and we could live right here, with a good horse for him to drive back and forth with. I should like driving down for him nice evenings, too. Ten miles isn't very far. Of course, gran, he's poor."

"He's a printer," said the old lady, as if that settled the poverty question.

"Oh, no, gran; a newspaper man. And I always did think it was so nice that we had money enough so that I needn't be looking out for a rich husband, as some of those poor girls at the Academy had got to do as soon as they'd finished their schooling."

Grandma put on her glasses and began poking about the table for a last tidbit of curly lettuce with which to finish her meal. Having found one to her liking, and sugared it in accordance with a taste educated ere salad oil was introduced in New England, she continued the conversation.

"You ain't engaged yet?" she asked, in the casual manner of a guardian who feels perfect confidence in the ability of the guarded to arrange her own life satisfactorily.

"No, indeedy, gran; I shall tell you first thing when that happens. Only I'd like to think it was all right to get engaged before I let him keep coming. It's horrid mean of a girl to let a man get to caring a lot for her, and then throw him over."

"We didn't think so when I was young," chuckled grandma. "The more the merrier, gals thought then."

"'Course, gran," Charlotte went on, "Mr. Lombard may be just a friend, you know. He's got to coming out here since I met him graduation day at the Academy."

"He's been here quite a few times," said grandma, nodding sagely. Then, with something as near suspicion as she ever indulged in, she said, "I do hope his folks are nice, or else will know enough to keep out of the way. Most any gal can get along married if his folks let her alone."

"I don't think he has any," said Charlotte. "His parents are dead, he told me that; his father died when he was a mere baby, he said once, and I think his mother married again and his stepfather was not always very kind to him. When he was talking about them, though, he said something like, 'Let the dead be dead,' and changed the conversation quick, so I imagine they are gone also."

"Good enough," said the old lady, nodding with the heartlessness of age when death is concerned. "If you like David Lombard and he likes you I don't see why you should not say yes when he pops the question. All I want to be sure of, Charlotty, is that you are saved any interfering relations."

Charlotte, sure as she had felt of grandma's confidence, was made yet happier by these words, so that she decided not to go far away from the house, but sit upstairs by the front window embroidering a bit of a collar to send to one of the girls who had a birthday next week.

The pretty work suited the day and Charlotte. The sun rose higher, the dew dried, the yellow cats came meandering back from the hunt, and sought out sequestered spots—like the very centre of the kitchen floor—for noonday naps. Matilda was way down in the spring-house skimming cream with which to make something nice for the two o'clock dinner. Sister was taking a nap on the calico-covered lounge under the morning glory vines that twined on strings beside the back porch. Grandma was vigorously trying to keep awake in her big chair by the window.

Suddenly the stillness was broken by a sharp "Ki-yi!" from the small dog, and a loud, gruff "Wow-wow!" from the table-tall mastiff. Charlotte looked far out at the window and discerned the top of a dust-colored felt hat among the bushes that hedged the roadside.

"Gran," she called, "if you've got your cap off or anything put it on. Mr. Lombard's coming."

"So's Christmas!" called grandma in return, with the usual chuckle.

CHAPTER IV

"Damn," said Ellyn. "Damn and damn and damn."

She was standing in the bare and not overheated hall, before the door of David's room. She had knocked, she had yelled "Supper" through the keyhole, then with a high tragedy air she had flung open the door and discovered not only that David was gone, but his best clothes. His workaday ones were flung on the floor, as if David had scorned the idea of ever meeting them again. He had even, as she ascertained by an agitated scramble through the top drawer of the bureau, taken his white necktie, the one usually kept for funerals and town meetings.

"Oh, dear," she cried, miserably, "why need he act so? Here I've tried to be so good, and now David makes me go damning."

Being desirous of proving David to blame for something especially vicious on her part, she decided that after eating the sardines and other portions of the meal upstairs which would not keep until morning, she would smoke a cigarette! She possessed one, stolen from the "devil," and though it was somewhat dry from three months' preservation in a handkerchief case, still it burned satisfactorily, and made Ellyn feel quite as uneasy as might another. "It's great," mused Ellyn, making an air castle meanwhile, in which she became a famous newspaper woman and sat all day before a roll-top desk, smoking violently and yet constantly consulted by highly respectful and greatly admiring politicians.

"And after I've dictated the policy and written all the eds, David shall come and take me home in a top buggy," said Ellyn. This final touch, however, brought up all the rage against David, in the midst of which there was a knock at the door.

Perhaps it was a belated David. And the smoke? Ellyn promptly turned up the lamp, so that it adds a share to the smudge in the room. She meditated throwing the cigarette into Old Baldy's face, but finally hid it under a plaster cast of Praying Samuel, for though on deception she was bent, she had a frugal mind, and it was probably none other than the girl next door asking for a match.

"Come in," said Ellyn, whereat a lank youth, himself smoking a cigarette, entered with so much impetus that he was well nigh out of the window before he stopped. It was, in sooth, the very "devil," from whose store Ellyn had fled. He looked like the kind you see in front of tailor's shops, marked: "This style, $1.20."

"Good evening," said he, sitting down suddenly, putting his feet on the table, as abruptly giving his flashily clad ankle a saucy slap, and saying sotto voce, "Get on to the floor, you impudent dog!"

Then he wanted to know, "Boss round?"

"No'p," said Ellyn.

"Know where he is?"

"Who wants to know?"

"I'm the one doing the asking."

"He's gone out to spend the evening," said Ellyn, with a brave air of having been consulted beforehand.

"Who you expecting to supper?" continued the inquisitor, gazing with effrontery at the table set for two.

"Girl friend o' mine," returned she, nonchalantly.

"They was a girl in down to the shop after you went home," said the youth, with such an air of innocence that Ellyn instantly suspected that he suspected her. "P'raps that was her."

"Who was she?" asked Ellyn.

"I'd know. Had red hair, patent leathers 'n a green veil. The boss 'nd she looked like a steam roller flirting with a cow."

There was a long pause, during which the youth informed all and sundry that his coal black lady was his baby. Then, because she felt she must do something, Ellyn began to pile up the dishes.

"Why don't you wait for her?" asked the questioner, who always took a 300hp interest in things in which he had no earthly concern. "I heard her say to the boss, 'Come on, it's time for supper.'"

Ellyn tried to look unconscious, but was obliged to bite her under lip to keep from crying out. So a girl had gone to the office, and David had put on his best things to meet her. David, who wouldn't dress up to take Ellyn to the Methodist strawberry supper, however she teased. And The Kid had come over just to see if she felt cut up over it? Well, he should go away thinking her just tickled to death, and knowing all about it in the first place.

"Yes," she said, with ready mendacity, well trained by lying about the circulation to people it was advisable to get to advertise. "They were here a minute and said they couldn't wait for supper, as they had to go to Ware on the trolley."

"That so?" said The Kid, with elaborate politeness, pressing in his chin amazedly until his extremely tall and very glittering collar actually cracked. "Then of course you've seen the boss since he wrote the note he asked me to bring over, and 'tain't no particular use."

As he spoke he drew from his pocket one of David's well-known notes, probably written with blue pencil on the back of an auction dodger thrust into the first envelope at hand, and sealed with a blow of the fist.

Ellyn started. Of course she longed for the note, longed with all the intensity of a woman whose curiosity is baffled at the same time that her feelings are hurt. Perhaps had she been sufficiently apt she might have framed an excuse and gotten it from The Kid, but it seemed to her that the only way to keep him in the dark as to her feelings was to continue dissembling.

"No, just throw it in the waste basket," she said airily, adding, "tear it up."

The Kid pulled down his unkempt sandy eyebrows and viewed her quizzically. Ellyn trembled. The Kid always did seem to see through folks, and she doubted not he appreciated her little scheme of getting the torn pieces into her power, and afterward pasting them together again.

"Naw," he said, in a sudden excess of conscientiousness. "Guess I better keep it and hand it back to the boss."

Ellyn began to carry the dishes to the table behind the screen, where she dumped them into a tin pan. Now she knew The Kid was obdurate she wanted to get rid of him in order to be as miserable as she liked all the evening. She was wiping away a surreptitious tear with the dish wiper when she became aware that The Kid was close on her heels, peering round the screen with the air of one to whom nothing was sacred.

"Say," he asked, "what you going to do with all them sardines and the oil that goes with 'em?"

"Nothing," said Ellyn, hoping her generosity would hide the choke in her voice. "Do you want 'em?"

"Bet yer life," said The Kid. He pitched his hat to one side, hitherto worn as carelessly as it was worn in Ellyn's presence at the shop, shot his immaculate cuffs, and sat down in David's place with the air of a man suddenly fallen into a fortune. It did not take urging to induce him to clear the table. He soaked bread in the sardine oil, he piled raspberry jam upon jelly roll, he drained the teapot and then asked Ellyn if she couldn't squeeze down the leaves and provide him with another half cup.

Despite her misery Ellyn began to laugh.

"My gracious goodness," she said. "Didn't you have anything to eat at home?"

"Nothing but my supper," returned the youth. "When a fellow's really hungry supper's only an aggravation. Now I've finished up this little snack I just feel ready for a couple dishes of ice cream and I guess I'll go and get some."

He wiped his lips as he spoke, and carefully folding the napkin placed it in the napkin ring marked "David L.," being a lad carefully reared by a grandmother whose one dread was "large washings."

Ellyn filled a little agate kettle, and placed the water over the flame to heat. The youth, although he was lighting another cigarette, observed that the water pail was emptied by this operation, and asked, "Say, do you have to lug that pail all the way up here from the pump in the yard?"

"David does," said Ellyn.

"Well, tonight while he's out with his mash he can't," returned The Kid.

Ellyn's cheeks burned, but she said nothing.

"'Tis his mash, ain't it?" pursued the youth, his relentless questions in no way softened by the fact that he had partaken of her bread and sardines.

"How do I know?" she returned, angrily. The Kid gave a shout of glee.

"Yah," he cried, "thought you knew all about it? Thought she was a great friend o' yours. But yer never seen her nor heard of her! Come now—"

"I certainly don't feel called upon to answer all your fool questions," said Ellyn, trying the last resort of ill-assumed dignity. "You might remember that Mr. Lombard is your boss and what he does is none of your business."

"Sure mike," cried The Kid with a grin. "Now you're talking. We're ain't neither of us next, an' you know it as well as me. Here, hand over that pail." And he was gone for five minutes, returning with the pail well filled and a fresh cigarette ablaze.

"Dropped the other on the stairs," he explained, "and the dirtiest little mick I ever seen picked it up. Catch me smoking it after he'd mauled it. Take it yerself, said I, and then his ma came out and bailyragged me for teaching him to play with fire. Come on now, ain't you got them dishes done yet? You're slower'n the Second Coming."

"Oh, I'll get them tended to between now and bedtime," said Ellyn airily.

"That's all very well, but I'm dying for that ice cream."

"Go ahead 'n save yer life," replied Ellyn, flippantly.

The Kid reassumed his chair and re-elevated his feet, this time without the reprimanding slap. "Not till you're ready," he remarked.

"I!" Ellyn stopped short.

"Sure. You're coming along."

"Who said so?"

The Kid rose and made a sweeping bow. "Arthur Sherlock Montgomery Hamilton," he replied, and then sat down.

Suddenly Ellyn's spirits rose. She giggled. "I didn't know but 'twas The Kid," she said.

"Nixy," said that individual. "I'm no kid outside the shop. You may think I be, but that's because you don't know me, only just as a proof-puller. Gosh," he continued, in a fervor of admiration for himself, "I could tell some things to the boss about folks in town he writes up that'd make his hair stand on end and bring them into the place with shotguns."

Ellyn turned him into the hall to commune silently with his own self-esteem, while she tore off the faded muslin frock and got into her second best white shirtwaist and bran' new linen skirt. For a moment she meditated putting on her very Sunday frock of white swiss, but thought better of it in the end. After all, perhaps all was not lost. David might have explained everything fully in that mysterious note which The Kid still possessed. Ellyn retained the best frock as a cautious whist player retains one trump to the very last. It might be better to play it, and thus show her despair to be irrevocable, but Ellyn hadn't the heart to spoil the pretty frock, though she was about to place in jeopardy the good opinion of David.

For David had very high and mighty ideas about Ellyn's holding casual conversation with "the help." Ellyn had been taught to believe them a vulgar lot, perhaps better off financially than herself and David, since they must be paid weekly whether or not the boss and his faithful little aide-de-camp bought necessities "on tick," but quite impossible socially.

David, when leading Ellyn to make her debut at the office, had provided her with a code of directions memorable and simple—"Keep your mouth shut, and don't let the comps get gay."

CHAPTER V

As Ellyn came into the open, where twilight struggled with afterglow, Arthur Sherlock Montgomery Hamilton arose from the doorstep and emptying his lungs of cigarette smoke inquired anxiously, "Say, do you want a pleasant evening, or the time of your life?"

"What's the dif?" asked Ellyn, with a giggle.

"It's no laughing matter," he returned, with an unwonted sternness. "If you just want a pleasant evening I've got the price right in my bloomer's pocket, but if you want the time of your life I've got to hock my watch."

"Goodness gracious!" exclaimed Ellyn, aghast at such recklessness. "I guess I better stay to home."

"Nixy, you don't," and he grabbed her arm, adding, "Pooh, 'tain't nothin' hanging up a watch. I've done it as much as—once. No, twice, when the circus was here, and the night the Bon-Ton minstrels played. A fellow introduced me to a real actress—she dressed the one that played Queen of the Air in the burlesque—and we had an oyster stew and three frozen puddings after the show. And I sneaked her name into the write-up after the boss had read proof on it, and he never got wise. Tra-la-la!"

Ellyn's blood ran cold at the revelation of duplicity being made on this eventful evening. It was very evident that a world existed, all around her, of which she was quite ignorant. While she sat reading Byron when she should have been keeping books, and sometimes bookkeeping, the comps were thinking, scheming, doing. And she had considered them dumb, uninteresting objects, who kept their eyes glued to their sticks as they walked down the alley between the cases, to tell the man at the stone that he could run the Railway's Ready Relief ad (only two years dead) to fill the space on the editorial page where Mr. Lombard was to have had his editorial on The Tariff Issue, only he'd sent word he hadn't time to write it this week. Everything was quite different from what it seemed—it seemed. And Ellyn's ever ingenious mind sought an analogy in the fact that even the stone was "Sacred to the Memory of Eliza Brown" on the under side, having been bought cheap from the local marble man as a misfit.

Just at this moment they entered the swinging door of Miss Parrott's Ice Cream parlor, and Ellyn realized that here was yet another world. Past the counters they went, looking furtively at the tin trays of peppermints and gumdrops, to the rear, where on either side were marble-topped tables and spindle-legged iron chairs, wondrously like the ones provided by thoughtful mourners on their own family lots in cemeteries. Each table was discreetly screened from any other by a curtain of Nottingham lace, looped gracefully with a strand of red rep. And every table was flanked by a youthful couple varying the absorption of pink ice cream with sips of ice water.

Presumably there is nothing criminal in invading an ice-cream parlor where all the places are taken, but Ellyn's face flushed as if she had been detected in a crime, and The Kid was visibly impatient of the result.

"Look at that pasty-faced one," he observed, in a more than stage whisper, "giving you the merry ha, ha's. The gent with her ain't her steady—he's a high school stewed cat. Say, let's pick a fuss and get the fellow done up."

"Oh, please not," cried Ellyn in distress. "It would be so—vulgar."

"Shucks on the vulgarity. I'm not going to smack him myself. He's not exactly in my class."

Which he wasn't, being a gymnasium product of some 140 pounds, while The Kid was an aenemic specimen of probably 95.

"My idea," The Kid went on, "is to look up her high school beau, put him hep, and let the two of 'em fight it out. Then we can grab their table and be all hunky dory."

He led the way out, once more past the peppermints and gum drops, while in Ellyn's ears never failed to ring the snicker of the daughter of the Congregational clergyman, who had apparently told her companion something about Ellyn's hair—or perhaps it was her clothes—Ellyn knew that both invited criticism, but would have died before acknowledging it.

She and The Kid were walking down Main Street now, by the cigar store where its wooden Indian offered to all and sundry a bunch of cigars that some wag had once painted cabbage color; by the trolley waiting room where the slot machine invited the reckless expenditure of coin; again past Tony the Dago's, where the automatic peanut roaster invited other expenditures. Perhaps it was the sight of a Boston drummer, extravagantly feeding a nickel's worth to the pigeons, that put a bright idea into The Kid's sleek head.

"Don't move," he exclaimed to Ellyn, and went up the street on the run. He was back soon, grinning from ear to ear. "Done it," he shouted. "Had 'em dead. Waltzed into the old dame's and hollered her from out back where she was just getting Miss Parson and her beau some more ice water. 'I want to buy some chocolates,' I yelled, loud enough to wake 'em all up. 'Op'rys?' she asked, '25 cents a pound?' 'Not on your life,' I answers, Huyler's, an darn quick.' She wilted and had to own up she didn't keep 'em. Wouldn't I have been in bed if she had, though! They're 80 cents a pound stale, I don't know what fresh—price of a farm with a cow on it, I s'pose. Come on, let's go down to the depot, and watch the 6.42 express come in at 8 o'clock. I guess all the old lady's ice cream won't melt before we get back. Anyway, I'm ready to make a night of it—don't care if I don't get home till half-past nine P.M."

"Was she having a good time?" Ellyn wondered. The mists creeping up from the river filched the starch from her badly cut pique skirt which it had yet taken her two hours of a precious Sunday to iron. The rising moon seemed tangled in the willow trees that grew by the roadside at the point where the houses ended and the railroad ownership started in. She looked and felt a great disgust for the youth, redolent of sweet caporal, who strolled so nonchalantly by her side. How should she ever face David, on the morrow, when in the office The Kid would presume upon this night's adventure with an insolence that she dimly felt had long waited for such an opportunity? What was she doing, wandering in the dusty road at this hour, an hour usually sacred to the companionship of David and a soothing chapter of *The Newcomes*. Perhaps even now David was at home, struggling man-fashion with the dishes, wondering why there were so many, and slopping water on his only good suit.

"I must go back," she cried, in a sudden panic. "I'm going to turn right straight round and go."

The Kid's skinny arm was about her waist in a nervous pressure, and she could see his yellow teeth in the moonlight. "Pshaw," he was saying, sniggeringly, "you're just a girl, even if you do put on airs down at the print shop. Guess you are willing to be beaued 'round, same's anybody. I told a feller in the press room—"

Ellyn did not lack the spirit proverbially accompanying red hair. She slapped The Kid in the face with no unwilling hand, and then promptly burst into tears.

"I'm not crying because I feel bad," she sputtered, into his amazed ear. "I'm crying 'cause I'm mad."

At which moment the 6.42 came in, rather earlier in its lateness than usual, and from it alighted two people—a man wearing a dust-colored felt hat; a man stout in figure, yet with the stoutness of youth, that is far removed from the unbecoming stoutness of age. To the form of David Lombard it lent dignity, a dignity also carried out by his earnest strong-featured face, and by a certain manliness of bearing that impressed even those from whom, day by day, he was obliged to solicit the small business that made up his living. They felt that somehow, though they might affect to despise him now, he was a man whom they would yet be proud to have known.

Just now his gaze was fixed, with an ardent interest, on the placid blonde face of the girl beside him—Charlotte Converse, perfectly equipped in white linen and a lingerie hat, the despair of little Ellyn, who gazed at the neatly shod feet, the immaculately gloved hands, the well-groomed hair, just showing beneath the floating veil.

The Converse carriage was in waiting—an old-fashioned brougham, to be sure, but a wonderful production in a town where a hack was "the" hack. David handed her in, then took off the dust-colored felt, and stood for a moment bare-headed as one might before a princess. They heard him say, "It will be a pleasant drive home, I hope," to her, and her reply, "Of course—and it was so kind of you to relieve Gran's mind by seeing me safe from town," and then she drove away, with a wafted, "We shall expect you to luncheon tomorrow."

Even after this David did not turn toward the place where he might reasonably have expected to find Ellyn, *The Newcomes*, and supper. Unseeing the onlookers, he wandered, still hat in hand, to the river, as if to walk and think of what had earlier befallen.

All of which might have been romantic, or might have been funny, if looked at rightly, only to poor little Ellyn it was tragic, so that she cast discretion to the winds, turned and slipped her feverish hand, unthinking, into that of the not unwilling Kid, exclaiming in a husky whisper, "Take me somewhere, Kid, take me somewhere—give me the time of my life!"

CHAPTER VI

Charlotte Converse would never again look on the world as "a sealed package in which there was probably a prize." The patch of red on her bedroom wall awoke her from a dreamless sleep to a day that was as a pleasant dream. Luxuriously she turned herself to find a cooler spot on the linen pillow and happily she looked forth from her window into the heart of the rising sun. It was early—so early that the yellow cats were still asleep, and that is very early indeed, as any know who have ever owned cats, of yellow or any other color. Matilda and Sister had not gone down to the kitchen, Charlotte found it wrapped in that wonderful quietude which seems to best like lingering in those places where usually it is noise and bustle.

Softly drawing the bolt Charlotte let herself into the just-awakening world. The lush grass had adorned itself with dewdrops as an unwise woman wears diamonds, until bowed with shame. Here and there the faeries' tablecloths were still spread—it had, without doubt, been a royal night with the wee ones.

Charlotte would have always thought it a beautiful world, but now she realized that beauty is wonderfully enhanced when seen through a medium of great joy. She had meditated going a long way off—quite into the wood on the hilltop—but it was so pleasant, and so quiet, here; and she wanted to think with such a great want, that she plumped herself on the wide doorstone, without further ado, and putting her white chin in her whiter hand, gave herself up to reverie.

Of her life before she had known David Lombard she did not care to think—it seemed colorless and flat. She supposed she was like other girls—but surely no other girl could feel as she was feeling on this morning. Mabel Sampson had been engaged, to be sure, before she graduated from the Academy, but all Mabel seemed to care about was her clothes. A full dozen of everything, and seven silk gowns—that was the height of her desire. Oh, yes, she should be glad to be married because Harry was very kind—he was going to buy her a Boston terrier! As for Harry himself, he was but a means to a material result.

Another girl was always having "affairs" and putting them down in a diary, and imploring the other girls to remember for her if it was Sunday evening that she met Herman in the Bon Ton drug store for soda—or only Saturday afternoon after the tennis match?

Charlotte needed no written record of that which was engraven on her memory.

First, graduation day at the Academy—the girls in a serried row of white muslin—and the proud parents and friends in a solid mass before the platform. How happy one felt—with just the little dash of sadness that by contrast makes happiness quite perfect. For it was a day of good-bye, so one could even afford to be real nice to the few girls who had been real horrid during the past four years.

Standing at the rear of the room, with a half-amused and half-tender smile on his face, was a man on whose brow there seemed to rest a dignity beyond his years. His fading hair swept carelessly in a way that Charlotte liked—it was so refreshingly different from the laboriously acquired sleekness that marked the heads of the youths who would presently ask her to promenade and eat ice cream.

Charlotte felt that she would like to know who this man was—he smiled as if he saw through all the silliness of this girlish exhibit of frocks and outgrown sentiment under the caption of "Beyond the Alps Lies Italy," while yet he somehow found it attractive. Presently, in talking with him, she found that this was true.

"You're such a lot of happy girls, with a whole lot of nonsense about you," he said, "and it isn't anything to laugh about because it's sincere. You don't know a thing about the real world—and please God some of you will never have to know anything about it. If I had my way all girls would grow up just like you, and every woman would lead the sheltered lives that I hope will be the lives of all of you in the years that are to be."

Charlotte had glowed with pleasure because he had considered her capable of understanding such opinions as these. He treated her like a thinking human being, instead of descending to small talk, as had a couple of snuffy professors to whom she had been introduced just before the preceptress brought up David Lombard. They were learned men, she knew, men of worth, but all they said to her was, "What a rosebud garden of grils—and you like the queen bee therein!"

Slush—she hoped she had stung them with her reply. At least they had gone back to their own rational talk, leaving her free for David.

She had given her valedictory, for an excerpt to be used in the report of the graduation, and instead of sending back the Mss. he had brought it. On an early evening in June he had come—when she was cutting roses for grandma's rose jar. Presumably Charlotte herself had made a picture doubly attractive to David's eyes, wearied as they must have been from the smoky town—she was standing in the gloaming, with the dogs and cats at her feet, surrounding the great flat basket into which she flung the flowers. She wore a fresh white gown of the filmy sort that no one could ever wear in the village because the smoke of the factory chimneys grimed everything in an hour—but David was a man, and could not know this, and perhaps wondered why he had never before seen a girl dressed, as it appeared, in a newly gathered cloud.

Charlotte, however, remembered him, carrying his dust-colored hat before him in the way some folks hold their hats in church, and which gave her an idea that he approached nature as others might a sanctuary—which was, in fact, quite true. What a happy evening it had been—they sat on the porch for a time, with grandma nodding in the window of the parlor, and later went into the parlor, where Charlotte had lighted the candles in the light of which the room appeared at its best—a light which I am afraid David compared to smoking kerosene lamps with an unwarranted bitterness.

He had come, next time, to a trifling evening party which Charlotte and her grandmother had given for the Academy girls and the boys who were their brothers—or the brothers of some other girls—with a sprinkling of the older folk whom grandma had known all her life. Charlotte had written him a note asking him to come, it was quite an informal affair with no fuss about cards or anything of the sort, and he responded with a real letter that she had read, shyly, more times than she cared to think about, since.

That, too, had been a successful evening. Charlotte's friends were not the snobs of the village, and everyone understood at once that David Lombard was not there in other capacity than as of guest. He had known what to do, too, afterward—he had not erred on the side of putting a flamboyant "notice" in his paper. This was a trifle, but Charlotte had a fastidious woman's desire that the man she admired should show the best taste, even in a trifle.

And now—to know that he preferred her above all others—to realize that the wealth of his heart and mind were laid at her feet—this was happiness unspeakable. He had said, deprecatingly, that he was not a successful man as the world counted success—"but I hope I am indifferent honest," he had added, quite as might a hero in a Shakespeare play. Somehow when she was with him all those things the other girls wanted seemed of very little consequence—fine clothes and automobiles and five dollar bunches of violets. He had never given Charlotte anything but books, and Charlotte loved that, too, because it had somehow ever appeared to her vulgar to be wooed with chocolates and American Beauties.

It was all perfect, and David himself was perfect. She knew she could trust him, forever. She felt that he would always be equal to whatever situation life might bring one into.

Serene and pleasure-sated, Charlotte mused, until the rising sun peeped over the hill and inquisitively into her very eyes. At that moment, also, she heard Matilda and Sister vigorously pursuing a left-over-night quarrel down the stairs. Charlotte fled into the dewy morning-world, longing to be alone—and yet not alone, because her happiness would be with her.

CHAPTER VII

It is so different—the wakening in the town. The room is hot and stuffy, and the sardine oil in the still unwashed dishes is beginning to smell. Ellyn sat unrefreshed on her couch that so eagerly pretended not to be a bed that it never succeeded in being a very comfortable one. She was conscious only of the wretchedness of life—the dust motes in the sunbeams, the badly varnished floor, the jangle of whistles and bells urging the factory help to the day of greasy toil, and the fact that she hadn't a clean shirtwaist to her name.

Wearily dragging her feet she went about the room, picking articles of clothing from the unlikely places where she had tossed them on the dazed night before, finally completing the process by donning a dirty linen kimono that only cost 39 cents in the beginning, and was now a shame and a disgrace. Then she sat once more on the edge of the tousled couch.

"I can't," she murmured to herself. And all the time she felt that she must. And she knew not which she dreaded most—the unsuspecting presence of David, or the smug winks of The Kid.

While still she sat, David's voice, from the floor below, roused her from her unpleasant reverie.

"Most ready for the office, little girl?" he asked, in the voice vibrant with a feeling which seemed to animate him whatever trifling matter was the subject of which he spoke, and which thrilled both Charlotte Converse and poor little Ellyn as no other voice was ever to thrill.

Ellyn dug her nails into her palms, while she answered in a would-be careless tone, "Almost."

"Very well—then tell them I won't be round till towards night—I'll get breakfast at the café, as I am in a hurry. I'm going—out in the country."

Was there a break in his tone as he said the last words, or did Ellyn imagine there was such a break? At any rate, she remembered the girl in white—and a promise to see her at a meal called luncheon, which was evidently quite different from lunch and a ham sandwich eaten over proofs at a stand-up desk.

Very firmly Ellyn rose to her feet, and unlocked the foolish little enameled desk that stood by the door. Within a pigeon hole stood a flask—how well she remembered the day when David had laughingly drawn it from his pocket, remarking "This is all I could get from the Gem drug store for its ad. Keep it safe, Ellyn, maybe it will come handy in case of illness."

And Ellyn was very ill, yet would the little flask prove a cure? Resolutely, as if she knew nepenthe lay within, she poured out half the contents and swallowed them hastily. The fire ran through her veins, and for a moment the physical shock brought forgetfulness of all else. Then she saw herself in the glass across the room—a wild-eyed creature, haggard, weird, looking hardly of this earth. She wondered, vaguely, if she really looked that way, or if her eyes were dimmed by the strong drink.

And she wondered, too, if it was a bad dream when a voice like The Kid's said, in her very ear, "Ah, ha, I caught you! Hitting the booze at this hour! Well, you are a nice young girl, upon my word. And I always told the feller in the press room—"

At least she had the spirit left to try to box his ears once more, and to be indignant when her feeble hand failed. He caught the little fist, squeezed it hard, and then observed, "Say, met the boss down here—he says he's going to cut it out again today. So I guess me'n you'll do likewise. There's a daylight dance over at Thorndike, and I think that's just about our limit."

"What's a daylight dance?" asked Ellyn, while the room bobbed up and down before her, and The Kid seemed to be lighting a couple of cigarettes with an innumerable number of matches taken from uncountable trousers pockets.

"Great fun—you dance till you're so tired you can't stand and then you pour a few beers into yourself and dance some more."

"And what else?"

"Oh, that's all."

"I don't think I'd care for it," said Ellyn, sleepily. "I think I'd rather stay at home and read a book."

The Kid gurgled with derision. "Books is all right," he observed, "but I like my Nick Carters only on a rainy night for a half hour before I hit the hay. Somethin' doin' all the time's my motto. Say, it'll cost us a quarter apiece and I'm the fifty cents short. Go along down to the shop, you, and sneak the wherewithal out of the money drawer."

Ellyn was so miserable that she did it. Already she had put far behind her the days when to moon over Byron's poems was the height of happiness. And the sad part of it all was that she had been so much happier then than now. She had envied the girls who went gayly by the office, escorted by merry-faced boys to what it had seemed probable were all sorts of social gaieties, but it now appeared that these haunts of merriment were only places where one tired oneself to repletion and then spurred weary nature to further exertion. Ellyn could almost have wept over herself, she found the walks of pleasure so distasteful.

Going down the street a half hour later, thinking in a hotly angry heart of how she hated The Kid—only a little less than she hated herself, she met the daughter of the Congregational clergyman, on her way to High School, who whispered to her companion, "Look at Ellyn Lombard—" and turned to look.

If Ellyn could have known, they thought they saw a little girl in a white dress, starting for a day's pleasuring. But she knew herself for what she was, and rather startled The Kid when he asked carelessly, "How you feeling after the spree?"

"Like a drunkard and a thief, thank you. And if you get fresh," she added, savagely, "I'm just as likely to be a murderer."

With which promising anticipation they were borne away through the summer sunshine.

CHAPTER VIII

Anticipation—even apprehension—seldom matches the event. El-lyn had seemed to see herself at this much-dreaded daylight dance, importuned by The Kid to those dalliances which disgusted, while they fascinated. She had scarcely dreamed of being deserted at the very steps of the platform under the pines, where perspiring couples swayed to the music of a funny little German band, very strong as to brass and drum, but otherwise weak, and absolutely devoid of tunefulness.

After tossing the half dollar to the man who sat in front of the gate that broke the expanse of picket fence, and who showed his utter lack of interest in the affair by reading a paper—yes, even when the prettiest girl on the platform did a cake walk, while the one with the best "shape" wriggled in what she called a "Sallyme"—The Kid shouted the glad news, "Gee, look who's here—all the bunch," and forthwith projected himself into a group of youths as like himself as they could very well be and not be printer's devils, but perhaps incipient plumbers, budding bricklayers or full-fledged clerks in general stores.

There were girls in the group, too. Ellyn looked them over, and recognized one or two as belonging to the "shoe shop crowd." They were wont to scurry to the factory at the hour when Ellyn was getting breakfast for herself and David. They wore, then, greasy skirts and old shawls for wrappings, often their hair was in curl papers. At night they straggled home, reeking of leather if you chanced to meet them, hands browned and faces smudged and unbeautiful. Now—what a metamorphosis! They wore such white shoes and silk stockings as Ellyn had only dreamed of, with flimsy dresses, and she whose hair was not marcelled was a wall-flower.

The Kid danced and The Kid smirked—he seemed to be a prime favorite—but his only notice of Ellyn was to send her a glass of beer that was two-thirds foam by one of the replicas of himself, who did not appear to fancy the errand.

"Say, Hamilton told me to bring you this," he remarked, as he see-sawed from one foot to the other in his anxiety to get away.

"Thank you—I don't want it," remarked Ellyn, in a voice that sound-ed strange to her own ears, so parched were her lips, and so weak was she from lack of a breakfast, and yet for that of a dinner.

In response she got an amazed stare, but no further remark, for the youth drank the beer himself, thus removing Ellyn's last chance to wring The Kid's heart by the pain of her refusal.

The afternoon wore on, and Ellyn watching the sun westering, and seeing its light caught by the tops of the pines under which was the dancing pavillion, felt an acuteness of rage that frightened her very self.

Had the world indeed fallen into chaos? Could it be but a day since she had sat in the office, peacefully reading stormy poetry, and afraid of nothing worse than a marauding mouse? Had she bartered David for the meretricious pleasure embodied by The Kid—or had David been actually lost?

She had thought she was doing all this because of sorrow, but it now seemed that she must have come to care for The Kid, since her chief desire was one to bring him again to her side, and to prove how much better a companion she was than the Maymes and Hortenses with whom he was wasting his day. By he went in what passed for a waltz in this company—aenemic, sallow, of meagre form, scrawny neck, red-eyed from want of sleep, his face puffed from much beer, the cleanest thing about him the cigarette stuck on his lower lip. She saw all his deficiencies, she knew he was fit to be despised, and yet all this but increased her rage that he should dare to scorn her. And then, too, she was exasperated at the fact that in the piece of gristle called his heart, and in the resounding vacancy of his head, there must have been hatched up some scheme, some plan, which had resulted in this day. He would not have brought her here, otherwise. She was aflame with curiosity to know what was this plan—she felt that she must soon cry out, and beat someone with her fists, unless she might know and understand.

Yet at the very moment when it seemed that something must happen to break the noisy monotony, The Kid walked down the steps, and out of the gate, and up the alley between the towering pines, with Mayme on one arm—in pink—and Hortense, in arsenic green, on the other, and Ellyn found herself quite friendless. Others were going, too, and the band ceased playing and began putting the instruments into felt bags. The beer kegs were tilted, also, and there was something of a scramble for the last glasses.

Ellyn alone, of all the company, had no farewell word to hear or speak. "Well, so long, Sister! Next time maybe we'll tell our real names!"

238

"Yes, I live down by the river—straight goods I do. When you're that way drop in."

"Say, walk with me. Your number tens might hold the sidewalk down—it keeps coming up and hitting me in the chin."

"Gee, ain't it sump-in' fierce—the way them boys is tanked up."

They trailed away into the gathering twilight, and Ellyn stood, tears of rage coursing down her cheeks, while she clung to the fence in an effort to keep from falling. She knew well enough there was something of revenge to do—if only she might think of it. It was impossible that she should remain in this wood all night—just as it was impossible that she should walk the ten miles back to town. Besides, it was more than ever necessary to make some move that should dent the dullness of The Kid's comprehension.

In a few moments Ellyn felt stronger, and walked aimlessly along the car track to the main road, whence she had come in the early afternoon. There, with a cigarette stuck to his under lip in exactly The Kid's fashion was the youth who had brought her the beer.

"Hamilton said for you to come down to the boardin' house," he observed, in a tone that indicated his errand to be one for which he had absolutely no taste.

"W—where's he?" asked Ellyn, trembling a little.

"Oh, I'd know. Gone up t' th' poolroom t'panhandle car fare, I guess."

Ellyn felt a little better—he hadn't quite forgotten her after all.

"Where's it—the boarding house?" she inquired.

Her companion made a vague sweep over half the horizon with the nicotined hand, and then observed, "I s'pose I c'n pike along down. Gee, I wish Hamilton'd look after his own bunches of skoits."

The boarding house stood big and bare in the midst of a barren field, through which they traipsed, their feet caught by tangles of witch grass, their toes stubbed against debris of tomato cans and broken bottles. It was lighting up time, and some of the windows began to glow.

Just inside the bare hall he spoke once more. "It's the room at the head of the stairs," he remarked, and forthwith vanished into the large room where was spread a table covered with plates of bread and doughnuts, and bright with bottles of catsup and jars of pickled beets.

CHAPTER IX

Ellyn never could remember quite what she expected to find in the room at the head of the stairs, because the picture of what she did find glowed for years in her memory. It was merely a pleasant little snuff dipping party of Mayme and Hortense and six or eight other damsels. The room was very small, and the two beds and one trunk nearly filled it, while the paper was of the large-figured variety, so that the walls appeared to be drawing together in a desire to contract the space even more. Thus the girls were perhaps obliged to sit curled up in grotesque attitudes, with their heads on each other's knees and shoulders—yet somehow, too, this seemed a result of the license of the day, and because no spine was very well able to hold itself upright. Dimmed eyes, somewhat malevolent, were turned on Ellyn as she opened the door, and the voice of Hortense, raised in shrill vehemence as she told a story that had set half of her listeners into agonies of laughter, was hushed. Yet not before Ellyn heard—"brung her just to throw her down, because he had told a feller in the press room—"

It was too much. Ellyn slammed the door in a way that caused snuff-laden sticks to fall from limp fingers of teetery nerves. She ran downstairs and out at the door. Over the railroad track she hurried, and for refuge into the very train that was puffing at the station. Stumbling up the aisle she almost fell into the first vacant seat—it was beside a man, and so strange had been the events of the afternoon that she was not at all surprised to hear him speaking.

"Mighty glad to see you, Miss Ellyn," he observed, in a tone of respect which struck her as amazing strange after the day's adventures. "I just had to come home for supper, but I'm going back again, for we haven't got but one side printed yet, and the paper ought to have been in the mail four hours ago. The Washington played hob with us, for one thing, and then you and the boss both being away the proofs piled up, and I was thinking of slamming the stuff in without correctin' 'em— just for once. Don't believe the readers would tumble."

While he spoke Ellyn's comprehension cleared. After all, there was something solid left. This was the foreman, Mr. Smith, he lived in this town, and rode back and forth four times a day on a pass marked "David Lombard—not transferable." He was handing it now to the conductor, who nodded and said companionably, "Hullo, Smithy, how's everything?" and then added, "Young lady with you?"

"I—I forgot to get a ticket," stammered Ellyn, whereat Mr. Smith grinned, and pointed to the words, "and wife," which in well nigh undistinguishable script appeared on the historic pass.

The conductor was so well-satisfied that after he had taken the rest of the tickets he came back and discussed Bryanism with Mr. Smith until Old Baldy was once more in view.

Though she might have seemed in happier plight than an hour before, still Ellyn was miserable. For one thing she longed to be comforted—longed as does a little child for comforting and petting of a mother—as a child longs more especially if she has done wrong and been punished therefor. Ellyn's mother had died when Ellyn was very wee, yet she could remember hours of bliss when after wrongdoing, and a good sound spanking, she had crept into mother's room and into mother's arms, there to be kissed and soothed and told that it would be "all right tomorrow."

Alas, no one was at hand to tell Ellyn that it would be "all right tomorrow"—and tonight, with an aching head, and every fibre of her ill-used body crying out for food and rest, she must read proof, and answer the many questions of the people who for want of better employment strolled in to ask why the paper was "late again."

To avoid them Ellyn moved into the composing room, where the smell of benzine battled with that of an ill-plumbed sink; where Smith, with a green shade over his eyes, bent above the stone; and two boys giggled into each others' ears as they corrected galleys of type, and a comp or so simultaneously chewed tobacco and spun yarns while throwing in the case.

Out in the press room the "feller" into whose ears The Kid had poured comment of Ellyn, swore none too gently at the Washington hand press, which stood, a mass of obstinate looking iron, obdurate at his efforts. Presently arrived two besmudged machinists from outside, who seemed to have come to help him swear, for that was all they accomplished, beyond a bitter quarrel as to whether the errant bolt was to go this way—or only that.

Through the windows came the sounds of the night—the puffing of an engine far up the road, the chirping of crickets, the wailing of a sleepless child, the shrill cry of a passing night bird—the mingled sounds of city and country that Ellyn was never to hear again, though this she knew not.

And with the reading of each galley of proof Ellyn's much-abused eyes dropped, while a great lassitude crept about and well nigh surrounded her. Never before had she felt as now—hers had been the elasticity of youth, and even when weary she had been able to rally herself for extra work, often asked for on occasions like this.

"Why—what is the matter?" she asked herself. "Did not David and I once work three days, without leaving the office, when we got out the tax book? And when it was over wasn't I just ready to use the circus comps?"

Yet now she knew the meaning of nature's "thou shalt not," as it is usually known only to the old and decrepit. She read a paragraph, and thought "I can never read another," yet still another was read. And Mr. Smith came and showed her a word misspelled, and a name uncorrected, yet so dulled was her brain that she did not care, or indeed quite comprehend what should be done to make things right.

And still through the open windows came the sounds of the night—the straining and coughing of the mogul engine as it labored up the incline with a long freight, the whirring of a tree toad, and curses of a homeward wandering "drunk," the tender call of one passing bird to another—these Ellyn was never to hear again, though this she knew not.

CHAPTER X

It was a mistake—that mad dash down the alley, in the hope of finding night air a cure for blurred intelligence. The alley, upon which the boiler room gave, was paved with refuse, and odorous of the beer saloon on the corner, its alley door yielding impartially dregs of casks and dregs of humanity—too far gone to be tolerated even in the all-tolerant back room. Ellyn felt it was a mistake, even as she hurried, she hardly realized whither, knocking against the ash barrels on the dirt sidewalk, stumbling over the marauding rats in the roadway.

She was going home, to her room in the face of Old Baldy. She would it had been to sleep, for weariness was in all her body, but there would be more proofs ere long, to say nothing of the "stone proof" impending. She had run away from duty—she, who had never run from duty before—and it would be impossible to return. But in the meantime there was the peaceful little room—and the touch of cool water for one's face—and there was also the flask in the enamelled desk.

And that was the greatest mistake of all. Ellyn found the flask, found it in the dark, since the evil-smelling lamp refused to light for want of filling. With shaking hands she bore the flask to the door, and viewed it in the light from the hall. Half its contents remained. What would happen should she drink it? Ellyn wondered. She tried to recall vague stories, told in the office on November nights while the men waited for election returns. Was there not a man, vaguely known to have reformed and become a pillar of some religious edifice, who once picked up a precarious living making bets he could swallow a vast quantity of whiskey at a draught, and invariably doing it? But what was the quantity? Ellyn wavered between the misty amount mentioned as "a bottle" and the more likely "all the other fellow could pay for."

To counterbalance this there was the harrowing tale of the child who "got at" the family medicine cupboard, and died in awful agony after taking "one swallow" from the brandy flask.

"I am not a child," said Ellyn, foolishly—for she was very tired, in mind as well as body—and then repeated, "I am not a child."

And while the flask clattered against the tumbler, she poured and drank it all; then, wide-eyed, waited the result.

There was no result. Ellyn's excitement perhaps acted as a counter-irritant, or her oft-denied body may have seized upon what nutriment there was in the Gem drugstore apology for whiskey. At any rate, Ellyn was merely a trifle more sodden in mind than before, but otherwise unchanged. She walked steadily downstairs, without the slightest idea that she was bidding goodbye to that room in which everything was eagerly pretending to be something else. She left the sardine oil smelling unto heaven in the unwashed dishes, David's socks unmended, the tumbled couch as she had crawled from it in the morning, the tell-tale flask upon the mantle shelf incongruously half-hiding the passe partouted William Ellery Channing "Creed" which David had presented to her the previous Christmas. For below stairs was The Kid, pale and penitent, and his arguments seemed to prevail that they both "cut sticks," though really I think it was Ellyn's own ill-regulated heart that urged her to shirk responsibility.

CHAPTER XI

The Kid talked at staccato intervals all the way to the station, where the 6.23 was rather more overdue than usual.

His arguments—

"I always said if I got enough money I'd cut this town. I got enough money. Never YOU mind where I got it. Or how. I got enough. Five dollars. I've doped it all out. A dollar apiece to Bosting, then you can get a room in Pleasant street, or Warrenton—a cheap joint, but that will be only till we get jobs. I know a fellow will put me up till I hep to something. Gee, he ought to. I've hid him in the press room lots o' nights, last winter, when he was razzle-dazzled, and afraid to go home to his old man. Kept him from freezing alive out in the snow."

"What do I want to have you pike along for? Say, you're a suspicious piece of cheese, ain't you now? S'pose I want to do you a good turn—get you out o' this one-hoss place. A smart girl like you can certainly make good in the city. Oh, all that fluff today didn't amount to a hoorah in hell. I'd a took you home all right, only you was so darn previous. And I know you can't dance. That's another thing to pick up in the city. Say, won't we just have the time of our lives? I wouldn't wonder if there was some sort of a toe-fest bein' held ev'ry evening in Bosting—no, I won't even leave Sunday out. Looks likely they can't have cops everywhere at one time—no, SIR!"

He bought the two tickets, and Ellyn noticed that he paid for them with a five dollar bill. Then he returned to her and went on, in a low tone so as not to be overheard by the one other passenger, "No use gettin' blue moulded workin' just for rags an' a place to doss in. The city's the place. Always something doin', and salaries somethin 'scanal'ous. Gosh, there was Hank Bennett—you know, clerked over to Whitney's, for $6 per. Came to Bosting, and was pulling out a thousand dollars a year. I know, 'cause his sister told a feller 'n the feller told me. A thousand dollars! Why, they ain't half a dozen in this town gets that, and what's the use, when there's nothing to spend it for. Not so much as a moving picture show, and the op'ry house only light two nights a week. In Bosting—grand shows, 100—count 'em—girl cut-ups, and such-like, while we've been moseying along with Uncle Tom—and only one Eva or dog—and Comical Brown. Say, that fellow was stale in Bosting years before you and I was invented. Hark! There she is. Come on."

The Kid's eloquence, as will be noted, was well worth preservation, but it had every bit been wasted on Ellyn. She had listened only to the anxious beating of her own heart, which grew tumultuous as the train rolled in. David—would he be thereon, as he had been the night before? And if he was would she take courage to run into his arms, and beg him to forgive her choice variety of crimes? Or at least would she not first confesss how she had deserted the proofs—and then she was sure he would tell her to run home to bed—tell her in that rumbling yet sweet and satisfying tone of his which was to her, now more than ever, the dearest sound of all those for hearing.

Well, David was not on the train; the daughter of the Congregational clergyman was. She came from two stations up, where she had played tennis all the afternoon; and was now rather scared at being out so late. As she passed Ellyn she condescended to speak. Her tone was scornful, her remark meant to be sarcastic.

"I suppose you and your beau are going to Boston for ice cream," she observed, choosing this pleasant allusion to the contretemps of the previous evening as about the best adapted to cut Ellyn to the heart—not that she had anything against Ellyn, you know, only Ellyn was such a ridiculous little thing, with her self-devised frocks, and her sore throat bandages of collars, and her chopped hay hair, that it would have shown lack of refined taste to have treated her as another girl and an equal.

The chance to be revenged, instantly, for many cuts direct was too good to be neglected by Ellyn. Grabbing the ticket from The Kid, she swept it under the nose of the minister's daughter, as she said, "Ya'as, that's exactly what we're going to do."

The Kid, too, with all his faults, rose manfully to the occasion. As the train carried them from sight of Old Baldy, he imperilled his precious neck by leaning from the car window and yelling back, "No more op'ry caramels for us—nothing but Heyler's!"

Crude boasting, but somehow it impressed the one it was meant to impress, who scurried home wondering, after all, if she had lost anything by not taking up funny little Ellyn. So what did it matter that Ellyn was crying miserably into the cold window glass that separated her from the night, while The Kid frankly snored in the opposite seat. Ellyn might feel that she was proving herself a failure by running away, nevertheless her slight triumph over the sneering girl but typified her start on a road to success.

So cynical, however, is life, that after the usual fashion, no inkling of this cheering fact was accorded Ellyn. She entered Boston, sometime to be a witness of her triumph, in a cringing mood.

It seemed to her that they walked through a series of back streets, badly lighted and very badly side-walked, until they arrived before a huge mass of brick, towering arrogantly over the narrow and winding street.

"Is this Pleasant Street?" asked Ellyn, and "No, it ain't," succinctly responded The Kid, breaking a silence of some hours. Then he abruptly plunged into the doorway, leaving Ellyn alone to brave the imagined horrors of the street. Though nothing happened worse than a couple of marauding cats she was glad to see his ugly face, after fifteen minutes.

"He don't doss here no more," said Arthur Montmorency, etc., as he implied they were to resume their march. The next stop was before a dark facade, whence came sounds of clinking balls.

There was firm determination in The Kid's aspect as the journey was once more resumed, nor was it long before he again halted Ellyn, and she ventured, "Is this Pleasant Street?" and again he answered, "No, it ain't." This time, however, his speech went on: "This is a Young Women's Chris'ian joint. The fellow I'm going to bunk with put me wise to it. They don't want no coin if a girl puts up a story about getting into the city alone at night, and being scared of lodgings. Tell 'em you want a job, too. They'll put you next."

"It looks—awful gone-to-bed," quoth Ellyn.

Just then two girls swung up arm in arm, ran up the steps, and pulled the bell with an accustomed hand. Aided by a vigorous poke from The Kid, Ellyn joined them, while that deserter scudded into the night.

"Hullo," said one. "You on a night job, too?"

"N-no," faltered Ellyn, "I just got in. I want to stay here."

"I suppose Miss Scudding wasn't at the station? She doesn't meet the last ones. I guess the night watch can give you something." This from the other girl—with the imitation Panama hat, which Ellyn respected because she thought it real. The one who had spoken flopped onto a settee and groaned, "I though we'd never get counted up, and the boss, instead of ordering a good feed sit us all down to—cold lamb!"

The night watch proved friendly, and in a few minutes Ellyn was in a room, largely hardwood floors and painted walls. She put up the shade, but the outlook was only a brick wall, and "So this is Boston," she thought, then a tap at the door, and the girl with the Panama whispered, "My chum and I noticed you hadn't any handbag. Don't you want a nighty?"

Ellyn accepted the disproportionate garment with a sense of gratitude.

So this was—Boston!

[to be continued]

WHO BROUGHT THE CHILDREN HOME?

The Duett, November-December 1885

"This river runs to the sea," said Lady Margaretta. At least that was what her Ladyship meant to say; what she really remarked was, "Dis wiver wuns to 'e sea." Her Ladyship was so taken up with the etiquette of her exalted station that she had not yet learned to roll her r's. The word of Lady Margaretta was law. Davy and Dimples stopped digging in the dirt, while Pet Phillips dropped the frog he had been admiringly holding in his plump hand, and inquired, "Do it?" Lady Margaretta nodded emphatically.

"I'th never theen the thea," lisped Dimples, putting out her lip, and beginning to cry.

"An' I know where there's a weal boat with oars," continued Lady Margaretta, who was the leader in all mischievous schemes.

"Where?" shouted Pet.

"We'll get it an' wow it," said Lady Margaretta, starting on a run for the red boat house which stood not far away. Pet rushed after her, losing his cap, while little fat Dimples fell down and scratched her knees in endeavoring to keep up with him. Davy followed more slowly. He was a pretty little Scotch boy, with long brown curls and a blue kilt suit. He was not used to playing with children, and the impetuous ways of Lady Margaretta and her companions somewhat bewildered him. When he reached the boat house he found Lady Margaretta tugging at the single knot which fastened a green row boat, known as the *Water Lily*, to the wharf.

"Tumble in," said she, "'n hurry 'fore anybody comes."

"Isn't it naughty?" asked Davy.

Lady Margaretta, who had just unfastened the boat, seated herself in the stern seat and pouted.

"Stay 'way," she said, "if you're 'fraid."

Davy looked at the little lady with his big brown eyes. Then he climbed into the boat and said very gently, "I'm not afraid if you aren't."

"Pooh!" said Lady Margaretta, "it's dust as easy! We don't even have to wow—do we, Pet? The wiver takes us wight along."

"Hurrah!" shouted Pet, standing upright at the bow, and waving his Tam o'Shanter. "We're a band o' jolly tars started on a cruise to—to the end of the world. Let's discover something before we come back."

"All wight," said Lady Margaretta; "cum over here, an' tell me what we'll 'scover."

And so the green boat, with its long rope trailing behind and its precious cargo of thoughtless children making gorgeous plans, floated gently down the current of the rapidly widening river. The water course was clear and blue, bounded by flat green meadows. The day was sunny, but cool and breezy. White and fleecy clouds fluttered over the sky and cast floating black shadows in the water.

The boat went under a bridge, where two country children were fishing for shiners. Pet twitched the boy's line, and made him believe he had caught a fish. This pleased the voyagers greatly. And once they found a few stunted pond lilies. But on the whole the voyage was an uneventful one. Pet took of out his pocket the yellow covered *Sailor's Yarn of Merry Mike, the Boy Mariner of Timbuctoo*, and nestling down in the bottom of the boat, pulled his jacket over his ears to shut out the sun, and read cozily. Dimples went to sleep, with her little round mouth wide open, and her curly hair blowing all over her face. Davy sat in the stern, leaning his cheek on his hand, while Lady Margaretta sat stiff and straight at the prow, looking steadily seaward with her little green eyes, while the wind blew her short sandy hair in a little stubby aureole all about her face.

By this description you will see that Lady Margaretta was not pretty; and by her running away you have already learned that she was not good. Even the name by which she was commonly called was not romantic like Dimple's or Pet's; at home she was known simply as Bob, from some supposed resemblance to a cousin in far off India.

High noon came; the sun slipped directly over the children's heads, and began to sink towards the West. Suddenly Lady Margaretta called, "The sea! The ocean!"

Dimples awoke and rolled over sleepily, rocking the boat violently. Pet slipped his book into his pocket, and looked around, half dazed. Before them was outstretched the wide green sea water, on which tiny white caps were just beginning to form. On one side of them was a long stretch of yellow sand; on the other a flat swamp, covered with rank salt grass. Above this swamp was a turf grown dune, crowned by three lofty trees, behind which the low sun lay. A number of huge rocks lay in the middle of the stream, directly across the boat's path. These only kept the children from sweeping out on the open sea. The boat grated gently against one of these crags and then stopped entirely, moving only slightly with the lapping of the waves.

Pet immediately jumped to the summit of the rock, shouting, "In Lady Retta's name I discover you, and name you the Isle of Margaret," adding, "Hand me up some water in your hat. I must sprinkle the island. That's always the way, after 'scovering things."

Meanwhile Davy pointed to the tree crowded dune, and whispered to Lady Margaretta, "Don't you see some one up there?"

Lady Margaretta shaded her eyes with her hand and looked earnestly at the hill. Then she jumped to her feet, crying, "It is some one, and they are beckoning to us!"

Dimples was frightened, and began to cry; Pet wondered if he could jump the two feet of space between rock and rock, and so reach the land that way, while Davy drew off his shoes and stockings, saying, "I can swim a little."

But Lady Margaretta threw her arms tightly around the lad, and holding him close, exclaimed, "You sha'n't! You sha'n't!" Davy turned his face up to hers and said, soberly, "There is some one there who needs help. They can't get away unless I go to them, and I must."

At this moment something shook the boat, and turning they saw that the person on the hill had come to the edge of the swamp and was throwing stones at them.

"Can't we wow the oars?" whispered Lady Margaretta, still clinging to Davy.

Pet came tumbling into the boat. "I know," said he, "tie a stone to the rope, and fling to shore."

Three pairs of busy hands hastened to draw in the long length of stiff rope which had trailed behind them all the voyage. Three times did they throw the rope towards land, and only the last time did it go near the shore. The third time the person in the swamp waded out into the water, caught the rope and drew the boat towards land. Pet, Davy and Lady Margaretta stood up and clapped their hands, while poor little Dimples lay in the bottom of the boat shaking her fat shoulders with sobs.

As they neared the shore the person holding the rope climbed into the boat, seized the oars, and began rowing up stream. She appeared to be a young girl not more than fifteen years old, with a very slight form. She had yellow hair which hung in two long plaits almost to her feet. Her face was very white, while her cheeks bore a hectic flush of red. She had no hat and wore a plain gray gown, with wet and draggled skirts. The dress was open at the throat, and showed her thin, bony neck. She rowed nervously with a quick, irregular stroke, never looking at the children, who were regarding her with wide open, awe-stricken eyes. Dimples stopped crying from very fear; Pet opened his yellow covered book, and examined the picture of the heroine, silently comparing her with their mysterious oarswoman. Davy clasped Lady Margaretta's hand, while the sandy locks of the latter grew bristlier than ever.

As they went on, the sun quietly sank out of sight, and gray twilight began to creep over the river. The banks became black, and the trees were outlined sharply against the star-dotted sky. Suddenly the strange girl began to sing in a high pitched, shrill, but not unmusical voice:

> "Early in the morning,
> Blooming fresh and fair;
> Bertha at the gate way
> Is watching everywhere;
> Up the road and down the lane—
> Watching, watching longest
> The way that Robin came."

After trolling this joyously she suddenly turned to Davy, and laughed shrilly. "Isn't that a nice song?" she asked.

"Yes," murmured Davy.

"Ha, ha!" she shrieked, "you're wrong there. Because he never came, you see."

"Lost! lost! lost!
Do you know I have lost my love?
Cold, and white, and silent,
He lies in the chamber above.
Lost! lost! lost!
Never again my own.
Would I were dead beside him,
With a heart as cold as his own."

And then she leaned on the oars, and laughed once more, in a discordant manner. Just then a voice broken on the darkness, shouting, "Boat, aho-o-o-y!"

"Yes, yes," shrieked the children, recovering their voices.

Steps were heard on shore, then a hand clutched the boat and drew it to the wharf. Some one came out of the boat house, bearing a large lantern.

"You bad, bad, bad children," the first speaker ejaculated, picking Dimples from the boat much as he would have handled a fat white rabbit.

"I'm hungry," said Pet.

"I'm theepy," moaned Dimples.

"I've had a—splendid time," said Lady Margaretta, stoutly endeavoring to pretend she was telling the truth.

"You'll get punished when you get to the house," said the young man with the lantern. "I can tell you that. But how did you get back?"

"The queer girl," whispered Lady Margaretta, clinging to the hand of her big brother.

He turned the light of the lantern directly on the boat, and found Davy standing on the wharf, with wide open, frightened eyes, staring at—nothing!

The boat was empty!

And to this day no one knows who brought the children home.

'LIZABETH PRUE?

The Palladium, March-April 1886

It was a cold morning of a day in late October. The sky was a deep, cheerless blue; the grass a frost whitened brown; and the trees were masses of gray, leafless twigs. The air was biting and keen, a "piping and an eager air," yet exhilarating and stirring in its effects.

'Lizbeth Prue, as she walked down the well beaten foot-path leading from the pasture to the barn, felt new joy in her placid nature, as she breathed the crisp air. 'Lizbeth Prue's way was through a long and crooked lane, boggy and wet in places, rough and rocky all along. On one side of the lane was a moss-covered stone wall, on the other a straggling Virginia rail-fence served as a support for bittersweet and frost grape-vines. The frost had partially opened the bittersweet berries, and the yellow shell parted to show the crimson within. The tiny frost grapes hung in diminutive deep purple clusters, under the shriveled brown leaves. Clumps of ferns—brakes, 'Lizbeth Prue called them—some yet a tender green, others brown and sere, still others bleached a pale yellow by the frost, covered the bank under the wall. 'Lizbeth Prue stopped to taste the grapes; to pluck a bunch of the bittersweet and tuck it into the belt of her calico gown; and to pick up a handful of the satiny, brown chestnuts, lying under a tree, among the fresh green burrs of this year, and the brown spikes of seasons past. Bits of dead blackberry briars caught at 'Lizbeth Prue's gown; and two pronged thorns of the weed called hound's tongue, fastened themselves to the fringe of her shawl; and it was only be extreme care that she escaped the burdock burrs, and the thistle-down, ever watching to catch the unwary. Even this peaceful lane had its Apollyons.

'Lizbeth Prue crossed a tiny brook by the bridge formed by a single stone laid from bank to bank, and climbed a little hill, at the top of which was a lofty bar-way. At this bar-way she stopped, and leaning on the top rail looked down into the valley. Before her was a wide ploughed field, rough with corn stubble, and the yellow pumpkins which had not yet been gathered. A single thorn tree, with crimson fruit, stood in the centre of this field. Below this, and half hidden by the brow of the hill, was a large brown barn, and a square white house, connected by a series of rambling sheds, in varying states of primness or dilapidation. 'Lizbeth Prue finally climbed the wall, and began to pick her way along the edge of the field, where weeds and grass held sway, avoiding the muddy ground, which was partially frozen in the night. By slipping down a bank, she found herself at the door of the barn. Pushing down the log which had been rolled against it, 'Lizbeth entered the barn. It was sweet with the odors of hay, grain, and apples. Several barrels of the red and green fruit filled the space known as the "Floor," and heaps of the poorer qualities were lying on the ground, just inside the door, partially covered with old sacks and blankets. The yard of the farm-house was alive with fowls, pecking apples, plucking grains of corn from some gnarled ears lying about, scratching the ground, or drinking sour milk from a stone trough in their usual ecstatic manner. Piles of shining milk pans were sunning on a superannuated ox cart; and a demure white kitten gravely chased its tail on the house steps.

'Lizbeth Prue, after carefully rubbing her shoes on a corn husk mat, lifted the latch, and, with a backward glance at the clear morning, reluctantly entered the house.

The kitchen which she entered was large and low. It had three windows, two looking northward, and shaded by a mass of lilac bushes, one on the south, but darkened by the vine shaded porch before it. The room furthermore had sixteen doors, nearly all of a different size and with a different method of fastening. To further vary matters, every door had its own way of opening, rather bewildering to strangers. But the family knew that the cellar door opened with a touch, on a precipitous flight of steep stairs; that the parlor door required lifting up; the chamber stairs door a pressing down; the pantry door a pushing; while the hall door could only be opened by heavy bodies falling against it. The shed door, opening into a cold and draughty place, was as difficult to keep shut, as the others were to open. It had a ghostly way of lifting its own latch, and swinging wide with a crash, when the house was very still, and no one expected it to do so. Every door also possessed an individual squeak. Besides these peculiarities, the kitchen had a smoky ceiling, a large number of shaky tables and uncomfortable chairs; and a cooking stove which required more ingenious treatment than all the doors combined. The kitchen walls were covered with dirty striped paper; several guns and rifles stood in one corner; and the end of the room opposite the stove was filled with wide shelves, on which rested every variety of odds and ends, from bottles of vinegar and goose oil to old china and powder horns. When it is added that the paint was worn from the floor in paths from one door to another; that cobwebs lurked by the windows; that a pan of fat was hissing on the stove; and also that the kitchen had two occupants, you see the room very much as did 'Lizbeth Prue on that October morning.

As 'Lizbeth entered, a pretty child, with blue eyes and a head covered with tangled curls, ran forward and clung to her gown, putting up his red lips for a kiss.

"I'se up, 'Lizbeth," he lisped, "I let mammy wath my fathe, too!"

"What a good little boy."

"But the tha'n't comb my hair, tho now!" continued Willie.

'Lizbeth passed one hand over his curls caressingly, and went forward to the fire. Her shawl fell off, and showed her lithe, girlish figure. 'Lizbeth's dark hair hung in a single massive braid down her back; her cheeks were somewhat pale, her brown eyes looked truthful and clear.

The well preserved matron who was busy with a pan of flour and a kettle of fat, frying crullers, had a light step, a cheery laugh, and a pleasant voice. She cast many anxious glances toward the stairs door, and remarked to 'Lizbeth Prue: "Tom ain't up yet, I'm thinkin' something must be the matter. The table's stood this two hour for him. But boys will be thoughtless—" Her speech was interrupted by the opening of the door, and the entrance of a young man. He came into the room without a word of greeting, advanced to the mantel shelf, seized a tallow dip, lit it at the fire, and silently marched down the cellar stairs. The matron stole a furtive glance at 'Lizbeth, and turned away, that the girl might not see the tears which glistened in her eyes. Tom came up bearing a huge earthen pitcher full of sparkling cider; he poured out a glass full and swallowed it at a draught, before extinguishing the candle. Then he drew an arm chair to the table, put his books on the stone hearth, and settled himself to drinking in earnest. Tom Bassett was a good looking young man, with heavy features, a becoming flush on his brown cheeks, and an expression marred only by a somewhat sullen frown.

While 'Lizbeth cleared the table, and washed the breakfast plates, with little Willie yet clinging to her gown, and the mother skimmed the cream in the dairy, Tom drank the pitcher's contents in solitary grandeur, then got up, yawned heavily, took a cartridge belt and game bag from the wall, and strapped the one about him, and slung the other over his shoulder, then lit a pipe with a blazing coal, seized a rifle, and left the house. While he was thus moving about, 'Lizbeth several times looked into his eyes with an earnest pleading, but elicited no word from that firmly closed mouth.

The day wore on, and 'Lizbeth and the mother worked on at the many household tasks, each one crushing down a grief which was nonetheless severe for being daily felt. The sun rose to the zenith, and then sank horizonwards, yet sent no ray into the dusky kitchen. The noonday meal was eaten, the table cleared, and tea time had nearly come, yet Tom had not returned. As it drew near candle lighting time, 'Lizbeth left Mother Bassett sitting by the northern windows, catching the last bit of daylight for her knitting, and went out into the yard. The sun's light had almost disappeared, and the evening star faintly glimmered in the last bit of rose tinted sky left in the West. The ground was cold and wet, while the chilly air was somewhat damp. 'Lizbeth put the slices of apples drying on an old table at the south side of the house, into a pan, and carried them into the shed. Then she went down to the barn, and swinging open the wide door looked up the lane. She saw a long line of brown and white cows coming down the path, each one shaking its horns and snuffing the air suspiciously as they filed past her. As the last one entered the barn, their driver came out of the dusk, merrily whistling. As he came to 'Lizbeth's side he held out a bunch of flowers.

"Blue gentians," he said, "I found them in the meadow—they'd have frozen tonight sure."

The freckled and red-haired Davy Hardin, the gentle-voiced and pleasant-faced "hired help," who was kind to even the cats and chickens, this poetic drudge, who had never known a home, or a mother or possessed twenty-five dollars of his own, loved 'Lizbeth Prue as tenderly, chivalrously, and almost as hopelessly as John Alden loved Priscilla of yore. That she accepted the flowers, and even thanked him for them, was sufficient to send him about the night's work with a cheery heart.

When 'Lizbeth, followed by Davy, entered the kitchen they found a most cheerful scene. The fire burned bright, and the stove doors had been flung open, so as to show the blazing wood, behind the iron bars. Little Willie, kneeling in an arm chair, was watching the chestnuts roasting on the top of the stove. Mrs. Bassett was setting the tea to steep, while a tallow dip, on a high shelf, faintly illumined the apartment. 'Lizbeth placed herself in the chair by the fire, taking Willie in her lap, while Davy busied himself with bringing in billets of wood, pumping water in the chilly shed, and locking the back part of the house for the night. When everything was done, he allowed himself the pleasure of standing in the dusk, leaning on the mantel shelf, and staring furtively at 'Lizbeth Prue.

Quite suddenly the placid scene was disturbed. The door was flung open, and a rush of chilly air swept into the room, followed by half a dozen dogs, who ran over everything with incessant restlessness, explored every corner, sniffed at every chair, licked everyone's hands, and barked at the fire and candle. After the dogs came Tom, who slammed the door vengefully, and began to swear at the restless animals.

"Be still, can't you, you——brutes!" he shouted, kicking one of them half way across the room.

"They are hungry," said 'Lizbeth, half timidly.

"No wonder—they've run some forty miles since morning," returned Tom. "But I'll feed them when I've had something myself."

"Supper will be ready right off," said his mother. "I'll make you some good strong coffee."

"No slops!" Tom brutally answered. "Dave, go down and draw some cider."

Mrs. Bassett came forward, and laid her hand on her son's arm. "Tom, dear, you had best not. You are tired—"

He shook her roughly off, and began drawing the soft plumaged partridge and woodcock from his game bag. Then he threw bag and belt to the floor, and threw himself into a chair. He drank, and cursed the dogs, then drank again, and watched carefully while his mother fed the beasts, and continued to drink himself into a savage fitness for retiring.

Later in the evening, Davy led the dogs out into the shed for the night, while 'Lizbeth carried the nodding Willie up the stairs to his crib. While the child knelt before his pillow, and repeated a prayer, with one arm about 'Lizbeth's neck, the girl looked out at the clear stars, shining undeviatingly in the black heavens, and thought of the time when she herself had been but a child, and how that then her cousin Tom had been as sweet, and kind, and pure as was now this little one, his tiny brother Willie. And 'Lizbeth also realized that the love which had grown up in her heart for the sweet boy Tom, yet clung to the rough, sullen, wicked man.

A harsh voice calling, "'Lizbeth! 'Lizbeth!" roused her from her reverie, and giving Willie a hurried kiss, she groped her way into the dark hall. As she went past the door of Mrs. Bassett's room, that good woman came out, rather shamefacedly, and whispered to 'Lizbeth: "Go downstairs, please. Tom—he wants you. You know why—we've all understood 'twas coming quite a while. Tom's better than he seems," she continued, pleadingly; meanwhile, she nervously fingered her apron, and avoided looking into 'Lizbeth's eyes. "He'll be a kind husband. If it was anyone else," she went on, hurriedly, "I—I might tell you different, but you've always been a daughter to me—I can't let you go away from me and the old place. Perhaps you can get Tom to do different."

"Aunt Bassett," exclaimed 'Lizbeth, letting her dark eyes flash suddenly on the cowering mother, "I know what Tom is. And I know that he will only grow worse—no man who is deaf to the wishes of his sweetheart, will change his ways to obey a wife. But I love your son Tom—and because of that I will marry him—drunkard though he be. I don't expect to be happy," she cried desperately, then, brushing away the hot tears which had rushed to her eyes, and choking down a tendency to sob, she left the astonished mother, and went down the stairs to the kitchen.

As she opened the door she saw Tom, still drinking at the opposite end of the room, while Davy Hardin stood near her, as if he had been waiting for her entrance.

Coming to her side he said, in a low and wistful tone, "He is savage—he is wild—I don't know what he may do. I shall stay here—if you need any help—"

"'Lizbeth!" shouted the demon.

'Lizbeth drew near to him, never looking at Davy. Tom turned, and stared at her from under his heavy eyebrows for fully ten minutes. Then he got up, grasped her wrist, and said: "Is your mind made up?

Will you take my name peaceably, or will you choose to be dragged to the Parson's? Have you done playing with me—contrary minx—or do you wish for more coaxing?"

As he spoke he grasped her arm tighter, and she inadvertently gave a little cry of pain. Davy Hardin sprang forward, his eyes flashing and his fist clenched. But before either of the two became aware of his presence, 'Lizbeth had looked up into Tom's face, and said slowly, "Yes, Tom, I will marry you."

Davy Hardin, feeling as if some one had dealt him an unexpected blow, left the room and the house. Out under the stars he stood, the damp wind lifting the hair on his uncovered brow, the sharp air nipping his bare cheek. He did not hear the chirp of a lone cricket, the shriek of an owl on the hill top, or the lowing of the cattle in the barn. He stood quite still, his eyes on the ground, his dazed brain unable to decide whether that which had stunned him was a great joy, or an overwhelming grief.

THE WOMAN OVER
THE WAY

The Ubiquitous, June 1887

Two women were gazing out at the early evening of a day in September. From opposite sides of a narrow village street they watched for a single object. The window enshrining one of the twain was in the attic of a prim, white-painted cottage. It had well-scrubbed panes, set in lead, and was shaded by a scrupulously clean cotton curtain, edged with ball fringe, and looped methodically. The house itself was embellished with green blinds and a narrow green door, on which shone a knocker of brass. A square courtyard, carefully fenced in by white palings and carpeted with clipped grass, separated the house from the weed-grown street. The narrow door was approached by a spotless gravel path, edged with box. A single evergreen tree was before the parlor windows. The yard resembled nothing so much as a "family lot" in an old-fashioned cemetery, and the plaster of paris urn standing on the opposite side of the yard, and balancing the evergreen shrub, completed the likeness. The cottage itself was very ugly, very neat and very silent. Every window was darkened excepting that at which Miss Elsa Norton, spinster, sat at work from a day's beginning to end. Miss Elsa had once been beautiful, and forty years had only subdued her face, so that it was handsome. Her thick brown hair was always becomingly dressed, and on this September evening she wore a gown of rich maroon silk, with frills of old lace, that softened the angles of her bony hands and subdued the sallow tone of her complexion. Her fingers were occupied in the manufacture of "tatting," and several valuable jewels, in old-fashioned settings, glistened regularly with each precise movement. The room in which she sat was square and bold, a window in the exact middle of the front wall, a door on each of the other three sides. A Brussels carpet with a "set" pattern in green and brown roses stretched from wall to wall. The gilt paper was offensively new, and the woodwork had so recently been painted a glaring white that the odor of its freshness was not yet obliterated. As a matter of course the room was furnished with a marble-top table, and several chairs upholstered in green rep; and each separate article, from Miss Elsa to the tatting-bobbin, gave forth an impression of calm sumptuousness, of respectable luxury.

The house from which the woman on the other side watched was a straggling, brown structure, abutting directly on the street. Ivy, now crimsoning with the first touch of autumn, clustered about its windows and helped to destroy the rotting clapboards with its clinging tendrils. The low-lying sun shone directly over the opposite cottage and in at the front windows, glorifying Mary Brown's modest parlor into a very mosaic of yellow and red. Mary's room was small and paneled with unstained butternut wood, its few chairs were rush-bottomed and old, and the table stood crookedly on the sunken floor. But there was a fire of apple boughs blazing in the rusty grate, a vase of yellow nasturtiums on the low mantelpiece, a willow cradle in one corner, and a copper tea kettle singing happily over a spirit lamp. Mary herself, though she had no claims to beauty, or even prettiness, was yet a fascinating little figure as she sat in the low rocker by the window, half shaded from the sight of her neighbor by the faded red moreen curtain. The sunlight, filtered through the crimson cloth, gave an artificial flush to her brown cheeks, and added a golden lustre to her hair of a glossless, flaxen drab. Mary's plump figure was clad in a brown gingham gown, and there was but a single ring on her fat left hand. But the treasure of all her treasures she held on her arm. The baby—as yet without a name—was very much like other babies. He possessed a rudimentary nose, pale blue eyes, dimpled cheeks and a flaxen fuzz of hair. His lungs were undeniably strong, and he seemed to derive great enjoyment from sucking his own pink fist. He was engaged in this engrossing occupation just now, as he lay over his mother's arm, his face against her shoulder and her cheek resting lightly on his nearly bald little crown. He was silently blinking at the moat of dust which the strong sunshine, creeping through the crack between the window-frame and the red curtain, was apparently driving directly at him. Meanwhile his mother was thinking earnestly, agonizingly. She was absolutely unhappy, and the fact could not at all times be crushed out of mind. The wife of her first and only love, Marc Brown, the mother of his child, sitting at this very instant in expectation of his return, sure of feeling his kiss upon her lips before she could run to meet him, she was yet suffering too poignantly for tears. There was in her heart the very same mixture of hate and jealousy which embittered each day belonging to the life of the woman opposite. Though Marc's brown eyes still looked lovingly upon her, though he was absolutely kind, though he knew no enjoyment beyond watching her and the baby, and no object beyond caring for both, there was omnipresent the memory that once he had planned for himself a different life, with another companion.

On this evening, while the sunbeams gradually dissipated themselves away and only gray twilight remained, each woman was living in the past—the past of Marc Brown.

Elsa saw herself the brilliant daughter of a New England "Squire," living in vulgar opulence, dressing gorgeously, as girls were then permitted to do, spending her days in a round of country pleasures. She danced her way into the heart of Marc Brown, then young, like herself, poor and handsome, earnest, truthful, talented. She again responded to his gay, trifling, ardent affection with a love as lasting and passionate as it was unreasonable, hence more did the solemnity of her nature rebel at his jesting courtship. Daily did she learn that he to whom she gave her whole heart and life was incapable, from very shallowness of character, of appreciating her utter abnegation. Where she longed for protection and adoration, he gave fantastic favors, warm, but mere affection. While she longed to worship him, he only wished companionship; her wish for self-sacrifice was utterly useless. At length, in an instant of fierce anger at the frivolity of her idol, she had wildly given him back her troth and sent him from her with a fire of words which only stunned him, while they stung her bitterly. His liberty once gained, he never returned to her side. It mattered not that she humbled herself in her agony, and besought him for only one look, one word of kindness.

A man must not wear his heart upon his sleeve, and so successfully did Marc Brown hide his wounds that the world never suspected him of having been jilted. He had loved Elsa with the ardor of youth, but it was as the love of man, capable of changing. But one man in a legion is capable of utter constancy, and Marc Brown was but an average man. He forgot Elsa, and he learned to love Mary. At least Elsa believed he loved her. From her post over the way she tortured herself by watching his quiet and happy married life and on this very evening there was a wail in her heart. Mary, sitting in a blaze of sunshine, with Marc Brown's baby in her arms, and bearing his name and wearing his ring, was to her typical of everything that was bright and joyous.

And yet—if she could only have known!—that same woman was bitterly envying her. For Mary Brown, basking in the sunshine of Marc's smiles, had ever with her the haunting memory that once his words of love had been said to another, that once the guide star of his life had been the woman across the way. Mary felt that she would forfeit all her happy married life, all her present pride in husband and child, to be the calm, narrow-lived woman in the white cottage. For, however little joy there was now in that woman's existence, she had yet and ever the surety that she had been his first love.

And that woman also was vainly wishing she might give up riches, beauty, love even, could she be the wife of Marc Brown, could she be near him, even though he hated her.

And while the usurper was envying the usurped, and the cherished wife longed for power to become the despised and lonely spinster, Marc Brown was striding down the street, his broad figure shadowed before him, by the watery beams of a slender new moon, and a coral rattle for the baby in his pocket.

THE OTHER ELIZABETH

The Nugget, November 1888

AUTHOR'S NOTE—This confession was found and given to me by the daughter who in the narrative is incidentally mentioned as Julia. She says: "I indeed lost two sisters named Elizabeth, but that my mother really was concerned in the death of the younger, as she asserts, I cannot believe. Mother described her own character in the darkest light, though when we were young we thought her harsh. But now I recollect the sacrifices she made for her children, and I am sure she was a better mother than some who were outwardly more tender. Regarding the close of the narrative, on the day my sister Elizabeth was buried, just as the casket was lowered into the grave, my mother, who was standing by, suddenly threw back her head and cried, 'Turn back! turn back! do not point your finger at me!' When we took her home she continually repeated, 'Still the child, the child!' From this it would seem as if she again saw the vision she saw when first her mind began to give way. For after that time my mother became a maniac, whose only peculiarity was wild good spirits, alternating with sad times, when she would refuse to eat and only sit and moan that she was a cruel mother. Last month she died, and this narrative was found among her papers. It evidently stopped just previous to the time when her mind wholly gave way. It is needless to say that none of the family believe it, nor do I count as worth anything the fact that I indeed saw what appeared to be my sister rocking in her cradle, at the same time that she was really in another room with my mother."

She was a pretty baby. She had big eyes, the color of a blue gentian, and long lashes giving them just the flower's fringed look. Her hair was yellow and silky and thin so you could see the pink scalp, but it curled in soft little ringlets round her ears and neck. She had a pointed chin and a very tiny face; she did not look like the rest of the children. Oh, I cannot deny she was a pretty baby. Her feet were all dimples and her skin was as soft as satin. But, deary me, the trouble she made. It was bread and treacle, and ginger cake and mud pies, all over her face, and on clean pinafores too, which was worse. People said, "What a pretty little one—like a flower!" They did not have to wash a crying baby a dozen times a day.

And her name was Elizabeth.

I never liked the name of Elizabeth, but Robert, my husband, would call her so. Our first baby, who died years before, had been called Elizabeth also. Somehow I never wished to remember the first Elizabeth. She had died when a little one, of a cold, and the doctor did say that with more care she might have—but then, that's neither here nor there. Robert never knew of it, and so when we came to naming the last baby he would have it Elizabeth, like the first one. As nearly as we could remember, she looked a good deal like the other Elizabeth. But people's memories of their first baby's face are not apt to be very plain when there are six others. The other Elizabeth had black eyes—we remembered that. The thought of those eyes as they looked reproachfully at me before they were closed in the coffin, had never quite gone away with all my after life. How they had stared at me!

The last Elizabeth was what I hated—an over-sensitive child. If she was tapped on the shoulder and made to get out of the way she whimpered. If because she had played in the mud and got her shoes wet I sent her to bed without supper, she never seemed to mind losing the supper, but would cry and moan until an hour's coaxing was necessary to make her eat any breakfast in the morning. Now how can a body bring up a child like that, I'd like to know? The other ones never were so. George and James bellowed if they were whipped, and stole cakes from the buttery when sent to bed supperless. Julia, and Mary, and Annie would lie any time to avoid a scolding, but only laughed when it was over. They always remembered the stick, but Elizabeth would be punished for mucking her pinafore, and then go to where she would muck it again, crying all the while like one daft. She never howled, either. When she cried, her underlip came out, and her chin quivered, and the big tears ran over her cheeks, and Robert declared it was the saddest sight he ever saw, and begged me never to whip her. But I never heard of bringing up a child without the rod.

And she was such a trouble. The others were all old enough for school, and I should have had some peace all day, and could have gone out for chats with the neighbors when my work was over, of an after-noon, but for Elizabeth. I never loved children, and who could help feeling angry with such a hindrance as she? And she was so daft, too, I feared she would never come to any good. Often she'd go out by the creek, and I'd find her sailing her own shoe full of violets or dai-sies, singing a queer little wordless tune all by herself. Now it's only natural for children to herd by themselves, but Elizabeth never cared for other brats. If she could get a flower she would kiss it and hug it for hours, but she was so afraid of other children that I was actually ashamed when the neighbors came in with the little ones. People said I spoiled her beauty by putting her into holland frocks, but I could not dress a dirty baby in lawn. She was a vain little piece, and on Sundays, when she wore her white embroidered frock, she would coo over it, and smooth the skirt with her hand.

My God, I cannot see how I was to blame. I had spent my life in bringing up babies I did not care very much for, and in doing work I hated. I did the best I knew how, my children were clean and whole, and always went to school. If they did wrong I whacked them, and if they didn't I never committed the fault of making them vain by prais-ing them. What was I punished for? I was not a bad woman. My kitch-en floor was well sanded, and a person could have died in the house any day and no cleaning would have been needed before the funeral. I could not spend my few hours of leisure in coddling children's fancies, in telling them fairy tales to fill their heads with nonsense, or in rocking them in my arms. If they must be rocked, there was the cradle, which I could jog with my foot, and read or sew at the same time.

What was I punished for!

Robert used to say it was wrong to punish the children without inquiring carefully who was to blame. But in that case they would often have gone unpunished, for I had no time to make inquiries. Yet if it was unjust, surely my punishment was wrong, for I was given no chance to defend myself. My punishment came on me suddenly—I remember well the day it came.

I had just got my work out of the way, and was in the parlor with my sewing. The parlor was a big square room, with wainscotted walls and a floor which I was always careful to keep well waxed. The furni-ture, though it dated from my wedding day, had been well rubbed also, and there were no scratches on it. There was a corner cupboard in the room, from which shone out my pink china—what of it the children had not broken. On the big table, which told of no saving of elbow grease, was the family bible, and a tray of decanters and glasses which we never used. It was a peaceful, quiet place. The windows were all darkened with dark-leaved vines, and through the open door, under the heavy roof of the porch, the grass looked dazzlingly green, and the odor of apple blossoms stole in. A row of red and yellow tulip blooms shone out just above the low floor of the porch. I was tired and hot that afternoon. So when Elizabeth came pulling at my skirts to be taken, I pushed her away. "You are a bad baby," I cried, "go and play." At that moment I looked up and saw her on the porch. I called her to come in, for she had just had on her clean frock, and she came, very slowly. As she entered the room she lifted her hand and pointed her forefinger directly toward me. I was startled at the baby's doing something she had never done before. At that moment I felt another pull at my dress. Now Elizabeth, as I saw her pointing at me, was across the room by the door. I looked down. Elizabeth was at my side. I turned to the door. There she still was.

There were two children in the room with me!

I took the one by my side into my lap and stared at the other. I saw that her eyes were black. The dead Elizabeth had had black eyes. She had the same little curls and the same face as the child in my lap. She wore a white frock with no sleeves, and her feet were bare. While I looked, she turned and went out over the porch. She did not vanish away quickly, but went down the steps creeping as she had always done, and then she ran over the grass until she reached a clump of bushes, behind which I lost sight of her.

I was terribly frightened, and it was the whole afternoon before I felt myself. But I did not speak to Robert of what I had seen, and by morning I had convinced myself that the whole thing had been an optical delusion—a waking dream—a trick of the imagination. Several days went by. One morning Julia came down stairs and exclaimed, "Why mother! how did Elizabeth get down here so quickly? I have just come from upstairs, where she was rocking in her cradle."

I caught Elizabeth in my arms and hurried up-stairs. There in the old wooden cradle, which had a head like a chaise and wooden rockers, in which all the children had been rocked, sat—the strange child. She was clinging with a hand to each side of the cradle, and was rocking herself back and forth. Elizabeth slipped from my arms and ran over to the cradle. She did not seem to notice that it was in motion, but climbed into it herself. The other child moved to make room for her, and Elizabeth sat down facing the other and holding on in the same way. They looked like twins.

While I was looking, the child jumped out of the cradle and ran across the floor, passing very near me and going into another room. I followed her, but she was gone. She did not look at me this time.

I began to feel very sad. I was still capable of being irritated by the children, but nothing seemed of very much consequence to me. It was such an awful thing which had happened. I had in some way done some great wrong for which this was the punishment. I knew my husband would think so if I told him of what I had seen. He was a good man, and I could not bear to disturb him, so I told him nothing. Perhaps I had never really loved him, but one does not live beside another for fifteen years without becoming attached to him, and especially fearing his anger. I knew he always thought me too careless and harsh with the children—I now came to have a terrible fear that I had been wrong all my life. There was a horror in my mind, a fear of seeing again that tiny avenging figure, with its finger pointing at me in scorn. I felt sure the end was not yet. I was apologetic in my mind toward little Elizabeth, as if it had been she who was constantly taunting me. I could not bear to look her in the face.

Sometimes in the night I would get up and go through the cottage chambers where the others slept, bending my head under the low ceilings, and pulling down the coverlids from the little figures, to see my sleeping children by moonlight. I wondered why they had never in some way avenged themselves upon me. Was not Julia afraid of the dark ever since I had shut her in the cellar all night without a candle, because she had broken the china plates? Had not George been whipped until his very skin was hardened? If I had treated little Elizabeth wrong, surely I had wronged them all. But it was through her alone the punishment came. I had never loved any of my children, but now I feared one—the youngest one. I could not bear to touch her skin when I was curling her hair and dressing her. She seemed to be to blame, and yet I felt very sure she had never seen the other Elizabeth. I hated her with a terrible hatred. It was not the general dislike I had always felt from her birth. Then I had not especially hated the child, but only the work she made. Now I hated her for herself. She had ruined my life. I knew I could never be happy any more.

Many weeks came and went, and there was no visit from the other Elizabeth. But my dread of such a visit, instead of decreasing, became the greater. I feared continually. When I was leading Elizabeth to bed another child seemed to cling to my gown and patter up the stairs by my side as well as her. When I tucked Elizabeth into her crib it was as if another curly head was on the pillow. When she ate the food seemed to diminish faster than one child's appetite could have made it. If she cried, I heard another wail mingled with the tones of hers. When I was with Elizabeth I feared of someone coming to tell me they had seen the specter, as Julia had once done. I was afraid when alone, and was never easy for a moment when others were with me, for I had begun to fear the end of the punishment would be the appearance of the avenging child some time when it would denounce me to others. So far no one—not even Elizabeth herself—had seen it and known what it was. But I felt certain in my own mind it would not stay hidden forever—it would come when others were with me, or in a moment of carelessness I would tell the secret myself. I became nervous, and hardly dared to sleep for fear of whispering the secret in a dream.

I did not consider that had I really wished the world to know, I should have found it difficult to make others believe what was so strange. I did not remember how I would once have scoffed at hearing such a tale from anyone. I knew what had happened myself, and it seemed as if a single word would tell the story to the world. The family began to notice my nervousness, my sudden starts, my haggard countenance. When Elizabeth was born, though I was thirty-five years old, I was yet a handsome woman. That was why I had been so angry at being kept at home to take care of another little one. I looked in the mirror and saw that I was yet comely. I knew my beauty would not last long—a few years at most would be mine for gaiety, and those I could not bear to lose. But I faded soon enough. After my sorrow I had no more desire to spend all the money Robert could afford me for coquettish bonnets and dainty gowns with which to deck my ugly careworn face and spare form. I became wrinkled and yellow, my eyes looked wild and glaring. I did not care. I was desperate.

My mind was made up to the doing of a wicked deed. The spirit had not come again. Very well. If it came I would kill Elizabeth. Then we would see what would happen. She alone was to blame, I felt, and as I gazed into her weak blue eyes I felt bloodthirsty.

It was only a few days after my resolve, but I had begun to think that the spirit would not come again. I was very glad—almost happy. I plucked up courage to scold Elizabeth when she ran in after dinner with her clean frock muddied and her mouth covered with dirt. I washed and dressed her again, and when I had tidied myself, we set out on a visit to a neighbor. I feared I had been solitary for too long a time. It was a beautiful afternoon. The sun shone brightly, and the grass and foliage wore the brilliant green it has in early summer, before toughened by exposure to the elements. There was a crisp freshness in the air which was sweetly suggestive of summer flowers. We went past a meadow purple with violets. The friend on whom I called said to me, "What a big girl Elizabeth is getting to be. Really, you need not stay at home so much now."

I looked at Elizabeth—she was actually growing. Mrs. Mason was right. She would soon be big enough for school, and then I could have my liberty. My heart throbbed with joy. After all, while I had been fretting, the weary time of probation had passed. I bade Mrs. Mason a lively good-bye, and started home with Elizabeth. She ran on ahead of me, and finally disappeared round a turn in the road. When she came running back, the front of her frock was covered with stains from the huge bunch of flowers she clasped in her arms.

"Naughty, careless child," I cried, jerking the blossoms from her, and giving her a slight shake, "you shall be well punished when we get home."

She turned her blue eyes up to my face. "Mamma whip I?" she said, whimpering. Then suddenly pointing down the road, she said, "Oh mamma, see the baby!"

I looked. It was the other Elizabeth. She wore a pink frock which I well remembered making for her in her life time. She had on a little lace bonnet, and a white flannel blanket, folded cornerwise, was fastened about her shoulders. She was ahead of us, walking along a grass grown rut in the road. She did not turn around. I noticed that when she walked under the trees the shadow fell on her as well as the sunlight. I walked rapidly on, but though she seemed to toddle along in the shaky way of childhood, yet I could not overtake her. She was always ahead of me. At length she neared a place where the road made an abrupt turn to the right, to avoid a brook which, also making a turn, flowed straight ahead in the former direction of the road. When we neared this place, the child before us, instead of turning, went directly on. My astonished eyes saw her walking over the water as if it had been land. She walked slowly on, and went from sight among the bushes in which the silvery windings of the brook were lost.

Elizabeth puckered out her under lip and began to cry. "Baby gone," she whimpered. I saw it was coming as I had feared. She had seen the other child. By and by others would see her—they would know it was a judgment on me. I put Elizabeth down by my side and clutched her firmly, half afraid she too would disappear as the other one had if I let her go. We went into the house. Elizabeth still prattled about "the baby that walked on the water." I heard Robert asking her about it. I felt that the end must soon come.

When I was undressing Elizabeth she seemed afraid of me. My fingers felt as if they were burning, and when she pulled away from, as children will when they do not like to go to bed, I caught her by the arm and held her until—as I saw when I took off her frock—my fingers had left a red mark on the flesh.

The end had begun. I felt very happy of a sudden—as I had been used to feel before the haunting, when someone would relieve me of the care of Elizabeth for a few hours or days. I was going to be rid of my burden. Elizabeth, I was resolved, should trouble me no longer. She seemed to know that something was going to happen, for she was a long time in going to sleep. After I had tucked the covers about her, as she lay in her narrow crib, she stared at me with wide open eyes, in which there was a frightened look. Finally she put out her tiny hand and grasped hold of one of my fingers, but I put her hand away. I did not like the touch of it. After a long while, during which the moonlight, as it fell on the floor, moved several degrees nearer the window, as the moon rose higher, she fell asleep. Her lips were slightly parted, and some people would have cried out that she was a pretty baby. But

I hated her. She had never brought me anything but unhappiness. I could see that other Elizabeth sitting on the floor beside the crib, half her body in the patch of moonlight. I felt that she would always be with me while Elizabeth lived. I bent over the crib in which the sleeping child lay, and clutching my fingers closely about her throat, placed my lips to her mouth and sucked out her breath.

A few minutes later all was over. The child was dead. I would have laughed had I dared, but I was fearful of being overheard. I looked carelessly at the patch of moonlight. I was not afraid of anything I might see there now. As I expected, the other Elizabeth was gone. I nodded my head triumphantly and went down stairs into the parlor. Robert looked up from his paper and said, "Is Elizabeth asleep?"

"Yes," I replied.

I slept well that night, something I had not done for months before. Everything was off my mind. In the morning I sent Julia to call Elizabeth. The child came running back to cry she could not wake her sister. On examination we found that Elizabeth was dead! The doctor says she had a defective heart. I hold my peace and can hardly help smiling, I am so happy. I only fear that in my joy I will whisper the cause of it to someone. I must be discreet and quiet, for I am happy—happy!

WHEN THE FOG LIFTED

The Nugget, May 1890

"Good-bye, Dorothy!"

"Good-bye—be sure the lobsters are live before they are broiled."

"Yes. Don't get drowned. I don't want the lobs to get cold while we're fishing you out of the raging deep."

"Good-by—y—y—e!"

Dorothy rowed around a jutting point of gray rock, and the last farewell was lost in the dashing of the waves. It was early afternoon of a day which had been rainy. Now the sun was shining and the fog bank had been driven out to sea. The harbor was full of craft; the sailors were singing, as they hoisted sail, their song being a rude sort of chant, interspersed with hoots. The sails were streaked with water and cockled up with the damp. On decks of the vessels lines were strung, full of newly washed red shirts and blue blouses. Dorothy pulled her dory through the water with a long steady stroke, leaving a slender white wake after her boat. She was rowing over the town to meet her husband, was Dorothy—her handsome Jack, whom she hadn't seen for a whole fortnight. Dorothy had been married all of five years, and the wee lassie in a sailor suit sitting quietly in the stern of the boat, was her own; but she was still glad to see Jack, especially when he hadn't been around to bother her for a whole fortnight. Dorothy was only 25, her hair was still fluffy and yellow, and she had bangs and a Psyche knot, and a white-ribboned sailor hat, almost like the young girls. She had left orders at the cottage for a sumptuous supper, however—she knew Jack would be better tempered for that. Wee Trixy looked like her pretty mamma, only she had Jack's own big brown eyes, and she was a silent child.

Dorothy was thinking, for some reason or other, of the time when she and Jack had been lovers. Dorothy had been a "summer girl" then, and had danced and flirted with many a gay young man. There had been a young West Indian at the hotel—a perfect waltzer, and somehow Dorothy always shivered when she remembered him. He gave her a fan of feathers, and he had taken a party out once in his yacht. Dorothy was with them, and a storm came up. Oh yes, Dorothy remembered it; and how frightened she was, and the lightning lit up Don Menela's face, and he knelt beside her and clasped her hand, and begged her not to be afraid, and told her of the terrible wind storms in his home near Havana, and how she would have to learn bravery when she went there. And then it had seemed to Dorothy that she would really go, for she allowed Menela to sail away the next day with a gentle kiss on his lips, leaving her with a big diamond ring in her pocket and a sinking in her heart. But he didn't come back, and Dorothy met Jack, and—well, the ring was returned, and that was all there had been about it. Jack was a good fellow, and he liked her, and life was very commonplace, but not so very bad after all. She certainly never had loved Don Menela, and she would have been scared half to death had fate compelled her to go and live in the terrible West India island with him. But there was a queer little thrill in her heart when she thought of him, and it was such a very long time since anyone had made love to Dorothy! Jack loved her, of course, and all that, but he had stopped paying her compliments, and he more frequently told her that the soup was too thin, than that she was looking well. After all, Dorothy was only 25, and she looked as young as at 20. She thought of her past good times and almost wished—. And then she looked down at Trixy, and gave herself a shake, and blushing a little, said, "What a horrid creature I am. An old married woman like me! Why, I shall soon be chaperoning Trix." She looked up, and saw a white yacht, which bore in gilded letters the title of *The Southern Cross*. She looked again, and saw—Don Menela. The recognition was mutual. For a moment he gazed solemnly, and then a brilliant smile came over his swarthy face. One hand fell carelessly on the yacht railing. Upon the little finger Dorothy saw gleaming—the diamond ring once given to her. He spoke.

"Mrs. Crawford?"

"Yes," answered Dorothy, with a poor attempt at bravery, and trying to stifle the fierce beating of her heart.

"I am here for the season. I shall see you again." As he spoke, he looked at her with the old air of proprietorship. Nay, he even gazed at Trixy as though he owned her too. Dorothy felt like a poor gilded fly caught in a spider's web. She mechanically rowed away from the yacht, but she felt very much afraid. He would see her again, she knew, and Jack was inclined to be jealous. Oh, there would be trouble, and perhaps the neighbors might talk. She hated Menela. She was glad she was going to meet Jack.

When she arrived at the wharf the steamer was already in, and the pier was gay with people. Jack was nowhere to be seen, and Dorothy surmised that as he had not expected her, he was gone to the hotel to secure a team for driving down to the cottage. So, leaving Trixy and the boat in the charges of a trusty sailor, she skipped up the slimy moss-grown stairs to the wharf, and hurried to the hotel. Just as she came in sight of the wide piazza, where the girls in mannish hats and neckties and the young men in feminine blazers and sashes were quizzing the arrivals, Dorothy caught sight of Jack leisurely strolling down the street. He had on a new hat, and—oh, horrors!—he had actually shaved off his moustache; but still it was Jack. Of course she knew her own husband. Dorothy began to think she did not, though, when she observed him climbing the steps and ringing the bell of one of the smart villas built on the rocks above the beach. And when Jack actually went in, and the door closed behind his broad back, Dorothy could hardly keep from screaming. Why, he hadn't seen her for two whole weeks, and here he was calling on folks he did not know. Then it occurred to Dorothy that maybe he was there on business. Dorothy knew nothing about business, only that it had interfered between her and Jack before now. She thought she would walk on a little further and become absorbed in the view, as people on this plank walk often did, until Jack should reappear. There was plenty of time yet to get back in season for the broiled lobsters.

Jack reappeared sooner than Dorothy had expected, but he was not alone. There was a pretty young lady with him, in a white gown that looked very very Frenchy, and a most elegant sort of bonnet. She had black hair, and on gazing at her Dorothy felt extremely dowdyish. Neither the dark-haired woman nor Jack took any especial notice of the little lady absorbed in the view, and they strolled down to the shore believing themselves unobserved. Probably that was why, in helping her down a slippery rock, Jack took her hand and forgot to give it back. Dorothy felt rather sick. The couple disappeared from her view. She altered her position, and saw them seat themselves side by side on the beach. Jack's arm stole around his companion, and Dorothy saw it for a moment before she unfurled a big umbrella, under which the two were completely hidden. For a minute Dorothy had an insane desire to roll a big stone down the hill and let it fall plump against the big umbrella. How they would jump! It seemed to her as if she must burst out laughing, the whole affair struck her as so very funny. Her Jack making love to another woman! Suddenly a gush of tears ran down Dorothy's cheeks, and at that instant, Menela's voice said, "So. The husband of the signora amuses himself as he pleases. Also the signora?"

The last was a question, asked with a burst of mocking laughter. Dorothy felt a wicked and strong desire for revenge. Yes, she would amuse herself with Menela, as Jack had ceased to care for her. She gave Menela her hand and said, with a dash of oldtime coquetry, "I will row back now, as my little one is waiting." And she walked towards the wharf. It was a short stroll, but when she got into the dory and started to row Trixy back to the cottage she had promised Menela to take a moonlight sail on his yacht that evening. Trixy wanted to know where her papa was, and why mamma hadn't brought the caramels she had promised to, and why Sailor Bill called a boat a bo-at. Dorothy said nothing, and did not even think. She looked around, as if she had never seen the harbor and village before. She saw the funny little shanty which bore a sign of "Fish Dealer," and also another legend asserting that "Paints, Hair, Grease and Cement" were sold within. Somehow she smelled the sickish musk-like odor of an evening primrose, though no one ever heard of primroses growing near the harbor. The shore looked dreary to her, with white granite patches cropping through the scanty covering of brown and green streaked turf. There was a pale moon over in the east, and the sun was setting, a perfectly round red ball. Overhead, the sky was a dull pale blue, flecked with what the sailors call mackerel clouds, from their resemblance to fish scales. Lower down there was a thunder cloud or so and one faint yellow glow accented to rose tint just below the sun. The sun rapidly turned to a deep orange red, and sank with a reflection in the water. The sea was streaked with pale yellow and pink, and for an instant a very path of glory seemed to be laid on the water. Then the air became opaque, and the next instant the fog came down, and all Dorothy could see was Trixy and her own boat. Sounds, however, came with strange distinctness. Someone on shore was musically asking "Where is my wandering boy tonight?"—and over in the village a brass band began to drawl out, "Kiss me again, I like it." Dorothy actually heard a cow cropping the grass, while a child's voice called solemnly, "Mooly, mooly." Suddenly there cleaved through the mist and shot by her a tiny blue dory, in which was a man and a straw-covered demijohn. Dorothy recognized him as a notorious toper who used to row once a week to Capitol Island for a supply of fire water, unobtainable in the prim, law-abiding village. She half-wished she were going with him for a roistering spree. She heard the steamer's whistle, and the fog horn off Leguin began to blow monotonously. The bells were ringing on the revenue cutter in the harbor, and some sailors had got out their tin horns and were making a terrible din, in their endeavor to "blow the fog away."

And she had promised to meet Menela on his yacht!

Dorothy saw before her, as in a series of pictures, all the consequences of her mad act, if it was committed. She would become a fast woman, and Jack would probably decline living in the same house with her. There would be no trouble, no divorce scandal—oh no. She would merely become a frisky little woman, living at beach hotels in the summer, and having a pretty apartment in the city for the winter. Women would be shy of her, but all their lovers and husbands and brothers would call on her, and make much of Trixy, and take her to the races. She would probably never be much talked about, because Jack, too, would call occasionally—when "business" would let him. All the women would pet Jack, and pity him because he had made such an unfortunate marriage. Trix would grow up frisky, and the men would trifle with her affections. The girl would fall in love with someone who would go away and marry a carefully reared rosebud of a conservative patrician family, and Trix—well, Trix's heart would break and she would go to the bad entirely. Yes, Dorothy saw it all. She would likely enough get to drinking too much champagne, and she would keep a bottle of liquor on the dressing table. It would all be terrible—terrible. On the other hand, if she did not meet Menela this night she foresaw that she yet would later on. Jack was gone from her, and Menela would haunt the place until he had acquired his old influence over her. She looked at Trixy. The child had pulled her mother's red peasant cloak about her and sat crouched on the seat. Her yellow curls, damp with

fog, were lying on her arm. She was half asleep—she was altogether innocent and lovely. Dorothy knew she was almost home. Since the fog
came on she had been rowing with the aid of a pocket compass, and
now, though she could not see the house, yet she could hear singing,
"There is a tavern in the town."

All at once her mind was made up. Jumping to her feet, Dorothy
seized Trixy and wrapped her, head and all, in the heavy cloak. Clasp-
ing the little one in her arms, she made a step over the edge of the boat
and sank under the gray water. The golden head rose once—twice—but
there was no cry, and Trixy, stifled in her cloak, died at once. For the
last time she sank, and the empty boat was thrown violently against
the rock from which Dorothy had embarked earlier in the day. Indoors
the lobsters were broiling to a beautiful pink, and the gray fog, growing
thicker with the darkness, wound itself into a shroud above the white
crested waves which marked Dorothy's grave.

FOR A BIG ROLL OF MONEY

Dilettante, July 20, 1890

I have just been told that I am too small a girl to be trusted with the ink bottle when I have a clean pinafore on, but there are always pencils in this house. If I had a clean pinafore oftener perhaps there wouldn't be as much fuss made as there is now whenever I get one on. When I am rich some day, and wear a silk dress before breakfast I wonder will I remember now—and how every Monday afternoon when dinner is over mamma says with a very fine air: "Go to your room, Theresa, and have on your fresh pinafore." And then soon Maggie comes up with her hands all wet from the washing, and steam coming from them as it does from horses' noses on cold days, holding out at full length my stiff, starched, crackly pinafore. One week it's tucked and one frilled. This week it is frilled. But really, I have no right to use up such a short pencil as this one writing about my apron. Only we are poor. I know that if I do wear a sleeved apron, and if people do see my knees when I sit on a high chair. Perhaps it's because we're poor that mamma did it. Maybe it's because we're poor that papa let her—I am quite sure Mr. Livingstone never would have asked them to do it only that he knew quite well how long I wore my pinafores without laundrying, and that papa smoked a T. D. pipe at home because it was cheaper than cigars. At any rate it was done, and I say it was a nasty thing to do, and one I would have been whacked for if I had done it.

I can remember very well the first time Mr. Livingstone came here, and how surprised everyone was. I was small then—for mamma is sure I have grown an inch in six months—and it was before my doll Polly was turned into Polyphemia and executed by Georgie Scott in a gullytine—a word I can't spell—made out of the carving knife and a chess board. So I had Polly with me, and I was putting court plaster on the hole Georgie made in her nose when she was an Indian princess and wore a ring there. It was a cold fall evening, and mamma was almost falling asleep over the stove, for the wood was wet and smoked. There was a big wind in the chimney, and I could hear it turning round and round and growling as if it was mad and wanted to get out and couldn't. We were in the office, for papa was away though it was the office hours printed on his card, and mamma sat there to talk to patients in case any came in. People would be angry if they knew it, for my papa is said to be a very wonderful doctor for a countryman, but mamma makes nearly all his prescriptions, and always tells him what kind of medicine to send everybody. It was growing dark, and I could hardly see the skeleton in the corner of the room behind mamma's chair, which seemed to be gnashing its teeth at me just because she wasn't looking that way, when the door opened.

The man that came in was very tall, he had not any beard or moustache, and some of his hair was gone. He was very finely dressed and he carried a cane. He did not look, though, like the kind of men who wear nice clothes in the fashion book plates. His face made me think of a view I saw once when I was top of a high hill, it was so full of funny knobs, and hollow places. Afterwards as I saw him sometimes he would look very handsome and young and bright, and again his face would seem ugly, as if he hadn't, as Maggie says, an idea to bless himself with. As he came in he looked around, and then said, "Where's Dr. Barton?" just as anyone would.

Mamma was pleased. She got up and held out her hand, crying, "Why Mr. Livingstone," and though he didn't seem especially pleased I saw he remembered her and they began to talk. He asked very carefully all about papa, and called him Fred, so I felt sure they must be great friends. Finally he left, promising to come back in the evening, and when papa came in mamma cried, triumphantly, "Guess who has been here—Tom Livingstone!"

When she said this she acted happier than I had seen her for a long time, but papa did not care for the news at all. He appeared disgusted, and began to plan for going out that evening, just as though mamma had not told him that Mr. Livingstone was coming back. That was often his way when mamma expected company, but I was astonished not to see him pleased at meeting such an old friend of his own. However, as it happened Mr. Livingstone came in before papa left, while we were at tea, and papa acted as if tickled to have some one to talk to, and told stories about himself until I honestly think Mr. Livingstone wished he hadn't come. Before he went away he said to mamma: "Do you ever hear from Miss Munsill now-a-days?" Of course mamma said "yes," for we had seen Minna only the week before. He then said, very carelessly, "It is a long time since I saw her. Really—I think I promised once to call there."

"'M," said mamma.

"I—wonder—that is, I shall come through here on business one week from today. Does Miss Munsill ever visit here?"

Mamma smiled a little as she said, "Frequently."

"It would be charming coincidence should she happen to be here next week," he said, very slowly.

And mamma replied, "I would be a very strange coincidence, indeed."

He shook hands then and went away. No sooner was the door shut than mamma crammed her hands over her mouth and began spinning about the room, laughing very hard.

"What a fool," she cried.

"What are you doing, Sissy?" papa asked. She came over and kissed the little bald spot on top of his head. "Don't you see that he doesn't care about us?" she asked. "He wants Minna, and he has renewed our acquaintance to see her again here. We must invite her down at once. As if I could not see his designs. But he makes $10,000 a year—Minna will do well."

"And what about Minna's other lover?" asked papa, as if he hadn't very much interest in the subject.

"Oh, he goes in for too much church. He and Minna will never agree. She should marry somebody with heaps of money, who will let her dance and take her to the theatre. All the same I think Tom Livingstone will need sharp looking after, and Minna will be the woman to do it. She is far smarter than any man in existence."

Papa hadn't heard half of this, and he then began a long story of his own about something which happened when he was a schoolboy, and I marched off to bed.

Minna Munsill is younger than mamma and very much prettier, I suppose, though I like my little mamma better than her. She—I mean Minna—has got long, silky, black hair which curls up around her face, and which she is always doing in a new way. This time she came she had it sticking out at the back of her head in a knob, with a silver pin stuck through it. She has got great big blue eyes with long, black lashes, and she is awfully jolly and dreadfully independent. I have heard mamma say she has had lots of beaux, and she treats them very carelessly, but they all keep on liking her no matter what she does. Mamma also used to say Minna was too independent ever to marry. When she came to see us the next Monday she looked very nice in a new dark green gown, all edged everywhere with tiny white braid and beads. It wasn't very often Minna had a new dress, and mamma had heaps to say about it. They did not speak of Mr. Livingstone all day, however, but papa at noon was making all sorts of jokes about the "coming anxious lover," and what sort of a greeting he was to get. But Minna was just quiet, and didn't seem one bit confused at any of it, though mamma was quite angry and scolded papa for it quite dreadfully under the cellar stairs.

That evening when Mr. Livingstone came there was no one in the parlor but Minna and me. She was sitting by the table with her hands on the red spread, bending over a book. Her front curls were almost touching the shade of the big lamp she was bending so. Mr. Livingstone had come in through the office and walked upstairs without saying a word. He came into the parlor with a long gray ulster flapping about his boots when he walked, and when he saw Minna he let go of his hat, which rolled along the floor, and just kissed her twice on the lips. She said, "Well—," and did not seem very much confused, so I thought they must have been really truly lovers some time before, and that this was the making up, like there always is in story books. When mamma came in she and Mr. Livingstone were very lively, and talked about a great many people whose names I have never heard, and who seemed strangers to Minna too, for she sat saying hardly a word.

And then, I was sent to bed! It was the first time in all my life that I was sent to bed. When I was little mamma used to rock me in her arms until I feel asleep, and when I was bigger she used to put me into bed and pin my clothes with a long pin to the mattress so I couldn't get away, but I had never been told to "go to bed, there's a dear." I felt just mad and when I took off my clothes I had a very great mind to imagine I had seen a ghost and scream so loud as to frighten everybody, only I was afraid I would spoil it all by bursting out laughing when I had brought them all to me. My room is a little one, out of the hall above the parlor. There is a bed in it, of the kind that shuts up and looks like the clothes' horse in the kitchen. Besides it there is one chair that I put my clothes on, and in the corner is a big box full of dolls and playthings. I undressed and got into bed, feeling rather jolly after all. I sat up and vowed I would not go to sleep until everybody else had. A little light shone up from the hall below on my ceiling. It flickered once it a while, or my eyes shut—and I went to sleep.

I woke up in what seemed just one second, I thought I had been looking at the light every moment and it astonished me to find it gone. I could not understand how it had gone without my knowing it. I was very wide awake, so I got up and went into mamma's room. It was very still in there, and a piece of moon with a cold, shining look like a polished brass basin, could be seen through the window. This moon, bright as it was, did not exactly frighten me, until I felt of the bed. It was just as hard and cold as could be, and the pillow was smooth, too. No one had slept in it that night. And at the very moment I made this discovery the clock down in the hall struck, loud and clear in the silence—one, two, three! Three o'clock and my mamma not in her bed! I knew something terrible had happened, and my hands began to shake. I ran into my own room and buried my head in the bed clothes, thinking, thinking what the awful happening could be, and what a little girl like me could do.

While I was thinking I heard a sound in the hall. I heard a step on the floor below, followed by a sob. Some one down there was crying and I thought I would just go down and find out about it. I wasn't afraid any more. The hall was all dark, and I went down the stairs in my bare feet as still, every bit, as a mouse. When I was half way down I heard the person who was in the hall step to the parlor door and with a push it came open. I could see into the room very plainly. The gas was turned partly down and in the doorway stood Minna. It was she that had been crying. It was Mr. Livingstone who had been in the hall and who pushed the door open. Minna stood there quiet, with her hands clasped, and the tears on her face, just like my old cat does when Rover wants to bite her kittens. I wondered where papa and mamma were. Then Minna spoke: "Mr. Livingstone, you are not treating me fair. I thought you were a gentleman and that you knew I was a lady, even though I am poor." Her voice sounded sort of shaky. "I may have been so foolish as to have come here to meet you, for I supposed you might remember our former friendship and wish to renew it, but could not conveniently come to my home."

He just stood there and played with his upper lip as if there was a moustache there—only there wasn't. "Did I ever ask you to marry me?" he asked.

"No."

"Did I ever give you to understand I wanted to marry anyone?"

"No."

"Now look here, Minna, darling," he said, trying to get hold of her hand, which she snatched away angrily. "I don't want to marry anybody, either. Not but what I love you well enough—and when I marry anyone it will be you. But for a few years it will be impossible. However, that need not prevent our being happy. About once in six weeks my business will take me here in the future. Mrs. Barton is your friend, what is to prevent your visiting her about that often? I have money—plenty of money—and all you want you know you can have without ever speaking of it. I will fix it all right with Mrs. Barton. We—"

Minna's eyes snapped. "And will we be engaged?" she asked.

"Well—well, yes of course, only you had better not tell your mother. Come," he added with a sudden change of manner, "don't haggle any longer, my Minna, give me a kiss and let's be happy." As he spoke he grabbed her hand. Minna gave one scream, and then I called right out from where I was on the stairs, "Don't mind Minna, I'm here."

Mr. Livingstone said "d—n," and Minna ran up and caught me by the shoulders. She was trembling all over.

"You are a vile, bad man," she cried, "and now I see all the scheme. I did not do wisely to call for Mrs. Barton—she knows enough to keep herself shrewdly out of the way. Probably the mysterious patient who called both her and the doctor down to the office an hour ago is a ruse also. I liked you once, Tom Livingstone, but now if you ever venture to speak to me again I'll—I'll kill you!"

And then, all in a moment, she pulled me upstairs, and into my own little bed room. The key was on the inside of the door and I heard her turn it. Then she lit the gas and sat down in my little rocking chair. She was shaking terribly, and I felt frightened, but she said, "Go to bed, Theresa, and sleep. I will stay here until light." Her voice sounded hollow and very hoarse. I went to sleep in a few minutes, for the bed was warm, and I had got awful cold standing on the stairs in my bare feet. But when I heard Minna move I woke all at a jump. It was broad daylight, and the sun was just coming through the window. Minna and mamma stood at the door and mamma was crying bad.

"Oh, Minna," she sobbed, "indeed I don't think Tom meant any harm. I wanted you to marry him, he is so rich, and I thought if you keep meeting him here he would marry you in the end. It was the Doctor's plan."

"I know it," said Minna, in the same hoarse voice. "But we can never be friends again. I hate that husband of yours—but never mind. I shall never come here again and I only hope when Theresa is grown up you will never play with her the game of chance you attempted with me, your guest, last night."

She never said another word, but went to the guest chamber where she got her hat, jacket and satchel. Then she came into my room, kissed me once, and walked quietly downstairs and out on the street. Mamma followed her to the door crying, but papa came out of the parlor and shouted to her to "hold her row."

I never knew where Mr. Livingstone went to, but he never called on us again. Mamma was very unhappy for a long time, and one day I saw papa trying to push a big roll of bills—really money—into her hands.

"No," she said, real cross, "I won't take it. We were vile to ever consent to such a scheme. I hate myself when I think of it."

Papa told her angrily to "stop her whining," and I never saw the money again. Perhaps papa did, though, for he went off on a big spree and mamma had to look after the prescriptions for over a fortnight.

I don't rightly know what all the trouble was about, but I say again it was a mean thing to ask Minna, good, nice, pretty Minna, here, and then leave her all alone in the parlor when it made her cry. I say again, I should have been whacked if I had invited Bessie Scott over to play with me and then had left her alone with some bad boys who plagued her and made her cry. Sometimes little girls know more about politeness than grown up folks. And it wasn't any nicer for my mamma and papa to stay out of the room and let Mr. Livingstone plague Minna, for that big roll of money, than it would be for me to take a bag of lollipops from Georgie Scott for keeping away while he teased Polyphemia. If a little girl is bound to protect her dolls, so I think big folks are bound to stand up for their guests and not let them cry.

So there now!

OVERHEARD ON THE BEACH

The Iris Magazine, September 1890

She (frigidly): Mr. Montgomery, will you kindly return me the use of my hand?

He (angrily): Madam, certainly.

She (spitefully): I wish to return to the hotel at once.

He (calmly): Just as soon as you please.

She (tearfully): You're the rudest man I ever saw.

He (sarcastically): With whom you ever flirted, you mean.

She (nervously): You men call it flirting if a woman is civil to you.

He (mirthfully): Well, I can't complain on that score.

She (curiously): Do you mean to insinuate that I'm not civil to you?

He (stolidly): Well I guess I shall trust my sisters after this.

She (excitedly): Oh, why?

He (slowly): No why.

She (frantically): If you don't tell me, I'll never speak to you again.

He (recklessly): Well, if I tell you I know you'll never speak to me again.

She (loudly): Tell me this very instant!

He (hurriedly): Well, they warned me that you were the vilest flirt on the beach.

She (faintly): Do you believe it?

He (firmly): I know it.

She (saucily): And I shall believe in Aunt Sue's prediction after this, too.

He (huffily): All right.

She (eagerly): Don't you care to know what she said?

He (quietly): Not by a d—— excuse me! sight.

She (quickly): Aunt Sue said that I had better associate with gentlemen, because they were well bred and never took advantage of one's kindness.

He (glumly): Pardon me for mentioning it, but all my family disapprove of you.

She (vivaciously): How nice of them! All my family positively hate you.

He (viciously): It was in the teeth of the strongest opposition that I've visited at your home.

She (loftily): And it was only by my pleading with tears in my eyes that pa allowed you to be received there.

He (airily): I suppose it isn't polite to mention it, but you never was my style at all.

She (firmly): I must have been crazy to have allowed you to say all these insulting things to me.

* * *

But in spite of her opinion, she sat on a rock for two hours longer, listening to variations on the same theme, and when she returned to the hotel it was to electrify her family by the triumphant announcement, "I'm engaged!"

MAGGIE

Quartette, October 1890

Maggie was a very little girl—so little that the "great big girls," those of eight or ten, refused to play with her. Two of these great girls were Maggie's own sisters, in whose charge she had been put by their mother, but they ran away with the rest, to play "Hi Spy" around the corner. Maggie did not mind this very much, but she could not bear to be deceived. Those bad great girls had sent her into Tod Burnham's yard, to see a "Brownie up in the pear tree." When she returned from an unsuccessful search for the Brownie—she hoped it would have been the Dude—she found that Nellie and May had gone. In fact, the street was quite empty, whichever way she looked. Not a child was to be seen. To be sure, there were plenty of houses where children lived. On the corner was the red and gray villa where Beulah belonged—but Beulah always had afternoon naps. Next door was the brown cottage in which Herbert Thomson stayed nights, but Herbert was quite a large boy—almost six—and he never was seen near home in the daytime. Over the way was her own house, but Maggie was not yet so lonely as to think of returning there. She had no love for her home, it was only by main force that she was induced to come in at bedtime. Further along the street was a big red brick mansion set in a nice wide yard. Leonora Montmorenci lived there, and Maggie could see her now, sitting in the red hammock, and eating bonbons out of a pretty box. Maggie was rather bashful, but Leonora was quite alone, like herself, and she did not believe there was a girl living who wouldn't prefer having somebody to play with—even Maggie—to being alone. So she shuffled up the street, making a little cloud of dust with her shoes, and pressed her little face between the gilt and iron bars of the Montmorenci gate. Leonora was not very far away, but she only munched her chocolate and stared at Maggie without a word.

Finally Maggie remarked, "Hullo."

Leonora still said nothing.

"Want I should come in?" inquired Maggie, cheerfully showing all her little teeth, black with the blueberries she had eaten for dinner.

There being no reply, she opened the gate and entered. She even came and leaned against the head of the red hammock.

"Want to play squat tag?" she inquired. "I'll give you ten squats if you will."

Leonora was silent. She had finished her bonbons now, and she turned the box bottom upward, shaking some quite large pieces of broken chocolate out on to the gravel. Maggie regarded them longingly. Then she said, "I'll give you twenty squats. Come on."

Leonora took that beautiful box, all lace paper and ribbons and pretty pictures, and deliberately crushed it out of shape. Then she began to tear it into scraps.

"My mamma don't 'low me to play any rough games," she remarked. "My clothes is too good. This is a Nindian silk I got on, and if I sh'd squat I'd bu'st the 'smocking.' My mamma says so."

"I got a best dress too," put in Maggie, pleasantly.

"Poh, this isn't my best dress. It's one of my very oldest ones," declared Leonora grandly. Then she looked at Maggie, from her head crowned with tangled black curls under a broken straw hat, down past the grimy gingham frock, to the dusty stockings and worn out shoes, through one of which Maggie's big toe protruded.

"I wouldn't be seen playing with you," said Leonora. "You look like sin. I heard my nurse say so."

For an instant Maggie could not understand just what had happened. Then her little breast heaved under the dirty frock, and she turned her back so that Leonora should not see her tears. When she got down on the street once more, she went into Tod Burnham's yard and sat down on the doorstep. As there was nothing else to do, she kept on crying, in a subdued way, wiping her eyes with the skirt of her frock.

Presently there burst upon her ears the welcome sound of something, evidently youthful, approaching. "Ding dong! ding dong! Tootle, tootle, to-o-ot! Bow, wow, wow!"—it was the "Tod Burnham" fire brigade coming out to subdue a big blaze on the Burnham ash heap. Tod was fire engineer, he wore a paper cap, and made the ding-donging. Herbert Thomson and Harry Hammond were the horses, and drew the red wagon with "Express" on the side boards, in which Tod sat.

Maggie's own brother Jo was the fire brigade's dog, he rushed before the procession and never left off barking. Budsy George was a fireman, he pushed before him a blue wheelbarrow, in which reposed about a foot of dilapidated rubber hose. On came the company, with a very real accompaniment of noise and confusion, around the corner of the gatepost into Tod's yard the express wagon was whisked with a celerity that overturned the cart, and sent Tod rolling out onto his head.

"Hullo Mag," he remarked, sitting up and rubbing his forehead. "What're you a-bawling about?"

"Cause I—didn't—have nobody to—play with," said Maggie, dolorously.

"Oh rats," remarked Tod, "come on and play with us. Can't she, boys?"

The boys, solely excepting Maggie's brother, were of the opinion that she could. Budsy George, in his anxiety to comfort her, pulled down his stocking and let her see his sore leg. It wasn't very much of a sight to be sure, being only a scratch covered with court plaster, but Budsy gave a thrilling account of how "the old cat did it 'cause I removed her kitten, and it bled pints and pints, and mother she put a compress on it, and then she said an air excluder 'd be a good thing." What with his big words and his injured limb, Budsy was quite the hero of the moment.

"If she'll be the dog she can play," remarked Jo. "I'm tired of barkin' forever n' ever."

So Maggie became the dog. After a time she was even promoted to the rank of a horse, and cheerfully tugged along pushing the blue wheelbarrow, with Budsy in it, in addition to the hose pipe. Maggie had a lovely time. Harry Hammond gave her his apple core, and Budsy traded his knife with her for a picture card and a set of jackstones. To be sure the knife was only a handle, with rusty indications of having been once a "sixteen blader," as Budsy called it, but Maggie thought she had made a good bargain after all.

"I like to play with boys," she announced at the top of her voice, in which tone most of her playmates' conversation was carried on. "You can have heaps o' fun."

"That's so," said Budsy, "I sh'd think girls'd get terrible tired o' playing together. They never do nothing scrumptious."

Suddenly Budsy pushed his hands deep down into his knicker-bocker pockets, and shouted.

"Tell you what, fellows, I'm going to ask ma if I can't get out the pony and give Maggie a ride."

"And me"—"and me"—shouted everybody. Harry Hammond tried to turn a somersault he was so joyful, but only succeeded in putting his head to the ground and reeling over sideways.

"No siree, not none of you," said Budsy, ungrammatically but firmly. "Ma made me promise never to take no boys out riding since that time Jo licked Mousy till she lay down in the shafts. But I 'most guess she'll let me drive Maggie up and down the street and you boys can walk along behind maybe, if you won't holler or make any rumpus about it."

The boys, all but Jo, were perfectly willing to accede to this. Jo ventured to insinuate that he didn't believe his mother would let Maggie go riding, and Maggie was obliged to give him her newly acquired knife to prevent his going home to find out. It had long been the height of Maggie's ambition to ride after the George pony—a pretty little animal belonging to Budsy's elder sisters in reality. A select deputation, consisting of Budsy and Harry Hammond, waited upon Mrs. George, and received her permission to harness the pony, and to drive slowly six times up and down the length of the street. It was stipulated that nobody but Budsy and "the little girl" should be allowed in the wagon. Maggie felt that she had arrived at an important crisis in her life. She would be the cynosure of all eyes—perhaps even Leonora Montmorenci would see her! At this thought, Maggie turned her attention to her personal appearance. She smoothed her hair and put her hat on straight, she also pounded her little fat legs to get the dust out of her stockings, and she moistened her handkerchief at her mouth, afterwards using it to brighten her shoes with. It was a proud moment for Maggie when Budsy led the pony out into the street, even though Jo tried to make her unhappy by declaring that she was nasty as a pig, and mother would be sure to scold her when she got home.

In the meanwhile Miss Leonora Montmorenci had been regretting having declined Maggie's company. Leonora had finished her chocolates and read her story book through, and she found that the wearing of an "Nindian" silk frock could not prevent one's feeling lonely. So

Leonora now came strolling down the street, anxious to know what the crowd in front of the George horse block was gathered to see, and afraid it might be vulgar to seem interested. But when she caught sight of the pony, and the yellow village cart, Leonora didn't pause, but rushed to the animal's head and cried, "Oh, isn't it cunning? I do love ponies. Whose is it?"

The boys fell away a little, and regarded Leonora with awe. They had never seen her outside of her own yard before, and her gay dress, fluttering with beautiful ribbons and sash ends, fascinated them. It made them think of a circus. "She's every bit as pretty as the girl what rode six horses to once in a chariot race," declared Harry Hammond, audibly. Herbert was heard to assert that his sister had hair as long as that, before it was cut off; while Tod remarked that he'd bet her dress was real silk, too. He said this in a whisper, and added that he'd give his air gun for her sash, to make a kite's tail of.

Such general admiration turned Leonora's head. She forgot her danger of being discovered outside of the gilt and iron gate. She didn't even remember that she had run away without a hat, and that these were the "common children" with whom she had been warned she was not to play. She turned to the crowd and asked, "Whose pony is it?"

Tod pointed to Budsy with his thumb. Leonora at once began to beg.

"Oh give me a ride? Won't you? Please. I'm going to have a pony myself when I'm bigger, and then—maybe—I'll pay it back."

Budsy shuffled his russet shoe back and forth in the sand.

"Well," he said slowly, "I—can't. I promised Maggie a ride, and I can't drive only six times up and down."

Leonora looked at the mouse-colored pony, and then she burst into the violent, uncontrolled weeping of a badly brought-up child.

"You're all real mean," she sobbed. "My papa always 'lows me ev'ything I want. You're—you're real mean, so now. I'm going home to tell, too."

Maggie stood beside Budsy, rather unnoticed all this time. She was feeling—well, a very tempest of feeling was surging under the grimy gingham. When Leonora began to cry, Maggie's face flushed, and a great lump came in her throat. For she remembered how she had cried herself not long before, and how desolate and lonely she had felt when she had no one to play with. Maggie remembered, to be sure, how ungraciously Leonora had refused the squat tag offer, but Maggie was dimly aware that nobody seemed to care much about being with her. Hadn't the big girls run off and left her? She had had a nice time with the boys, but they didn't care for her now. Maggie felt very sorry she pleased no one, it must be the hole in her shoe, she thought. But then, this ride. Could she give it up? Could she? At first Maggie felt that she could not. But then Leonora was crying. Maggie had cried too much in her short life, not to know how unpleasant it was.

"She feels just as I did when she told me I looked like sin," thought Maggie. Suddenly she made up her mind. Sweet and clear her childish treble rose above the hubbub caused by Leonora's wailing and the boys' clumsy attempts at comfort, as she exclaimed, "You can go if you want to, Leonora. I don't care about it."

Her voice choked a little as she made the last assertion. Leonora's sobs were checked in an instant. Nimbly she leaped into the cart.

"Come on," she called to Budsy.

That youth paused a moment, and then followed her, saying somewhat shamefacedly to Maggie, "See here, Mag, I'll take you 'nother time."

Maggie turned away. She felt that the "'nother time" would never come. She was only a very little girl, it must be remembered, and so she watched, through a mist of tears and with an aching heart, the yellow cart and the gray pony, Leonora's pink dress and Budsy's red cap, go up the street at the head of a procession of boys. But after all, Maggie dimly knew in her own little mind, that she was happier than Leonora. She saw it very plainly when the procession swept its way back, for Leonora was again in tears, of rage this time, because Budsy refused to allow her to whip the pony.

"You're a bad unpolite boy," she was saying. "I won't ride anymore unless you let me."

"Get out then," said Budsy, stopping the pony in the middle of the road. Leonora descended, and went home in high dudgeon, shaking her elbows violently.

"She's a nasty cross girl," said Budsy. "I don't want to play with her. Come, hop in, Maggie."

And Maggie did hop in, and her ride was twice as delightful as if it had not been shortened by one of the six turns up the street. For there is a sweet kind of feeling which comes to bless whoever does an unselfish deed—be they old or young. Maggie being such a very little girl, only understood that she was very happy indeed, and she didn't mind it at all when the great big girls came around the corner, having finished playing "Hi Spy," and called her a "little Tom-boy," because she was playing with boys. For did not one of those same boys—Tod Burnham—whisper in her ear, to comfort her, "Don't mind 'em, Maggie. Someday I'm going to ask my mother for a turniper, and maybe she'll give me one, and then I shall have a party, and you can come to it, Mag."

AN UNKNOWN MYSTERY

The Ideal, August 1891

Alicia Hammond-Flack sits in a broken-backed, wheezing rocking chair, a baby in her arms, a yearling child squalling at her feet, a young bully of three pulling at her back hair, a husband scolding in the next room because he has to catch the train for Boston at four o'clock, and it now wants thirty minutes of the time. It now wants thirty minutes of four, and there are no buttons to any of Jacob Flack's shirts, while his go-to-meeting suspenders have taken unto themselves wings and got lost. Alicia Hammond-Flack holds in her right hand a letter, for which the baby makes ineffectual grabs. While the baby makes ineffectual grabs, Alicia reads:

> My Dear Miss Hammond,
> You will doubtless be astonished when you recognize this hand—if you do recognize it—and when you remember the bearer of the name I am soon to sign—if you do remember it. Perhaps this will never reach you—may return to me via the dead letter office. You may be dead, married, living out West for aught I know. Fifteen years ago I asked you to marry me, and you said no. Since then I have been in China, in Africa, and in various other parts of the world, and I have never regretted your refusal since a twelvemonth of unavailing grief. I have now returned. I have little hair and less heart, but I want to see you. This note I send at a venture to your old home. I shall call on you there on Wednesday next, and if you are gone, or the place sold—bless me, what a snarl I'm in. Anyway I'm coming, in suspicion that you are a charming old maid and that you will be shocked at my bad manners, as you were when we were lovers.
> Truly yours, Melville Browne.

"What for are you laughing, ma?" asked Jacob the second. Alicia was thinking, "He never used to put an 'e' at the end of Brown." Sadly she contemplated the baby. Melville Browne was coming to see her on Wednesday, and today was Wednesday. He evidently knew nothing of the addition of Flack and a hyphen to her name. How would he be affected when he learned the existence of the hyphen and the Flack? Would he not laugh at Jacob Flack, as he had laughed at him when they had been fellow students at the Baptist Academy in the village?

Jacob Flack entered the room. He wore a straw hat and heavy boots, slightly molded with blue mold. His coat was of heavy woollen material and his trowsers of faded linen hung affectionately to his bony legs. For the first time in years Alicia was affected with disgust for a man who wore blue mold on his boots. "Button up your vest," she said. "No. I don't want people to see that you wear a white bosom pinned over a gingham shirt."

Then Jacob Flack left the house. As he passed the window he cried, "I forgot to kiss you good-bye, Allie. Never mind, I'll remember when I come back."

Melville Browne's letter seems like a benign influence, but the crying children, so dirty and so rude and so many, are like jarring elements. Alicia gazed about the old room which had been hers since her marriage as well as before. It is unchanged; always shabby, it had remained the same. She wonders, for the first time in her life, why she married Jacob Flack. And for the first time in her life she wonders why she refused Melville Browne. At the time, she had not been heart-broken. Melville had been only one among others who were refused by her. He had been one among others, but he had distinguished himself by going away. The rest had remained in town, and had married other girls in time, and she sees them weekly at church, with varying-sized flocks of children. Melville had gone away. She had married Jacob Flack, perhaps because he was a well-to-do man, more likely because he was the last one to ask for her hand, and there had been a wide interval minus proposals just before. Twelve years she had made Jacob Flack a faithful wife. It is the way of New England girls to be flirts before marriage and household drudges after. Alicia Hammond-Flack might insert a hyphen in her name, but the last twelve years had been busy ones for her. Each year she sold pounds of butter and cheese, besides moulding countless loaves of bread and baking thousands of ginger cakes. There were also three living children, and a row of little graves down in the cemetery clustered about the Flack monument. Alicia was a faithful wife and a hard-working woman. The neighbors said, "there was never anything slack about her."

Alicia wondered if Melville Browne needed to see the children. There were so many, and they all held their mouths open. It was a Flack trait. Even Jacob gaped a little, only his moustache hid the fact. Alicia went into the kitchen where a frowzy-haired girl in scant skirts was washing dishes.

"If you'll take the children out in the orchard back of the barn, and keep them there all the afternoon, away from some callers I expect, I'll give you my newest white apron," Alicia announced, with an unusual briskness in her voice. Without a word the girl drew her hands from the dirty water, threw the baby over her shoulder, and with the second child under her arm, his worsted shoes kicking vigorously, she quitted the house. Young Jacob followed her. Alicia was alone.

Alicia was alone. She went to her chamber, and musingly viewed herself in the mirror. Her skin was pale and colorless, her lips even looked bloodless. Her lips looked bloodless, but she brought back the color by rubbing them with a bit of scarlet flannel. Her thin faded hair she disposed as it had been worn long years before—in simple loops above her neck. Perhaps there were wrinkles it was best to hide. With trembling fingers she heated a slate pencil and curled the rings of hair about her temple. Once Alicia's hair had curled naturally, but somehow sickness had done away with that. Her one best dress, a black silk, was too old-fashioned and matronly. She cast aside the old-fashioned and matronly black silk and slipped into a fresh, white muslin, which, girded about her waist with a blue sash young Jacob wore with his Sunday frock, did very well. She slipped off her wedding ring—her hands were whiter without it. Yes, without it her hands were whiter, and besides she might want to play a trick upon Melville, and make him think she was unmarried for a time. Yes, for a time only she might pretend to be unmarried. It would be a joke, and Melville was always fond of jokes. And it was such a pleasure to think of something else besides stockings and cream, that Alicia did not see a man drive to the gate, and getting from the rickety top buggy, secure a piece of rope from under the seat, with which he tied his horse to the fence. While the horse was twitching its velvety lips and showing two rows of black teeth, in

298

an endeavor to devour the leaves off Alicia's pet rose bushes inside the yard, the stranger was lifting the tarnished brass knocker on the green door. Five minutes later he and Alicia are seated in the parlor.

Five minutes later the dim, rose-leaf scented parlor, ever kept sacred from invasion by the children, holds Alicia and Melville Browne. They are seated side by side on the green rep sofa; it is not a very large sofa, but is just about right for two. Melville's greeting had been characteristic. He had grabbed Alicia by the hands, and after closing the green door with his foot, waltzed into the parlor, and giving her one corner of the sofa, plumped himself into the other. Then he removed a tall, white hat and rubbed a silk bandanna over the red mark it had made on his forehead. He looked at Alicia with evident approval, then he said, "Upon my word, Lishy, you're prettier than when I went away. All my other old girls are like the roses which weren't the last rose of summer—'faded and gone'—that is gone and got made into Mrs. Somebody. You're like the last rose—'standing alone'. Sure!"

Alicia remembered that "sure." It suddenly came over her that she had lost a good deal in not having heard it for fifteen years. As for Melville, he was better-looking than ever. When she refused him he had worn long hair, a full beard, loose clothing, and had had a fat figure. Now his hair was clipped extraordinarily short, his face was cleanly shaved, his thin, erect figure was cased in closely-fitting garments of broad cloth. Such are the changes made in a man by time and fashion, that Melville Browne now had a mouth full of dazzling white teeth, where when he had left home there had been a row of aching snags.

"Why, Lishy," exclaimed Melville Browne, "you look exactly as you used to when I went away. You haven't grown old a bit, I declare."

"You're grown young," returned Alicia brightly.

Melville clasped his large, white hands over one knee and regarded Alicia with his head on one side.

"I suppose one year has been just the same as another to you," he remarked, "living here in this dead-alive town, and never seeing a new face from year's end to year's end. Oh, I remember the place of old, sure! While, as for me—oh, good Lord! I can tell you, business is the career for a man. When I remember how I planned to buy a farm and go to raising cows and potatoes, if you had married me fifteen years ago, I declare I'm glad you said no that evening, Lishy, though it was blamed hard at the time. As it is, I've seen something of the world, I've made some money and spent more than I saved, had an all-fired good time spending it, too, Lishy. Only when a man gets to my age he's sort of lonesome, you know, without a wife. All the old fellows that married at the age I wanted you, Lishy, have got daughters now, and they keep firing 'em at my head. I say, Lishy, how pretty you are! That's because you've had nothing to worry you, I suppose. But don't you get sort of blue down here all alone on winter evenings?"

Alicia nervously twisted the fringe of little Jacob's sash about her finger. "The neighbors come in sometimes," she said in a low, sweet voice. The low, sweet voice in which she spoke bore no resemblance to the sharp, irritated tones in which she habitually yelled to the young Flacks. Alicia hardly knew herself. She felt quite young and coquettish. All her cares had gone from her, and even the thought that Debby would be sure to let young Jacob eat green apples brought her no qualm of trouble. The wearied house-mother had bloomed again into a slightly chastened edition of what she had been as a young girl.

Melville Browne, with his hands clasped just above the buttons on the rear of his well-built coat, began to roam about the room, staring at the shells and china mugs on the walls, the dead flies in the corners of the window panes. Presently he returned to the sofa with an antiquated leather-bound album. "I gave you this, do you remember?" he asked. "Gracious, goodness, don't try to take it away. I want to see if you've got my old phiz still in here." The first leaf enshrined the portrait of Jacob Flack, bald and tired-looking, his head screwed to an impossible angle. Melville Browne let off a big, hearty laugh at his formal rival.

"If there ain't Jake Flack," he cried. "Good Lord, is he still in town? Poor old chap. Is he married?"

Alicia nodded.

"Sure! Well, I needn't have asked. He couldn't look so forlorn if he wasn't. Anyone can see that he's wondering where the next round of shoes for the youngsters are coming from. Who'd he marry?"

"She was no one you ever knew," said Alicia, evasively.

Melville continued to skim his way through the album. "Who are all these kids?" he inquired, as photographs of children in various awkward attitudes passed before his vision.

"Oh, they are Jacob Flack's. His wife is something of a friend of mine; she gave them to me," remarked Alicia.

Suddenly Melville Browne pitched the album on a table, narrowly escaping from overturning a kerosene lamp, and putting one arm around Alicia's waist, he gave her a resounding kiss upon the lips. She blushed prettily, and exclaimed, "Why, Melville Browne, don't you know we're too old for such nonsense?"

"Sure!" he returned, laughing, and kissing her again.

"After all these years—" she protested.

"Never too late to reform, you know," kissing her a third time.

"Really, now, Melville Brown—"

"I say, Lishy," he broke in, "I'm the same old fellow I always was, ain't I? You know you never could keep me in order. Come, now, ain't you glad to see me a little bit? Ain't you? Gosh! I came pretty near dying last Christmas. I had the cholera in Hong Kong, and it was a blamed close shave for life. While you was eating your plum pudding, I was almost going off my hooks entirely."

Swiftly Alicia's mind returned to the last Christmas day. She herself had been at death's door at that time, for scarlet fever had passed through the house and had carried two of her children down to that well-filled lot in the cemetery. She had cried then, but now there were no tears in her eyes. No, with Melville Browne's arm around her waist, her heart was beating rapidly, and she felt happy. Nothing seemed of very much consequence, only to have a good time. To have a good time seemed the only thing of consequence in the world. So she looked up in Melville Brown's face and smiled, whereupon two charming dimples came in her cheeks, and Melville felt under the necessity of kissing her again. Suddenly he drew her closely to him with his strong masculine arm. Her cheek rested on his breast. She could feel something square and hard in his coat pocket against her cheek. She could hear the ticking of his watch.

"Alicia," said he, "do you know what I came to see you for? I just made up my mind that if you was single, and if you was as dear a girl as you were fifteen years ago, I'd ask you to have me again. Don't begin to trouble now, Lishy. I haven't asked you yet, remember, and I'll be eternally flabbergasted if I do ask you until I'm sure you'll say yes. I can't stand a refusal at my time of life, Lishy, 'twould break me all up. It took me a year to get over your saying no before, and a year out of my life now would mean the loss of more than one $10,000, I can tell you. Now, do you blame me, Lishy?"

"No-o-o," she said slowly.

Pinching her ear, Melville went on, "Well now, Lishy, what shall I do? Will I ask you?"

"If you want to," she whispered. Her eyes were shining, and her breath came in ecstatic little gasps. If you had asked her the number of little graves down under the Flack monument, she couldn't have told.

"Then, will you have me, Lishy?"

"Yes."

"When? Come now, when?"

"Oh—I don't know."

"Today? Now?"

"Oh, no. There's so much to do."

"Do? Why, all we've got to do is lock the house, give away the cat—by the way, have you got a cat?—and fire what victuals'll spoil out of your pantry window. I'll help. I can eat some of 'em; I'm mighty hungry. Come now, I've got to go to New York tonight to see my boss. Just get in the team with me, and we'll take the next train. When we get to the city we can be married and start in for a good time. I've no desire to hang around this God-forgotten town any longer. I had enough of it when I was a boy, and I bet you haven't quitted it once all these fifteen years. Come now, Lishy, let's vamoose the whole ranch."

Then he kissed her again.

Alicia did not stop to think why this man seemed more akin to her than Jacob Flack and the little Flacks. She felt as if it would be impossible to support an existence apart from him. Not that she loved him so very much, but in some way their interests seemed to have suddenly become the same. She projected her mind into the future. It seemed perfectly natural and proper that she was henceforth the companion of Melville Browne. She could not, however, try as she could, imagine herself darning the stockings and washing the faces of the little Flacks anymore. It was funny, she had always been so good, so prim, so hard upon any woman who committed an unconventional act, but now Alicia never once thought that she was doing anything wrong. She was happy and contented. To send Melville Browne away and return to her old life never once occurred to her. It did not seem as if it were possible to send Melville Browne away. He was part of her life now and forever. Perhaps her conscience had died suddenly. Perhaps she never had had a conscience. At any rate, this was no commonplace yielding to temptation. There did not seem to be any temptation, on the contrary, as it would be absolutely impossible to do anything except ride away with Melville Browne.

And so it happened that a woman wearing a white dress and a blue sash, a large straw bonnet and a thick grey veil, drove away in the gathering twilight with a tall, well-dressed, clean-shaven man. The few people out on the country road at that hour—small girls going for the evening's supply of milk, or weary-footed men or boys driving home the cows—noticed that the carriage was shabby and the horse a livery stable hack; they also noticed that there was a dark coat sleeve about the woman's white gown. Owing to her veil no one noticed the woman's face, but several afterwards said, in talking the matter over, that she seemed to be laughing loudly. That she seemed to be laughing loudly all agreed, but none connected the laughing woman with the disappearance of Alicia Hammond-Flack. As her clothing lay in a disordered heap on her chamber floor, and as there was a beaten path through an oat field to the river—a path which either a cow or a woman might have made—it was decided that Mrs. Flack had wandered away and drowned herself. After all, her mind never had seemed quite right since Christmas, when all the children had had scarlet fever, and the baby had been born at the same time. So in time Jacob Flack married Debby, the frowsy-haired girl, because his children needed a mother, and all the neighbors agreed Debby would never learn the worth of milkpans and how to wash them properly until she owned some of her own.

But all agreed that the strange woman who went away in a shabby carriage was laughing loudly.

CINDY'S CHILD

Ink Drops, December 1891

I

At nine o'clock Sunday morning the village street was nearly empty. It looked very bare and clean, the yellow sand glistened in the spring sunshine, with a beaten path at one side, and the festering garbage in the gutter now hidden by newly sprouted weeds. There was an old brown house standing so close to the road that passers-by could see in at the windows. The unpainted clapboards were shriveling up, and great black bugs crawled from under them into the sunshine. The faded green door of the house was open into the kitchen. The floor of this room was sunken and discolored, with streams of dirty water radiating from a leaky pail in one corner. Some pale cockroaches, that looked as if a touch would crush them, crawled languidly in and out of the crevices in the wall. A big man with a red chin whisker sat on a low chair with his back in the sunshine that was streaming in at the window. His boots were reeking with offensive-smelling mud; and he was drinking a mixture of eggs and cider out of a rusty tin basin.

Two girls who had just come in to make a call were seated on a calico-covered lounge in one corner of the room. They were snigling at some jocose remark made by the man. He was pressing them to drink some of the egg-nog.

"Oh, if you won't drink out of the same dish as me," he said, "if that's it."

Lilla Mason, the big girl with a flat face and nose, who wore her light hair in a tight frizz like a negro's, and with a dagger of red glass thrust through it, protested warmly. It wasn't that she was proud—oh, no; egg-nog never did agree with her.

The other girl was quite stout, and her plaid dress did not match evenly above her waist. She did not talk, but looked impatiently around the room, while Lilla made great efforts to be polite.

"Just think of a great fat thing like her running after the men," she remarked. "That last story? Oh, it's too funny. You see she gave a berry party, and she, and the schoolmarm, and Jack Dalton and another man went off in a team, with little pails, to pick berries. And when they came home, you know, Jack Dalton was drunk, and it was dark, and he drove up to the livery stable in great style and fell out of the wagon. In clearing out the wagon the schoolmarm's boots were found there. That's how she lost the school. Oh, it's all true. Jack told me all about it himself."

The man laughed a great deal at the story, and proceeded to cap it with another even more outrageous. The silent girl, finding the edge of her rough woolen dress irritated her neck, pushed her fingers over the chafed places. Then she cried, in the midst of the story,

"I say, how's Cindy? It's Cindy I want to see."

The man took another drink. "Cindy's in the bed room. You can go in, if you want," he said.

The two girls got up and went slowly into the bed room. They had only one door to open. The bed room had a window on the street and anybody going by could have seen all there was in the place. That was not much—only a wooden bed, a small table with a nursing bottle on it, a tub of dirty water, and a heap of soiled linen on a chair. On the bed, leaning against grimy pillows, was a girl. Pretty—oh very pretty, with big blue eyes, and feathery yellow curls around her temples. Her cheeks were pink, and when she smiled they were full of adorable dimples. Lying by her side was a fat, red-faced baby, with little twinkling dark eyes. The girls were rather embarrassed to see Cindy lying so still and weak, so after saying, "Howdy, Cindy?" both sat on the bed and looked at the baby.

"Ain't he fat!" said Lilla.

"Twelve pounds," replied Cindy, with a bit of real motherly pride in her voice.

"Anyway, he looks good enough to eat."

Here the infant squalled.

"Well, that's like you anyhow, Cindy," said Lilla, giggling.

"What's happened while I've been in?" asked Cindy.

The two talked very fast. Oh lots had happened, yes, lots. Emma had got a beau, it was the best she could do, poor girl, but how he did look when she was out walking with him. He was so bow-legged—his legs as crooked as anything.

"For my part," said Lilla, "I never walked yet with a bow-legged man, and I never will. I'd rather go alone. Whenever I'm introduced to a man I look at once to see if his legs are straight."

Then the other girl began to talk about Delia. She was putting on so many airs, you couldn't think, over a new green poplin. Well, if she didn't know green made her look like a sick cow, it was time someone told her. And Loo Burns was getting ready to be married. As to that, it was quite time if she wanted to keep him, for he was going over to Longmeadow to work in the stone quarries, and Loo was the kind it's out of sight out of mind with.

Cindy listened, stretching herself lazily. If girls knew anything, she said, they would leave the men alone, and not get married. 'Twasn't so nice when their husbands ran away and left them in the situation she was left in.

"Yes," said Lilla, rather flaunting, and leaning back against the foot-board of the bed, "you're in a nice mess, Cindy, you are."

Cindy grew confidential in relating her troubles. Why her husband should off and leave her with a baby to support, she couldn't see. He wrote her a letter saying he was gone for good. She hoped he had. Her mother said maybe he had another wife hid off somewhere. Anyway, he'd gone. The worst of it was that her engaged lover was coming up from Boston that very night. Lilla got interested. Any prospect of a row was nuts to her.

"Doesn't he know you're married?" she asked, pointing to the baby.

Cindy grew irritable. Did Lilla think she was a fool to throw away all her chances by telling? When she was married ten months before, of course she had had other things to think of besides writing letters. He hadn't been to see her for a year, but he wrote real often. He was rich, too. He made boilers in a shop of his own, and hired help, he had a house and a housekeeper to do for him. Her father had been there. He had sent her an emerald ring, and had asked her to marry him. He had written that he would get there Sunday night. He had business in Longmeadow and would drive over. It was a wonder, she said, beginning to cry, that he hadn't come even before.

The plaid-dressed girl comforted her. "After all, he didn't," she said.

Lilla was more practical. "Some one'll tell him," she observed.

"Oh, father'll see he don't speak to anyone in town, and the baby's to stay in the garret till he's gone. And no one would be so mean as to tell."

Lilla denied this. There were some awful pigs in the world, she declared. Old fatty Lutien, for instance, would tell anything she made up and pretend it was about a real girl. But then, such people were not respectable. Oh no, Lilla called them dowdies, they did not even know how to wear becoming clothes.

Cindy, having once begun crying, could not stop. It was so horrid!

"I've got to get up and dress," she sobbed, "and I feel so weak. I feel as if I should fall down. When I get up my legs are all trembly, you know."

"If it was me," said Lilla, in a business-like tone, "I should just take a big drink of whiskey, and then I'd feel equal to anything."

Then the two got up to go. They promised over and over to come again, and the plaid dressed, who was a sentimental sort of a creature, kissed Cindy. Then they went off down the sun-glaring road, and the sun being high a couple of black squat shadows travelled along with them.

Lilla rid herself of all present thought of her old comrade by re-marking, "Well, Cindy's got herself into a pretty kettle of fish. For my part, I wouldn't try to marry two men at the same time."

The more sentimental creature in the plaid dress, being interested in the romance, whose apotheosis she had just witnessed, sighed and said, "One thing I'd like to know is who's the father of Cindy's child?"

II

Toward evening, when the sun was sinking like a great red ball in a cloud of dust, Cindy got up. There was a great deal of trouble in getting her dressed. One of her gowns was out grown and would not come together, while the other was so tight it made her cry. However, at length all was done. Cindy looked very nice in a blue dress, with some pink ribbon quilling around the neck and wrists. Her mother told her she was getting to be an old fat, and scolded her well when once Cindy broke down and burst into tears. The baby was put into the garret, with a bottle of milk for company, and Cindy took Lilla's advice as to the big drink of whiskey. The consequence was that in her weak state she really felt drunk, just sleepy and boozy, as if she didn't care what happened. When all was ready Cindy and her mother went into the little parlor. A bright brass lamp was blazing away on the marble-topped table, showing off the autograph and photograph albums, the brussels carpet, the cane chairs, and the chromos—"Rock of Ages" and "No Cross No Crown"—on the walls. Cindy's mother had black hair and high cheek bones, she had lost her upper front teeth, so that her lip fell in. While they were waiting she gave Cindy some good advice.

"Don't keep him dangling any longer," she remarked. "First thing you know he'll come up here and find out something, if you let him keep coming. Just bring him up to scratch, and once you're married to a rich man you're all right, Cindy."

Further counsel was made impossible by the arrival of Cindy's father and her lover, John Hedderman. The father and mother went into the little entry for a moment and whispered.

"He ain't heard nothing. I took precious care he shouldn't gab with anyone in the village."

John Hedderman was a big, stout man, a good many years older than Cindy. His head was rather bald, and his beard had turned gray. He kissed Cindy a great many times, and pinched her cheeks. Then he gave her the presents he had brought—a silver bracelet and a pair of coral earrings. Cindy admired the earrings, but privately thought the bracelet very ugly until John told how the stunning Boston girls wore them over long gloves, and how they hung silver dimes on them, given by their lovers. Cindy thought that was lovely.

The old man and woman were very polite. Red beard insisted on his dear friend, Mr. Hedderman, joining him in a glass of cider, and they drank Cindy's health. Cindy's mother talked very slow, so as to get in no objectionable words. She deplored the fact that Cindy had no society in town. The factory girls were so vile, she never let Cindy associate with them. Some were not even respectable. Here the old man, in spite of some nudges from his wife, insisted on repeating the story of Mrs. Lutien and the berrying frolic. But it went off well. John Hedderman laughed, and Cindy blushed very prettily. The poor girl felt all the time as if she should faint, she was so weak. In the midst of the conversation the older two would occasionally go out of the room for a few minutes, and then John Hedderman would leap nimbly from his chair and run over to kiss Cindy or give her a rough hug. Occasionally he pulled her on to his knees and called her his little duck.

Finally he asked her when they were to be married. He had not really thought of doing this when he came, but Cindy looked so pale and pretty that he felt very much in love with her, and it had just entered his head that it was dull for a pretty girl in the country. When it got to be ten o'clock he boldly told Cindy's parents to go along to bed, for he and Cindy were going to talk about their wedding. The old people toddled off as pleased as possible.

Cindy and John sat on the sofa. John had turned down the lamp until only a blue flame was left, and then he put his arms tight around Cindy.

"We'll have a jolly old time when we're married," he whispered, "you shall go to the show every night in the week if you want to. And get some nice clothes, won't you, now? I want my wife to beat 'em all. I'll foot the bills, you know, Cindy."

The proximity of her lover, combined with that gorgeous promise of unlimited theatre going, was too much for Cindy to take in unmoved. She put her arms tightly around John's neck and whispered, "Oh, I love you so much, and it will be just elegant." In her exalted state she forgot her recent trouble and her weakness and pain. John got a box of burnt almonds out of his overcoat pocket and they had a good time crunching the candy until midnight. Cindy simpered, she was so modest, whenever her wedding was spoken of, but at length it got settled for two weeks from then. And John was so well pleased that he whispered some very affectionate words into Cindy's ear, making her blush quite red. And then, as the candy was all gone, they went to bed.

Cindy slept up in the garret that night, to be near the baby. Her mind was so easy that she never woke until nearly eight o'clock.

John Hedderman had told Cindy's mother and father all about his arrangements, and he gave Cindy's mother the money for the wedding clothes. He wasn't as much in love as he had been the night before, and excess of burnt almonds had made him rather ill, but he was not of the sort to go back on his word.

When Cindy came to bid him good bye, she was overcome with a whim of tenderness, and throwing herself into John's arms she began to cry and to say, "You'll be good to me—good—won't you?"

Her father was frightened, for he didn't know what the sick girl might tell in her maudlin state, so he shouted harshly, "Cindy, I'm ashamed of ye."

John crushed her close to him, and told her to cheer up, and then he with the father drove off in the morning sunshine. After they were gone Cindy went into the bed room and buried her head in the foul-smelling pillows. The baby was wailing on the bed, but she did not pay any heed. She felt physically broken and worn out. She didn't much care what became of her. The baby was allowed to cry as loud as he pleased, now there was no John Hedderman near to hear him. Cindy began to wonder what would become of him, and then she fell asleep.

III

Cindy and her mother were making wedding clothes. John's present had been liberal, and it allowed for the purchase of two silk dresses, and boots and gloves, as well as underclothing. The fame of Cindy's trousseau had spread quite through the village, and all the girls in town came to see it. Cindy's father had used up all his cider treating the gentlemen who came with them. Cindy had been over to Long-meadow and had bought a lot of things, some had never been seen in town before. For instance, a pair of red hose suspenders attracted much comment. The girls all tried them on and laughed loudly at the idea of wearing such things. But Cindy assured them that such things were worn by everyone, the shop girl had told her so. And even Lilla acknowledged that they might be the thing for Boston. But when the girls went away they laughed well at Cindy's airs.

"Positively that girl makes me tired," said Lilla, "putting on all the airs she does and making wedding clothes with that baby in the room. I wonder if she'll take the young one to Boston with her?"

The baby was troublesome, always crying to be taken up whenever Cindy tried on a new dress. One day, while Cindy and her mother were sewing, the latter remarked, "Well, what lunkheads we are to keep that child here anyway. He must be given away before the wedding."

Cindy began to cry, hurriedly putting away her work so as not to spot it.

"Well, you are a fool!"

"I don't care, give him away. I wish he was given away. I ain't a-bawling for him, you needn't think. Oh dear, everything is so hard on me."

"You ought to have known better than to have married a man you didn't know nothing about. I always knew you'd come home in some sort of a mess when you wrote you was married to a stranger. You're a fool, Cindy, however you put it. Stand up and let me see if this skirt is too long. I only hope he won't appear here before you're married to Hedderman and gone. I'll send him packing. He'll never find you in Boston and nobody in this village will tell him. All the folks here are your friends, Cindy. Just keep a stiff upper lip and you'll be a rich woman yet."

The baby, lying on a pillow in a rocking chair, now set up his insistent wail, wrinkling his red mottled face. Cindy's mother shrugged her shoulders with vexation.

"It's a pity he won't die," she remarked, "such heaps of babies die when they are wanted, and this brat—"

She looked out of the window meditatively. Cindy stared at her open mouthed a moment, and then got up in a hurry.

"I'll go and get his bottle," she said. "That's what he wants."

She was gone a long time and when she came in her face was very white. She had the bottle, however, and she gave it to the child. It was empty. Cindy had just rinsed it with milk, so that for a moment it looked as if full. The child attempted eating an instant, and then recommenced crying. Cindy's mother seemed to understand what was going on, for she began talking loud to drown the infant's wail.

"Lilla was telling another funny story about Mrs. Lutien," said the older woman. "It seems the new minister they've got up at the Advent church went to call on her. Jack Dalton was there, and some other men, having a great time, with the girls. They got the parson out to play croquet on the grass, and they had lemonade with rum in it. The deacon drove by and he was fit to split he was so mad, when he saw Dominie out there playing croquet. And parson never know what gang he was with until they got into the house and Mrs. Lutien said her hair was too heavy for her and took off her false crimps. I shouldn't wonder, fat as she is, but Jack says the parson just jumped out of the window and ran off lickety larrup. I guess he ain't been there since."

The baby was still crying.

"I'll take the bottle away," said the mother, preserving the fiction that the child had eaten. "He'll get wind on his stomach if he has it empty."

The baby went to sleep in the evening and did not wake up until Cindy was in bed. Then he recommenced his hungry wail. At first Cindy tried to sleep, tossing and turning in the darkness until she tore a hole in the sheet. It was a sultry night, every few minutes there came a rumble of thunder and one vivid flash of light, but no rain fell. Cindy finally sat up in bed and gritted her teeth together, her fingers in her ears, and her knees drawn up until her chin rested on them. She was so sleepy that her eyes would not stay open, but she could not rest. The baby wailed on.

Toward morning the thunder ceased and there came a pink tinge in the air. Cindy felt feverish and shaky, she was still weak from her recent illness, and it was the first time in all her life she had kept awake all night.

"After all," she said to herself, "I can't stand this. I can't sleep while he cries. I shall be sick, and then mother will feel worse."

And just to get some sleep, as she thought, she crept out and found a bottle of milk. The baby drank and went to sleep contented. Lying on the outside of the bed Cindy fell into a stupor of exhaustion.

Cindy's mother, in her own bed, had heard the crying, and forty times during the night she had been on the point of "going in to help Cindy." But then she reflected that Cindy would probably prefer to be alone, though she deplored the weak mindedness of her daughter, who listened to the crying all night, instead of getting the job done quickly so as to get some sleep. When the sudden silence came the grand-mother was so pleased that she turned over and went to sleep with a grin on her ugly mouth.

In the morning she was very pleasant indeed, and even went so far as to ask her husband how he slept.

"Well enough," he responded, "only for the squalling of that brat."

For an instant the old hag felt a great tenderness in her heart, as if this was the red-haired lover of years gone by, and she had a whim to be confidential and tell him that he would not hear any more squalling, but then she reflected that in one of his sprees he might give the whole story away, and so she held her tongue. Just then Cindy came in, her eyes wandering restlessly around the room.

"How's baby?" asked the fond old woman of the broom in the corner.

Cindy, with a great air of weariness, was eating curds out of an iron kettle on the stove.

"He cried all night," she remarked. "But he's quiet now."

At that moment the wail arose on the air. The old woman got up with the air of a Lady Macbeth, and gripping Cindy's arm exclaimed, "Good God, the child is crying."

"Why not?" said Cindy with an irrational laugh. "I'll go take him up."

That afternoon Cindy and her father went over to the village. The mother watched them off, the girl tall and handsome, with her curly head crowned by a white bonnet, the old man having a straw-covered demijohn slung over his shoulder by a worn bit of rope. After they were quite out of sight, she went and looked at the baby in a business-like way. He was growing whiter every day. His plump hands had dimples in them.

"Cindy's a silly fool," said the woman, wagging her head, and pressing her lips together over the hollows in her teeth. She took a small bottle full of dark fluid out of her pocket and began feeding the paregoric by spoonfuls to the child. It was sweet, and he swallowed it eagerly, sticking out his tongue to lick the poison off his lips.

He was soon alseep, and the woman went out into the yard, and flung the bottle down the well. Then she drove away an adventuresome chicken, which was scratching up the row of balsams growing from seed below the bed room window, and before she went in the flowers were protected by a row of sticks driven around them until they formed a miniature fence.

Then she went and looked at the baby. He was sleeping quietly, but there was a big brown spot on his dress where some of the paregoric had been spilled. The woman hurried to change his clothing. The child lay on her arm as heavy and limp as a little dead animal. She tucked him up in the bed, and went out to wash the stained garments. While she was kneeling on the floor, scrubbing at the washtub, her memory again reverted to the days when big, red-headed Bill Hammond was her lover, and she even sung, in a cracked voice, a song which she remembered from those days:

> "Oh Evalina, Sweet Evalina,
> Under the willows she's sleeping"—

She could not remember any more of it, but she repeated this over and over, until Cindy and her father came back from town. The man was rather drunk, and his wife hustled him upstairs to bed in short order. In the meanwhile Cindy went into the bed room. A glimpse of cambric edging caught her eye, and she called out, "Ma, why did you put on baby's best dress?"

Then, coming closer, she said, "Anyway, he's drooled all over it. What've you been giving him that's black?"

"I gave him some paregoric," said the old woman, leaning back in a creaking rocking chair.

Cindy came out, with the baby on her arm. His eyes were open and he was coughing vigorously. Pretty quick he began to cry and to beat the air with his fists. He was still alive, very much alive. Cindy's mother got up to look at him, and then sat hard in her chair. In her excited state of mind she paid no attention to feeling in her spine.

"Well, that child is tough," she exclaimed. "It must be he was born to be hung, for I'm sure he'll never die a natural death."

IV

It was a hot day, no sun, but a moist heat in the air that was more unpleasant than any amount of sunshine. Cindy's father was quietly getting himself drunk by slow degrees, her mother had gone out, Cindy sat by the kitchen window, leaning back in her chair, and thinking how she would look in the new fawn colored silk she would wear at her wedding. Once in a while a gush of rain would blur the landscape for a moment, but all the time the air grew more oppressive. Cindy was watching for her mother to come back with the doctor, who had been sent for to come and see what was the matter with the baby. He had been ailing for a day or two and Cindy had made a strong point of the doctor's being called. After one look at the child her mother, with a satisfied grin, went out to call him herself.

It was a relief to see Dr. Weber's cheerful face, with the big yellow mustachios he was so careful of cherishing. He came into the kitchen, pulling off his gloves, and talking in a loud, round tone.

"Well, Miss Cindy, you're not so white as when I saw you last," he said. Then he told facetiously how the old lady refused to trust herself to his two-wheeled gig, but walked home in the rain, and how he had splashed her with mud about halfway there. The doctor then sat down and poured himself out a glass of cider, drinking it with a slow earnestness which the old drunkard admired open mouthed. Then Bill Hammond began to dilate at length on his troubles. Crops were so bad, this wetness was killing all the potatoes, and the neighbors were sure he would come to ruin because he cut hay on a Sunday when that was a fine day and the rest of the week was as wet as the river.

Oh well, the doctor observed, there were degrees in all things. Probably those very people did not hesitate to make love to their neighbors' wives after church. And then the doctor began to relate some scandal which so delighted old Bill that he toddled to a cupboard and brought down a bottle of brandy to spice the cider with.

But the doctor did not quite forget he had come to earn a fee.

"Business is business," he said, getting up and wringing the cider out of his mustachios. "Where's the youngster, Cindy?"

Cindy led the way into the bed room. The baby was laid upon a chair, set close to the window. He was no longer fat, his bones seemed coming through the skin in places, he was crying faintly and his lips were blue.

"He don't look much like a youngster to take to Boston," said Dr. Weber, smiling in a slow, beautiful way at Cindy. Then resuming his professional air he took the baby into his arms. The child gave a further irritated cry when moved, and the doctor could see through the thin muslin night gown that his tender skin was chafed in places until raw and bleeding. The doctor whistled a moment under his breath, and then looked sharply at Cindy. She was standing awkwardly by the window, looking out.

The baby began to gasp for breath. Dr. Weber calmly laid him back on the chair.

"He's got cholera infantum, I should say," he remarked gravely. "There's no hope of saving him. You had better fan him, Cindy, and keep the flies away. I'll wait a while in the other room."

He went out, leaving the door open. Cindy took the baby on her lap and began to fan him with a newspaper. Some large green flies crawled over the child's dress and buzzed at his eyes and nostrils. When they once lit on his flesh it was well nigh impossible to get them off, they hung as if glued.

In the stillness their buzzing sounded very loud.

Cindy's mother had got home and was in the kitchen. She had taken off her wet shoes and was drying her soaked feet in the stove oven, while she wiped the sweat off her face with her apron.

"I heard you was calling down to Dolly Parsons' last night," she said to Dr. Weber.

The doctor, who was now sipping more cider, nodded heavily. Then, observing her expression of interest, he consented to give her some details. Dolly was a woman who had been notorious, first as the hand-somest woman in the village, and then for having eloped with her husband's brother, going to live in a remote farmhouse.

"I never was in so queer a place," he said. "It seems young Parsons broke his leg a spell ago and wouldn't send for anyone to set it. He's been lying a-bed there ever since, and Dolly did everything. Finally she got hungry; a woman can't stand that, you know, and when she came to the village to buy food she asked me to come up, too. Parsons was in bed in the kitchen, and it seems Dolly saws the wood right there. Old fence rails were what she was burning and when she can't saw them she sticks one end in the stove and shoves it up when it gets burned off."

Mrs. Hammond exclaimed loudly. Good gracious, what a way to live! Well, Dolly Parsons always did put on too many airs. For her part, she liked living respectable, and having regular meals. Then she asked Dr. Weber if he was going up there again?

"Well, yes; I've got to see about Parsons' leg. And I shouldn't wonder if the undertaker was called up that way before long. Dolly had a bad cough."

The old woman leaned forward, licking her lips in anticipation of a nice gossip to come over the grewsome details of a funeral. She always knew Dolly would come to a bad end, she declared, when she used to make her little Tommy wear calico long gowns years before. One thing she could always be thankful for. And that was that Cindy's child had been well dressed. They'd nothing to reproach themselves with. But poor Dolly—

"Oh," cried Cindy, "Oh, my baby is dead!"

Dr. Weber and the mother hurried into the bed room. The child had indeed stopped breathing and the corpse was even then stiffening. The doctor quietly ascertained this, then he gently closed the black eyes, and impelled Cindy to lay her burden on the bed. All three left the room, closing the door. Cindy threw herself into a chair, but her mother went up to the table and drank a mug full of raw brandy.

"I'm afraid that walk got my feet wet," she said.

The old man paused in his tippling for a moment and looked at the closed door. Then his bleary gaze wandered around the room, and with trembling forefinger he began to count.

"Doctorsh, one—Cindysh, two. Ole woman—My Gawd, I'm four! Wheresh the baby?" he ended by calling in so loud a tone that it seemed to surprise himself.

Dr. Weber forced him back into his chair.

"Why don't none o' th' —— fools stay with the baby (hic)?" he asked of the doctor.

"The baby is dead," replied the doctor, somewhat impatiently, and looking around for his hat.

Slowly the old man closed his fingers around the handle of the pitcher, and began pouring out a glass of cider. By an inadvertent movement his hand turned, and the stream of brown liquid went on the floor. When it was all gone the old man raised his glass to drink. It was empty. He looked into the pitcher, but that too was empty, except for the carcasses of a half dozen drowned flies. Realizing the state of things, he burst into tears and buried his face in his hands.

"He wash the only grandchild I had," he moaned. "Doctor, he wash the apple of my heart. The first and the lasht."

The doctor was now standing in the door way.

"I'll speak to the undertaker, and have him come up," he said.

Then he flicked his gloves in the direction of old Bill and continued, "You'd better put him to bed. I don't want to come back here to a case of shakes before morning."

V

It having rained in the morning, and the clouds not being entirely dissipated, there was a pale watery sunshine out of doors. Quite a festal air prevailed in the house. Some strange old ladies were cooking in the kitchen, and in the parlor a crowd of men were being treated to cider by old Bill. The latter, in his Sunday clothing, which was never worn on the Sabbath, looked most uncomfortable, but his eyes glistened at the thought that before night he would be delightfully drunk, and revenged on the women folks who had forced him to keep sober ever since the baby's funeral.

The marriage ceremony was over and the parson had gone away, so all hands could freely give themselves up to merriment, only the bridegroom had it on his mind that he must be sober enough to take Cindy and the four o'clock train from Longmeadow to Boston.

Cindy, in her fawn-colored dress with tight sleeves, had just cut the big black cake John Hedderman had brought from the city, and all the girls were getting pieces to dream on. Lilla Mason went out into the kitchen to carry a slice to the girl who had visited Cindy two weeks before, and who now refused to come into the parlor because she was still wearing the plaid dress that did not hook together. Cindy's forefinger was rough from the sewing she had recently done, and she felt rather tired and nerveless from the same up the back cause. She sat and idly picked icing off the cake, while she watched one of the group of men drinking and laughing with her father. It was Jack Dalton she looked at, a gay young fellow with black eyes, who was welcome anywhere, though he wore poor clothes and never had any money to spend like the mill hands. He would not work and so he was called "Gentleman Jack."

"All the same," Cindy muttered to herself, "he had better have staid away. Yes, he had. I would have staid away, at all events."

Then she went into the kitchen where the girls were. Lilla was whispering to the rest, "Why, you never saw such a little corpse as they said he was. All raw and chafed, too. And they did not even have a parson to bury him. The old man and Dr. Weber went out in the morning and saw it done, that was all."

"Dr. Weber—what made him come?" asked Delia, a big girl with a flat nose.

"Oh, my dear, you must not ask such questions. They say he wouldn't mind being in the bridegroom's shoes today. Who knows?"

A chorus of amazement greeted this remark. Much complimented by the attention she was arousing, Lilla went on, "Oh yes, it is probably so, though what he can see in Cindy—"

Then, as Cindy came in, Lilla lovingly put her arm about the other's waist and murmured, "Oh girls, she's Mrs. Hedderman now. Isn't it funny?"

At this everyone began to praise Cindy's husband. He was so distinguished, not young, of course, but then young men did not have any money to go housekeeping with. Lilla said that for her part she preferred an old man, for he had seen something of the world, and there would be lots to talk of evenings. And Delia asked if they had heard how Sue Brewer set up housekeeping?

"Oh, it's so funny, you can't think. She would marry Ben, though he has nothing saved—oh, nothing at all. He borrowed $35 from his brother, the butcher, and you ought to see their home! Home—it's one room, and the bed in a corner, and two wash tubs, and all the dishes left on the table because there's no cupboard."

Cindy turned up her pretty nose at such squalor. For her part, she had never eaten in a room with a bed in it, and she guessed now she never would. And Lilla said folks must be sick to marry and take in washing to help support the family, when all the while they could work in the shop if they were single and have their wages for their own. Only Delia whispered to Cindy that it wouldn't be safe for Gentleman Jack to speak of marrying to Lilla unless he meant business.

The uproar in the parlor grew louder, and Mrs. Hammond with several female friends withdrew to the bed room for a last look at Cindy's "things" before packing them up. Gentleman Jack had drank until his face was red as his necktie, and feeling hot he said to the bridegroom—who was having a dull time, as he took but one glass to his companions' three—"Let's go out of this cursed hole. Let's take a walk."

Hedderman consented, and picking their hats out of a pyramid of headgear on the entry table, they went outdoors into the cooling. Cindy, in the kitchen, ran to the window when she saw those two going away together. She watched them follow the road a little way, and then turn aside into a field where some fir trees grew.

"Gosh," said she, turning to her friend, "what do they want in the graveyard today?"

The girls began to feel a sort of evil omen in the occurrence, as well as Cindy. They looked at one another and nodded their heads. Cindy burst into tears and hid her face in Lilla's lap. She wailed that she was the most unlucky girl on earth. Just as she had gone through so much, and was going to Boston to be happy, that nasty Gentleman Jack must come and spoil it all. Lilla did not quite understand. Said she, "Why, Jack's a good fellow. He won't tell anything."

Cindy forgot prudence in her sorrow.

"He might not tell," she sobbed, "but he will about me. He's just as spiteful. He wants me to marry him, myself. He wants to come here and have father support him. He's a jealous pig, that's what he is. Oh, what shall I do, what shall I do?"

Lilla consoled her. At any rate she was safely married, and even if John Hedderman wouldn't take her to Boston he would have to take care of her, for he had got money. Cindy finally went and washed her eyes at the pump, and then all the girls took a cup of tea with some brandy in it, all around, to cheer each other up.

Gentleman Jack escorted John Hedderman out into a little graveyard on a hill top, where only a picket fence interposed between the graves and the blue sky. It was a quiet enough place, with tall, lush grass, taller than the leaning headstones, and a half a dozen sparrows chirruping in the branches of a partially dead tree.

"It's still up here—we can smoke in peace," said Jack, sitting down on a little fresh heap of yellow dirt in one corner of the place.

At this John Hedderman handed the other a cigar. After smoking in silence for a while, and amusing himself with planting twigs in the fresh mound, Jack remarked, "I suppose you'll be putting up a headstone here one of these days?"

Hedderman looked at his companion, thinking his liquor had gone to his head.

"I'm sitting on a relative of Cindy," Jack remarked, grinning like a man with a pleasant recollection.

Hedderman himself, being none too sober, resented this.

"Call her Mrs. Hedderman," he said, with the stiff solemnity of a man who is drunker than he thinks he is, "or I'll brain you."

"I wish't had been Mrs. Dalton," replied Jack, getting up and beginning to kick the loose dirt of the mound into the grass.

Hedderman arose also, and laboriously began to relight his cigar. When he got it drawing he said, "You'd better be leaving Mrs. Hedderman's relatives' graves alone. You're drunk, Mr. Dalton, that's what you are."

And in a slow way, with an occasional lurch, he walked toward the house. Jack stood as if paralyzed for a moment, and then it occurred to him that after all he hadn't told him about Cindy's baby, as he expressly intended doing. He started to run after Hedderman, but came to grief among the graves, and fell on his face, getting a nasty forehead cut on a stone an hundred years old. Cursing, he pulled himself up, and went on, pausing to take a long pull from a bottle he had brought with him, and which he had intended to share with the bridegroom after the fun of telling him the little story.

Gentleman Jack, though he had wandered from any faith, had been brought up devoutly, and it suddenly occurred to him as a pity that Cindy's baby had never been christened.

"Poor little thing's in hell now," he kept repeating. "Poor little thing."

He went back and leaned against the picket fence by the grave.

Meditatively he took another drink, but it sickened him after his broad potations, so he spat it out.

An idea struck his maudlin brain. He looked at the liquor in the bottle.

"I do' wan' it," he soliloquized, "I'll baptize the baby."

Reeling rhythmatically in order to stand upright, he slowly emptied the bottle over the earth. When the bottle was empty he stood and looked at it for a few minutes, and then he began to cry.

"If I could only be jolly wi' th' boysh," he murmured, "but I'm such a quiet chap. I'm all alone."

Then his legs collapsed, he fell into a heap by the side of the mound, and went to sleep with his mouth open, and his tongue lolling out into the dirt.

VI

It being quite the style to drink that day, Cindy and the girls were not slow in increasing their potations of tea and brandy. Toward two in the afternoon the house, set full in the sunshine, became like a furnace. More neighbors and friends arrived and remained to drink. An old hag, who earned a precarious living by scouring knives and cleaning spittoons down at the hotel in the village, ventured into the kitchen, and being unmolested, remained. She amused herself by building and keeping up a blazing wood fire, seating herself in the warmest corner, as if in revenge for the many days when she had suffered from cold in the winter.

Cindy and the girls reclined on the lounge in a friendly huddle. Cindy had unbuttoned her collar in order to cool off, and was lying in Lilla's arms, shedding tears. She had long ago forgotten why she was crying, but having begun she could not leave off.

As Hedderman entered she looked up.

"Hullo?" said Lilla. "Where's Jack Dalton? What makes you come back alone?"

With great gravity, Hedderman replied, "He was drunk. He was no company for a gentleman, and I left him. He was kicking your relatives' grave to pieces and I left him. I brained him first."

Here Hedderman sat slowly down with the air of a profound thinker.

There being no chair at that particular place he went on to the floor, and then, after several abortive attempts to get up, he remained there, leaning against the wall in perfect solemnity.

Cindy began to laugh.

"Jack's so funny," she said, "I like him better than any man I know."

Then she recommenced crying. "You've killed him," she yelled, glaring at Hedderman. "You know you have. You took him up there and you murdered him because he loved me. There was a dog howled this morning, and I knew something would happen. Oh, you old fat wretch," she cried, jumping to the floor and catching Hedderman by the ears, "take me out to my Jack and we'll all die together."

Hedderman struggled vigorously, and the girls pulled Cindy off, slapping her hands to make her leave go. Hedderman was then helped to his feet, and led to the pump, looking rather bewildered. He still had the same expression when he came back, sobered by a liberal application of cold water.

The men in the parlor were now singing, and it occurred to Hedderman that if he was going to catch the 4 o'clock train from Longmeadow he had better be starting. The truth was, he had not the slightest idea of the time. In going through the parlor his father-in-law insisted on his taking a glass of cider. Thinking it might further clear his brain, Hedderman stopped.

Old Bill, very drunk, began to apostrophize his son-in-law.

"There sits," said he, "the noblest man in this Commonwealth. He not only married my daughter, but he paid for the refreshments. Yes, boys," he added, as if trying to convince an unbelieving audience, "he paid for the refreshments."

Although everyone had known this before, there was a murmur as of surprised approbation, while old Bill, feeling he had said a good thing, added, like one announcing a discovery, "Out of his own pocket!"

"You'd better have paid him to marry Cindy, you old hypocrite," said a voice at the window. Everyone turned and there, looking in from outdoors, his hair and clothes covered with yellow dirt, was Jack Dalton.

"Gentleman Jack, come in and have a drink," called old Bill.

Jack shook his head.

"If I come in there," he remarked, casually, "I shall feel it's my duty to kill your son-in-law, Mr. Hedderman. Yes, and to keep your wife's carpet from blood I ask him to come out here and I'll do him up in five seconds. First I want to bite his wife. Bring out Cindy, the girl who killed my child with neglect."

At the last word, Gentleman Jack brought his fist down on the table by the window, and made all the glasses jump.

Attracted by the noise, Cindy and the girls crowded into the room behind the chairs of the men. Two of the least drunk had gone into the yard, and were endeavoring to make Gentleman Jack go quietly away.

Mrs. Hammond, quite disgusted at the row which presented her neighbors in such a bad light to her Boston son-in-law, was saying, "Oh no, we didn't invite him. But he isn't always like this. He must have been mixing his drinks."

Gentleman Jack, fighting his captors, was yelling for Cindy to come forth and be chewed up. Then, seeing he was overpowered, he made the most of the time left him, and shrieked, "Ask her, anyway, ask her. Whose child was it she killed? Whose—"

Cindy, her pretty face aflame, quite light-headed in fact, rushed to the window.

"You're a great hulking booby," she cried out, quite as if that statement settled matters. Then, giggling, she went on, "I kill your baby, indeed! You killed it yourself. You left it to starve. Without a cent!"

As Cindy was tossing her head, Mrs. Hammond grabbed John Hedderman by the arm and began to explain. She wasn't used to quite such good times, it crazed her. Cindy was a good girl, she would never deceive anyone. The company, glad to pay for their good liquor, chimed in corroboration. Cindy was the best girl in town, it was declared. She had never had a word for any of the fellows. Cindy and a child—indeed! Well, one hoped she would have plenty of them now she was Mrs. Hedderman, but the past was quite another thing. It was only that funny Gentleman Jack. He was bound to have his joke. And he was drunk.

Old Bill tried to say Cindy was as pure as a dew drop, but being very far gone had to give it up.

John Hedderman stared in amazement from one protesting face to another. His slow brain prompted his thick tongue to a final comment.

"After all," said he, "I don't take in what you're talking about Cindy for. The drunken fool said it was his child that died. Anyway, Mrs. Hedderman and me can't stop to talk it over. We got to take the four o'clock train from Longmeadow. Where's the rig?"

A sound was heard, but it was different from that of any approaching horse and top buggy. Cindy had taken up her father's rusty gun, which always stood ready loaded in the corner, in case of an attack by hawks on the chickens. Putting it to her breast, she pulled the trigger. She staggered against the wall, and fell to the floor, carrying with her the ruins of glasses and bottles.

The fumes of the spilt liquor arose like incense in the sun-lighted air. A fly, imprisoned in a bottle, buzzed loudly. The sound of its wings beating against the glass could be heard distinctly all over the room.

"Whoa!" cried the half-grown boy who drove the livery stable turn-out into the yard.

As for Cindy, she was dead.

A REARWARD GLANCE

The Varied Year, February 1909-Spring 1910

T he life of the Amateur Journalist is made up of many ages—not including the nonage, before he discovers the magic circle that is ever after to fence in his joys and sorrows, his intellectual achievements and his political throwdowns. Feeling that I have perhaps a right to claim "Anecdotage," I am going to begin a narrative of my stay in the world of amateur letters—as much of it as has happened.

* * *

The first feeling amateur journalism induced in me was one of regret. Not regret that I hadn't heard of it earlier—because, as some one has said of the 1876 convention, "I couldn't have been there unless taken by my nurse." (Only, as it is not worthwhile to put on "side" with those who are so thoroughly acquainted with you as are amateurs with one another, I'll admit I never had a nurse to guide my infant footsteps, but tumbled up naturally.) No, the regret came from the fact that I supposed amateur journalism to be entirely "boy's play," with "no girls allowed" as a sort of catch-word. I read the famous *St. Nicholas* article, written by Harlan H. Ballard, and which has been making amateurs ever since its publication way back in the early 80s. I studied this article so intently that many of its phrases made a burnt wood decoration on the tablets of memory, and the scratches are there still. I remember particularly one apt quotation from an amateur paper which had struck Mr. Ballard as a sample of literary skill. It read thus:

> So-and-so has gone to Somewhere-or-other. Bring a washtub for our tears.

I don't remember who had gone where, but the touching and refined idea of a washtub brimming with tears appealed to me with irresistable force, and I yearned to be writing such paragraphs myself, and seeing 'em in print. Alas, the article described N. A. P. A. conventions—of boys—elections—of boys, by boys—in organizations composed of boys. I sighed, resigned myself to the awful fate of being a girl, and continued to "compose pieces" which I carefully copied in red or violet ink—I despised plain black in those days—little suspecting that all the while those Mss. were being prepared for amateur papers.

* * *

One morning in May, 1883, I took up the Worcester (Mass.) *Spy*, and because there wasn't much of anything else in it worth reading, turned to the advertisements. There I learned that some one called Finlay A. Grant, president of the N. A. P. A., would like to hear from boys—and GIRLS—who liked to write, and might care to belong to an association of writers. I looked again to be sure "girls" were really mentioned, ran for *St. Nick*, and ascertained that it was the same N. A. P. A., then wrote in my prettiest style to Mr. Grant. received an immediate reply couched in that language of enthusiasm for the cause of A. J., which he knew so well how to employ. I often think nowadays what an unfortunate thing, for me, if that advertisement had never been printed. Mr. Grant once observed that the ad. "cost him 25 cents, and he got to it one reply"—mine!

With reading bundles of papers such as Grant's *Boy's Folio*, Shelp's *Brilliant* and Sanderson's *Bay State Press*, the amateurs soon seemed good friends; the *Boy's Folio* I admired more especially then, and still do so. There has never been another paper exactly like it, with its crisp paragraphs, each a combination of news and comment thereon, each showing an independent spirit, entirely free from prejudice. The *Folio* was a real "newspaper" in miniature, and it has probably never been even imitated, because there has never been but one Finlay Grant in our little world.

* * *

Amateurs were soon to be more than mere names to me, for one hot July morning I started from my home in Worcester, escorted by Finlay Grant and Frank S. C. Wicks, and followed by anxious looks from my mother, who had never before allowed me to go a pleasuring alone. There had been a family conclave, I remember, before I got permission to even think of going, but the explanations of Grant as to what A. J. really was and how a convention acted did much to win me the coveted bliss. Frank Wicks sat by, I recollected, but he couldn't say anything because it was to be his first convention, too—the New England meet at Gardner. On the train were more boys and girls, and in Howard Sanderson, candidate for presidency of the New England (an honor hard fought for in those days), I discovered a sort of cousin, since his uncle had married my aunt. Also on the train was a brilliant youth who had used his nice new rubber stamp inscribing all the tickets with the initials N. E. A. P. A.—whereupon the conductor refused to take 'em, and general mob ensued.

* * *

A story of this trip which I have often told is how George E. Day was "discovered" on the train—a brown-eyed youth, who sat very mum, and pretended he knew us not, until we were almost at Gardner. Then Finlay Grant, to keep up his vaunted record of "talking amateur journalism to every man, woman or child in town," went over and started a vigorous oration, which came to an abrupt stop when the presumed recruit held out his hand and observed, "You are right in saying I should not miss this convention—I've come all the way from Westfield to take it in."

* * *

At this convention I met so many who were to become good friends in after years—Willard Wylie, even then the most graceful of speakers; Truman Spencer, so shy that he seemed proud and cold (he has confessed since how scared he was of the "Gardner girls," and how he actually ran away from the convention before it was over because something called a "promenade concert" was scheduled for one night—perhaps the only instance on record of an amateur quitting a convention while he had money in his pocket. There was also Alexander Stewart, another quiet chap; Dennie Sullivan, presented as the dryest sort of a fossil, but in reality training for the presidential race two years later; and Charles Wilson, of raven hair and face of marble pallor, who amazed my untutored mind by relating the ease with which one could dash off "blood and thunder" stories, a dozen chapters an evening. I returned to my Worcester home after three days of happiness, having cemented an undying friendship for Gracia Smith; and registered an undying hatred for Charles Heywood. Yes, I know he was afterward a brilliant writer, and the finest of our critics, but to me he will live ever as the bad boy who cheated in a baseball game—Gardners vs. Visitors—and came chuckling down the street rejoicing in the success of his own duplicity. I hadn't heard of plagiary then, so cheating at baseball stood to me for the blackest of (amateur) crimes.

* * *

The next thing that happened was delicious:

> Miss Edith May Dowe, a young lady of marked talent, has entered the ranks, and would be pleased to contribute to the amateur press.

So the *Boy's Folio* had said, trustingly, before ever its editor had seen anything to justify the statement; its publication aroused my ambition and I felt bound to at least do my best toward its justification. My first two published contributions were a story called "Bert Gifford's Masterpiece," in the *Cincinnati Amateur*, and "A Visit to the Wayside Inn," in *Langill's Leisure*, both published in 1884. It seems to me that authors were treated better then than they are now. I know my little sketches brought lots of nice congratulatory letters, and many printed notes, too. I am afraid we pay less attention to writer-recruits today. In 1884, I began the publication of a wee paper. Frank Roe Batchelder printed it. I remember he used to write "Letter Carrier Please RUSH" on the outside of all the envelopes containing proofs which he sent me, which was a huge joke, because I was stopping in the country at the time, and R. F. D. wasn't invented, and things laid in the post of-fice, sometimes for days and days, until someone happened to go for them. The best thing about my first paper, the *Worcester Amateur*, was its printing, aside from the contributed matter—for contributors I had my mother and Joseph Dana Miller. I was very proud of receiving a poem from the last named, and prouder yet when he began *criticis-ing* my work. Twenty-five years ago he was a writer with a finished and admirable style, and a critical sense of wonderful acuteness. For some years I benefited by his advice, improved through reading the books he recommended, and enjoyed a wider outlook on life through his letters. Oddly enough, we never met until 1902, when he had been induced, through friendship for Burger and Carter, to lend his dignity to the Wills cause; we tried to speak of things that interested us, but a delegation of New York boys ruthlessly forced us apart—I suppose they thought for political "enemies" there was no possibility of friendliness.

* * *

The New England met twice yearly in the 80s, my next convention was of that organization, at Worcester, in January of 1885. It was a tame affair, with no banquet. I thought it better fun to stay at home writing letters than attending such stupid "meets." And so I did stay home, until 1885 arrived, and the Boston convention of the N. A. P. A. loomed up large in the view. In the meantime I had managed to get myself elected one of the three vice-presidents of the New England, and to issue a number of the *New England Official* containing the nine-column message of President Charles Wilson, which starts gracefully thus:

> Amid the involutions of association affairs, Time's insuperable sway ushers us once more onward to the conventional era when one executive lays down the grand old standard, only to be immediately taken up by him whom the political voice of our convention may indicate.

I got into hot water, I recollect, because the *Official* was bigger and costlier than it ought to have been—on account of this message. Some members said nine columns of it (all just like the sample) weren't worth paying for. In the light of the present I think they were mistaken.

* * *

I had also become associate editor of a paper called the *Bayonne Budget*, and afterward the *Rising Age*, which was gotten out by a lively youth named John Moody. This is the same John Moody who now issues *Moody's Magazine*, and fills in odd moments going around lecturing to associations of bankers on how to better their business. In his amateur days he was a sort of Harry Konwiser, ready to perform any sort of literary antic, if thereby he might win fame. As a starter we took opposite sides of the fence—he was a Heath man, I favored Sullivan for the N. A. P. A. presidency—thus making the paper a political double header. I also roused a good deal of a row by criticising the writings of a Miss Minnie Irving, who had just entered our mimic world. Miss Irving was even then a widely known professional writer, and she resented my comment. It ended in a friendly correspondence between us which lasted while Miss Irving was in A. J. I enjoyed the correspondence, but I am glad to recollect that I never gave in as to the worthlessness of my criticism! Miss Irving had attacked Tennyson, and she deserved all she got!

* * *

I think this is a good place to stop, until these "I remember" tales are resumed in another *Varied Year*. It is 1885, I have been two years an amateur, have to my credit thirteen contributions to amateur papers published in 1884, and eighteen to those of 1885. I have helped to organize the Young Women's Amateur Press Association, made up of amateur "girls," and designed to "get the better of the boys"—it failed, presumably through lack-worth in its *raison d'etre*. I am bound to the July conventions, that of the New England in Providence, and the N. A. P. A. in Boston. It will be my first visit to the latter city, and it will also be the first N. A. P. A. convention attended by womankind. To complete the "firsts," I have been mentioned (without my consent being sought) for the office of third (or was it fourth?) vice-president, this being the first campaign in which anything female has been allowed to run for office. How I wrestled my first laureateship from a much-disgruntled "old timer," how I assisted at a very pretty political game played by Dr. E. B. Swift, and how Frank Wicks (Rev. F. S. C. Wicks of Indianapolis, Ind., now, if you please) smashed my new hat, must be told at another time.

II

The first thing that happened at the National convention of 1885 in Boston was the New England convention in Providence. It was held the day before, and to it came most of the great and notable from the N. A. P. A., whom the Metcalf boys gleefully escorted down Narragansett Bay and fed bountifully on clams—which were not welcome viands after paying an excess of tribute to Neptune. However, the girls who were at this convention, together with some fossils so ancient as to be positively venerable, were better cared for. As today, I remember the old-fashioned home of the Metcalfs on one of the most interesting streets of Providence, and of the hospitality of Mrs. Metcalf, mother of the amateuristically famous "Metcalf boys," Ralph, Fred and Guy. The last named was a little chap at this time, he never became as prominent an amateur as his seniors—younger brothers seldom do. I suppose they take up A. J. not from personal bent, but just because it's in the air.

* * *

Apropos, next day some of us who were at the Metcalf dinner went to have our picture taken. We were eight, and we started on tintypes— suddenly pausing in our mad career when it was borne in upon us that we should be obliged to pose eight times—and the day was just as hot and the gallery just as stuffy as the hundred odd days and galleries on and in which I have since suffered for the sake of "souvenir groups." We switched to ordinary, everyday photographs, and mine is before me as I write. Where one may see a presentment of Miss Jennie Day and Miss Helen G. Phillips, both looking quite ready to emulate Clarissa Harlowe in her chief stunt—graceful fainting. Alfreda K. Richards is somewhat more animated, but perhaps that is because Ralph Metcalf *elegante* of that day (only then we said "dude"), stands tenderly holding her parasol. Parsons and Schofield are also of the party, as well as George Dunn of Gardner. As for myself, I have spent most of the rest of my life trying to decide which of the spikey things seemingly growing from my head were so growing, and which came from a cactus on the pedestal against which I am leaning. I don't like to show the picture very much, because the onlooker always says, "What funny hats they wore then." And it takes too long to explain the cacti.

* * *

There, I meant to have mentioned that this long screed about the photo was introduced simply to state that in 1908, Smith of the Collection, sent me a battered reproduction of this work of art, with the glad news: "Suppose you don't know you're in this," and a surmise that this was the only copy in existence because 'twas a tintype. Evidently some of the eight was too nearly broke (and it was only the first day of the convention) to pay for the finished photo. I wonder who?

* * *

While I'm speaking about photos will mention the official group of 1885, taken outside the Quincy House, most a hundred people in it, and not a head bigger than a quinine pill. No one can tell who, in the back row, is a famous old timer, and who is a perfect stranger looking out of the hotel barber shop. Smith, of the Collection, has labelled every one, but Spencer (of good memory) denies a good deal of the labeling, and there you are. But I know myself, sitting with James H. Ives Munro on the one hand and Dr. Swift on the other. And if you like you may see me with Munro on the one hand in a group of 1904, and with both Mr. Munro and Dr. Swift in the group of 1907, so strong a hold has precedent on the amateur.

* * *

Of course there was a great deal done at the 1885 convention besides being photographed. A merry crowd of us went from Providence to Boston by train, and on the way Ralph Metcalf very condescendingly wrote his name in everyone's autograph book, in Greek! We thought it awfully clever of him to be able to do it—it wasn't until later we realized that whether 'twas the real thing or not, 'twould be all Greek to us.

* * *

The first person whom I met at the hotel was Zelda Arlington Swift, whose bright eyes and vivacity of expression bespoke the wit and enthusiasm which she brought into our little world. Our meeting was generally interesting because we alone out of all the young women in A. J. had been selected to run for a N. A. P. A. office. Mrs. Swift had been making a sort of a "home run" that seemed eminently "safe" under her best known pen name of Zelda Arlington, when some wise youth popped up, declared she could never be elected under a *nom de plume*, and promptly started a campaign for Edith May Dowe. I was amazed when I got wind of the thing—of course it couldn't be kept from my knowledge forever—and gladly wrote Dr. Swift that the glory was none of my seeking. This letter he had in his pocket when, shortly before the convention, some of the politicians of that day were discussing matters with him. They, secure in the fact that Worcester, Mass., was a full day by mail from Cincinnati, Ohio, declared they would believe Miss Dowe not a candidate only if such a statement could be secured over her hand—telegrams didn't go, and wireless not then invented.

* * *

I suppose Dr. Swift chuckled when he drew from his pocket just such a statement from me! And to think that I waited twenty years before I knew what was done with that note of mine.

* * *

Zelda, as I remember, was full of indignation at the time of my first meeting her. First, Clarence E. Stone was all put out because his entry for the serial laureate had been scored by the judge (Converse, the writer for boys), and the honor had gone to a chit who had written a yarn called "Back o' the Mountain." As I was the chit she was glad for my sake, but it was too bad to see Mr. Stone so disappointed! Then again she had Charles N. Andrews on her mind, and I was taken right upstairs to meet him. Mr. Andrews looked very unhappy; I was told it was because he had not been put on the slate for treasurer. I recollect that he shook hands and bitterly bade us all to beware of ingratitude. Then he went away and I for one did not meet him until "quite some" few years later as they are said to say in New York. At the time I could not understand how any sort of ill treatment could drive one away from that delightful diversion called a convention. I presume that by-and-by Mr. Andrews came to wonder, too.

* * *

Not everyone who was turned down left is disgust. There was Jud Russell, with as lean and meagre a countenance as Don Quixote himself, and on perhaps as helpless a quest, trying to get A. J. to take him seriously. I think, at this time, he was seeking readmission to the N. A.

P. A.; the boys spent most of their waking hours declining to let him have enough of the floor to stand on in the convention hall, refusing to introduce him to the ladies, and finally locking the doors and forcing him to stay and see himself voted still an outsider; while at night, when they ought to have been alseep they made his life miserable with pillow fights and ice-water shower baths, pausing only long enough to invade the room of William S. Moore, who had come to Boston to secure "Frisco in 1886," and who went back to the Coast with just that inscribed upon his chest in red paint, "warranted to stick."

* * *

Such were the gentle and refined gambols of a convention that had for its chief emblem a paper bag, supposed to have been introduced by Frank Wicks, on which was printed some scurrilous "news," with the inscription "Blow it up an' Bu'st It." We girls went discreetly away at sundown, we didn't even attend the banquet, but let the "animals" feed in peace. Afterward Joseph Dana Miller burst out into editorial invective because the boys had been "too stingy" to invite us! Ah, those were days when courtesy was carried to something of an extreme in the N. A. P. A. Girls weren't even allowed to pay any dues. Luckily this last went out of style before 1902, or Burger and Anthony Wills might have been considerably less out of pocket.

* * *

Finlay Arnon Grant, the amateur who with Spencer probably would share the highest honor of all, was married, at the time of the convention, to Bertha York, even then our most admired writer of both prose and poetry. On one afternoon they gave a reception at Young's Hotel to the amateurs, and the amateurs, not to be outdone, gave them a silver ice pitcher. We didn't mean anything sinister by it, we merely picked out the gift of the period. I started for the reception, but inadvertently got lost—it was my first trip to Boston. I remember wildly dashing up to a kind looking stranger and gasping out, "O, sir, will you please direct me to the Common?" and the prompt way in which he replied, "Why, my child, you are standing on it." It was the only spot in Boston that I thought I knew, and it seemed I didn't know that. Despair set in, I never reached the reception, but I must have found the Quincy House again, because I'm somehow back there, and acting as secretary of the Massachusetts A. P. A. (which Joe J. Lane is trying to revive in this year of 1909), while Frank Wicks as president thereof gets so excited in the joy of presiding that he hits the table with Ralph Metcalf's cane and smashes my new hat, which hadn't any business to have been there, anyhow, and so he made no bones of telling me, for we were from the same burg and almost on terms of real brotherly and sisterly frankness by this time.

* * *

After this detour into the N. A. P. A., we New Englanders turned our attention back to local affairs. On returning to my home in Worcester I found a letter from one John T. F. Miniter, asking for directions in forming an amateur club, and before long one was formed in Haverhill that was probably the largest on record, outside of Gardner. It published a handsome paper called *Haverhill Life*, and two of the publishers, Miniter and Chamberlain, were at the New England convention in Leominster in December of 1885. There was also Frank Wicks, from a military academy at Peekskill, whom "we girls" robbed of all the glory of brass buttons on coat and overcoat ere the convention ended. We supposed, of course, he could pick 'em up by the bin full when he returned to school, but he told me under the rose that he couldn't—that it wasn't allowed—that he went round all winter without a coat button to his name. I felt so sorry then—I wonder now was he telling the truth?

* * *

But Wicks did suffer most terribly in that boarding school—it equaled the convents of novelhood for ingenious torture. They read his letters, I recollect, in the principal's room—and must have been highly edified at references to "the cause," "fossilism," and "new recruit." There was always supposed to be a particularly secret and valuable message hidden under the stamp, which had presumably passed the eagle-eyed inspector. How anxiously we recipients used to peel off the stamp, and how eagerly we read some such important news as "George Day's a chump and the *Round Table* may go to grass."

* * *

They didn't, for that—but it seems, as I write, that the woodbine came all too soon to twine over a great deal that made life notable in A. J. Consistent activity has appertained to but few of us, others, like Wicks and Emery and Day, have been lost and rediscovered, with much rejoicing on both sides, and perhaps their day has seemed greater than ours, but I maintain that the one who gets the most out of amateur journalism is not the one who treats it as a childish affair, to be gone through with as one goes through the measles, but those like Dr. Swift, John T. Nixon, James F. Morton, who have taken its pleasures and some of its duties along with the serious work of life, who have never been too busy to forget their real alma mater, whose days are never so filled with the assembling of bread and butter that they haven't an hour for picking daisies in the meadows of youth.

III

Haze is apt to hover over the memory of most of us, and there are times when it settles almost earthward. Such, to me, is the obscurity of the years following the extremely vivid remembrances of how I got into A. J. and attended my first N. A. P. A. convention. They must have been busy years, because over a dozen stories with my name hitched to them appeared before 1887, not to mention a funny little novel, "Phillis the Fair," which got published in Dunlop's Amateur Library in 1886, and a would-be weird serial, "The Solitary," for which, in the year, I got $5 from S. Scott Stinson, and an unlimited amount of "cussing" from the amateur public. And letter writing! How proud I was when the carrier on our route told my mother that her daughter received more letters than the tin plate factory in the next street.

* * *

A lot of these letters were political ones. The affair should have made a great impression on me, but it seems not to have. I can only guess that it was about this time a youth named George Hough, who lived in New Bedford, sprang me on an amazed public as candidate for president of the Eastern A. P. A. He neglected to ask my permission, a mere incident, as it turned out, because when the time for the convention came I was not in Brooklyn, where it was held, neither was any other person of the female sex, excepting Johanna M. Brown, a well known author of that day (*nom de plume* "Stuyvesant"). The way in which she tried to attend this convention, and was made not welcome, was a scandal of the period. I never knew her a little bit, but for years I wondered if she was induced to be among those present by the anticipation of seeing a girl made president. The farce was soon played out. I am sure this was the last Eastern convention held. Wicks and Hoppin of Worcester attended, Wicks came home president and Hoppin came home with a pathetic story of how he had lost his hat on Brooklyn bridge. One was as important as the other, for Wicks' folks sent him to the cruel boarding school before mentioned, so he could do nothing as president, and the only good that ensued was the getting out of some handsome *Round Tables* (George Day's paper) solely in order to score the recreant Wicks. As for me, I never even learned the true pronunciation of George Hough's name.

* * *

I must hark back, a moment, to the Boston '85 convention, because there a number of far reaching results started, the Virgil B. Clymer affair for one. Mr. Clymer was connected with a chap named Wyckoff (afterwards of the Remington typewriter) in getting out a paper. It was in columns of this sheet that I made myself forever famous by signing a screed,

"I am, And always shall be, Yours very truly, EDITH MAY DOWE."

George Dorr had one of these papers, carefully marked, in his collection, when displayed at the banquet of the 1892 convention. And I think it was in the same issue that Mr. Clymer "attacked" the ladies of the N. A. P. A. for attending the banquet at the Boston '85 convention, when that meant their sitting at table with the vile and unspeakable Jud Russell! I believe I've mentioned before that in those halcyon days girls weren't supposed to be able to fight their own battles. A lot of champions bubbled right up, went for Mr. Clymer tooth and nail and directed him to make a public apology or—! What the ellipsis represents I can't say, but Clymer apologized in the paper, and in the summer of 1887 came to Boston and did it all over again *viva voce*. Truly, he was a glutton for humble pie; I remember his standing in the "dim religious light" of that famous basement convention hall of the old American House, holding out his hand and in a would-be winning voice beseeching "Miss Dowe" to shake hands. I suppose she did. Unless my memory plays me false she would have been a chump if she hadn't, for he was a remarkably handsome youth and probably meant nothing sinister by stirring up this tempest in a teapot.

* * *

What made me maddest in the aftermath of the '85 convention was Antisdel's saying, right out in print, that I hadn't written the stuff I had written, because I was too small to have written it. For years and years my anger grew whenever I thought of that paragraph. I was going to have revenge—oh, yes. Some day I'd meet Mr. Antisdel, and I'd tell him to call a jury of able amateurs, and they'd shut me up in a room with pens and paper, and give me a subject, and see me turn out a story right before their very eyes. So now! In imagination the scene was enacted many a time and oft (I think I got the idea partly from the famous sermon composed by the notorious Stephen Burroughs, who when accused of using his pa's old sermons—which he did—had his congregation give him a text, and floored 'em flat with an able discourse on the not over-inspiring topic "Old shoes and clouted on the feet.") The revenge remains an idle fancy. When Antisdel and I met next 'twas 1901, at the twenty-fifth anniversary; we had both acquired avoirdupois and grey hairs, so that in 1907, when my mother and I had him for guest at Christmas dinner, I kindly refrained from poisoning the turkey.

* * *

I haven't said anything about achieving fame, but that I did achieve it will be pretty obvious when I observe that in 1886 John Moody got out a book called *MEN of Today*, and I was in it!

* * *

As the only conventions available for my attendance at this time were New England ones, I took them in pretty regularly. It was at the N. E.

A. P. A. in Lowell, in the summer of 1886, that I met Mabelle F. Noyes, who with her sister Minna B. Noyes, then unknown to A. J., but afterward to become one of the immortal Quartette, I now count among my best friends. Gracia Smith traveled with me to this convention. We had been friends ever since the days of Gardner, '83, when we swapped confidences all night in a room of the Windsor Hotel, hastily opened for that convention—how time flies, I read only the other day of it as a "landmark"—never stopping even when the man in the next room banged the wall with his boots and ordered us to "stop that eternal chatter." About all I recollect of the Lowell convention are two comparatively unimportant incidents. One is Mabelle Noyes and myself taking a twilight stroll about Tyng's Island, a pretty place where the Lowell boys escorted the visitors for the evening. And just as we were swearing an eternal friendship a rough man dodged up from somewhere and informed us that we were sitting right over the place where the ferocious bear had tunnelled out the day before—"And he's liable to do it again any minute, young ladies, and think how you'd feel, hugged to death by a bear!" Didn't we run shrieking away, while after us came his apologetic remark, "I'm going to fix it tomorrow." Do we ever meet to this day without recalling the incident? Never!

* * *

The other happening was more terrifying then and funnier in remembrance. While we three girls were huddling in one room for companionship, talking over the events of the day, we heard a horrible thumping at our window and probably would have rung in a burglar alarm had one been handy. As it was we barricaded ourselves with furniture and slept with the gas burning—and the thermometer at what in the shade it always is when conventions are going on—only to learn next day that the supposed robber was not after our bangle bracelets and German silver watches, but instead was a lad who had run away from home to attend the convention, and being unsupplied with money enough to attend the convention, was being sneaked into the room of better supplied fellows, via the fire escape—and making a trifling mistake in the floor he was to get off at!

* * *

At the New England convention of '87, in Boston, besides the Clymer handshaking affair, there was my first meeting with Harriet Caryl Cox, who had just dawned upon an amateur world that was presently to pay her homage never accorded any girl before or since. Her bright stories had won her instant fame, and I shall always remember the first time I saw her, wearing a blue gown with swandown trimming, and carrying an immense mass of garden posies with which she proceeded to decorate the table of the convention hall. We did not "take" to each other at all, I recollect, and neither had prescience of the hundreds of days when we would range the woods and fields together, and call one another "little h." and "Granny." Why should we? It would be nearly ten years ere such things would come to pass.

* * *

It was truly a brilliant lot of girls who were assembled in Massachusetts in these years, and who got out such papers as *Duet* and *Quartette*. Gracia Smith, big and earnest, with large eyes and the most magnificent head of hair I ever saw, was a faithful worker and an industrious, but not a brilliant writer. She lived in Springfield, and spent her summers in North Wilbraham, the little town where I also "summered." Her stopping place was miles away from mine, I used often to go down the road a bit and gaze at a big red barn—oh, miles and miles away, gleaming on a hill top, and think that there she was, perhaps at that minute reading the very same amateur paper that the morning mail had brought me. Infrequently we met, most romantically, in a glen by the river, nearer my home than hers, but a long way from either. And how our tongues would run on politics, laureateships, and "the Metcalf boys." Alas, her fate was a sad one. She was married in the fall of 1887, caught cold on her wedding trip, developed consumption, and sank rapidly. Her young husband, named Woffenden, whom she eagerly asserted she "met through amateur journalism," because he was employed in the Springfield post office, and made her acquaintance through selling her stamps to put on amateur papers, soon fell ill of the same disease, and was sent South in search of health. He was caught in the famous blizzard of March, '88, and died. She survived him a brief while, taking a pathetic interest in A. J. to the end, her last written words being letters planning to get out a paper and be once more active in her loved pursuit.

* * *

Others of the girls of that day have less hapless fates. Jennie M. Day, a charming little blonde poetess, sister of George Day, to whom her attachment was notable, is still a school teacher in her native town of Westfield. Her best friend, Frances Parsons, was a teacher there until recently, when I believe she retired. Mabelle F. Noyes has always retained her interest in A. J., she has attended any number of Boston "affairs," as well as the conventions of '92, '94, '98 and '07. She it was who started *The Quartette*, a little "blanket sheet" paper, the editors of which were always four girls though not always the same four, and which came out last as late as 1902.

* * *

In 1888, having proven the falsity of my assertion that "I am and always shall be yours very truly Edith May Dowe," I thought to embalm my new name of Edith Miniter in an amateur paper. It was called *The Webster Amateur* (I was then living in a town of central Massachusetts, Webster by name), and was notable for nothing, save the particular kobosh which it put upon the large and flourishing professional office where it was gotten out. Innocent four-by-seven, for months afterward nothing happened—a form pied, a comp. out how-come-you-so, press day late, press cranky, safety valve blown off the boiler—that the intelligent help in this establishment didn't trace the happening to "that week, you know, when we got out the amateur paper."

* * *

And then Frank Denmark Woolen had the "coolth" to say: "In her new publication, Mrs. Miniter calmly takes out her little yaghtaghan and flays us neck to heel." I wonder if I did? And if so, why? Not having set eyes on *The Webster Amateur* for at least twenty years, I can't say. And above all, what is a yaghtaghan?

* * *

Must I stop for now? It seems so—when we old folk get to reminiscing we're hard to break off. I want to talk about amateur loot, and why it shouldn't be called junk, as Ethel May Stuart Johnston Myers does call

it; and about some of the letters I swapped with amateurs, and especially about the visiting amateur and what we did to entertain him in
the '80s that we don't do today, but it all must wait a while.

IV

[NOTE—Since publication of these reminiscences began, last February, two mysteries have been cleared up. This first by Mrs. Bertha Av-
ery. She, it seems, was treasurer of the Young Women's Amateur Press
Association, which was born and died young—as the good are reputed
to do—way back in the '80s. When it expired a smallish sum of money
was left in her hands, and this for many years has been a trouble to her.
She knew not how to whom it ought to be returned, she kept it hoping
that some time there would be another organization of young women
in A. J., to whom it might come as a rightful inheritance. At last, when
all hope of such had died, there came into her mind an idea of the right
thing to do. The sum was expended in violets, and these flowers were
placed upon the grave of "Zelda Arlington," the much loved first and
only president of the Y. W. A. P. A. I feel sure that the members of
that girlish association, who are still within hearing of A. J. doings, will
feel that this was a fitting way in which to employ the last emblem of
the organization which existed for so brief a while, and which owed its
existence to "Zelda."]

[NOTE 2—From W. M. Emery, of New Bedford, Mass., whom I met
in the winter of '83, and never since, has come the pleasing information that George Hough's name is pronounced "Huff." I knew Hough
in 1885, and have this information in 1909, but better late than never.
I shall not quite go to my doom wondering if it might be "Howe."]

* * *

Speaking of mysteries, I would really like to know whether or not I attended the first Boston conference? For be it understood that during
the first part of my amateur life I was not a Bostonian—indeed, I could
not, with the eye of prescience or any other old eye, see that I was to
presently become one, and be long and loudly cursed for that very fact

in the years of 1902-3 and 1909. If I had seen this I should probably have died of joy, so it's just as well. I lived in Worcester, a city of central Massachusetts, until 1887, and my only glimpses of Boston were when I stole away to New England A. P. A. conventions. After that my home was for a brief while in Webster, then in Manchester, N. H. This last place seemed very far indeed from amateurs. I can remember the letters of James F. Morton, Jr., as oases in a desert, and once when one was dropped in the mud on the way from the post office to me, and made undecipherable, I was as ready to sit down and cry as the child who discovered that her doll's sawdust.

* * *

Yet in this very year of 1909, at the New York convention, I discovered that I was literally surrounded by fossils at that very time. It was in Manchester that I had my first "job"—as a proofreader on a sensational paper called the *Telegram*—and C. Fred: Crosby informs me that the owner and editor thereof, a man named Taylor, was once an amateur. And on the second "job" in this same burg, to which I succeeded after being there three months, and which consisted of being city editor(?) of a penny afternoon daily, both the owner, Frank Challis, and a stoop shouldered friend of his, Herbert Eastman, who called daily, were of the fossil breed. I cannot tell why I failed to discover these interesting facts—I suppose because I never proclaimed myself an am. In those days I don't think one did—one rather kept it, like an unreciprocated passion—hidden in one's heart, a secret cherished all the more because a secret.

* * *

It's just occurred to me that that's why I've never been an awfully good recruit agent. I've never cared to talk much about A. J. because I cared so much about it. We do not like, you see, to run any chances of hearing our dearest abused.

* * *

But about the conference? I well recollect coming to Boston one 22d of February to some sort of an amateur affair. There was a banquet, I remember, and James F. Mortons both Senior and Junior were there, and the Senior delighted us highly by instantly getting up and opposing whatever was proposed by Junior. The latter, I recall, at this time was all for having resolutions of total abstinence passed by everything he was connected with, and never let a chance go by for suggesting such resolutions to collections of amateurs. And he never succeeded. This time we had his father's advice to strengthen our resolve.

* * *

Was it not on this occasion, also, that Dr. Swift, leading me to a window, gave one comprehensive glance at my teeth, and then observed, "How I wish I had brought me instruments!" But it is only fair to add that I have told this once already, in *Ink Drops* for 1902, and Dr. Swift has since denied the story almost *in toto*—at least he observes that never, never, never did he say "ME instruments."

* * *

A few words as to the bright torch of amateur enthusiasm set blazing in Boston some years before I came to live there. There had been numerous Hub Clubs that were invented, that lived a little while, and that died, for THE Hub Club, now probably immortal, like the N. A. P. A., was built on the ruins of numerous others of similar name and aims. When I first entered A. J. Boston proper had almost no amateurs, and only a few outsiders were well known, such as Wylie, and Mr. Capen of Canton, as that merry wight was called. Then Harriet Caryl Cox of Abington began to write, and to make recruits. In her own little town, but a few miles from Boston, were Susan Brown Robbins, a wonderfully original writer, Flora Atwood, less well known but a great favorite, Alfred Nash, an editor of ability, "Hilda," one of amateurdom's mysteries, introduced (I think) by James Morton, and keeping us all guessing at her identity for a time; with John Robbins, Emma Paty and others. And in Boston itself there was Ella Maud Frye.

* * *

Mrs. Frye came to Boston from Nova Scotia some time in the late '80s. She had been prominent among the amateurs of her own country, who were then existing in considerable numbers, owing to the efforts of the Grant brothers, J. H. I. Munro, and especially to those of George Edgar Frye, always referred to as "father of amateur journalism in Nova

344

Scotia." Coming to Boston almost as a stranger, Mrs. Frye organized the Hub Club as a sheer cure for loneliness. She says she was discouraged in her first efforts by the boys, but she went ahead and called a meeting, borrowing, for the purpose, the home of a friend in Maplewood, a suburb of Boston, as her own was not large enough.

* * *

Of those at the first meeting none now attend regularly, but during the first year Walter Herbert Thorpe and Mrs. H. M. Small (Helen Sullivan) began to come, and they have been coming ever since. And I, far away from the Hub of the Universe, read of these gatherings, and felt miserable indeed in that I seemed fated ever to live where there were no ams. For long 'ere I left Worcester the little group of amateurs there was dissolved. Frank Wicks was lost from our ken, we knew not where, and we were never to find out until 1895, when he was to appear in Boston, at a conference, a full fledged minister of the gospel, or whatever it is Unitarians preach. Charles Hoppin, his best friend, had also disappeared, and we heard of him later in an insane asylum. As for Frank Roe Batchelder, the amateur who wrote such clever rondeaux and ballades, and with whom I carried on a ream-of-paper-to-a-letter correspondence, all about books and ideas and general hifalutin, the letters being convoyed back and forth to him at the Worcester High School and to me at my 18 Mason Street address by a girl amateur, Mary E. Hyde, associate editress on Charles Hoppin's paper—he, too, had left Massachusetts. For he failed to graduate from Worcester High (I wonder if the interminable letters furnished anything of cause and effect), but took away what I am sure he liked better, fame as editor of a rival school paper that was far more clever than "the" paper and organizer of perhaps the first real "politically managed" school election held in that town. And then we learned of him as private secretary to Congressman Walker in Washington, the only senator who secured a passport to fame by removing his coat in the Halls of Congress.

* * *

This long preamble brings me to 1892, when I attended my second National convention. It was in Boston, of course, and I came to it through Methuen, where I paid the first of many happy visits to the

Misses Minna and Mabel Noyes. We lolled in hammocks all day Sunday, wondering what the next or convention day would bring forth, and Monday came down to find out. It was a smallish convention, owing to the existence of the famous "split," a hang over from Philadelphia, but very enjoyable. Truman Spencer was made president and Brainerd Prescott Emery official editor, and we bothered ourselves very little about the folks off in Buffalo "electing" Harry Hochstadter and Harry Sizer. The Boston one was a very jolly convention. One of the features, I recollect, was Ernest Capen's there starting his afterward famous collection of hairpins from the heads of girl amateurs—he collected all I had and in this state I was taken in the group picture. And after I was forced to return to my home in Manchester, the rest of the convention went out to the resevoir and rolled down the embankment, an historic "doin's" since much celebrated in song and story.

* * *

What I most disliked, however, was that eternal feeling of being an outsider. I heard of all sorts of anecdotes of Hub Club goings on, and I wasn't in 'em. So when, the following August, I saw a chance to come to Boston to live, I grabbed it forthwith, and attended my first Hub Club meeting that fall.

* * *

My recollections of this meeting are very vivid. It was held in the *Woman's Journal* rooms on Park Street, a dingy hole that never seemed exactly worth the $2 or so which we had to pay for the privilege, and which it was the first and principal and generally the only duty of the meeting to raise. Miss Sullivan (Mrs. Small) was treasurer, and when all else failed she would lock the doors and call on a stalwart young man named Nathan Willard Small to assist her in wheedling coin of the realm from the pockets of those present. When she thought she had enough she would retire into the hall to count, and if she cried triumphantly "I've got it," then either James Morton or Mrs. Frye would call the meeting to order and we would proceed with the rest of the programme. I say Mr. Morton or Mrs. Frye because one or the other was generally president, electings being then held at six monthly intervals. The meetings, I recall, were largely attended, and James Morton was always called upon to recite something cheerful and usually responded with "'Ostler Joe"!

* * *

In September of this year I attended the first gathering of amateur journalists which was neither a convention, a conference nor a club meeting—how many have I been to since? It was Mr. and Mrs. Frye's wooden wedding, held at their home in Maplewood, and thereby hangs a tale. I went to Malden in a trolley car (we said "electrics" then) and being instructed to take any car that came round a certain corner for Maplewood, did so, and was soon blithely proceeding back to Boston! Coming to my senses after a time, I turned back, but various waitings so long delayed me that when I got to Mrs. Frye's home P. B. Emery and several of the guests were saying goodbye, and James Morton had just finished his usual cheerful recitation—not "'Ostler Joe" this time, but something "bludgy," as the renowned Budge and Toddy would have said, so that he waded to his knees in metaphorical gore, while the dead were strewn all over the parlor floor.

* * *

An amusing incident of my getting there had to do with my entering the last of a series of cars, and gasping to the conductor, "Do you go to Webster street, Maplewood?" And at this two perfectly strange ladies rushed at me and exclaimed, "Are you going to Mrs. Frye's party, too?" To which I replied, "Yes, but I've lost my card, and can't remember the number." At this they cried, "So have we, and we couldn't even remember the street until we heard you speak the name." They were Miss McKenzie, afterward well known in the Hub Club, and a sister of Miss Katie Cameron, a sweet girl whose influence in amateur affairs was very potent a few years later in Boston. They, too, had been riding in "electrics" all the evening, and we gladly assisted in rescuing each other.

* * *

At this time, I remember, the Hub Club had the theatrical bee, and was employed in rehearsing for a performance to be given at the March anniversary. "Tom Cobb" was the piece selected, Thorpe was Cobb, and a very pretty lady the heroine, to whom Tom makes love. I hadn't then read *Mansfield Park*, but I have since been reminded, in the immortal account of the theatricals at the Park, of Thorpe in "Tom Cobb." Do you not recollect what the vivacious Mary Crawford says of "those indefatigable rehearsers, Agatha and Frederick"? In the Hub Club affair "Tom Cobb" was quite as indefatigable as a rehearser—of course with assistance. We had our rehearsals in the extremely chic millinery establishment of Misses McKenzie and Cameron, in the Phillips Building, Boston.

* * *

I suppose this place was a haunt of fashionable in search of headgear in the daytime, but I only remember it in the evenings, as an amateur hangout. The hats and bonnets were a shadowy background, on the pin bestrewed carpet of the spacious rooms we walked as we chatted, laughed and watched "Tom Cobb" rehearse. In the little cubby of a kitchenette we brewed cocoa. And all the while Ernest Capen, as stage manager, stormed and tried to infuse some idea of order. I remember that finally, urged thereto by his talk of "unities," I went so far as to provide two sets of aprons and caps for the two servant girls I was cast to play, but this was looked upon as an undue expenditure of energy. And so it proved, for in February of 1893 I went away, and "Tom Cobb" was done without me.

* * *

Minna and Mabel Noyes attended me to the station in the ice storm amidst which I left Boston, as I thought forever, torn with a racking cough, for which I blamed the east winds. I believed I was never coming back, and I regretted the Hub Club with a keen regret. Yet the following December was to see me once more a Bostonian, and this time for good and all.

V

Somebody comments on these reminiscences by asking "Because we have cakes and ale, shall we never be literary?" Of course I was always trying to be literary, to the best of my ability, but somehow memories of cakes and ale cluster rather more thickly than memories of stories for amateur papers, and what happened to the papers that printed 'em. Only there had to be stories, or their equivalent, or I wouldn't have been remembered when the cakes and ale were passing 'round. We "authors" are a modest lot, anyway, when it comes to talking about how we do our work! If I remember rightly Bobby Burns was about the only writer chap who dared to say he got any pleasure from actual writing—in one of his poems he does say "I ha' been happy thinkin'." Only he spoiled it by letting "drinkin'" rhyme with it, and represent quite an equal sum total of happiness. And neither, if I remember rightly, came up to strolling in fields with a beauteous damsel named "Anna."

* * *

I believe I may claim to be about the first amateur writer to write about child-life, which seems odd, when you think that generally a lot of amateur writers are of immature age. But I started a series of little sketches of children which "went" well, and which stood rather alone until Harriet Caryl Cox and Annie Laurie Lynde came to the fore. I didn't think so much of them, however, as of other yarns. In '91, while laboring under the influence of Amelie Rives' "The Quick or the Dead?" I produced "Cindy's Child" and a tale even more "realistic." The last was never published until years later, when it appeared, immeasurably toned down, in Truman Spencer's *Investigator* under the title "Wabbits." But "Cindy's Child" has always retained its character as a real hair raiser. That *enfant terrible* of A. J., Alson Brubaker, at the beginning of his career, published it with the design of "knocking 'em dead to rights" and seemed to be satisfied that he had done it. And even at this late date this "Child," like other faults of one's extreme youth, will not down.

* * *

Which reminds me that one should never essay to repeat one's self. To please Sam Steinberg I tried "knocking 'em dead to rights" again, with "For a Big Roll of Money," but got for it only condemnation for myself and publisher. Even Truman Spencer, whose mildness was more cutting than any other's invective, sends this last to perdition in the *Encyclopedia*. I've always supposed the result was because "For a Big Roll" was founded on fact, while "Cindy" was made up. Truth is shockingly inartistic, you know.

* * *

But let's get back to the cakes and ale. In December, '93 I was once more in Boston, and found it going on just as I had left it, because a year more or less, while perhaps a whole lot to clubs in Brooklyn or Poke-machunk, is nothing whatsoever in Boston. Just as ever we were having evening seances at the Cameron-McKenzie millinery parlors, trying on everyone's hats with the utmost sang froid, and objecting to the look of the $40 ones when we had only fifteen cents in our pockets. About all Boston was talking about on this occasion was the impending convention of the N. A. P. A.

* * *

Mrs. Frye was chairman of the reception committee, I remember, and I was honored with a place on it, as indeed was about everyone else in Boston excepting James Morton, and this omission showed James to be really the most important object in our amateur world, since it had been done a-purpose and of malice aforethought.

* * *

Quite as nowadays in Boston the committee began eating early in March, and James invariably attended as a special guest, but quite as invariably went into the hall or thrust his head from the window when business was being discussed so that technically he might be absent. For James ever was a conscientious person! This, however, didn't interfere with his taking animated and even acrimonious part in the conversation whenever it interested him, as for instance when we planned to go to the United States Hotel and he waged manful war for the Quincy House. Of course, he said, he knew its reputation wasn't what it had been in '92, but he believed something should be accorded to sentiment, and then again, "It has the finest ice water in Boston—why, Wylie and I always drop in, when passing, for a drink."

* * *

Well, at last everything was in readiness. Ernest Capen and myself had prepared a bogus map of Boston having on it all the things strangers asked for and never saw—"T wharf, place where Tea was thrown overboard," "Grave of Mother Goose," etc. James Morton had secured the promise of Stephen O'Meara, a really first-class professional journalist, to come down and talk to us at a time when with our usual egotism we'd far rather have been talking to ourselves, and Mrs. Frye and I had made arrangements similar to those of the young lady in Tennyson's poem who was to be queen of the May.

* * *

Thereby hangs a tale. Prancing, she and I, over to the old Providence Station in Boston, at the unearthly hour of 7 to meet a strange girl from New York, Emma J. Hauck, whom should we run into but Charley Burger and J. H. Stover. How happily we convoyed our catches to the hotel, not caring a whit that the girl had entered Boston by the Old Colony Station and been met by James Morton, without the preliminary of explaining her switch of plans to us. The eve of convention, I remember, saw a lot of folk in town, and we took them out and walked them all over the Common on such a damp evening that the curl came out of my Cameron-McKenzie hat's feathers and I was a "sight" all the rest of the convention.

* * *

It was this convention Susan Brown Robbins called to order, being the first girl to go down to fame as performing such a feat. It was this convention which politely reopened all its old wounds and fought them over again on the last day, though quite amicably settled before, to please Brainerd P. Emery, who turned up 48 hours belated, and regretting there was "no excitement." It was this convention which, because Seattle and San Francisco were at loggerheads over the next convention, calmly ignored the claims of both and elected Cincinnati next meeting place. This last of course was a mistake, because Cincinnati hadn't done a thing to justify such honor, which was never hers next July, anyhow. And of the disgust of San Francisco and Seattle with Boston of '94 I've heard quite enough of late years from one John Leary Peltret, who apparently came east in '98 to bury the hatchet in

Boston's head-piece, but after seeing Boston thought better of it, buried the hatchet elsewhere, and became a resident Bostonian himself.

* * *

But "What larks!" as Jo says to Pip, in *Great Expectations*. Most of the convention girls stopped at a lodging house where lived my mother and myself, on Beacon Hill, and what a stream of them—of course gallantly escorted—trailed from the U. S. Hotel in the wee sma' hours after other festivities were over. And didn't we march "Handsome John Henry" Stover out on the Public Gardens at 2 a.m. to see the "Ether Allen Monument" (i.e. a statue to the discoverer of ether), and perpetrate other idiotic jokes, the memory of which is still fresh and green. I think for pure childish hilarity it was only excelled by the New York convention of '09 and that may yet be eclipsed by the Cleveland one of '10, for some of us do get "fooler and fooler" as we get older, and glory in it, and that's a fact.

* * *

The evening of the first convention day every one distinguished himself by going to Nantasket and getting as near lost as possible—some entirely so. Thus most of us lost the last boat and came up on the last train, and two of us—one "Jim" Munroe, too—lost the last train and couldn't come up at all, and Wylie, having caught the boat, lost his note book and went back to find it and got carried to wherever boats spend the night, and stayed there until morning. Munroe avenged himself by getting up at an unearthly hour and writing a poem as he strolled the beach waiting for the sun—and the other "left behind" one to arise. But was that poem ever published?

* * *

It was at this convention that Rev. James Henry Wiggin first appeared. I believe he was induced to attend by James Morton, inveterate ferreter out of notables. Mr. Wiggin was even then a man of venerable age. Many years before the existence of organized amateur journalism he and a brother, who afterward died at an early age, issued a real boys' paper, the numbers covering some years. The brother had been editor, a girl cousin was chief contributor, and "our" Mr. Wiggin, as he afterward became, did the mechanical work. The bound volumes of this little magazine now form an interesting feature of the Edwin Hadley Smith collection.

* * *

Mr. Wiggin had been most things in Boston—writer, lecturer, clergyman, clubman, dramatic and musical critic, and in his old age he became a loyal Hub Club member, attending everything with delight, and entertaining us most hospitably at his home.

ON $40 A YEAR

How a Bright Woman Manages to Dress
Her Ideas May be Homely, but the General Result Isn't
She Talks for the Benefit of Readers of The Globe

The Boston Sunday Globe, January 4, 1891

"How do I dress on $40 a year?" exclaimed my friend. "I flatter myself I do it well. I mean to look—decent on every occasion. I don't go to many balls or parties, but I take in the theatre or a concert once in a while, and I never heard of my escort's being ashamed of my appearance yet."

"But on $40 alone?" I queried. "Aren't you guying me? Or do you have things given you by some wealthy aunt whom I never heard of?"

"I haven't a relative who isn't poorer than myself," was the prompt reply. "I buy all I wear, and I get it out of four $10 bills. It is the honest gospel truth, and now I'll tell you all about it."

I was making a call on a little friend of mine, and, as girls always do at most any season of the year, we were talking about clothes: why we had this and didn't have the other; what we wanted and wouldn't have, and what we should get because it came within our means. My friend is a pretty little creature, with blue eyes and fluffy, yellow hair; she earns a sort of precarious living by addressing envelopes and occasionally copying papers for a law firm in Boston. But while I knew she was not able to spend very much on clothing, I certainly never had dreamed that all the stylish frocks and dainty underclothing she wore during the year came out of $40.

"It's awfully easy if you know how," continued my friend. "Women who spend hundreds of dollars every year for very ordinary clothing simply throw their money away. I'm acquainted with some such. They buy silk and wool stuff that cockles the first night they get caught out after the dew falls. They spend goodness only knows how much for hideous jackets and hats, which they are sick of in a fortnight. They don't take care of their clothes, but put their dresses away unbrushed, throw their bonnets around anywhere, give away their half-worn dresses, and never mend their gloves. Oh, 'I know their tricks and manners,' as the dolls' dressmaker said. I'm not one of them."

"That's all very well; I know you were careful. But $40 is very little money."

"I call $40 a good deal of money. It takes one a good long time to earn that much—and collect it. But I suppose I must sink into details and tell you just how I do it. In the first place, I make my own under-clothes. Oh, I know you can buy pretty things which fit nicely, very cheap, but they won't wear like the home-made article. I bought one of each garment I wanted, ripped it up and used it for a pattern. A paper pattern would have been cheaper, but it would have needed more fitting and been harder to copy.

With a Finished Garment

only half of which need be ripped for a pattern, you can see just exactly how everything goes together, where the bindings, etc., belong and all. I get 36 yards of bleached cotton cloth at eight cents a yard. This will make me three suits of underclothing—drawers, corset cover, under-skirt, long skirt and nightdress.

For trimming I use the knitted or crocheted stuff I make myself, if I have time to do such work; sometimes I buy a piece of cotton edging for 20 cents, and use that. Cotton edging looks almost like crochet work, and wears heaps better than hamburg embroidery or lace. In summer I wear black cotton hose, in winter black merino. Three pairs of each kind do me. I buy for 37½ cents a pair or three for $1. In the summer I get the jersey undervests, three of them cost 75 cents. They fit themselves to the form, being seamless, and they laundry beautifully. For winter flannels I pay 37½ cents; they are not all wool but they are warm and thick. Three of each will last me two seasons I find.

"I wear low shoes in summer on all but rainy days. They are chic, you know, and the cost is about half that of boots. I generally buy one pair during the summer, at $1.25. The russet or morocco ones are better than the black ones at that price, and they are what I generally choose. In the fall I buy a nice thick-soled pair of Dongola boots, for which I pay $3.50. As I take them off the instant I get into the house one pair will last for street wear all winter and spring, and do well enough for rainy-day wear in summer. Boots get worn out more by house than street use, I believe, so I wear slippers at home. I get a pair for $1, and they generally last two years.

"By the way, I must tell you how I fooled the public last spring with my boots. I had bad luck with my winter pairs; they split just where they were sewn on the ankle, a great ugly gash that showed the lining every step I took. I just wore them down to the store where I bought them and the clerk offered to allow me $1.25 on the next pair I purchased. But that did me no good then, for I had no money, and yet could not wear boots with holes all the spring and rainy days in summer.

"Can't I have it sewed up?" I asked.

"Then the clerk showed me that the leather was so torn it could not be sewed. I was about to bolt out so that he shouldn't see the tears in my eyes when I caught a glimpse of a pair of pretty brown gaiters buttoned on a wooden foot in the window. The gaiters were cunning as could be, yet they covered all the boot but heel and toe.

"How much are those gaiters?" I inquired.

"When he replied $1.25 I just jumped, as I told him I'd take a pair instead of waiting for that allowance on the next pair of boots. He was reluctant to close the bargain, but I insisted, and the end was I went home with the gaiters hiding that hole in my shoe. I wore them all the spring, and when they are worn out I shall make me a second pair, using the old ones for a model.

The Metal Buttons

and leather straps won't be worn out then, and I'm sure a bit of ladies' cloth won't cost any $1.25.

"I have an awful grudge against patches, but once I wore a patch on my shoe, which was in plain sight, and yet no one ever suspected it. It covered a hole on the top of my foot. The patch was a long strip of leather, running over the hole and fastened into the sole on each side. It needed no glueing, and when the shoe was well blacked could not be noticed.

"In the winter, to save my white skirts, I wear a red flannel one. I make it myself, and one will last two winters. Knitted edging, quilled braid, or even a plain feather-stitched hem, finished one nicely at the bottom.

"Two pair of rubbers are all I wear out in a year. I get good ones. The cheap rubbers are made out of old rubber, I suspect, for they fall to pieces with half a dozen wearings.

"I can get a good pair of corsets for $2. As I seldom wear them at home, or in the summer, a pair more than lasts a year.

"As for hose supporters, I know some women who buy new ones every time the elastic gives way. That is ridiculous. Away back in the dark ages I bought a set for 20 cents, and the catches and buckles from that pair are doing duty now. I buy elastic ribbon and fix my own whenever they need it, just transferring the nickel fixings, you know.

"I guess this finishes the list of things which don't make any show in dressing, yet must be had, and which cost more than anyone would think. Now for my dresses.

"Of course I have different frocks each year, so I can't generalize quite as much as I did in telling about my underclothing. 'Mother Hubbard' for house wear, a primrose cloth gown, a white frock, a red sateen, and a mohair. They weren't all new, however. The 'Mother Hubbard' cost 60 cents when new, and I wore it mornings two summers. The red sateen I had the summer before; it cost 25 cents a yard—$2.50 for the dress—when new. The basque was worn some on the edges, and the overskirt was faded. I took off the overskirt and wore the skirt plain, the basque I put on under the skirt, and for 50 cents I got a belt to wear around my waist. I took the high collar off, and wore a toby frill of the sateen. It made a pretty suit for cloudy days, when starched dresses would grow limp.

"My primrose-cloth dress cost six cents a yard; it was a sort of cambric, with white ground and big pink roses on it—very pale and summery looking. I got 10 yards at a bargain-counter, made it with a full skirt, leg o'mutton sleeves, a full waist and a sash. My gray mohair cost me 39 cents a yard. I made it myself with a plaited skirt, full sleeves and a coat-tailed basque.

"I will tell you how it is that I get a good-fitting waist, and a properly hanging skirt. I went, some time ago, to a first-class dressmakers and had her cut me a skirt and basque, which I have used for a pattern.

The basque fitted me to a T, and

When I Ripped It Up

I left the basting threads in to mark where the seams were to be sewn. The pattern I cut has the places marked black with pencil, so I can't go astray.

"As to draping skirts, I keep my eye on the store windows where full costumes are displayed, and from them I get lots of ideas. Dress-makers acknowledge that they do the same, so I am not ashamed. However, about once a year, I go to a good dressmaker and have one dress cut—generally my winter wool frock, which is my best one. I pay $2.25 for the cutting, basting and draping, and get up with the styles once a year.

"My sailor hat last summer I trimmed myself. The hat cost 50 cents, ribbon and some black quills brought the whole thing up to $1.25. I did not buy my ribbon of a milliner, but in a dry goods store, where the price asked was half that tacked on by the bonnet man. For five cents I got a white vail that is still good, and for 39 cents a pair of black silk gloves. I bought them at a bargain counter, but they are thin and silky just the same. I would not wear the thick taffeta gloves which are gen-erally offered at that price, but if one watches the stores one will find special sales of real, silky, cheap gloves every spring. A pair of mitts left over from the year before did for every day.

"My white frock was manufactured from the cross bar muslin chil-dren's aprons are made of. It was six cents a yard. I made it with a full skirt, puffed sleeves, surplice waist, and sash. Around my neck, with it, I tried a bit of black velvet ribbon, and it did for hot Sundays as well as for street wear. I can tell you my 60-cent gown felt very much complimented when young Hammond, the artist, called me a `study in black and white.' You see, my dress was white, my hat, mitts and beck ribbon black.

"The mohair, being a very dark gray, will do for a stormy day frock this winter. My sateen I shall wear for a home dress in addition to this tea gown. You think it's chaille, do you? Well, 'tisn't. It's only indigo calico at eight cents a yard, well lined to give it firmness. You see, I got a calico with a blue ground and yellow sprig, which does look like woollen goods. I have made it with a shirred back, a full, baggy front, full sleeves and a pleating of the same around the neck. I shall wear it all winter in the house. My new dress is a dark brown tricot. I would have preferred black, but black in rather cheap goods doesn't wear as well as other colors. I got nine yards for 59 cents a yard. This makes me a dress and a short jacket. The jacket has full sleeves and is bound with fine worsted braid. Some use silk braid, but it wears worse and doesn't look much better. The sacque is lined with silk lasting, so it goes on and off easily, and looks neat hung up anywhere. Next spring I shall wear it without anything extra. For cold weather I have a fur cape. I could have got me a pretty plush jacket for about what the cape cost, but I should have been obliged to get a second wrap coming spring.

So I Thought Better of It.

For $5 I have a pretty seal plush cape which will wear two winters, and which looks real stylish, if I that bought it do say it.

"My bonnet is partly old. I bought a frame for 40 cents, and covered it myself with brown velvet, putting a puff up from the face. I got cheap velveteen, it will wear one season, and when new it looks as well as velvet. I got this dodge by once buying a nobby hat ready trimmed at the milliner's, paying for silk velvet. I wore it one season, and when I ripped it up found I had bought velveteen instead of the finer article. Since then I get the advantage of cheating the public myself. After disbursing 50 cents for the velvet, I refused to pay out any more.

"My bonnet has narrow velvet strings, and on the crown are some bows of brown ribbon which I had in the house. I pinned the ribbon in places with some yellow headed pins which I once purchased for 20 cents a dozen, and which have been used in bonnets or bodices ever since. To save myself a Tam o'Shanter cap of black worsted.

"For best wear I paid $1 for a pair of black dogskin gloves, and for everyday I cover my hands during the cold season with black silk mittens which cost 75 cents in the beginning and have lasted two winters. They are knit of good quality silk, and I lined the thumb and palm with old black cloth, so that the friction in those places hasn't made a hole yet.

"My tricot dress was cut by a dressmaker, so the style is no credit to me. However, I do feel proud of this article which I wear around my neck. I was at a church sociable not long ago, and I was introduced to a young girl who had just returned from a trip to Europe, and who spent hundreds on her clothes where I spent dollars. She had on the darlingest fluffy white thing around her neck, and it was quite a while before I took in the fact that it was an awful simple affair, which I could easily copy. You see this fac-simile of it is only a yard of tulle veiling, gathered one side of the middle, and sewed to a bit of white ribbon large enough to go around the neck. The tulle hangs over in two ruffles, one a bit narrower than the other, the woven edge making a pretty finish. I made mine extra full in front, so that it falls in a jabot almost to the waist, you see. It cost me only half a dollar, and yet I hear it admired everywhere. This ends the list.

"I might add that I buy handkerchiefs at Christmas time, when they are always cheap. I pay 25 cents apiece, generally, and as I get only those with white or red bordered, they wash well. Blue or pink borders are pretty when new, but they fade. A half-dozen a year is the most I need, for it takes lots of wear to use up a handkerchief. I don't make mops of mine, nor wash rags, nor dusters.

I Don't Use Them for Napkins

when I eat a bit of fruit at home. I don't wipe dirty windows nor inky fingers on them. In the summer, when I like a real dainty 'kerchief to stick into my sash, I use my one handsome embroidered one for that purpose, but I don't use it in a 'handkerchief' way. I have a 'shower and a blower,' as the boys say—it sounds vulgar, but it's efficacious in practice."

While my friend talked, I made jottings in pencil. Here they are:

20 yards cotton cloth at 8 cents	$2.88
3 pair black cotton stockings	1.00
3 pair black merlino stockings	1.00
3 jersey undervests	0.75
3 sets winter flannels, to last two years, one year's wear	1.00
Summer shoes	1.25
Winter boots	3.50
Slippers at $1, one year's wear	0.50
Flannel skirts, 4 yards flannel at 20 cents a yard	0.80

"Mother Hubbard" wrapper, 10 yards at 6 cents	0.60
2 pair rubbers at 40 cents each	0.80
Sateen dress, one year's wear	1.25
Belt	0.50
Mohair dress, 10 yards at 30 cents	3.00
Black sailor hat	1.25
Lace veil	0.05
Silk gloves	0.39
White dress, 10 yards at 6 cents	0.60
9 yards tricot at 59 cents a yard	5.31
Plush cape	5.00
Material for bonnet	0.90
Gloves	1.00
Neck wear	0.50
Total =	34.03

Allowing for the "lasting over" until another year of the plush cape, the white dress, flannel skirt and the tricot dress, which will certainly be "made over" in 1892, there is margin enough left to pay the dressmaker for one cutting and basting and to buy dress linings, elastic for hose supporters, thread, sewing silk, darning cotton and worsted for a small amount of fancy work, as well as about the half dozen handkerchiefs and the few ribbons, which eke out my friend's successful dressing at $40 a year.

ABOUT THE EDITORS

Born in 1948, Ken Faig has been writing about H. P. Lovecraft since the early 1970s and was a founding member of the Esoteric Order of Dagon (E.O.D.) amateur press association in 1973. He founded his Moshassuck Press in 1987 to publish specialized works by and about Lovecraft and his associates, and published two large collections of work by Edith Miniter (1995, 2000) and *Susan's Obituary* (1996), a novel by Lovecraft's uncle, Dr. Franklin C. Clark. He has made a specialty of Lovecraft's family background and published a genealogy of Lovecraft's branch of the Phillips family in 1993 and (with collaborators Chris J. Docherty and A. Langley Searles) a monograph on Lovecraft's paternal ancestry in Devonshire, England in 2003. He is also very interested in Lovecraft's participation in the amateur journalism hobby, and edited *The Fossil*, the quarterly journal of the history of the hobby, from 2004 to 2012. *The Unknown Lovecraft*, a collection of Faig's essays on the great writer, was published in 2008.

Sean Donnelly is assistant to the director of the University of Tampa Press, where he is also editorial assistant on the literary journal *Tampa Review*, a contributing co-editor of the series Insistent Visions, and an associate of the Tampa Book Arts Studio. He also collects supernatural and fantastic literature and mystery/detective fiction from the late 1800s to the 1950s, with a special interest in the pulp era. His previous books include *Willis T. Crossman's Vermont: Stories by W. Paul Cook* (2005) and *W. Paul Cook: The Wandering Life of a Yankee Printer* (2007). He is also the author, with J. B. Dobkin, of *The Peter Pauper Press of Peter and Edna Beilenson: 1928-1979* (2013).

The book was typeset and designed by
Sean Donnelly at the office of the
University of Tampa Press
Tampa, Florida.